MAUNA KEA

A NOVEL OF HAWAI'I

TOM PEEK

ALL NIGHT
BOOKS

Praise for Tom Peek's *Daughters of Fire*

Winner, Benjamin Franklin Silver Finalist Award for Popular Fiction, Independent Book Publishers Association

"If you've never been to Hawaii, this novel will take you there. If you've been there and love it, this novel will reveal things you never knew about our fiftieth state. If you have no particular interest in Hawaii but just want to experience a countdown to cataclysm in a tropical setting, this is one highly recommended thrill ride of a book." —*Huffington Post*

"Set on the island of Hawaii, *Daughters of Fire* keenly captures the boiling point of long-simmering tensions between traditional lifestyles and Western development." —*San Francisco Chronicle*

"Set amid the beauty, volcanoes, and intrigue of Hawaii, *Daughters of Fire* is an original novel exploring the meeting point between cultures. . . . An engaging saga of suspense, crafted with a deep understanding and appreciation for Hawaii's unique history and culture, *Daughters of Fire* is highly recommended." —*Midwest Book Review*

"This is a book about power and justice . . . one of the most factually aware novels I've come across." —*Maui Time Weekly*

"The rifts in the earth at Kilauea volcano are mirrored by the rifts in local society in Tom Peek's debut novel *Daughters of Fire*, and although it's a work of fiction, there are forces at work that anyone who lives in today's Hawaii will recognize." —*Hawaii Public Radio*

"Tom Peek has lived a life worthy of Melville, Twain and Stevenson. . . . The book, with multiple plotlines . . . has drawn comparisons to Michener's *Hawaii*. . . . A portrait of Hawaii with an unflinching realism absent in tourist brochures." —*Hawaii Tribune-Herald*

"Places come alive for the reader on every page of this taut, deftly constructed novel. . . . Peek is a storyteller extraordinaire, cut from an older cloth seldom seen today." —*The Contemporary Pacific Journal*

"*Daughters of Fire* tells the story of modern Hawaii, with its political problems and controversies. Peek brings it to life through his experience and knowledge, gleaned from years of studying with local Hawaiians and living among them as brother and friend. . . . He shares this knowledge and perspective with the reader in a far more knowledgeable and detailed manner than other writers who visited Hawaii occasionally, such as Michener and Robert Louis Stevenson. . . . Find the mystery, adventure, excitement, and wisdom from this must-read novel." —*Journal of Humanitarian Affairs*

"*Daughters of Fire* offers a window into the complex reality of life in contemporary Hawai'i. Tom Peek's understanding of place, culture, and current issues is deep and respectful without being heavy-handed. . . . This is a terrific read." —Maile Meyer, founder of Native Books / Na Mea Hawai'i

"An enthralling ride that introduces the reader to virtually all the forces at work in Hawaii today. From the historical to the scientific, the spiritual to the political, to corruption and eruptions, this carefully researched thriller MUST be made into a film!" —Victoria Mudd, Academy Award–winning producer of *Broken Rainbow* and *Tibet: Cry of the Snow Lion*

"Drawing on years of experience living and working with Native Hawaiians, Peek takes us into the spiritual and cultural depths of Hawaiian traditions, masterfully presenting a worldview that deserves our consideration as rampant development threatens to destroy traditional cultures worldwide." —Edwin Bernbaum, author of *Sacred Mountains of the World*

"A page-turning thriller on the surface, a deep meditation on culture one level down, a spiritual tour-de-force at the core." —Arthur Rosenfeld (aka Monk Yun Rou), award-winning author of *A Cure for Gravity*, *The Monk of Park Avenue*, *The Jade Boy*, and many other Taoist-inspired books

"Earthquakes, volcanoes and a romance in paradise . . . *Daughters of Fire* hits the trifecta of a South Seas adventure."

—John C. Dvorak, critically acclaimed author of
The Last Volcano, Mask of the Sun, and other science history books

"Vividly imaginative in its storytelling, yet stunningly accurate in its rendering of Hawai'i's history and contemporary scene . . . Tight, gripping drama that exalts the power and mystery of nature over the supremacy of man. For anyone who can see and feel and know there is sacred all around us."

—Nelson Ho, past chair, Sierra Club Hawai'i Chapter

"An epic tale . . . a mystery of social and political discord . . . a story steeped in culture, mythology, and spirituality. . . . Peek writes about the land with respect [and] the Hawaiian spirit with reverence."

—Misty-Lynn Sanico, cofounder of *HawaiiReads.com* and
independent book reviewer for the *Honolulu Star-Advertiser*

"If it is dynamic, strong women you like in a story, then this is going to be a favorite. If you are intrigued by the mysticism of the Hawaiian gods and goddesses . . . then *Daughters of Fire* will be both exciting and educational. . . . There is something for everyone in this great fun book."

—Sheryl Lynch, Librarian, Hawai'i Public Library in Waianae

"Like a local plate lunch special, [*Daughters of Fire* is] a mix of many different genres, an unexpected combination of flavors and tastes that work well together. . . . If you're looking for a book to take on a trip—or to remember your Big Island vacation—this one satisfies."

—Lehua Parker, author of *One Boy, No Water* and *Nani's Kiss*

"Peek's prose flows through the pages with all the rhythm and feeling of the old Hawaiian legends. . . . This one is a treasure."

—*ABookAddictsMusings.com*

"As someone who grew up on the Big Island of Hawai'i, I appreciate that the book honored the island and its local people. It was hard to put down."

—June Kaililani Tanoue, Kumu Hula of Halau I Ka Pono in Chicago

Paperback ISBN 978-1-63226-120-5
eBook ISBN 978-1-63226-121-2
Audiobook ISBN 978-1-63226-122-9

Published by All Night Books
An imprint of Easton Studio Press
PO Box 3131
Westport, CT 06880
(203) 571-0781

www.allnightbooks.com

Book and cover design by Alexia Garaventa
Cover painting "Lilinoe" by Catherine Robbins
Map and illustrations by John D. Dawson

For Aunty Leinaʻala Apiki McCord and her ʻohana,
and to the other Native Hawaiians whose commitment to aloha is
inspired—and protected—by the extraordinary mountain Mauna Kea.

Love and hate cannot occupy the same space.
—Contemporary Hawaiian elder

ʻAʻohe waʻa hoʻohoa o ka la ʻino (No canoe is defiant on a stormy day.)
—Ancient Hawaiian voyaging proverb

The opposite of a great truth is another great truth.
—Physicist Niels Bohr (1885–1962)

History is littered with the remains of great civilizations that chose to die rather than to change their organizing myths.
—Sam Keen, from *Hymns to an Unknown God*

Author's Note

Mauna Kea, on the Big Island of Hawai'i, stands 14,000 feet above the Pacific Ocean, higher even than the Himalayas when measured from its basalt base four miles beneath the sea. Its colossal cinder peaks tower above the coastal clouds, creating the distinct impression of an island in the sky.

Native Hawaiians consider the dormant volcano the archipelago's most sacred place. Here dwell ancient mountain deities—among them the luminous snow goddess Poli'ahu—and the bones of Hawaiians' most revered ancestors rest close to the heavens on this, the highest burial ground in all of Polynesia. Numerous stone shrines built by Hawai'i's earliest inhabitants dot its windswept upper slopes, and Hawaiians still brave long treks in thin, chill air to pay homage at these holy monuments.

Stalwart hunters have long trekked Mauna Kea's upper slopes to stalk mouflon sheep and goats to feed their families and to marvel at its majestic terrain. In more recent times stargazers from afar huddle inside their summit domes, gathering on giant mirrors faint waves of energy emanating from worlds and galaxies light-years away.

Just as oceanic storms blanket the volcano's peaks with ice and snow, ancient secrets guarded by Hawai'i's oldest families cloak Mauna Kea in mystery, so the particulars of this story are by necessity fiction—though not entirely untrue. One notable event did occur as portrayed: Three men died in a fire while building the Japanese Subaru Telescope, and islanders widely believed some grave offense on the mountain had caused the tragedy.

Contents

PACIFIC OCEAN   Hamakua Coast

Lunchroom
UH 88
Gemini   UKIRT
CFHT

NASA
IRTF   Summit Cone
13,796 ft.

Keck I·II

Subaru

North
Plateau

JCMT
SMA   Waiau Trail

TMT Site

Pu'u Poli'ahu   Lake Waiau

Pu'u Waiau

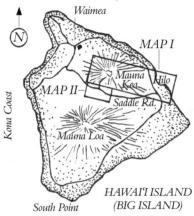

Waimea

N

MAP I

Mauna
Kea   Hilo

MAP II

Saddle Rd.

Kona Coast

Mauna Loa

HAWAI'I ISLAND
(BIG ISLAND)

South Point

MAUNA KEA SUMMIT AREA
Big Island of Hawai'i
Mauna Kea Telescope Acronyms

CFHT • Canada-France-Hawai'i Telescope
IRTF • NASA Infrared Telescope Facility
JCMT • James Clerk Maxwell Telescope
SMA • Smithsonian Submillimeter Array
TMT • Thirty Meter Telescope
UH88 • University of Hawai'i 88-in. Telescope
UKIRT • United Kingdom Infrared Telescope
VLBA • Very Long Baseline Array

Hilo Bay

Keaukaha

HILO TOWN

To Saddle Rd.

u'u Lilinoe

VLBA
Antenna

Ancient Adze
Quarry

To Base Camp

J. DAWSON

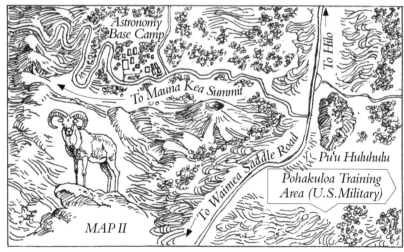

Astronomy
Base Camp

To Hilo

To Mauna Kea Summit

To Waimea Saddle Road

Pu'u Huluhulu

Pohakuloa Training
Area (U.S. Military)

MAP II

PROLOGUE
A Navigator's Honor

❧ 1268 CE

Hetu and his seven companions hid in a thicket of yellow-blossomed *mamane* trees, praying the king's men would not see them—or their precious burden. The choir of yellow-crowned *palila*, whose birdsong had greeted their dawn arrival, fell silent. Darkness had masked the pilgrims' nighttime climb up Mauna Kea's forested flanks, but now, nine thousand feet up, brilliant sunlight exposed the open slope of cinder and scattered trees.

Their discovery of warriors camping on the cross-island trail near Pohakuloa had slowed their clandestine ascent to the summit. Five thousand more feet towered above them, but the next five *hundred* would be the most dangerous. Beyond that, ancient *kapus*—taboos set a thousand years earlier—would protect Hetu's mission from the king's warriors, now alert to their presence and determined to stop them. Even the *ali'i*, whose royal blood gave them every privilege—including the right to kill or enslave those "from the time before"—dared not pass that sacred line on the mountain, for above it was the holiest place in the archipelago, a realm of female deities where weapons and war were not allowed.

In the fifteen years since arrival of the Tahitians' harsh regime, Hetu's chief had been routed and his people subjugated. Their community lands had been confiscated, their social and religious customs replaced, and their deep-seated Hawaiian values compromised. The Tahitian empire, in its quest for new territory, had carefully selected the Hawaiian archipelago to expand its domain. A charismatic priest, Pa'ao, was sent ahead to befriend the affable natives, catalog their resources, and assess potential resistance to colonization. The welcoming *aloha* his party had received—during which his hosts innocently showed him all the riches their supreme god had bestowed upon them—convinced Pa'ao he had not wasted his effort investigating the far-flung volcanoes of Hawai'i. On his next visit he brought armed warriors, and the Hawaiians, whose families had lived there peaceably for fifty-three generations, watched the priest's people overrun theirs. Hetu, now forty, had seen all this firsthand, for it was his father's cousin, Chief Kapawa, whom the Tahitians had deposed.

That morning, seven others from Hetu's clan climbed beside him: four strong men to carry their sacred burden, one at each corner of the seven-foot litter; his beautiful and courageous cousin Mahina to provide moral support; the village *kaula*, an oracle priestess with the rare gift of communicating directly with the gods; and Hetu's fifteen-year-old nephew trained to blow the holy conch. The day before, as they had traversed the broad saddle between the island's two highest mountains, Mauna Kea's distant summit peaks, dotted with moon-white silverswords, had inspired them with a feeling of holiness and peace, dissipating their despair from all that had happened to their homeland . . . until they spied the band of warriors.

Now, with ali'i soldiers in pursuit, Hetu's group fought their reawakened fears. Hetu's jaw clenched as he recalled the kaula's stern rebuke the night before.

"We could easily bash their heads with rocks as they sleep," Hetu had proposed. "Why should we, who lived peacefully before they arrived, not assail these heartless men of the warlords!"

"We cannot violate our moral traditions," the wise oracle snapped, her long white hair gently fluttering in the alpine breeze, "not without becoming less than human ourselves . . . as they have through their horrors. Those men are themselves terrorized by their rulers and now know only one way to survive. We must call upon our ancestors and the gods to show them another way."

The dim starlight had hidden Hetu's disappointed face.

Now, as the group climbed amid giant cinder cones, scattered clumps of trees, and silverswords, Hetu scanned the steep terrain to find somewhere to hide. Following instinct lodged in his *na'au*—wisdom gathered on previous mountain journeys, including those of his ancestors—he guided the group along the base of a mammoth cone that shielded their movements from the king's men. Rounding its broad base, he noticed an eroded gully running through a cluster of old mamane trees, a stony route that would leave no footprints. Within moments, all reached the shallow ravine, and setting down their heavy burden, crouched close to the ground.

"Hamau!" whispered Hetu, a command to silence that hushed even their panting breaths. Then Hetu alone crept up the embankment and peeked through the gnarled mamane. He spotted his royal adversaries, the red-and-gold feather cape of their commanding chief flitting among the trees, and shark-toothed clubs, daggers, and spears in their hands. Hetu's party carried no weapons, save for their slings to hunt birds for food along the way, for these sailors and fishers were on a holy mission. If caught, they could be sacrificed, mutilated, or enslaved for having "fouled" the royal lands. Trespass by lesser humans—"those with the little mana"—was bad enough, but Hetu's pilgrims had also killed and eaten two nesting *'ua'u* during their trek and were now thieves of the king's property as well.

The kaula, descended from the oracle aboard the first canoe of Polynesian migrants, chanted in whispers as the ten warriors searched the stark terrain. She called to ancient gods known for generations in the islands far to the south, and to new gods discovered on Hawai'i, including those dwelling on the mountain. This much divine help would not have been necessary before the Tahitian conquest, but now their hallowed trek was spurned. Many practices of the old religion had been forced underground, including the kaula's summit pilgrimages and families' visits to their mountain shrines and to the high holy lake—to say nothing of burying the extraordinary on Mauna Kea's highest cones.

The old priestess, flanked by the four muscled carriers, rested her hand on the litter's secret load, a six-and-a-half-foot bundle wrapped in white tapa cloth stained with ornate symbols of sea and sky—stars, sails, waves, birds, and wind. Inside was the body of a *hoʻokele*—a navigator—one who had known the ancient star maps of the heavens and embraced the corporeal and occult codes that ruled travel on Pacific waves. But this special sailor had also been the island's principal navigation teacher, responsible for keeping alive these most revered practices. In fact, the departed had been the last to know the full details of the very first voyage to these sacred isles, until he'd passed them on to Hetu the night before death took him to his ancestors.

It was imperative—for Hetu's clan, for "those from the time before," and for all humans—that the bones of this man of great mana, of spiritual power, be interred on the highest peak of Polynesia, to that place closest to the heavens and where the bones and spirits of other venerated ones reside.

Hetu watched as the warriors emerged from the trees into the open. The aliʻi chief waved his division onward, then stopped suddenly as if struck by a thought. He gazed intently toward the gully that hid the pilgrims. A pure white cloud, moving swiftly up the mountain, framed his bold form.

"Hetu," murmured the kaula, approaching from behind, her enormous eyes gleaming.

"Please stay down," Hetu whispered, respectfully motioning her toward the ground, but it was too late. The white tapa cloth of the oracle's robe flashed in the morning sun.

"Hoʻonana!" blurted the chief, pointing at the kaula. Look!

The soldiers bolted forward, but the oracle remained calm.

"We will be safe over there," she said, "inside that next cluster of mamane."

Hetu was perplexed. Those trees were too small to provide sufficient cover, and the towering cone behind them would block any escape.

"Do not worry, Hetu," assured the kaula. "I'm told there is a cave."

Hetu obeyed the oracle and motioned everyone toward the trees. The crouching carriers shuffled forward with the corpse, followed by Mahina and the boy with the conch.

Seeing more movement in front of the cone, the king's men raced forward, determined to pounce upon the prey they had tracked since dawn. But the expanding cloud behind them also hastened, enveloping the rear soldiers in cold, misty fog.

The ancient priestess strode up onto the embankment and addressed the mountain's goddess of mists. *"O Lilinoe, huli mai nana,"* she chanted with a robust, undulating voice that reverberated off the giant cone. *"Eia kau pulapula i hele mai nei i ou la no ka po'e pilikia!"*

The warriors, recognizing the words of a kaula from the time before, hesitated.

"Rush them!" cried their leader.

The soldiers crept forward with apprehension; they had heard stories of the mountain's mystical powers and of the aging bygone *kahunas* who knew how to call upon them.

Hetu leaped into the cluster of mamane, pushing their branches aside to find the prophesied cave. Yellow blossoms tumbled onto his skin as he pressed ahead. A tangle of tree limbs and three huge lava bombs spit out eons ago by the cone concealed the cave's shallow entrance. Hetu directed the carriers and corpse inside first. Mahina followed, but the boy with the conch stopped to blow the sacred *pu* while the kaula chanted the prayers. The haunting moan of human breath blown through the seashell raised bumps on the warriors' skin.

"Come!" Hetu whispered loudly. "All are inside!"

The two moved into the cave, first the boy, then the priestess— still chanting. Before dashing after them, Hetu glanced above the embankment. Only the chief, still two hundred feet away, was visible, all his warriors swallowed up by the fog.

By the time Hetu slipped his broad-shouldered frame into the opening and with the boy muscled a fallen chunk of cave ceiling over the entrance, Mahina had lit a candlenut lamp and taken the lead. The pilgrims' shadows danced along the ceiling and walls as they moved up the old lava tube. Hetu heard the warriors' voices as they approached the ravine outside, and he halted to listen.

"Where did they go?"

"I can see nothing in this fog!"

"Auwe! They have disappeared!"

"There must be a cave!" shouted the chief. "We will find it!"

"But the fog! It's dark as dusk now!"

"All of a sudden the cloud was upon us! From where did it come?"

"The magic of the kahuna," the chief mused. "She has spirited them away, or we would certainly have them in our hands!"

Hetu then heard footfalls racing up the cinder slope. "Ikaika is missing!" Fear in the soldier's voice. "He was right behind me!"

"Could he have stumbled along the route?"

A weighty silence followed.

"This mountain is strange," said the chief finally, goose bumps erupting across his back. The others muttered their agreement. "We must go find Ikaika," he declared, "and get out of this wretched fog!"

Hetu smiled as the warriors' footfalls faded. He thanked Ke Akua—the Supreme One—for providing the cave, and the goddess Lilinoe for the fog. By day's end, another great ancestor had found his resting place on the holy peaks of Mauna Kea.

The early Hawaiians who had risked their lives to honor their revered ones would all but vanish under the new regime. A clandestine remnant survived for many generations, but apparently they, too, disappeared. But not their legacy. That lived on in the ancestral memories of the men and women who, despite generations of intermarriage with the conquerors, still carried their DNA.

The Tahitians brought a contentious seed of competition to the volcanic archipelago, and centuries of interfamilial conflict ensued. Despite the bloody turmoil played out at the coast, the bones of the great navigators buried high on Mauna Kea remained undisturbed for almost seven hundred years, guiding those who felt their spirit toward peace, light, and love—virtues honed by generations making long voyages at sea and living simply on small islands.

Later, a new empire took over the archipelago, a continental people less familiar with the sea and ignorant of the cooperative rules that voyaging and island life demand. The new conquerors had little regard for the past, even their own, a strange rootless people looking only to the future.

PART ONE

CHAPTER 1
Back to "The Other World"

❦ Seven hundred and fifty years later ...

Erik Peterson, his strapping frame hunched over the sloop's navigation station, gazed at the captain's chart of the Hawaiian Islands, and his heart sank. Under the swaying lamp, light and shadow swept over the young sailor as he recalled the last time he'd sailed these waters, three years earlier on his desperate escape to the South Seas. Had he not been sailing back to Hawai'i from the lovely South Pacific islands, this boat delivery might have pleased him, but to Erik, after three years happily out of America, approaching the shores of its fiftieth state felt like being blown off course.

Nothing but the urgent need for money could have compelled the expatriate's return—real money, the kind you could make quickly in the States, even in Hawai'i, which to him, in the twenty-first century, had looked more like California than the South Seas. He ran his fingers over the raw scar under his shirt and cursed the only bad luck he'd had in the south islands. Every dollar of his pitiful savings had gone into that sewed-up hole, to pay an American doctor on Samoa who'd cut out his burst appendix.

"Goddammit!" he hissed, clenching so hard his jaw muscles flexed. "I'm heading back to the *other* world."

The specter of Jack's wan, lifeless body nudging the weedy riverbank floated up into Erik's mind. Suddenly claustrophobic, tangy sweat dampening his shirt, he pulled a Marlboro from his pack. "Shit," he cursed under his breath, remembering the captain's below-deck smoking ban, and jammed the cigarette behind an ear.

Erik pushed himself up from the nav station and stepped into the galley, where cool sea air drifted down the companionway. Braced between spar and cupboard, he poured a second mug of coffee, forti-fication for the four-hour watch ahead. Although usually his favorite stint at the wheel—when night turned gradually into day—the solo monotony of these watches afforded only the company of his mood, and on this long passage that nightly companion had been dark. Indeed, Erik was again smoking a pack a day.

From Samoa to Hawai'i was a third of the way back to his for-mer home in Minnesota—way too close to the source of unhealed wounds from all he'd lost there. For half a decade Erik had vac-illated about leaving his beloved Mississippi River until finally his grief overwhelmed his roots, and he abandoned the life he'd built there. The balmy winds, affable islanders, and soothing beauty of the South Seas had pushed his woe beneath the surface, but his heart still carried the wounds, and going back now would only invite danger. Never good at sorrow, Erik's paternal Viking blood could default to anger, and while he'd also inherited his mother's tender Irish American heart, half of him was fiercely Danish.

Pouring his black brew, a picture of his rustic houseboat beside the river washed into his mind, Becky sunning naked in a deck chair while his buddy Jack, sequestered in that tiny rear cabin, rewrote yet again his doomed manuscript. More images came unbidden: his vacant Peterson Pictures' studio downtown; ten years of photographs stored in his brother's attic with his father's yellowing *Cottonwood Weekly* editorials; that final swim in the river before shuttering his houseboat. His body shook. *How many times can a man start his life over?*

For three years Erik had wandered the South Sea Islands, using his lifelong familiarity with boats to earn subsistence wages as a deckhand on yachts. He was surprised at how much he felt at home on the sea and how quickly he'd picked up the nautical skills to crew sailboats. He'd also discovered that the far-flung Polynesians had much in common with the down-home river folk of his youth.

The islanders' custom was to welcome strangers, and over time Erik developed friendships—even a few brief romances—throughout the islands. Life had been good, far from the turmoil back home, and the optimism he'd inherited from his parents began to reemerge as he sailed through a remote part of the world that still seemed enchanted. He'd even started taking pictures again.

And then, just when he'd decided never to return to the States, his appendix burst.

Irritated by the way his trembling hand shook the coffee mug, Erik climbed the companionway and peeked out into the cockpit. Manu, the Samoan crewman, stood at the wheel, a bold silhouette beneath a halo of stars.

"Good morning, friend," Manu greeted, noticing that Erik's cheeks, easily flushed with the slightest emotion, were bright pink.

"Spotted Hawai'i yet?" Erik asked, feigning buoyancy.

Manu shook his head.

Erik settled into a cockpit seat with his coffee and scanned the dark horizon, but his mind was on the river. As he steadily emptied the mug, anger rose in his chest, and he grieved afresh how everything he'd learned growing up in a remote Minnesota river town became irrelevant in the America emerging in the new century.

He retrieved the Marlboro from behind his ear and dug into his khakis for a match, his tropical shirt fluttering in the stiff wind. Inside it, suspended by a leather thong, dangled an urchin spine etched with a bold tiki image of a Polynesian god given to him by a Mangarevan for protection.

"You look cold," Manu said, the Samoan bundled up in blue jeans and a thick cotton sweater.

"Vikings thrive on cold," Erik laughed, but his hand still shook as he shielded flame and cigarette. His shock of blond hair, bleached pearl from the southern sun, caught each gust of wind, and his dark-blue eyes glimmered in the glow issuing from below deck. "This is nothing compared to Minnesota."

"Lucky we missed Hurricane Wanana," Manu said, adjusting the main sheet to let out more wind. For more than a week, the captain had tracked that Central Pacific storm through NOAA dispatches. It had passed just south of Hawai'i two days earlier, but fortunately had brought only strong winds and downpours to their passage.

"Last of our South Seas luck," Erik muttered bitterly, but the wind kept his sneer from Manu's ears.

The ship's bell rang eight times—four o'clock—and the two young men switched places. The captain's weathered face emerged above the companionway, his eyes caulked with mucus and his tangled gray beard torqued comically to one side. "What's your heading, Ishmael?" he said, using his droll moniker for Erik. An avid reader in port, the old salt often nicknamed transient crew, matching what he'd noticed in them with South Seas literary characters.

"Still holding five degrees."

"Any sign of the light at South Point?"

"Nothing, sir," said Manu. "It's been slow going . . . no letup in the wind."

The old sailor cursed quietly, then returned to his berth, where he would doze until eight o'clock bells signaled his turn at the wheel. Manu followed him.

"Would you wake me, Erik, when you first notice Hawai'i Island?" the Samoan said from the companionway. "I've heard about it all my life . . . the volcanoes and the snowy mountains. I can't wait to see it!"

"I'll do that," Erik replied, wishing it was Tonga, Mangareva, or Mo'orea that lay ahead. A feeling of foundering gripped him, bringing to his mind Melville's image of the maelstrom that had seized the remnants of Captain Ahab's whale-shattered *Pequod*.

Alone, Erik settled into his nightly contemplation, watching stars rise and set at the rim of a gigantic stellar bowl under which the tiny boat rose and fell atop great breasts of wave. The primal beauty of the rolling sea and a starry sky streaked with meteors temporarily salved his grief, but anxieties kept intruding on that calm.

"I never wanted to leave this," he muttered sadly. "Why? Why am I forced to leave now?" And again he worried that his share of the boat delivery fee would barely set him up in Hawai'i. More vexing, could he find sufficient work there to save the money to get back to the South Seas? Another picture of his rustic houseboat beside the river floated into his mind, but by force of will, he sank it.

CHAPTER 2

Signs

An hour after changing the helm, Erik noticed a reddish glow dead ahead, visible whenever *Albatross* rode high up on the swells. It remained off the bow, barely growing as the sloop advanced, so he concluded that it was on land rather than a ship. When dawn's first pinks began to backdrop the rising star of Arcturus, Erik noticed the broad silhouettes of two giant mountains visible above the sea. A band of gray clouds hugged the island, a patch of which glowed red.

"Kilauea must be erupting again . . . ," Erik muttered to himself, recalling its fiery lava pouring into the sea three years earlier as his vessel of escape skirted the Big Island on its passage south. A moment after that realization, the snowcapped summits of Mauna Kea and Mauna Loa turned peach with dawn's first light.

He was about to inform Manu when a sudden commotion in the waters off the starboard side startled him. Instinctively he steered the sloop to port, and the canvas, suddenly full of wind, leaned the boat over. Erik righted the sloop and the turbulence passed astern. No fin broke the surface, and no spume either, but late autumn had arrived, when humpbacks return from Alaska, and a surfacing whale could deal a nasty blow to a boat, perhaps even sink her.

When Erik turned forward, he spotted a brilliant white light atop the taller mountain to the east, Mauna Kea. Its luminescence was as primordial as the sun, and he stood spellbound at the wheel, noticing that it cast a soft shadow off the jib.

Again the waters stirred beside the boat, this time to port. Unable to point higher to windward without luffing the sails, Erik held steady and felt the turbulence pass beneath the aft quarter.

"What the . . . ?" Again seeing no fluke, fin, or spume, he hailed the captain. "Skipper! Up top! Quick!"

Within moments both the captain and Manu were on deck. As the sun bathed Hawai'i's distant peaks in yellow light, Erik described what had happened. But he made no mention of the intense beacon he'd seen atop the mountain, now gone.

The puzzled captain scanned the empty seas with his own eyes, then sat down beside the binnacle. "Did it look like a patch of eddy beside the boat?"

Erik nodded, and Manu shook his head.

The captain grasped the rail and peered into the passing waves. The young men watched the face of the aging vagabond who'd spent forty years plying the South Seas.

"So you've seen this kind of thing before?" Erik said.

"Aye," he allowed. "Some odd permutation of the currents, I reckon. But a Marquesan I crewed with off Nuku Hiva claimed it was the sea itself sending a message." He pressed flat his crooked beard and thought for a long minute. "Safe anchorages are rare in this wily world," he mused. "I think we should sail on to Honolulu and skip that Big Island layover we'd talked about. Let's set a course for the leeward side and get out of this squally wind!"

The skipper went below, but Manu lingered on deck, his eyes fixed on Mauna Kea and its sunlit cap of snow.

"All my life I've heard of that mountain," he muttered in reverie.

"Really?"

"Oh, yeah . . . stories told by elders on Samoa. And *matua* from Rarotonga and other islands."

The next morning at 4:00 a.m., the boat having spent a full day passing the Big Island in the calmer lee of Kona, Erik was again alone at the helm, beginning its crossing of the legendary ʻAlenuihaha Channel between Hawaiʻi and Maui. Here, strong currents converged between the two mountainous islands while their flanks funneled the prevailing trades into fierce gales. Those winds and the waves they spawned—primal forces Hawaiians attribute to the ancient sea deity Kanaloa—created channel conditions capable of swamping vessels, even on crystal-clear nights like this. Indeed, these were the same seas where fierce winds had famously dismasted British captain James Cook, forcing him back to Kealakekua Bay—and his death at the hands of Hawaiian warriors. Another mythic maelstrom came to Erik's mind, the one that had seized Captain Nemo's misanthropic sanctuary, the *Nautilus*. "He'd tried to run from the madness too," Erik muttered.

Unprotected in the channel, *Albatross* already heeled 30 degrees. The rigging howled and constant spray off windblown swells kept Erik buttoned up in his yellow slicker. Manu and the captain slept fitfully below the battened cockpit hatch. Wet and already weary from an hour steering through these adrenaline-stirring conditions, Erik watched the bow dive under yet another swell.

"Damn sea!" he cussed.

The ocean replied with a mountainous swell that tossed Erik into the binnacle. Goose bumps erupted under his slicker, a chill he recognized, that internal call that had warned him off the Mississippi in high water or at the first inkling of approaching storms. An inexplicable urge compelled him to glance back at the receding island of Hawaiʻi, its snowcapped volcanoes silhouetted by purple predawn light. High up in the following swell, protruding above its frothy wake, rode a small pale head with dark round eyes staring at him.

Erik squinted through the spray. "Now what?" he gasped, his heart racing. *Apparition?*

He twisted rearward from the wheel and peered over the aft rail. "What the hell do *you* want!" he blurted.

The ghostly face dropped into the swell.

The captain slid open the hatch and peeked out from the companionway. "You call me, Ishmael?"

"Now what?" Erik gasped. Apparition?

Erik's cheeks reddened. "No, skipper . . . just cussing the wind."

The old sailor shook his head and returned to his berth. When Erik looked aft, the ghostly face, streaming with seawater, had returned, now only a boat's length beyond the transom. Its sheeny eyes gleamed from inside a furrowed robe of moon-colored fur.

"Taunting me for leaving the South Seas, are you?" Erik muttered with disdain.

Another wave broke over the boat, drenching Erik in an icy shower. He wiped the saltwater from his eyes and glared at the face. Its probing gaze seemed not to belong to an animal, and yet reason told Erik it must be. *Are you some kind of seal?* he wondered. *In these remote waters?* That notion seemed almost as crazy as his first reaction.

"*Auuooooooowaa!*" the specter yowled in a low rumbling voice that raised more goose bumps but also brought to Erik's mind the soulful, haunting hoots of the great horned owls that had greeted him on his nighttime journeys down the river.

"You have some message?" he replied.

The apparition rolled back toward Hawai'i Island and vanished beneath the swell. Every few minutes Erik glanced back from the wheel to see if his ghostly companion had returned, but it never did.

The eerie mood of the passage dissolved with the rising sun and the need to call the captain and Manu back on deck to reef the mainsail in the strengthening daytime winds.

"Anything to report?" the captain said, taking the wheel.

"Spotted some weird flotsam, that's all. If I'd been drinking I'd have sworn I'd seen an ivory seal."

The skipper laughed. He knew that monk seals—oldest pinnipeds on Earth—inhabited these waters but rarely showed themselves. "Ya sure it wasn't a mermaid?" he scoffed.

The unsettled weather persisted, and after passing the calmer lees of Maui and Moloka'i, the Kaiwi Channel was almost as windy as the 'Alenuihaha. In the daytime the ghostly specter did not reappear, and by nightfall, as the lights of Honolulu twinkled far to the north, Erik decided his imagination had just run amok.

Early the next evening, as the craggy volcano Diamond Head appeared off the starboard quarter, the three sailors chatted in the cockpit.

"I'll be glad to be done with *this* boat delivery," the captain said, sipping a whiskey at the wheel, his whiskered face aglow in the day's last light.

Manu nodded. "Long passage," he said, relishing the first can of beer the skipper had allowed since they'd left Samoa, "almost always against the wind."

"And wet half the time," the captain added, "what with that typhoon dancing around the neighborhood!"

To say nothing about that strange crossing of the 'Alenuihaha Channel, Erik thought, drawing deeply on his cigarette.

The old vagabond shook his head. "Why in hell anyone would name his boat *Albatross* is beyond me."

"Why not?" Manu said. "It's a splendid bird."

"Aye, and there was a time when its appearance at sea indicated good fortune, but now that bird carries a mixed message. You don't want an albatross around your neck, eh?"

The Samoan shook his head. "I don't understand."

"It goes back to an old Pacific yarn about an ill-fated voyage. The providential bird guides the crew out of the ice and fog off Antarctica, but the unnerved mariner shoots the albatross with his crossbow and all goes bad. As penance, the crew forces him to wear the dead bird around his neck."

"Oh, I see," Manu said, "a good sign not recognized turns into a curse."

The old sailor rattled the ice cubes in his glass. "Yep."

Erik's cheeks flushed. "I'm with you, skipper," he said, dropping his cigarette butt into his spent Budweiser can. "The sooner we're off this boat the better," by which he also meant, *the sooner I can earn some money and find my way back to the South Seas!*

Three F-22 Raptors shattered the quiet as they soared high above the boat on their way back to Hickam Air Force Base. *The other world,* Erik thought, shaking his head. An hour later, in dusky twilight, the skipper spotted a Navy submarine setting out from Pearl Harbor.

"Captain Nemo would have sunk that warship too!" Erik quipped, by then feeling his second beer.

The skipper grinned. "If it didn't sink the *Nautilus* first."

"Captain Nemo?" Manu asked.

"Another renegade hiding out at sea. You'll find that novel stowed in *Vailima*'s library," he said proudly, referring to his own little sloop anchored in Pago Pago. "I'll show you when we get back to Samoa."

That night *Albatross* moored under the gaudy lights of Waikiki's Ala Wai Yacht Harbor, where its tired crew would wait on board for the sloop's San Francisco owners. Between myriad tasks to ready the boat, Erik searched for work, checking newspapers and the employment bureau downtown. Bumper-to-bumper traffic, big-box stores, throngs of tourists, and the constant racket of new construction further darkened Erik's mood. Here was Minneapolis with palm trees and shave ice!

He couldn't believe all the people striding down sidewalks with cell phones at their ears or staring at texts and emails on their screens, oblivious to the tropical scene around them. He smiled bitterly, recalling how he'd ceremoniously tossed his own iPhone into the ocean off the coast of Niue during his first months at sea.

As the days passed, some new elements made urban Waikiki even more difficult for Erik. Homeless islanders he saw one day near the beach disappeared the next, swiftly removed by police as part of the city's Clean Sweep Initiative. "About time they got those vermin outta here!" commented a fashionably clad yachtsman moored in an adjacent berth. Meanwhile, thefts—almost unheard of in the south islands—occurred regularly in neighborhoods near the harbor, and sailors warned Erik never to leave anything of value untended on the beach. "It's 'cause o' da drugs, brah," said a local bartender, "ice and heroin."

Most disturbing of all, the locals, even the Hawaiians long renowned for affability, had taken on a surly edge. Indeed, he sensed something unsettled in the Oʻahu air, like the early gusts before a squall, a feeling he picked up whenever he caught a tortured look from a local or noticed another DEFEND HAWAIʻI graphic on a truck, T-shirt, or cap, its avowal accompanied by a drawing of an AR-15 assault rifle.

A week of job interviews passed without success, and Erik realized that his being a just-arrived *haole*—foreigner—didn't help. He, too, grew surly, twice lashing out at Manu, who had only sensed Erik's submerged anger during their weeks at sea. One Sunday morning Erik sat on Waikiki Beach cursing his bad luck when the classified section of the *Honolulu Star-Advertiser* blew across his feet. He snatched it off the sand and mocked each help wanted ad aloud—until he came upon a new state posting for a part-time job as a cook's assistant on Mauna Kea. "Candidates must be able to work with minimum supervision in a remote base camp 9,300 feet above sea level," read the ad, "and be in physical condition to travel to the mountain's 14,000-foot summit," two aspects of the job that no doubt explained its better-than-usual wages and benefits.

The next morning he mailed in the required forms with a letter pitching himself as a "thirty-three-year-old deck hand just back from the South Seas, in excellent health and eager to work on Hawai'i's tallest volcano." He also boasted his "solid cooking skills" from several years of galley experience on many different boats. It was the most intriguing application that camp manager Moses Kawa'aloa had received, and he called the captain's cell phone to invite the young man to interview the next day at his office in Hilo, the Big Island's largest city.

The captain asked Manu to stay aboard while he walked Erik to the bus stop, just inland on Ala Moana Boulevard. Erik hugged the islander. "I'll see you back in Samoa . . . soon as I can!"

Erik slung his big duffle over a shoulder and strode down the dock with the captain. The chorus of boat rigging clanging against masts chimed a soulful farewell. When they reached the noisy road, the approaching bus to the airport was just a block away.

"You're good crew, Erik," the old sailor said, finally dropping the nickname Ishmael. He put his callused hand on the young man's shoulder. "No way you can control the winds, the currents, or the passing storms . . . or what greets you in each port along the way. But how you react to all that is completely up to you." He curled his lower lip and peered into Erik's youthful face. "Whether you find what you're looking for out here in the Pacific ultimately depends on you. Deep down I think you know that."

Erik nodded. His cheeks flushed and a lump formed in his throat.

"If it's any consolation, son," the old wayfinder said, "though the ship that Ishmael boarded sank—downed by primal forces more powerful than Captain Ahab's will—Ishmael himself survived, saved by a coffin expelled from the sinking ship. Remember that."

The captain stayed on the curb as the bus pulled away, his raised arm still visible out the back window for a block.

Erik sat on the Mauna Kea–facing side of the plane, and that day a creamy swirl of thick clouds obscured the summit with an early snowfall, a leftover from the lingering remnants of Hurricane Wanana. Erik could not have recognized the omen, let alone understood its auspicious portent. When the plane flew over the coconut-lined bay fronting Hilo, the town reminded Erik of the larger South Seas cities into which he'd sailed—Papeete and Suva—where urban sprawl quickly gave way to farms and jungles at the foot of the mountains. *This might not be so bad,* he thought as he walked through the open terminal in moist ocean air scented with flowers.

During the interview, held in a tiny office in the vehicle yard for the observatories, the elderly camp manager watched the young man intently as he explained his culinary experiences at sea. But it wasn't the sailor's words that convinced Moses he'd found the right man for the job. The Hawaiian had noticed something else, a quality more vital and elusive, discernible only to his native instincts.

CHAPTER 3

To a Land above the Clouds

Erik immediately liked Moses Kawaʻaloa, a sturdy man in his six-ties with a kind, caramel-colored face, penetrating brown eyes, and a thick crop of silver hair that gave him a distinguished look. Like other Hawaiians whose ancestors had abandoned Protestant churches for other faiths after missionary descendants overthrew Hawaiʻi's constitutional monarchy in 1893, the camp manager was a Mormon and bore the name of the biblical prophet and liberator.

Moses' choice for cook's assistant was accepted without question by his bosses at the Mauna Kea Base Camp Cooperative, a University of Hawaiʻi affiliate funded by the observatories atop the mountain. The world's most influential science institutions operated almost two dozen telescopes, half by the US government and the rest by three American universities—Hawaiʻi, California, and Caltech—and a cadre of foreign nations. They'd all come to use the last clear, dark sky above Earth's Northern Hemisphere, the others muddied by air and light pollution. The cooperative ran the astronomy base camp where scientists ate and slept between nightly summit observing, as well as a small construction camp that housed workers when a major building or refurbishing proj-ect was underway. The cooperative also operated a tiny visitor center between the two camps, where guides organized daily tours of summit telescopes and conducted nightly public stargazing.

The enclave of dormitories and utility buildings stood two-thirds up the mountain amid a remnant forest of yellow-blossomed mamane trees—just below the tree line but usually above the clouds. The mountain's last five thousand feet rose so precipitously that steep switchbacks had been bulldozed to carry vehicles up its cindery face. The astronomers' quarters and commons resembled a ski lodge, in contrast to the homely construction camp with its mess hall, TV room, and sleeping cabins. All this was built at a place islanders still called Hale Pohaku—"the house of stone"—named for a public hunting shelter built in the 1930s by FDR's Civilian Conservation Corps and eventually commandeered by astronomers for dead storage. Astronomers later named the entire complex after Ellison Onizuka, an island-born Air Force astronaut assigned to the space shuttle program to conduct classified military experiments. America's first Asian American astronaut, Onizuka died aboard the *Challenger* with six others when a design flaw caused the craft to explode during a cold-weather launch in 1986.

Moses had chosen Erik, but Mauna Kea would also have to approve. Erik didn't know it yet, but to keep his new job his body would have to endure the steep ascent to the summit. Up there each breath contained half the oxygen inhaled at sea level. This final test occurred after their long chatty lunch in the dining room, Moses' stratagem for giving Erik's body time to acclimate.

On the way up Moses stopped briefly at the guard shack to introduce Erik to the mountain's senior ranger, Jill Kualono, a half-Portuguese, half-Hawaiian ex-cop from Honolulu. She happily interrupted her current detective novel to chat with Moses, but barely acknowledged the new haole employee.

As Moses' classic red Bronco groaned its way up the switchbacks of the four-wheel-drive road, he introduced Erik to Mauna Kea's history while observing him for signs of mountain sickness. Within minutes they were above the afternoon clouds, giving Erik his first panorama of Mauna Loa, a 14,000-foot hulk so massive that the 8,000-foot volcano protruding from its western flank—Hualalai—seemed diminutive. Another five minutes brought them so high above the base camp that the views beyond the steep embankment were like those from an airplane.

Islands in the sky, Erik thought, as separate from the coastal bustle of Hilo as the South Sea isles had been from the rest of the world.

Moses mentioned an ancient Hawaiian trail that paralleled the route, but Erik, wide-eyed at the vistas and already a little woozy, didn't register the comment. Above the switchbacks, the Bronco climbed into the heart of the mountain's volcanic landscape. Colossal cones of red, brown, and black cinder loomed over the desolate terrain, no tree in sight. Between the cones lay vast washes of cinder swept downslope by meltwater of giant glaciers that had capped the mountain ten thousand years earlier. Boulder-strewn heaps of glacial moraine lay piled along the cones' flanks, left by the scouring, shifting ice as it melted. To Erik it seemed as if Moses was driving them not just up toward space, but back in time, to a primordial place of creation. "This journey makes me feel like I did on my first blue-water passage," Erik mused. Moses smiled.

Twenty minutes and more than two thousand feet above the base camp, Mauna Kea's summit cone came into view, a mammoth feature that on almost any other terrain would be considered a singular mountain. Fresh snow on the peak from the snowstorm Erik had seen from the plane reinforced this impression.

When the Bronco reached the paved upper portion of the access road—its dust-inhibiting tarmac, steel guardrails, and reflective orange stripes more indicative of an industrial thoroughfare than a remote mountain road—Moses stopped the vehicle. Erik hopped out to unlock the four-wheel-drive hubs, and when he got back in, he was breathless, red-faced, and dizzy.

"First rule," Moses admonished, "don't run, no matter how excited you get. And make sure to breathe normally—no shallow breaths—as we continue up." Moses knew that if the young man was having difficulty at 12,000 feet, he would never adjust to the summit's even leaner air.

Moses' advice helped along the next mile and up the next half-thousand feet, but when the Hawaiian pointed to several ancient habitation caves visible from the road, Erik had trouble comprehending him. His mind felt dull, as if he'd downed half a six-pack at lunch. "People lived here?" he said, squinting to see the shadowed caverns in the distant ridge.

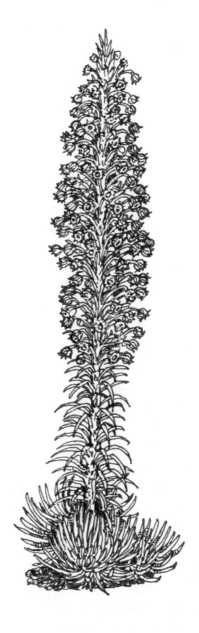

*"In ancient times ʻahinahina thrived all over the mountaintop . . .
a white mountain even without snow."*

"Pilgrims have trekked to the summit for generations."

Erik, disturbed by his labored breaths and dizziness, didn't reply. He inhaled deeply and let his eyes drift over the Mars-scapes along the road, reminded of nauseous passages over turbulent seas, waiting for his body to adjust. He ran his tongue over his lips, surprised to find them parched in the bone-dry air. The intense sunlight had also heated the closed cab, and Erik perspired, even while patches of ice marked the terrain outside. He rolled down the window and let the crisp air blow across his face.

"You OK?" Moses asked.

Erik nodded half-heartedly. His eyes defocused and the landscape turned surreal—pink cones, dazzling blue skies, and cotton-ball clouds floating above the distant sea. A small colony of the weirdest plants he'd ever seen clung to a cinder slope—knee-high pompoms of spiky leaves the color of moonlight. Two had thrust up six-foot stalks bearing dozens of purple flowers.

"What are those?" he asked dreamily.

"'Ahinahina. Scientists call them silverswords, because of their sharp silver leaves. In ancient times—before ranchers introduced goats and mouflon sheep for hunting—those plants thrived all over the mountaintop. A white mountain even without snow."

Erik blinked, but it was all still there.

"See that cone over there?" Moses said, pointing to the left. "Inside that puʻu is Mauna Kea's lake."

Water? Up here in this desert? But Erik's growing disorientation kept him from voicing the question.

He turned back to the window. A young Hawaiian woman in native garb appeared at the road's edge, as if out of the thin air. A sudden gust of summit wind ruffled her long mane of hair and the pink tapa wrap she wore over her jacket and jeans. The garland of green leaves around her head trembled. As the truck drove past she stared intently at Erik's face with her dark, luminescent eyes. He lurched back against the seat, his spine tingling.

"Who's that!" Erik asked, turning to grasp Moses' arm.

Moses looked over. "I didn't see anyone."

Erik craned his neck to scan the steep embankment, now behind them. "I saw a Hawaiian woman standing out there! Just below the guardrail!"

Moses shrugged, a hint of knowing smile at the corners of his mouth. Erik didn't notice it.

I know I saw her! Erik thought, rubbing his eyes. A portentous feeling settled into the young man's chest. *But who would hike all the way up here alone?*

The Bronco soon drove through a narrow cleft between two enormous snow-dusted cones, revealing a third, even whiter *pu'u* straight ahead—as if they'd transited some portal into a fabulous frosty realm. "That's Poli'ahu," Moses commented, pointing at the third cone, "named for our goddess of ice and snow."

Just then the observatories came into view, and the landscape abruptly turned industrial, the giant high-tech buildings like props for a science fiction movie. Numerous steel domes crowded the cones, some as large as ten-story buildings, and eight radio dishes sprawled across the north flank of the mountain, the Smithsonian Submillimeter Array. Only two of the upper cones remained undeveloped, the summit and the snowy cone Moses had called Poli'ahu. As the Bronco angled up the summit cone's south face, Erik spotted yet another huge radio dish two thousand feet below them, hidden between two cinder cones.

"Are these . . . um . . . towers . . . I mean, antennas . . . ah . . . military?" he mumbled, frustrated that his oxygen-deprived brain hadn't correctly formed the words.

Moses, now alert to the young man's deterioration, eyed him with concern. "They say not," he said with a shrug, ". . . but who knows?"

As they passed the old United Kingdom Infrared Telescope (UKIRT), Moses pointed at its tarnished silver dome. "Now *that* one may be doing military research. Lockheed Martin started conducting sky surveys there after the Brits quit their funding."

Moses pulled off the road next to an even older dome, the University of Hawai'i's 88-inch telescope (UH88), one of five atop the uppermost ridge whose peaks had been removed to build the observatories. Only the mountain's summit cone still rose above that ridge, its broad cinder base dropping fifteen hundred feet to the lower slopes below.

"Take it easy when you get out," Moses cautioned as he turned off the engine.

Erik inhaled deeply and opened the door. He got out gingerly as if stepping onto the moon. *Don't faint now*, he thought, but the effect was the opposite. Standing upright with fresh, cold wind in his face, Erik suddenly felt better. Moses motioned the young man to meet him at the edge of the ridge. Erik's heart pumped from the walk's exertion, but as his blood flow increased a flush of energy pulsed through his body.

His jaw dropped at the 360-degree panorama. Far below them an airliner passed through puffs of cloud drifting over the mountain's steep face, and the broad bay at Hilo marked the distant coast.

"This is unbelievable!" Erik grabbed a handful of brittle snow and munched it down, the first white stuff the Minnesotan had seen in three years. He trotted along the ridge, his mouth finally working with his brain. "I've been on mountains, but never like this! God, look at these cones! The wild terrain! The ocean way out there!"

Moses smiled with relief.

After a few minutes, Moses walked Erik to the little cement building below the 88-inch dome, where he would deliver hot summit lunches to the telescopes' daily work crews. They sat down at its outdoor picnic table, framed on three sides by a stunning panorama. Moses opened a small cooler he'd brought from the Bronco, inside which he'd packed cans of fruit juice and two small bags of potato chips.

"For almost forty years this was the finest observatory site on Earth," Moses commented, casting a hand over the sprawling complex, "but now some mountains in Chile are in fierce competition." Over their snack, Moses briefed Erik on each telescope facility and mentioned that the only construction work currently underway was replacing some wind- and ice-damaged panels on two domes and repairing an antenna on the Smithsonian's sprawling submillimeter array.

"I thought they were gonna build another huge telescope up here," Erik said. "I read about it in my father's newspaper before I left Minnesota."

Moses' eyes darkened. "Yes, California's Thirty Meter Telescope . . . TMT. It got hung up. They bulldozed a road and started clearing the site, but that's as far as it got."

What Moses didn't tell him was that the TMT had created turmoil on the mountain—years of protests; Native Hawaiian occupations near the base camp and later on the Saddle Road; and mass arrests after the self-declared "protectors" repeatedly blocked the road to prevent construction crews from further desecrating their sacred mountain. The island community was still on edge after the eighteen-story observatory—and the unseemly political machinations that had secured its state approvals—became the latest symbol of native oppression during two hundred years of American colonialization, unifying Hawaiians more than at any other time during the state's six-decade history. Nor did Moses tell him that queer things had happened on the mountain during the clash, including summertime blizzards, inexplicable bulldozer breakdowns, and the brakes going out on the state vehicle returning the governor and his armed bodyguards from the summit.

Instead they just stared at the scenery. Erik recalled the brilliant light he'd seen approaching the island, but he saw no beacon on the mountaintop. He surmised from his new vantage point that a vehicle's headlights would have been too small and dim for him to even notice at sea. *Could it have been dawn's first rays glinting off one of the domes?* he wondered. Even that seemed not bright enough for what he'd seen.

Turning to the summit, Erik noticed a small wooden tower perched on a foundations of lava rocks atop the cone. "Is that some kind of science experiment?" he asked.

"Far from it," Moses laughed. "That's a lele, a Hawaiian ceremonial altar. Just the other morning I noticed some new offerings."

Erik pondered that a moment, then gazed over to the island of Maui, whose ten-thousand-foot Haleakala peak also stood above the clouds. "This really is the top of the world, isn't it?"

The Hawaiian nodded.

Having passed the mountain's test, Erik began working his Friday-to-Tuesday shift, most days assisting "Braddah K," a reserved, fifty-something Hawaiian who served as chief cook on weekends. Breakfast prep began at 4:30 a.m., an hour before observatory technicians, camp staff, and any astronomers not observing via teleconferencing from outposts across the globe showed up to eat. The morning shift ended by 8:30, giving Erik a two-hour break before starting lunch prep at 10:30.

Within weeks he began exploring the unusual terrain around the base camp, his Canon Rebel DSLR camera in hand. His artistic eye quickly revived, opened wide by the lofty cinder cones, weathered lava flows, and old volcanic craters and lava tubes near the camp. Basalt spatter, including lava "bombs" of all sizes, littered the ground, their odd shapes and frozen drippings stimulating Erik to compose a series of photo abstracts. Most challenging were his attempts to capture telephoto images of the last of the once abundant yellow-crowned, parrot-beaked palila that flitted about the gnarled trees of the remnant mamane forest, searching for seeds, caterpillars, and insects.

Often he drove hot lunches to the summit, his favorite task because he did it solo, with spectacular views going up and down. Now and then he'd notice hunters far out on the distant moraines stalking mouflon sheep and goats. He took another break in the midafternoon—napping, shooting pool, or throwing darts—and finished his dinner duties by 7:00 p.m.

At first Erik spent evenings socializing with camp staff or astronomers in front of the TV—watching DVDs, science programs, or reruns of *The Big Bang Theory*, *Star Trek*, and other sci-fi favorites. As weeks passed, he discovered more pleasure reading nature and astronomy magazines in the camp's little library or wandering about the nearby cinder cones under the stars. He also reread *Moby Dick*.

The winter nighttime skies were even more dazzling than at sea, the stars the brightest he'd ever seen. He imagined what these heavens would look like if he still had his trusty 4.5-inch reflector, used for teenage galaxy hunts on moonless nights down on the sandbar below the old Indian mounds, and before long he started mixing with the stargazing crowd at the visitor center. Seeing with his own eyes the misty nebulas of long-dead stars and spiral galaxies far beyond our Milky Way reminded Erik of how inconceivably vast the universe was, and how shortsighted he'd been to let all the changes back home get under his skin, replacing his sense of wonder with rising rage. Now, the beauty of these celestial objects provoked contentment not unlike what he'd felt on the river and later at sea.

Daytime views were also arresting. Under sapphire skies stood the austere summits of all the Big Island's volcanoes, three active enough to merit geologists' constant attention—Mauna Loa, Kilauea, and Hualalai—handiwork of the legendary goddess Pele who, according to local lore, had built the archipelago. Of these, it was Mauna Loa, Earth's largest active volcano, that most intrigued him. Almost as high as Mauna Kea and still fuming from its 2022 eruption, its massive hulk brooded in the distance with a countenance that at first seemed severe, especially when snow shrouded its vast caldera. Erik came to admire its formidability, a strength his father had exemplified and which he felt he lacked.

He also enjoyed his three days off the mountain, often swimming at beaches near the dumpy little Airstream trailer he rented on the lush Keaukaha coast outside Hilo, especially once the windward rains let up with the arrival of summer. Erik bought a 2002 Toyota Tacoma pickup with decrepit struts but a working AM/FM radio and a moonroof. He affectionately named it Baby Blue for the sky-blue color of its rusting body and because he believed nicknaming junkers prolonged their lives. It gave him access to the base camp and everything else—the vast, fumy crater of Kilauea, sunny beaches in Kona, and picturesque old plantation and ranching towns throughout the island.

Here was a remnant of America not yet overwhelmed by the urban culture that he'd seen damage so many communities. Living on the Big Island stirred in Erik a long-repressed teenage memory of him and Jack hanging out after school at the Cottonwood city beach park between the river and downtown. They sat in the old WPA-built pavilion made of river stones and watched the comings and goings of townsfolk on Main Street, Jack jotting down vignettes in his ever-present journal. "Count your lucky stars we were born here," the young writer had declared, "far from the rat race with its unclean air and tinsel gods!"

Much as Erik enjoyed his days off, he always delighted at returning to the mountain, where the primal beauty of the Big Island took on majestic proportions and the cool high-elevation winds ventilated his wounded soul with the purest air he'd ever breathed.

Erik's perceptions of all this grandeur, though muddled on that first summit trip so many months ago, were now clear, and he began to recognize his good fortune. It was the second time fate had uncannily blessed him, his vagabond journey having placed him in the South Pacific islands during the pandemic, the only part of the world virtually untouched by the virus.

Then, on a full-moon night in June he drove to the place where Moses had pointed out the habitation caves, dwellings he'd since learned were part of a vast, ancient adze quarry where Hawaiians once chipped out the archipelago's densest stone for blades perfect for honing their renowned outrigger canoes and surfboards. As he trekked across the cinder and stone in a cold but mild wind, a deep boom faraway broke the mountain's silence. By then the crew had told him about the Army's nearby camp—the Pohakuloa Training Area (PTA)—a hundred thousand acres in the remote, high-elevation saddle between the volcanoes, and he wondered if nighttime bombing practice was underway. But the boom he'd heard, and the next one, seemed to come from the opposite direction.

It wasn't until Erik had hiked all the way out to a high ridge that he spotted distant thunderheads rising above Hilo, their billows softly illuminated by moonlight.

"My God, I'm *above* the storm!" he said, shaking his head in disbelief.

Lightning flashed inside the towering clouds, followed by muted thunder. Several particularly bright flashes revealed a set of tall upright stones nearby. It was an ancient altar, a *marae* like those Erik had seen in the jungles of the South Pacific. A feeling of mystery swept over him, of powerful and primordial forces in the land, and of something else—a sense of benevolent but formidable spirits astir on the mountain.

"Sometimes even ill winds can lead you to a safe anchorage," he murmured, gazing across at the distant flashing thunderheads. With stars and moon above him, and with stone monuments of an ancient Polynesian culture around him, he actually felt grateful his money had run out in Pago Pago. "It may not be the South Seas," he said, "but this island in the sky is pretty damn far from the other world. I might just anchor in its lee awhile, save up some more dough . . . and think about all that's happened to me since I ran away from home."

CHAPTER 4

The World of Dreams

Fifteen years before Erik Peterson discovered his high-elevation sanctuary, others had launched their own plans for Mauna Kea over cocktails in the Athenaeum Club at the California Institute of Technology. Under the prideful gaze of Caltech's forty-six Nobel laureates hanging on the wall of the Hayman Lounge, a previously obscure trust-fund child, Alfred P. Haisley, had pledged the largest single astronomy donation ever made. The $1.5 billion gift was the lion's share of the money astronomers would need to build Earth's most powerful telescope, with a light-collecting mirror so gargantuan it was bound to yield the first clear pictures of an Earth-like planet orbiting some nearby star.

At least that's what Haisley hoped, once engineers figured out how to manufacture a 60-meter mirror that could focus light without warping under its 75-ton weight. They'd also have to design a cathedral-size dome that wouldn't shake in Mauna Kea's high winds or buckle during the erupting island's frequent earthquakes. Haisley's "GOD"—the astronomers' acronym for "Giant Optical Device"—would be six times larger than the world's giants at the time, including the Caltech–University of California's twin Kecks on Mauna Kea, and twice the size of their planned Thirty Meter Telescope (TMT). Indeed, the "Haisley Big Eye" would even dwarf the Europeans' 39-meter Extremely Large Telescope (ELT) slated for Chile and would capture images twenty-five times sharper than those from the Hubble Space Telescope. All this would permanently secure Haisley's place in science history, a remarkable feat for the second son of America's fourth-largest beer manufacturer.

At that time, just after the turn of the twenty-first century, skeptics still held sway, but Haisley's donation to Caltech was so huge that even the harshest design critics hoped engineers would perfect feasible mirror and dome technology. The others relied on faith, a reasonable leap considering that the Big Eye would make discoveries otherwise possible only with temperamental space telescopes that were even more expensive. As for finding the other $1 billion, well, astronomers said they could work on that later.

Haisley's private dream fit perfectly with Caltech's less publicized long-term plan to use TMT as a prototype for a much-larger 60- to 100-meter telescope. Even more urgent, the title of "world's largest telescope," long held by their Keck 10-meter scopes, had just been snatched away by a Spanish-Mexican giant in the Canary Islands (if only by half a meter). Even their hoped-for TMT would eventually be "outgunned" by the Europeans' ELT. The Haisley Big Eye offered them the only chance to regain the trophy.

Back then, Haisley had also secured Caltech's promise to give him a more intimate, unpublicized tribute as well, something that would mark his contribution even after his family's beer business was long forgotten.

All this dreaming happened years before disparaging Mauna Kea telescopes—especially Caltech's TMT—became the cause célèbre of Hawai'i's burgeoning Native Hawaiian rights movement. No one in the international astronomy community had anticipated that the decades-long Hawaiian cultural renaissance would spawn an anti-colonial political movement that would one day target their Mauna Kea projects, let alone waylay them with incessant litigation and mass protests. Indeed, few of them knew enough about Hawai'i or Native Hawaiians to realize that such a renaissance was even underway.

At the Athenaeum Club ceremony Caltech administrators had accepted Haisley's pledge and an initial check of $500 million, but the scientist actually deserving credit was a short, ruddy-faced Irish American eclipsed by the other dignitaries. Dr. Willy McCrea was so devoted to astronomy he could not resist naming his only child Andromeda (after the galaxy and lovely Greek goddess) despite his wife's misgivings. In college he drove an old Mercury Comet. When its rebuilt V8 finally gave up the ghost, he bought a Saturn, eventually replacing that with a Chevy Equinox. Already renowned as Earth's most prolific discoverer of extrasolar planets—long before NASA's Kepler space telescope would accelerate the hunters' quest and its James Webb Space Telescope was still plagued with delays and cost overruns—Willy McCrea's quest so captivated him that he gave little thought to his place in astronomy annals or his faculty rank at the University of California at Berkeley. He just wanted to search for life—and, if possible, *intelligent* life—beyond our own solar system. To him the mission was nothing less than holy. "Our concept of ourselves and our Earth-bound nations will never be the same," he would declare, "when we see that first actual color picture of our blue-green cousin on the front page of the *New York Times.*"

His pursuit—in fact, just taking up astronomy—had cost him his father's acceptance. Had he followed the advice of the senior Willard McCrea, noted geneticist and chair of the Harvard Medical School, Willy might have become a wealthy patrician too, living in a fine house "back East," with a well-connected wife and a brood of promising children. As it was, Willy lived in a small middle-class home in the Oakland hills with a sculptor wife who taught part time at a community college.

Andromeda, then thirteen, was a good student and fascinated by science, but with broader interests than her father's. She had, however, inherited whatever gene fueled her father's independence. Eventually she, too, would attend Caltech, but Andromeda was determined never to be *that* crazy about any one thing. Whenever Willy forgot school appointments, soccer practice, or family gatherings, Andromeda would tease him about the time he "completely spaced out" at a dinner honoring Berkeley's foremost creative minds. So absorbed was he in a conversation about NASA's SETI project with the UC president's wife that he forgot to eat anything after the soup course. Mindlessly waving away each attempt by gloved waiters to provide new plates of food, he'd missed three courses while his gazpacho congealed in its bowl. When finally called up to accept his award—the dignitaries spooning their cinnamon flan—Willy thanked the group for "this disproportionate recognition of my happy research," then mentioned in parting how he looked forward to the rest of the meal. The remark had puzzled the guests, save for the president's wife who, while having managed to exchange her own plates, later reported, "that crazy astronomer was absolutely enthralling!"

Despite being upstaged at the Haisley celebration by eager Caltech administrators, Willy McCrea had worn his characteristic jowl-to-jowl smile, replete with large crooked teeth. He had good reason to be elated; *he* was the one who had engineered the Haisley contribution and obtained National Academy of Sciences cooperation in shifting its Decade of Astronomy priorities to include Haisley's ground-based GOD. Although money talks loudly in academia—and $1.5 billion was an astounding pledge—it was Willy's charismatic enthusiasm that had convinced the NAS astronomy scientists to go along with his vision.

As the dignitaries in the Hayman Lounge grew tipsy on their cocktails and dreams, Dr. Adam Jacob, the renowned—and notoriously ambitious—rising star of Caltech astrophysics, had slunk over to Willy. "I trust you'll figure out a way to make this monster work," Jacob said under his breath. Willy nodded vigorously, his wild crop of red hair trembling happily. But making it work would be the engineers' job, not his. He would be busy readying the science for the giant telescope. Bigger mirrors and breakthroughs in observational methods had yielded major discoveries in the 1990s, and the race to grow the roster of planets outside our solar system was on. Willy, a regular on the Kecks, had long been at the forefront, hunting for planetary systems around nearby stars whose bright shine masked Earth-like "Goldilocks" planets that might harbor life.

It had never occurred to Willy that Caltech would have difficulty coming up with the rest of the money. That was before fat budgets for pure science like astronomy felt the full blow of post-9/11 military priorities, and then got further slashed during the crippling recessions that followed the 2007 Wall Street crash and the 2020 pandemic. Fortunately, public anxieties during these economic crises bolstered the beer business, and Haisley's trust fund actually grew, as did his clever accountant's investments in Walmart and Dollar Tree.

Alfred Haisley, a rotund Californian with bushy sideburns and bulbous eyes the color of pale ale, had accepted Willy's thank you, but the oddball philanthropist was the grateful one. Willy had originally proposed that he put his money into the TMT, but the billionaire Gordon Moore had already given $200 million to stake his claim to that project, and Haisley didn't want to share the limelight with anyone as famous as the Intel founder and father of Moore's Law. Besides, he fancied himself as having even greater astronomical ambitions than Moore, "and I certainly have a bigger pillar of telescope coins than him," he'd say. No, Haisley was fixated on something grander, determined that no other telescope in his lifetime would outshine his.

From Haisley's unschooled point of view—having barely completed two years of college—brewing beer was also a science, with vats and formulas and laboratory standards of hygiene. He longed to move among the scientists he revered, people he believed held some kind of secret knowledge about the workings of the universe. As a high schooler, he'd watched *Star Trek* and *Cosmos* on TV, and always wished he'd met Gene Roddenberry and Carl Sagan before their deaths. With a computerized 16-inch Meade telescope at his sprawling vacation "cabin" in Marin County, Haisley entertained with stargazing parties at which he served planet-shaped hors d'oeuvres and specially brewed beers "to put my guests into nebulous states of mind," as he so fondly proclaimed.

It was at one of those parties that Willy McCrea had met Alfred Haisley. The McCreas were on the guest list because Haisley's wife, a fan of community art programs, had invited Willy's wife to the gathering. As soon as Haisley realized he had a bona fide astronomer on the premises, he sought him out, pumping him for the latest astronomy news. It was a perfect match—the enthusiastic Willy with his obsession for discovering life-bearing planets and Haisley, a screwball amateur astronomer with a family fortune burning a hole in his pocket. Before the evening was over, they'd hatched the idea of building a new telescope twice the size of Moore's TMT.

They had even talked about its location, high atop Mauna Kea. Willy had cautioned Haisley that the TMT would probably be built there and that the mountain's other best sites already had observatories on them, save for the summit and a cinder cone begrudgingly left vacant out of cross-cultural respect for a Hawaiian snow goddess. But Haisley insisted that such a telescope could be built nowhere else, even if one of the older telescopes on the summit had to be removed to make space for it. When Willy suggested other suitable sites in the Andes Mountains in Chile, Haisley retorted that putting "America's grandest discovery machine" in a foreign country was unpatriotic and a sacrilege to US scientific ideals. "Do you want the byline of every news story announcing the Haisley discoveries to read *South* America?"

To Willy, back then, the telescope's location was a detail to work out later, not fully comprehending that from Alfred Haisley's point of view, unless it was on Mauna Kea—the highest observatory site on US soil—there would be no telescope. This fixation was fueled by more than concern for newspaper headlines or Haisley's delight in seeing his observatory dwarf astronomers' other GODs, for it was on the summit ridge of Mauna Kea that Alfred Haisley intended to have his bones buried. Like James Lick on Mount Hamilton in California and Charles Yerkes under his namesake observatory outside Chicago, Haisley would lie beneath the great instrument bearing his name for all posterity—or no such telescope would be built, at least not by him.

CHAPTER 5

The Mountain Village

One July morning after his breakfast shift, Erik sipped coffee at a table on the long sunny deck suspended off the base camp dining room. His thick cotton cook's smock kept him snug in the midmorning chill. Relaxed and contemplative, he watched trade wind clouds move up the windward flank of Mauna Loa and again felt grateful for his remote mountain sanctuary. Now and then Erik turned his head to gaze through the tall windows of the dining room and watch the comings and goings of the camp.

Braddah K, the portly chief cook on weekends, had already retreated to his dormitory room for their late-morning break. *The ghost has gone back to his cubbyhole*, Erik thought. Like other Hawaiians on the crew, Braddah K was affable, but he kept to himself more than the other islanders, who socialized with Erik once he'd settled into camp life enough to let his friendly, river-bred nature show. But not Braddah K. He was like a shadow, fully dimensional in form but impossible to see inside of. The camp rumor was that some horrible tragedy had shaken the man in youth, leaving him as remote as the mountain itself.

The kitchen crew called him "K," or just "Braddah," so Erik had never learned his real given name. *Maybe Moses knows it*, Erik thought. *They act more like father and son than boss and employee. I won-der if they're related?*

At that moment, Jill Delima Kualono strode into the empty dining room to refill her giant plastic mug with Orange Crush. The camp's senior ranger was one of the few women thick-skinned enough to work with the mostly male crew.

"Faka!" Jill cursed at the soda machine, which dribbled only a few orange drops into her cup. "Asshole!" she cursed again, no doubt referring to Jeffrey Drake, the irascible haole cook who refilled the machine every other day. She took it personally—assumed it was out of spite—since she was the reason Moses ordered Crush for the dispenser, a flavor not particularly popular with the astronomers and observatory staff.

Jill was a *"tita"*—sharp-tongued and independent—and generally unfriendly to haoles, but the ex-Honolulu cop was also highly skilled and a keen observer of all that went on in her little mountain world. Some male employees, resentful of her gruff man-ner or threatened by her seasoned competence, dubbed her "Tita Jill" or "Ranger Bitch" behind her back, nicknames of which she was well aware. Erik, however, had quickly recognized her com-petence and treated her with deference. That, and his masculine good looks, had stirred Jill's curiosity—perhaps even aroused some attraction—so when Moses and the other Hawaiians had made clear through their actions that this haole was OK, Jill started interacting with him.

The clincher was that Erik had given her a copy of a portrait he'd shot of her—something he'd done for others in the mountain village—printing the glossy 8x10 with a computer in the camp's library. Taken inside her guard shack, Erik's camera had caught a sparkle in her severe black eyes, and her hunter-green uniform hand-somely displayed her buxom figure. She'd adorned herself with full ranger regalia—badge, nameplate, radio, and baton, even displaying her rarely worn Glock 19 on her duty belt. No one had ever taken a more beautiful picture of her, and she was impressed with Erik's photographic skills and moved that he would share the product of those skills with workers at the camp.

Grumbling hoarsely, she filled her mug with Sprite, grabbed a few cookies from the big pottery jar on the buffet, and marched back up the stairs and out the front door.

"Hey, buddy!" said a voice directly beneath Erik.

Startled, he cranked his head in all directions.

"Down here!" said the voice, and a moment later the camp's handyman, Freddie Hartwig, stepped out from under the lofty deck's wooden planking. "Break time, brah?"

The tall, athletic haole wore a skimpy, faded tank top over his lean torso, despite the chilly breeze blowing across the mountain, and he had a canvas tool bag slung over his shoulder. He carried a large shipping box in his muscled arms.

"Yep," Erik said, leaning across the rail. "Just cruising, as you say. What are you doing over here?"

"Moses asked me to replace a light fixture down at the visitor center," he said in perfect English rather than his usual colorful pidgin. "Maybe there's some cute chicks down there," he said, resuming his shortcut through the scattered mamane trees between the buildings. "Not that I'll bite," he said over his shoulder.

Erik laughed warmly at the thirty-nine-year-old man who had become his closest friend, an islander who at first blush had little in common with the Minnesota vagabond. Born and raised in Hilo, he had no interest in traveling beyond the island and was by outward appearances a muscle-brained jock. But there was more to Freddie than met the eye, something Erik would not have discovered had Moses not intervened. "You and the new cook have things in common," he'd told Freddie, pointing at Erik one day when the handyman was repairing a kitchen faucet. Freddie caught the hint and sat down to have coffee with the new *malihini*. The "island newcomer" and the *keiki o ka 'aina*—"child born of this land"—hit it off immediately.

Despite Freddie's haole upbringing—grandson of the manager of what had been the largest sugar plantation on the Hamakua Coast and son of Hilo's most successful real estate agent—he considered himself a "local boy." He spent most of his youth on surfboards and fishing boats, his love affair with water equal only to his affection for the islands of his birth and the gracious Polynesian culture that was reviving beneath Hawai'i's glitzy tourist exterior. Even now, as middle age loomed, Freddie remained a regular at the Honoli'i surfing beach just north of Hilo. His friends were mostly locals—that ethnic "mixed plate" of Hawaiian, Asian, Portuguese, and Puerto Rican blood—and he often spoke pidgin, much to his father's dismay. While his parents had encouraged "Frederick" and his siblings to dance hula, play 'ukulele and guitar, and even learn a little of the native tongue, their interest in things Hawaiian fell off when it came to the local girls Freddie brought by the house or the growing native sovereignty movement, with which Freddie was naturally sympathetic.

Along with those little tank tops—sporting evocative "Hawaiian Force" designs by a native artist and activist in Hilo—Freddie wore formfitting Levi's, much to the agitation of the few female graduate students who came over from Honolulu to use the telescopes. But even the prettiest of the scholars didn't turn Freddie's head; his tastes ran more on the local side, and most of his girlfriends had been some mix of Hawaiian, Chinese, or Filipino. While his father believed that this was yet another rebellion against the mainland-style manners and aspirations he'd tried to instill in his youngest son, in truth Freddie just preferred island women for their spontaneity, spunk, and superior looks. Indeed, he'd even been engaged to one, a Chinese merchant's horny daughter who'd mistakenly believed that once out of college Freddie would "buckle down" and follow in his father's footsteps. He backed out on Susan after an oddly shaped wave at Honoli'i threw him up on the rocks, knocking him senseless. He took it as a *ho'ailona*—a sign—warning that she would only bring him unwelcome responsibilities. He decided it was best to live alone in his Hamakua Coast cabin up on Kolekole stream (a short jaunt to Honoli'i) and relish his status as a fun-loving bachelor. Rumor was that he and Ranger Jill had twice had flings.

Freddie taught Erik how to surf and explained traditional uses of the native Polynesian plants he grew on his streamfront property, including taro for making poi, and kava, a South Seas pepper plant fashioned into a mildly narcotic drink. In turn, Erik used his boating binoculars to introduce Freddie to galaxies, nebulas, and globular clusters.

Erik's other best friend was an adopted member of the mountain village, Sam Chun, a frequent camper on Mauna Kea whose long friendship with Freddie guaranteed him free breakfasts at the base camp. Of mostly Chinese ancestry, the thirty-eight-year-old outdoorsman was short and brawny, with a smooth, affable face and jet-black hair. When he smiled or laughed, his earth-brown eyes all but disappeared behind the broad, arched lids he'd inherited from his Buddhist father, revealing only an expressive spark between those thick folds. His quarter-Hawaiian ancestry, inherited through his mother, leavened Sam's analytical temperament with potent intuition and native devotion to nature, beauty, and anyone with sentiments for both. Moses always greeted Sam warmly when he stopped by the camp, which signaled the staff that "this guy is one of us."

Sam was a halftime attorney, mostly on call for Island Defenders, a coalition of environmentalists and Native Hawaiians. Ten years earlier he'd escaped Honolulu's rat race (and his socially ambitious haole ex-wife) to practice law out of his Hilo condominium while pursuing his real loves—fishing, surfing, and ocean kayaking. Imprinted by his parents—both products of Hawai'i's rebellious 1970s—and with a Native Hawaiian grandmother who'd taught him to "follow his heart," Sam had decided that his life would center on reveling in nature's marvels and occasionally defending them in court. In so doing he had chucked some deeply rooted Chinese American expectations, forsaking a steady income and stockpile of savings for a lifestyle more suited to a man born and raised on O'ahu's beautiful North Shore.

Sam often joined Erik and Freddie on their days off, to swim, surf, or fish, usually ending up at Erik's trailer in Keaukaha, the old Airstream tucked behind the oceanfront bungalow of Erik's landlord, a colorful disc jockey named Sunny Boy Rocha. Sometimes the trio hung out at Freddie's funky cabin in the jungle along Kolekole stream, skinny-dipping in its cool, rockbound ponds by day, then eating supper on Freddie's sprawling screened lanai, looking out into the dark valley with its night sounds of tumbling water, chirping frogs, and the croak of a fat cane toad living under the house. Each had a culinary specialty—Sam's smoked fish or fresh *poke*, Freddie's chicken luau (baked with taro leaves from his garden), and Erik's cheddar-draped brats—which they always consumed with ice-cold beer (and sometimes a puff or two of *paka lolo* if Sam's cousin had lately slipped him a baggie of it). Depending on their impairment, one or more of the trio would crash on the floor of Erik's Airstream or in the ratty rattan couch on Freddie's lanai.

The three "talked story" about all manner of things, but it was their mutual love for Polynesian culture that deepened their bond. Freddie and Sam taught Erik about Hawai'i's native traditions and the fifty-year-old cultural renaissance that had brought back the language, dance, music, crafts, spiritual practices, and ancient knowledge of navigation and astronomy. In turn, Erik shared the experiences he'd had with South Pacific islanders and his knowledge of the ancient Midwestern Native Americans who had built great effigy mounds on bluffs overlooking the river. Whenever Sam was around, Freddie became even more "local," the two slipping into heavy pidgin, cracking island jokes (that Erik was only just starting to get), and gravely complaining about all the changes wrought by haoles after statehood.

Hanging out with the two islanders called up Erik's own Mississippi River heritage and evoked happy memories of his "river rat" adventures with Jack Alvarson, recollections that his sorrows had too often obscured, and he affectionately named the Hawai'i trio "The Three *Muskrat*eers." One night, with the three well lubricated on Kona beer, Sam had thrown his muscled arm over Erik's shoulder and declared, "You're one a da few malihini I evah met dat truly digs livin' like us locals!"

Freddie emerged from the trees near the visitor center, and leaped down into its parking lot. Two comely tourists turned their eyes from the solar telescope outside the center to observe the handsome "eye candy" striding into the building. Erik laughed.

It was then that he noticed a familiar car struggling up the steep mountain road—Jeffrey Drake's old Isuzu Trooper, oily exhaust pouring out of its tailpipe. "Shit!" Erik blurted, his serene mood abruptly shattered. *I thought we were free of that jerk today when he didn't show this morning.* "Goddammit!"

Unfortunately, Jeffrey Drake had also become part of Erik's base camp circle, not in friendship but as a persistent irritant, like the fat, noisy fly that kept sneaking into his dorm room. Drake was a skinny mainland haole raised in Hilo, with graying blond hair, icy-blue eyes, and pale, almost jaundiced skin. Drake, middle-aged, had worked in the kitchen almost fifteen years and no one in the camp was more unlike its calm and conscientious manager. Drake showed up for every shift the same ten minutes late and usually in a crumpled white frock splashed with a wild abstract of food stains from the past week's meal preparations.

Drake grumbled constantly, and when he got agitated his head trembled, causing his snarled, shoulder-length hair to quiver. He was most that way when he complained about cops, building inspectors, county officials, or anyone who represented authority—except the camp manager. His biggest beef was with the US government, which he charged "spies, lies, and steals from the public, then taxes us to pay for it!" The only times Drake acted mellow was when he reeked of paka lolo or had just finished "balling" Lucy, the randy blond housekeeper who filled in when the regular crew called in sick.

Paradoxically, Drake was also one of the smartest guys at the camp and college educated. He devoured books and newspapers, seldom missed the evening news, and Erik had occasionally spotted him in the Hilo library's stacks on history and literature. Even so, Drake felt no affinity for the visiting PhDs, ridiculing them as "over-educated sots drunk on space data." Yet he also disparaged anyone he judged to be a "knuckle brain," even though he chummed up to the camp's blue-collar workers, feigning their pidgin, calling them "comrade" or "braddah," and provoking their contempt for "the overhead" (i.e., management)—a hypocrisy Erik disdained. As far as Erik was concerned, the best shifts with Jeffrey Drake were the ones where he failed to show up.

Until recently Erik had managed to avoid any direct conflict with Drake, but as the camp staff's affection for the newcomer grew, particularly from Moses, Drake began turning his snide remarks toward Erik: "Hey, Paul Bunyan, wat'd you put in today's mac salad—Miracle Whip? Minnesotans may love dat oily shit, but islanders prefer real mayo!" And, "Wat's in dis soup! Salt and pepper da only spices dey know back in polar bear land?" Erik sensed more ahead but kept his cool to avoid fueling a fire that could make his camp life miserable. So far his strategy had worked.

Erik got up from the table, grabbed his half-empty cup, and took it to a smaller table at the far end of the deck, where his presence would be less obvious from the dining room. He sat down in the chair facing away from the windows. But Drake spotted him anyway, and a few minutes later, having donned his kitchen smock for the upcoming lunch prep, stepped out onto the deck. That day a splatter of week-old tomato sauce adorned his frock, its left cuff rimmed with mustard.

"Hey, Erik," he said with his usual mocking voice. "I was just thinking about you on my drive up the saddle."

"Oh, really."

"Yeah," he said, plopping down across from him. Drake leaned forward and fixed his glacial eyes on Erik. "How come a guy like you, with brains and mainland education, takes a job making hash for a bunch of pointy-heads so far up in the clouds they can't distinguish a black hole in space from the one they sit on?"

"I need the money," Erik replied, fingering his coffee cup.

"There's *lots* of ways to make money, brah. What are you doing up here with us losers?"

"Moses isn't a loser, and neither is Freddie."

Drake changed the subject. "I heard you used to be a wedding photographer or something."

"A long time ago."

"I also heard you spent time in the South Seas."

"So?" Erik feigned indifference but felt his ire rise. He downed the cold remnant of coffee in his cup.

Drake's head began to tremble. "Aaahhh. A romantic fantasy. Think you're Gauguin or something?"

Erik's ears flushed. "I went there because it was beautiful . . . and the people *down there* are decent."

"You mean the white man hasn't ruined those islands too?"

"Not so much."

"Well, give him more time and he will!"

Erik pushed his cup aside and peered straight into Drake's eyes. "At least here on the mountain we're isolated from all that crap, unless . . ." He stopped himself, but still thought it: *unless some asshole rubs our nose in it.*

Drake leaned forward, clutching both sides of the tabletop. "Naw, we just took over the whole damn mountain, flattened the cinder cones, and put up a bunch of shit-ugly buildings so eggheads from all over the world can ponder the cosmic equivalent of their navels!"

Erik laughed tensely, willing himself not to lose control.

"I bet you notice lots of things, huh, Erik?" Drake leaned so close that Erik could smell the dope on his breath. "You're a smart guy. I bet you see all this for what it really is—a prick-tease for ambitious academics, a gold mine for Oshiro Construction, maybe even a clandestine outpost for military research, and not some grand illusion of exalted science or a hallmark to technological wonder."

This guy's smart, Erik thought, but crazy. Sweat dampened the T-shirt under his smock. *I don't need this. I don't want this. Get up! Leave!*

"It's simple, really," Erik replied, his jaw tensing. "I was flat broke. Either I got a job in Hawai'i or I'd have to go back to Minnesota. And I didn't want that. Besides, it's really beautiful up here."

"Yeah, yeah. But you're just on a long vacation, right, brah? A little break from Minnesota monotony . . ."

At that moment, a drowsy young astronomer, having gotten up for lunch, stepped onto the deck with his Red Bull.

"You can hang out in Hawai'i," Drake continued, his voice rising, "visions of paradise dancing in your head . . . till you see what *really* goes down here." His eyes flashed. "Then, when your image is tarnished with truth you can move on to the next *beautiful* place . . . or just go home to Mama."

Erik was on his feet before he knew it, his face red and fists clenched. Drake rose too, and the astronomer, observing the clash 20 feet down the deck, slunk back inside, leaving his Red Bull on the rail.

"Is that what *you* do, Drake, when you don't know what to do next! Go home to Mama?"

Moses, whose sixth sense always discerned trouble anywhere in the camp, stepped out of his office and crossed the lobby to look over the dining room. He spotted the two men outside, standing nose to nose on the deck.

Before Erik could swing, Drake slipped around him and strolled away. "My mama's too busy with the milkman to bother about me," he sneered over his shoulder. By then Moses had reached the sliding door to the sundeck, and Drake whisked past him.

"What's his problem!" Erik sputtered, jabbing his finger toward the retreating cook. "He's been at the camp too long," Moses said softly, stepping close to Erik. "He knows he's wasting his time here."

"Then why the hell doesn't he get a better job and leave the rest of us in peace!"

"He doesn't believe he can get a better job."

"Because he's an asshole?"

"No, because he's been to federal prison."

CHAPTER 6

The Lady of the Lake

That night Erik slept poorly, and the next day a simmering, jaw-clenching anger shadowed him, making it difficult for him to focus on kitchen tasks. Drake's goading kept bubbling up in his mind. *Was anything I've done these past three and a half years truly constructive? Am I still just on the run?*

By noon his foul mood had become obvious to everyone at the camp.

"Paradise finally getting to you, vagabond?" Jeffrey Drake taunted in the kitchen.

"Shut up!" Erik screamed, shoving Drake so hard he nearly dropped the bowl of fruit salad he was carrying.

"Jesus . . . ," Drake said, quickly stumbling to the other side of the prep table.

Erik marched to the back door and slipped outside. He sat down on the loading dock and lit up a Marlboro.

Within a minute, Moses appeared around the corner of the building. "What's going on!" he said in a commanding tone.

"I lost it again with that sonofabitch Drake. If I'd done what I really wanted to you'd have to fire me." He exhaled a cloud of smoke. "I'm sorry, Moses . . . I'm out of sorts today."

"Is it really just Drake?"

Erik's face paled. "No . . . not just Drake . . . Don't worry. I'll figure it out."

The elder eyed the young man deeply. "Erik, trust the mountain to help you see your way through it . . . as it helped you when you first came here months ago. I'll also talk to Drake."

That afternoon between meal preparations Erik collapsed in bed, and he soon dreamt of the mountain's lake, a shining diamond surrounded by white clouds. In the dream, he knelt down at the shore and plunged his hands into the glassy pond. He saw his serene face reflected in the water cupped in his hands, then drank it.

It was not a surprising dream for one who'd made it a habit to imbibe waters at enchanted places, a ritual that began when Jack and he discovered an artesian well in the cottonwoods near the base of the limestone cliff across the river. Prostrate on the sand, mouths in the gushing spring, the two teens had drunk all they could hold, then vowed their allegiance to a "brotherhood of joy." On the road Erik had continued their tradition to honor Jack's memory, drinking from pristine springs high in the Rockies and down along the Big Sur coast, sipping dew in the folds of huge taro leaves in Samoa, and guzzling sweet water from coconuts in Tonga and Kiribati.

Erik described his afternoon dream to Moses at the start of the dinner prep. A few minutes later, the camp manager returned to the kitchen. "Take the rest of the day off," he whispered, ". . . go sort things out. Take the Explorer up top and stretch your legs. I'll tell K you're doing something for me."

"Thank you!"

"But watch out for the uhiwai," Moses warned, "the thick fog that comes when afternoon clouds climb the mountain. It's wet and cold and can take you by surprise. Many a hunter's gotten lost in the uhiwai."

The sun hung low over Mauna Loa by the time Erik reached the trailhead to the lake, located just downslope from the old James Clerk Maxwell Telescope submillimeter dome. Temperatures were already falling and Erik slipped a jean jacket over his hooded sweatshirt and donned his sailor's watch cap. His trusty hiking boots, shipped from Minnesota by his brother, would provide traction on any snow encountered. His little red backpack bulged with two water bottles, a dinner sandwich, binoculars, his camera, and a flashlight as he headed down the cinder trail below Pu'u Poli'ahu. Millennia of wind, rain, and snow had sculpted the cone's auburn cinders into sensuous curves that glowed golden yellow in the last hour of light. Icy snow patches and thin air made hiking the upper slopes more challenging than at nine thousand feet, and Erik's heart pounded, his lungs strained, and he soon became lightheaded. The sensation was not unpleasant, but it put him on guard.

The narrow path lay on the outwash plain between Pu'u Poli'ahu and another towering cone. A quarter mile ahead of Erik stood the top of Pu'u Waiau, its cinder rim just visible above the plain. He could see that the afternoon clouds were still five hundred feet below him, save for a single white swirl that teased the southeast lip of the cone. Erik picked up his pace, but the exertion soon made him pause to catch his breath and quiet the vascular throb in his head. He sat down on a large red "lava bomb" that the cone above him had spit out thousands of years earlier. Inhaling deeply, his mind defocused. *Otherworldly*, he thought.

Gazing across the volcanic terrain, he noticed a row of upright stones a thousand feet to his right and took out his binos for a look. Different from the Tahitian-style *heiau* on Hawai'i's coasts, this marae looked similar to the one that had flashed in the lightning that moonlit night above the adze quarry. Erik considered hiking over for a closer look, but his spacey fatigue kept him on the rock. His thoughts drifted on his own internal currents, stirring spiritual sensations lately obscured by his negative preoccupations. *Amazing light*, he mused, scanning the wildly bizarre landscape. *Van Gogh stuff. Beautiful.*

How long he drifted he did not know, but by the time his reverie faded, great wisps of cloud, backlit by the descending sun, danced all around the rim of Pu'u Waiau. *Better keep moving to avoid the uhiwai*, he thought, remembering Moses' warning. Erik took a deep breath and pushed himself up off the rock. As he pulled on his backpack, he noticed a flicker of movement among the distant stones.

Mountain goat? Mouflon sheep? Intrepid hunter? Whatever it was had already dashed below the ridge.

Erik continued along the trail, moving slowly, willing his feet forward. He paused again to catch his breath and drink some water. In a few minutes he reached the rim of Waiau, its outer slopes dropping precipitously. Nestled inside the cone's bowl was an oval pond sparkling in the low alpine sun. So brilliant was the jewel that Erik had to shield his eyes to study its contours. Again he puzzled over why such a small body of water didn't dry up in this arid environment. Late afternoon clouds seldom brought up more than fog, and the rarified atmosphere evaporated most winter snow. *Does some subterranean source recharge its waters?* he wondered.

Then he remembered what he'd read in a thick, dusty—and obviously never opened—archaeological report that he'd stumbled on one windy night in the base camp library. In Hawaiian lore the lake was a *wahi kapu*—a sacred place—where dwelt two mountain deities: a water goddess, Kapiko o Waiau ("the umbilical of the swirling water"), and a protector of the mountain, Moʻoinanea, a goddess who could take the form of a giant lizard dwelling in the lake's "bottomless depths." That same tome had mentioned that the ash-lined lake held the "sacred waters of Kane," the god to whom Hawaiians attribute creation, light, waters of life, abundance, and procreation.

These thoughts gave him pause before descending into the cone. *Dare I trespass into such a legendary realm?* And yet a strong compulsion—bolstered by his dream and Moses' encouragement—propelled him forward. With each step down the cinder slope he felt energized, as if the spirits he'd sensed on that moonlit night above the quarry were there and helping him along.

He was halfway down to the lake when over the lip of the cone came a delicate mist that enveloped him.

"Uhiwai," he said in a hushed voice, stopping. He held up his hands to feel it. *But this is a fine mist . . . not a heavy fog . . . and carries no sense of foreboding. In fact, there's still some light in it.* Then he recalled something else from the anthropologist's report. In his interviews old Hawaiians had told him about the misty goddess Lilinoe, who dwelt in a towering cone a short distance from Puʻu Waiau.

"Lilinoe . . . ," Erik said and resumed his descent. He trekked through the now swirling mist until the lake's cindery shore appeared at his feet. As in his dream, he knelt before the crystalline pond and scooped up a mouthful. The icy water tasted fresh and pure, and his whole body tingled.

"And one for Jack," he murmured as he cupped a second drink. It seemed to rinse away the bitter taste his mouth had taken on in recent days. He rubbed his damp, cold hands all over his face.

"What are you doing!" said a voice behind him.

Erik spun to his feet and peered into the mist.

Out of its wild swirls stepped the young Hawaiian woman he had seen on the roadside his first day on the mountain. As before, a garland of green leaves, now dripping moisture, adorned her head and a pink tapa wrap stained with native symbols draped her black jacket. But it was her face that struck him. Its smooth contours framed dark smoldering eyes that looked uncanny for one as youthful as she—too seasoned and heavy with somber authority. Her sun-bronzed skin perfectly matched the cinder landscape, and her train of lava-black hair swayed in the wind.

"Did you forget to bring water with you?" she asked.

"Why no . . . I . . . I have water. I always drink from places like this . . . places of wonder."

She walked slowly toward him, her damp, shiny hair trailing behind in the misty wind. She stopped a few feet away, crossed her arms, and stared sternly into his face. Her eyes were a paradox— opaque yet luminescent—and they peered at him with probing intensity. "This place is kapu," she said. Sacred.

"Have I done something wrong?" he asked, unsure if somehow he had reentered his dream or was hallucinating in the thin air.

"Why did you come?"

"I dreamt it," he said, answering as honestly as he could.

"Hmmm." Her persistent gaze unnerved him.

"And my friend Moses encouraged me," he added quickly.

"Who?"

"Moses Kawa'aloa."

She dropped her arms, and her eyes softened.

Out of the wild swirls stepped the young Hawaiian woman.

"I'm a cook at the base camp," he explained, wondering if a mountain goddess could comprehend such an inane thing. "Moses gave me the evening off."

"So you actually live on the mountain?"

"Most of the week . . . so here I am. And you?" he asked with apprehension. "Why are you here?"

"I belong here." She turned and walked away, down the shoreline and into the swirling mist.

By then dusk had come and in the gray twilight a cold, heavy fog replaced the mist. Erik sat down on a rock to gather his senses, and he realized that the apparition he thought he'd encountered had worn a leather jacket under her tapa wrap—that he had neither crossed into another realm nor lost his mind. And yet . . . was she not the most arresting and mysterious woman he had ever seen?

The primal mood of the lake and weather kept Erik fixed to the rock, but he decided he'd better head back. With difficulty, he followed the trail, dogged by Moses' warning about the *uhiwai* and aided on the last half mile by his flashlight. Moving carefully from one rock cairn to the next, he slowly found his way back to the Explorer. By then, it was pitch dark and the wet wind was frigid.

Moses had stayed late to watch for Erik out his office window after the observatories' webcams revealed that fog had overtaken the summit. He jumped up from his desk when the young man finally pulled into the orange illumination of the base camp parking lot, and met him at the door.

"What happened?" he asked, handing Erik a wool blanket to replace his wet jacket. "I started to worry."

"I ran into a Hawaiian at the lake . . . dressed in ceremonial clothing . . . that same woman I noticed the first day you took me up the mountain."

The camp manager's eyebrows rose in surprise.

"Who is she?" Erik asked, swabbing moisture off his face with the blanket.

"Some Hawaiians go to Lake Waiau for religious practice."

"Do you know her?"

Moses paused. "Late twenties, early thirties?"

Erik had to think a moment because for some reason she seemed timeless. He nodded.

"That's probably Hoku Holokai. I'm surprised you've encountered her—in fact, twice. She's often on the mountain, but rarely seen."

"What can you tell me about her?" Erik's tone was strangely urgent.

"Not much. Her mentor, also a cultural practitioner, lives in your neighborhood, Keaukaha, but I've never met Hoku. I also know that she's an artist because I once saw her work at a show in Hilo. At that time she painted in very dark colors."

"What would she be doing at the lake?"

"That's *her* business." Moses began packing up his belongings to go home. "You did the right thing coming back when you did. There'll be another day to visit the lake."

Erik couldn't get the young woman out of his mind as he sat alone in the dining room eating the sandwich he'd packed for the trek. He kept flashing back on the way she'd peered at him, as if searching for something. A sense of unreality about the whole experience—the hike, the shrine, the swirling mist, the Hawaiian—took hold, and he shivered.

CHAPTER 7
Retreat to Keaukaha

Erik breathed a sigh of relief when Tuesday evening arrived and his weekly stint on the mountain was over. As his old pickup Baby Blue rattled down the Saddle Road, his thoughts dipped in and out of a pool of memories from the last two days—his two rows with Drake, his dream of drinking from the lake, Moses urging him to trust the mountain's healing power, and his lakeside encounter with the mysterious Hoku Holokai. *Why, at that moment, were we both there?* he wondered. All this left Erik with a subtle anxiety like that he'd experienced sailing in fog, his bearings confused despite what he read on the compass. He turned on the radio to clear his mind, but the melancholy Hawaiian songs playing that night kept him in a pensive mood.

He dropped off his timesheet at the cooperative's base yard in Hilo's industrial area, a homely outpost compared with the astronomers' imposing complex of bluff-top headquarters overlooking Hilo. After four days up top Erik was usually ready to engage with the broader island society again, but not that night. He decided to skip his routine stop at the always-teeming Ken's House of Pancakes for a stack of whole wheats almost as tasty as the Minnesota variety. Nor would he go to Mama Choi's, a lively neighborhood bar that served free pupus with their beers and whose assertive Korean waitresses were a welcome provocation after four days in the company of mostly men. Neither of his regular haunts seemed right that night and he headed straight home to Keaukaha as a light rain fell.

His dumpy little Airstream trailer, shadowed beneath a towering avocado tree and hemmed in by tropical foliage, looked lonely in the orange light of the neighborhood's low-pressure sodium streetlamps. The pleading cries of coqui frogs calling out for mates just amplified Erik's somber mood. The only welcoming things about the scene were the illuminated windows of his landlord's seaside bungalow a hundred feet in front of the trailer and the strum of the old disc jockey's 'ukulele issuing from his lanai.

Erik got out of the pickup and headed to the trailer. The aerodynamic shape and aluminum walls of the 1955 Airstream Land Yacht made it look like a Cold War Quonset abandoned in the jungle. As soon as he stepped up into its tiny living area he regretted not having stopped at 7-Eleven to buy a Spam musubi or a hot dog. "I guess it's chips and beer," he said, reaching into the mahogany cabinet above the galley sink for the half-empty bag of One-Ton Chips that Sam had left during his last visit. He opened the little fridge under the counter and found a Kona beer left from that same night, a Castaway IPA. "How fuckin' appropriate is that?" he muttered.

Erik stretched out on the built-in sofa to drink his ale and munch his chips while he stared at the moths flitting about the illuminated screen door with its odd array of patches. The 22-foot Airstream was small and leaky, but it was Erik's first private domicile in years, for which he happily paid Sunny Boy Rocha $500 a month in cash under the table, a modest supplement to the disc jockey's paltry Social Security check and meager salary at KAAO-FM.

With Hawai'i's ever-rising cost of living, the septuagenarian had twice remortgaged his little bungalow, built by his grandmother after the 1946 tsunami washed away her home. Sunny Boy had crammed it with Hawai'i radio memorabilia—posters, photographs, and antique microphones sporting defunct station call letters. Its covered oceanfront lanai was furnished in the 1950s, with weathered koa wood furniture and a Caldemeyer "rocket recliner" inspired by that decade's space craze. There, Sunny Boy spent most of his free time, gabbing on his cell, reading newspapers, or humming to the strum of his 'ukulele with Mauna Kea looming in the distance across the nearshore waters. Sunny Boy had chosen talking for a living because he was a natural gab—to a fault. Delighted his renter was the son of a newspaperman, he'd drop in on Erik's days off to share the latest scuttlebutt, opine about current events, or lampoon what he called "lolo mainland politics."

Despite the DJ's gossipy nature, Erik had grown to appreciate his down-home verve, and the three Muskrateers sometimes ended their days of ocean play on Sunny Boy's lanai. They'd buy a twelve-pack to share with the disc jockey, and Sunny Boy would launch into lively rambles about growing up in Hawai'i. Some evenings Freddie played slack key guitar while Sunny Boy strummed his 'ukulele and sang along.

After finishing his impromptu supper, Erik stripped off his mountain clothes and exchanged them for the *lavalava* Manu had given him in Pago Pago, the red sarong printed with Samoan tapa designs. With the fabric skirt knotted at his waist, Erik dashed through the rain to the outdoor shower attached to his crudely plumbed outhouse (the Land Yacht's defunct head now used for storage), and he took a long steamy shower inside the thickets of fern that provided some semblance of privacy.

"Whew. Finally back at sea level," he muttered as he rinsed away the emotional residue from his time on the mountain. "And good to be in Keaukaha."

Keaukaha was mostly local, including Native Hawaiians, many of whom lived on Hawaiian Home Lands lots just inland from the ocean. Under a 1921 federal law, those lots had been given to qualifying Hawaiians—those with at least 50 percent native blood—a last-ditch effort to keep remnants of the original islanders on the land and to assuage haole guilt for their displacement.

But the Hawaiians living nearest Erik dwelt in a jungly "squatters village" adjacent to Sunny Boy's property. It was founded in the 1980s to protest the infamous Home Lands waiting list of applicants, most of whom died before receiving their tiny parcels while the agency leased huge acreages to commercial developers and for government projects like Hilo's airport and sewage treatment plant.

Residents of the village had revived something of the land-based life their ancestors had lived before annexation and statehood. But as real estate and rental prices soared, followed by the Great Recession and the COVID-19 pandemic, the village had grown into a permanent "homeless" camp of three dozen islanders crammed into Walmart tents or shelters made of blue tarp. Erik often saw residents spear-fishing offshore, picking 'opihi from rocks, or throwing net from the lava ledge in front of Sunny Boy's place.

To Erik, living in this largely native community felt more like being back in the South Seas than the United States, and he got to know many of Keaukaha's waterfront regulars. Yet he hesitated to introduce himself to the Hawaiians right next door. This made no logical sense to him. Erik had always enjoyed easy relations with Polynesians, and the surly attitude he'd observed among Honolulu's locals was rarely apparent in the village. Even some of the rough-er-looking neighbors—their spirits dimmed by poverty or drug abuse—smiled or nodded when they noticed him through the ferns. Yet some apprehension had kept him distant.

No doubt, some of this was because of the peculiar old Hawaiian woman in her banana-leaf sunhats who tended the community's gar-den of ti plants. On mornings after Erik returned from the mountain she seemed always to be waiting among the plants to smile at him as he emerged from the trailer. Sometimes he would look up from a book he was reading in his lawn chair, or glance over at the village from the galley window, and there she'd be, staring at him with the most intense concentration. Although her face was pleasant and her smile sweet—albeit missing several teeth—her expression always unnerved him. When he finally asked Sunny Boy about her, he said her name was Aunty Moana Keali'i Kuahiwi and that she was about seventy—and reputed to be half-crazy.

After toweling off, Erik strolled back to the Airstream in his lavalava and downed the last swallows of his Castaway. He crawled into his cramped berth at the back of the trailer, and despite its dank, lumpy mattress, fell sound asleep.

He awoke late the next morning with a wedge of hot sunshine on his face from the window above his bed.

"Hey, Erik," came the deep voice of Sunny Boy Rocha, followed by three loud knocks on the trailer's screen door. "You up?"

Now I am, Erik thought, rubbing his face. "Yeah . . . just a minute."

He pulled on a pair of shorts and stumbled to the kitchen. "What's up?" he said through the door.

"Gee, you look terrible," the chubby old DJ said, leaning on its jam. "Rough night, eh?" Bright sun illuminated the burlesque features of this Portuguese descendant of Azore Island immigrants—sparkling brown eyes, thick whimsical brows, a pug nose, and an immense mouth that formed a gaudy grin.

"Rough morning too," Erik replied glumly.

"Eh, big news, Minnesota boy!" the DJ declared with a smirk. "Remember yer nutty ex-congresswoman Michele Bachmann?"

Oh God.

"Nice looking wahine but shit fo' brains? Yer nevah gonna believe da lolo 'ting she w'en say about Biden dis morning on Fox!"

"I don't give a damn what that idiot said!" Erik slammed the door and stepped over to the galley to make coffee.

"Aww, c'mon, Erik," Sunny Boy whined, pressing his broad face against the screen.

"Forget it!" Erik snarled without turning around. "I told you before. I left all that crap behind. Don't take me back there. OK?"

"Sheeze," Sunny Boy said, stepping away from the trailer.

It wasn't until Erik finished his first cup of coffee and smoked two cigarettes on the rocks in front of Sunny Boy's place that his annoyance with the DJ's ill-timed intrusion waned. Only then, after gazing up at the mountain, did Erik's thoughts turn back to his encounters with Drake and the woman at the lake. He recalled an observation his father had once shared—though he was talking about Cottonwood and the river valley people. "There's no escape from community conflict, Erik," he had said, looking up from a draft editorial on his newspaper desk, "or from other maddening human frailties. But beauty and companionable relationships put those hassles into proper perspective and give one the heart to endure them." Later that day Erik apologized to Sunny Boy.

Erik kept his father's wisdom in mind as the summer wore on, and it improved his experiences at the coast and on the mountain. He chose to ignore Drake as much as possible rather than attempt a truce, but it turned out that his having defied Drake twice—and Moses intervening on Erik's behalf—had dampened the irascible cook's impulse to needle him, and from then on Drake directed his attacks on others.

Hoku Holokai remained a vivid presence in Erik's mind that summer, but many months would pass before he'd see her again.

CHAPTER 8
A Disappearing World

Three months after Erik's encounters with Jeffrey Drake and Hoku Holokai, in an old brick building above a sea cliff at the foot of Mauna Kea, the board of directors of Williams & Company Shipping adjourned an early-morning meeting that could well affect the future of Mauna Kea.

After everyone left, Thomas Williams Jr. rose from his chair at the head of the immense boardroom table and gazed into its koa wood surface, darkened by more than a century of use. His somber mood from the meeting clung to his psyche. Frowning, he pushed his portfolio, calculator, and notepad into a neat heap, then shuffled over to the window. His flesh hung heavy on his bones, weight accumulated during forty-some years of responsibility, although in youth he'd been as slim and agile as his son, Tommy—Thomas Williams III—who'd just left the room. A Camel smoldered between Tom's lips. He brushed the shock of white hair off his forehead and stared out through the sea-speckled pane, his turquoise eyes still as brilliant as a Polynesian lagoon. Outside, a turbulent October sea thundered against the cliff below and flooded the breakwater on the other side of Hilo Bay.

"We've been overwhelmed by a tsunami of change," the old shipper muttered, drawing hard on his cigarette. Behind him, on the wall above the table, hung an imposing oil painting of his great-grandfather's bark, the *Phoenix*, its square-rigged sails full of trade winds as white foam dashed her bow. The challenges facing Williams & Company were even greater now than in their pioneering days. Then, their fortunes lay *ahead*, in the dreams of adventurous descendants of brave missionaries like his great-great-grandfather, who had set out to bring civilization to these rich but "barbaric" islands. What bothered Tom Williams most—though he dared not speak it—was that neither he nor his bullheaded son could think of anything that would define a future worth pursuing in the islands. It wasn't just that sugarcane, whose trade had made them wealthy, was dead, or that their once thriving commercial goods trade was foundering in an island economy still suffering after the Great Recession and the pandemic. It was that the time-honored values of the island community were dissipating just as surely as the depleted soils of the Hamakua Coast were now dispersed daily by autumn winds.

"Sorry, Tom," Marilyn Cooper said, stepping into the cavernous room to tidy up after the meeting, a task she'd done automatically for thirty-some years. "I didn't realize you were still here."

He turned from the window and snubbed his cigarette in one of the antique brass ashtrays on the table. "It's fine, Marilyn," he said, "go ahead," and strolled over to one of the captain's chairs lining the front wall—artifacts from the long-ago mothballed *Awiki Mai*. He watched Marilyn stack the coffee cups on a silver tray salvaged from another company steamer. She was still enormously attractive to him, even though middle age had long ago compromised her curves and her blond curls had turned ashen. Working side by side all those years, Marilyn knew Tom's soul far better than his devoted wife did and was now his most important business confidant. Certainly more than Tommy, whose Stanford education and ill-mannered impatience could not replace the sensitive instincts of the chairman's secretary. Williams' Congregational heritage had kept him from acting out their mutual attraction, and so, uncluttered by passionate intrigue, he could trust her implicitly.

"You're not keen on this 'new initiative,' are you?" she said.

Tom closed his eyes and shook his head. "I know we need some quick capital for shipyard improvements in Honolulu, but what's the sense in selling off our landholdings to enterprises that will have limited shipping needs?"

Marilyn set the tray on the ʻohiʻa credenza beneath the painting and walked over to take a chair next to Tom's.

"I mean, hotels and timeshares for Christ's sake! That acreage used to produce enough cane to fill three hundred barges a year. What a waste!"

"Is that what really bothers you about Tommy's proposal?"

He glanced over at Marilyn, her olive eyes probing in that old familiar way, and lit another cigarette.

"No. You're right." He got up and paced around the long table. "I hate to see our company contribute to the change. I hate to see productive land—great-great-grandfather's land—turned into more hotels and golf courses. And I hate to see my own son advocating it."

"But the company *does* need capital . . ."

"No!" Tom stopped, glancing up at the painting. "Land is irreplaceable, especially on these small islands. Hotels are nothing more than . . ."

"The future?" Marilyn rose to move toward him. "Tom, the world you and I knew is gone."

"I've always refused to play a part in that!" he said, addressing the empty chairs as if the men of those earlier eras still sat at the table. His cigarette, idled between his fingers, waved a trail of smoke with each gesture. "The Hawaiʻi *we* knew—the Hawaiʻi that made my family and our forebears what we are—was a visionary spot, where people had jobs and everyone knew their place in the community. For years, I watched the plantations downsize their crews, juggle finances, and finally beg for government aid to keep the old camps going. How many thousands were laid off? How many had to find work on Oʻahu or the mainland, or didn't find work at all? At least *our* leases were among the last to grow cane. I kept lowering the rates to keep it that way."

"What about the new farms? Those are keeping people on the land."

"'Diversified agriculture'—bananas, tomatoes, orchids, shrubbery for subdivisions . . . cannabis, for Christ's sake! How many locals does that keep on the island? Manini!" Insignificant! His eyes watered. "When people leave, there goes your haulage."

"But isn't there *new* haulage?"

"You mean 'consumer goods'"—he almost spit the term—"mainland-style junk for big-box stores that wipe out our own merchants . . . Chinese products for the flood of malihini retirees."

Marilyn studied Tom's face. His turquoise eyes had suddenly lost their luster.

"Maybe you need a new vision, Tom. That's what your son's trying to do."

"What Tommy's proposing won't take these islands anywhere! You can make money on hotels and timeshares short term—God knows the Realtors and builders always do—but you don't build real communities with tourism and retirees, and you can't sustain growth with construction alone."

"At least he's trying *something* . . ."

Tom slumped into the chair directly below the painting. "And I'm not."

"Tom . . ."

He shook his head. "That's what *really* bothers me, Marilyn. I've racked my brain for ideas. I've hired consultants to advise me. I've read everything I can get my hands on that might shed new light . . . Tommy's read it all too. Face it. Life here is going the way of the old Northeast industrial towns."

Just then the intercom buzzed on the credenza phone and Marilyn answered. "Sam Chun, from Island Defenders, is here for his 4:15 appointment."

Tom scowled at his watch. "He's here about that fuel spill."

Sam strode into the boardroom with an athlete's brisk gait, wearing crisp blue jeans, surfer sandals, and a neatly pressed aloha shirt. He'd also put on his serious lawyer's persona and was already thinking in the King's English.

"Aloha, Tom," he said with a familiarity reflecting a long adversarial history with the Williams & Company patriarch.

Tom grunted back, but firmly returned Sam's handshake.

"What is it this time?" Williams said, uncharacteristically brusque, a holdover from the earlier meeting. He took a chair at the corner of the immense table and motioned Sam to sit down.

"The diesel spill," Sam replied, waiting. His dark eyes sparkled beneath the broad lids that hid them.

"Yes?"

"When we last spoke you said you'd investigate a better, long-term solution if we'd delay seeking an injunction on your pier operations," Sam said calmly, knowing that rattling legal sabers sometimes stirred action.

"Look, Sam," Tom said, leaning forward over the gleaming table, "it was an unintentional discharge into the bay—"

"A rusted tank that had been leaking for months, if not longer," the young lawyer interjected. "Hundreds of gallons of contamination."

"Like every other old island business, we've got infrastructure problems, Sam, facilities we're trying to upgrade, in this case an old storage tank long ago slated for replacement." He looked up at Sam's affable but impenetrable face. "We've been trying to raise the capital, but with the economy what it is . . ."

"I appreciate your situation, Tom, but what about Hilo Bay?"

Tom withdrew his cigarettes and tapped one out of the package. He stuck it in his mouth and then remembered Chun didn't smoke.

"Do you mind?" Tom asked politely, pulling a lighter from his breast pocket.

"Well . . . actually."

Williams set the unlit cigarette on the table.

"Island Defenders is relieved that the leakage was halted, but the Department of Aquatic Resources is still very concerned about how long you intend to store fuel in those small temporary tanks." Sam folded his hands above the table. "Of course, we too, look forward to a permanent—*legal*—solution to the problem."

Williams' face flushed. He'd already spent $75,000 for those tanks. A new fuel-handling facility compliant with the latest regulations would cost more than a million! Fortunately, harbor authorities had agreed to overlook the cumulative daily fine. "Seriously, Sam, what difference could a year or two make when it comes to the health of the bay? Nothing's leaking now."

Sam eyed his adversary with sympathy, but shook it off. "You've already avoided the fines, although that might be changed in court too."

Williams rose from his chair and thrust a finger at his adversary. "I've had enough of your legal blackmail! If Island Defenders wants to waste its time and everyone else's, go ahead. I simply can't respond any more responsibly than I have."

Sam also stood, quietly nodding. "OK," he said with a tone that meant, "I've warned you," and extended his hand to the businessman. They shook perfunctorily and Sam left. Williams slumped into his chair and watched the environmentalist drive away in his Honda CR-V, kayak paddles rattling in the back and its bright aqua bumper sticker—SEA>I—flashing in the sun like a taunt.

Some minutes later Marilyn found Tom alone at the table, smoking. He was gazing at the portrait of his ancestor's *Phoenix*, his moist eyes gleaming in the last sunlight coming through the window. He hadn't noticed her enter because his mind was firmly rooted in the past, recalling one of those youthful days when he and Bobbie Castle rode the cane sluice from Wainaku camp down to Puʻueo. The plantation foreman had chased after them, but they got away by splitting up in one of the gulches, laughing about it later at their favorite skinny-dipping pond.

He gazed into the table's dark wood, wiping away tears with a bare palm. Marilyn backed out of the room and had almost eased the door closed when Tom's face contorted with an anguish Marilyn hadn't seen since the day his father died.

"Bastard!" he shouted, standing erect before the *Phoenix*. "Wouldn't even let me smoke in my own boardroom!" His eyes turned to fire. "Things are gonna start changing around here," he announced, his stout lips in a straight line.

Three days later, Tom met privately with his son, arriving early to place himself directly beneath the canvas of his great-grandfather's square-rigger so that Tommy, sitting opposite, would have to face it as they spoke. The younger executive, still wound-up from his property sale scheme, hustled into the boardroom in a cloud of agitation, his new iPad Pro tucked under his arm. Although each man possessed a trace of Hawaiian blood from the original marriage that had yielded the land to their missionary ancestor, both were haole in business temperament and "wasted" no time on small talk.

"Tommy," his father began, "I called this meeting to tell you I've found a way to raise substantial capital without selling the land."

The son frowned. "We've been through all this before, Dad."

"I know, but this is crisis time, so I decided to step over a line I haven't crossed in years. I called in some of my chits."

Sweat gathered under Tommy's collar. He was wary of his father's connections to the aging cabal of Democratic Party "old boys," and wasn't convinced the company needed those ties anymore. Indeed, when he'd turned forty, he risked his father's ire by contributing company money to some Republicans.

"I didn't know anyone still owed you anything. And with Senator Inouye dead and buried . . ."

Tom's cheeks flushed, and he lit a cigarette to steel himself. "I called Hashimura."

Twice the "old boys" had offered Henry Hashimura the chance to be governor and both times he'd declined. He believed money held more power than votes and that it was easier to make or break political careers than to have one. Two years in the territorial legislature and one term in the state senate were sufficient to make all the connections he needed to join his older cohorts in their quest to get out from under the white plantation oligarchy and shift who controlled land, money, and power in the burgeoning economy of the new American state. Hashimura and his comrades had paid plenty of dues to haoles in those early days, what he called "investments in our revolution."

By the time the "old boys" asked Hashimura to run for governor, in the early '70s, he was already so prosperous from Waikiki real estate schemes that he didn't need the job. He'd also demonstrated a talent for recruiting ambitious young liberals willing to transform Hawai'i into a thoroughly American place so they, too, could gain social acceptance—and make money. His recruits had included Nisei Japanese, Chinese entrepreneurs, ambitious haoles, and even a few Hawaiians. Hashimura's immigrant parents had given him the auspicious name Noburo—"to ascend"—and instilled in their bright son a creed that would come to be known as "locals first—Palaka Power," named for the iconic checkered palaka shirts worn by plantation workers. Their goal: "to loyally serve the group so all can rise." And rise they did, to heights that made even members of the white oligarchy, like Tom's father, have to play in the new "old boys'" game. The last time Hashimura was asked to run for governor, in the early '80s, he was by then so rich from international deals that even the needs of his insatiable ego could not sway him to compromise his secure position of power outside government. Hashimura even used his given name as a thing of clout, granting to a select few the private privilege of calling him Noburo. Though it was long ago when Williams & Company held a virtual monopoly on island shipping, Tom was still one of those granted that honor.

"He's made calls to Washington to hold up the Department of Defense contract to a mainland shipper for transport of Stryker combat vehicles and Army training drones from California to Hawai'i. He's assembling a deal to make us the shipper."

Tommy bolted upright in his chair, flabbergasted, not only because that old goat Hashimura would still do this for his father but because he'd already told Tom his misgivings about making deals with the military, especially after 9/11.

"What's this gonna look like to our board of directors—the company dependent on the fed's biggest and dumbest bureaucracy!"

"Don't be so negative, Tommy."

"Look, Dad, DOD has locked up a quarter of Hawai'i's developable land for their bases! And what does Hawai'i get for that? Nothing except a few no-bid contracts to the same Hashimura-indebted construction companies." His eyes narrowed. "And I don't trust them. Look how they stonewalled the Red Hill fuel leaks at Pearl Harbor, downplayed sickening all those people who drink from the Navy's water system, then dragged their feet in shutting the damn tanks down!"

"Noburo will make sure we're not shortchanged." Yet even as he said it, Tom knew his son was right to be apprehensive. Military officials had also repeatedly lied to Big Islanders, about everything from secret missile silos to the clandestine testing—and later dumping—of chemical weapons. The business community had looked the other way because decades of pork barrel appropriations from Senator Daniel Inouye, and subsequent congressional leaders aping his example, had brought Hawai'i billions in military investments—particularly construction. This made the US government the single most powerful interest group in the state, with most of the spinoff benefits going to businessmen on O'ahu.

"Noburo assured me that we'll also get the lucrative contract to shuttle all that military hardware—and troops—between islands," Tom continued.

"And what did you have to give him in return?" Tommy replied incredulously, "I mean besides the last of your 'chits.'"

"A commitment to support that new Mauna Kea telescope in the Big Island chamber of commerce. As you know, some members, especially the Hawaiians, are lukewarm to the idea after all the *pilikia* over the Thirty Meter Telescope."

Now why would Hashimura give a shit about that? Tommy thought.

His father answered the unspoken question. "I take it Oshiro Construction has its fingers in that huge construction pie again. Noburo's on that board too."

Tommy laughed bitterly. "I see. Now that TMT's been derailed, Oshiro needs another fat building project, eh? Nothing ever changes with those guys!"

"Listen, son, if we get this Army contract, we'll have plenty of income to diversify our portfolio without having to sell great-great-grandfather's land. And it's still about shipping."

"I'll be honest with you, Dad. I'd rather sell off real estate than get ourselves tangled up with the military." *To say nothing about owing Hashimura*, he thought.

Tom leaned over the table. "In an earlier time I'd agree with you son, but with the ongoing 'war on terror' and growing worry about China, the generals continue to beef up forces in the Pacific. That means the military will keep expanding in Hawai'i, including up at Pohakuloa. We might as well get the shipping piece of that gravy train while it's running."

Tommy got up from the table. "This will have to come before the full board."

"Of course," his father said confidently, rising to walk his son to the door. He knew that even though Tommy was now running day-to-day operations, the elder Williams still held more sway with that group.

Tom closed the door behind his son and a thrill passed through his old body. The Hashimura option had given him new hope in a desperate time and stimulated a verve he hadn't felt in years. That these came with a renewed tie to the old establishment's kingpin filled him with both excitement and trepidation.

CHAPTER 9

Star Wars

As the Williams men wrapped up their debate, another meeting was underway across the Pacific, in Pasadena. Three men—one with four stars on his blue uniform—finished their coffee on the veranda of the Einstein Suite at the Athenaeum Club. Air Force General Michael Todt and the young captain serving as his adjutant had flown in from Washington to be hosted in Albert Einstein's former rooms by Dr. Adam Jacob, now installed as Caltech's astrophysics chair. The three had spent an hour strategizing the best way to tell Dr. Willy McCrea the real—and classified—reason the Air Force had committed the rest of the money for the Haisley Big Eye.

Two years earlier General Todt had secretly persuaded Dr. Jacob and Caltech's president to accept Air Force funding for the project in exchange for access to the telescope. With Hawai'i hearings on the Big Eye now being planned, Jacob would soon have to make public the Air Force contribution. Willy had received a partial phone briefing on the arrangement the previous week, interrupting his latest attempt on Keck I's Planet Finder spectrometer to verify a possible Earth-like planet identified by the Kepler space telescope. The news that the Air Force would get telescope time to produce extremely high-resolution images of potentially dangerous asteroids had dismayed Willy, but he wasn't really surprised. Vigorous negotiations with other universities, research institutes, and the National Science Foundation had yielded pledges for only half the $1 billion short-fall—and those were garnered only by implying that the Big Eye would likely be built near the other giant telescopes in Chile rather than at the long-controversial Mauna Kea site. Now, with TMT relegated to its second-choice site in the Canaries, Caltech couldn't afford to be left empty-handed in the competition for who would own the world's most powerful GOD.

In the days since the phone briefing Willy had come to accept sharing the telescope with the Air Force, especially after Haisley told him he was actually "stoked" that his telescope would "help save the world from killer asteroids." Both were relieved that the funding uncertainty was finally over—but what they didn't know was that asteroids were only part of the military's plans.

At a private contract signing two years earlier, General Todt had insisted that Caltech keep the Air Force involvement under wraps—even to Willy, who had secured the philanthropist's money—until the Big Eye's technical design was complete, its funding pledges acquired, and all backroom congressional com-mitments in the Intelligence and Armed Services committees secured. That NORAD—the North American Aerospace Defense Command—would have classified authority to periodically over-ride the telescope schedule for strategic imaging of enemy spy and communication satellites would be explained to Willy later, and never to the public or the donor. Decades of asteroid impact studies, along with several popular Hollywood movies, provided excellent cover. Even schoolchildren had been frightened into believing that unchecked asteroid collisions could imminently destroy life on Earth. For Jacob, this arrangement had finally solved the tele-scope's funding problem and in an era when so much science money had been diverted to military projects.

Keeping this secret from the public would be quite manageable. The Air Force and Caltech both had a long history of obfuscating on behalf of the military with well-tested protocols to prevent discovery and oversight, and after 9/11, claims of secrecy "to protect national security" usually won the day. Haisley, they figured, would never find out and wouldn't give a damn anyway, as long as his legacy telescope got built.

Getting Willy McCrea to go along that noon could be a different matter, but he was already too involved on Big Eye committees to keep the two-year-old secret from him any longer. Unfortunately, Willy was not among the majority of American scientists now working directly or indirectly on military projects. Devoted to pure science, he could be a troublesome idealist in the world of realpolitik. Now that funding shortfalls would not stop the Big Eye, the day of reckoning had come, and Willy McCrea was on his way up to the Einstein Suite for a private catered lunch on the veranda.

Willy dreaded the meeting. Since the agreement was already a done deal, he felt annoyed having to disrupt his research and wary that a general would be at the meeting. He wondered what "additional details" they now felt compelled to share with him. It was not the first time men in uniform had joined Caltech scholars at the table. With a planetary physics doctorate from Caltech and his daughter Andromeda now a PhD candidate there, Willy was well aware of Caltech's central role in America's military-industrial complex. Though his apprehension had made him a tad queasy on the plane, he conjured up the delusion that he was about to hear exciting news and strode out onto the suite's veranda with his usual charismatic aura.

"Good afternoon, gentlemen!" he declared, offering his hand all around. "A beautiful October day in Pasadena!"

Willy took the one unoccupied chair at the rectangular table, elegantly set with china plates and silver utensils. That the stony-faced general sat at the table's head aggravated Willy's tinge of nausea. A smartly dressed waiter brought in spinach salads as the discussion began.

"Thank you, Willy, for interrupting your work to fly all the way down from Berkeley," began Jacob.

"No problem," feigned Willy. "Gives me an opportunity to confer with several colleagues about my recent planetary observations, as well as stop by to see my daughter. I'm sure the trip was more inconvenient for the general."

Jacob set his fork down and cleared his throat, an uncharacteristic pause for this haughty man that further unsettled Willy. "General Todt has additional news he wants to share with us," Jacob said, "and with the environmental impact studies of the Chilean and Hawai'i sites near completion, it seems the right time to do that."

A bubble of gas traveled up into Willy's throat and he shifted in his chair.

"You remember, Willy, how concerned we were a few years back . . . when we couldn't find the money to match Haisley's contribution? And you'll recall your own concerns about, well, that *odd* commitment you had to make to Haisley?"

The astronomer winced at Jacob's reference to Haisley's burial under the telescope.

"Well, I didn't want to discuss it over the phone the other day," Jacob continued, "but Caltech had to make another concession to ensure that the Big Eye—and all its potential discoveries—actually becomes a reality."

Willy's apprehension moved right up into his head and back down into his stomach. He stopped eating.

"I know you appreciate just how sensitive negotiations can be, Willy, especially with so much money and science at stake . . ."

The general, better suited for command than tender diplomacy, interrupted Jacob's presentation: "The Air Force has agreed to contribute funding to the Big Eye in exchange for use of the telescope."

"Yes, I know . . . the asteroid thing," Willy said, mustering his last vestige of wishful thinking. "When your Pan-STARRS sky-survey telescope on Maui identifies an asteroid on a potentially dangerous orbit, we'll schedule some Air Force time to do high-resolution imaging."

"Yes, but there are *other* near-Earth objects we're interested in. Because of national security considerations, you were not fully briefed on the extent of our agreement."

Willy's heart dropped and his stomach went berserk.

"What we are going to tell you is classified," the general continued, "privileged information that cannot be shared, even with Mr. Haisley. However, because you are the key scientist on this project and will play a critical role in structuring the observatory's scheduling and interagency communications, we realize you—and for the moment, you alone—will need to know some of the national security aspects of our plans."

"Must I?" Willy mumbled at his abandoned quiche.

"We'll be coordinating the Big Eye imaging with our Pan-STARRS telescope and the Maui Space Surveillance System on Haleakala. Obviously, NORAD will also be involved. We've scheduled meetings with people from all these units, and of course we've included you in those deliberations." The general paused to sip his coffee.

Willy raised his blue eyes from the plate, their sparkle gone. *The Big Eye was supposed to discover life, not contribute to warfare*, Willy thought, his heart pounding. The faith underlying his science was that other intelligent beings were out there, and that knowing that would make Earth's warring tribes realize that their differences were less important than what they had in common as members of one species on one planet.

Willy absently scanned the campus view off the veranda, forming words of protest—that identifying asteroids is one thing, imaging war satellites for NORAD quite another; how turning his dome on Mauna Kea into an Air Force spy compound was like doing battle recon from inside a holy church; and that the community of planetary scientists would naturally stand opposed. Willy's roving gaze eventually returned to the table and the placid face of Dr. Jacob, the old bull of Caltech's research machine. Jacob's cold gray eyes twinkled with involuntary glee as he watched an old-fashioned dreamer face the hard truths of academia.

Willy looked straight at General Todt. "I have important science work to do. I don't need to be on those committees . . . I'd prefer not."

"That's no problem," Dr. Jacob said to the general, taking swift advantage of the moment. "*I* can do that."

Willy felt a hard thud in his chest. Others would now decide the telescope's priorities. His queasiness also shifted, from that caustic ache that comes from biting bullets to an unsettled feeling of weakness. To Willy, the latter was more digestible, though it left a sour aftertaste of cowardice in his mouth.

"Rest assured, Willy," Jacob said, feigning solidarity with an aberrant warm tone. "In light of your key role in creating the telescope I'll make sure you're allocated ample time on the Haisley for your own research."

The general's adjutant suppressed a smile, and he motioned the waiter to bring in the last course—strawberry tortes. Willy passed on the Athenaeum tradition, excusing himself on the pretense of an early-afternoon reunion with his daughter.

"Today's lunch could not have gone better!" General Todt boasted to Dr. Jacob after the astronomer had left, "although I trust the food here was better in Einstein's day. Frankly, I anticipated more argument from McCrea. Indeed, I thought we'd have to struggle with him every time the Big Eye planning committees met. Any chance he'll have a change of heart?"

Jacob rose from the table and sauntered over to the veranda's balustrade. "Once the Haisley's up and running, Dr. McCrea will be too preoccupied hunting for planets to concern himself with the telescope's military component. And he's not the type to leak classified information to anyone—too timid—especially if it would jeopardize building the Big Eye. No, the real problem ahead—for all of us, including McCrea—will be the islanders' reactions when we release the draft EIS next month and they find out we're not as serious about building in Chile as we've so often implied."

"Could it hold up the Big Eye?" the general asked, his buoyancy dropping a notch.

Jacob paused to assemble his answer, looking out over the campus. "We really thought we had the TMT in the bag after we got through all those state approvals and finally a positive nod from the state supreme court. It cost millions in PR, community concessions, and lawyers' fees, but we did it, and Hawai'i officials assured us that the broader public was with *us* and that they could quash any residual local resistance. Then all hell broke loose . . . the road blockade, massive native protests across the state, unfavorable national and international media, and American celebrities showing up to support the so-called protectors. None of that was on our radar . . . Too bad Haisley's so damn committed to Mauna Kea."

The general frowned. "What are you saying, Jacob? Mauna Kea is perfect for monitoring foreign satellites in *both* hemispheres. As far as we're concerned the Chilean site is worse than second best."

"I understand completely, General." But to Jacob building the Big Eye in Chile would be far better than having it derailed. As Jacob walked back to his seat, he bitterly recalled how NASA withdrew its funding of four small "outrigger" telescopes to augment the Kecks when that project started losing in court and how TMT's foreign partners wavered at the prospect of building in the Canary Islands. *Might the Air Force do the same to the Big Eye if Hawaiian litigation backed by protests tied it up too? Or could the federal clout of the Air Force actually keep that from happening?*

"Rest assured, General, Mauna Kea is also Caltech's preferred site," Jacob continued, "but frankly we've been hassled by the Hawaiians and their environmentalist friends since the 1990s."

"Sounds like the University of Arizona's war with the Indians over Mount Graham a decade before that," said the general's aide, referring to when astronomers successfully transformed an Arizona mountaintop sacred to Apaches into a multi-telescope mecca.

"Yes," Jacob nodded, "but the affable natives of Hawai'i, unlike the Apaches, didn't really go on the warpath until TMT. Before that they just shed buckets of tears at the hearings. During the TMT blockades they actually hugged the arresting officers and said they loved them as the police dragged them off in paddy wagons. Even hard-bitten riot police dispatched from Honolulu wept."

General Todt curled his lip. "That's disgusting."

"Frankly, we were blindsided," said Jacob, sipping the last of his coffee. "We did not anticipate a new generation of opponents showing up—millennials and Gen Zers who aren't placated by educational grants . . . militants unafraid to go to jail."

"Like what's happened here on the mainland," the general's assistant said. "Occupy, Black Lives Matter, Standing Rock."

Jacob nodded. "Just imagine those young Hawaiians' reactions when they find out that our preferred site is actually Mauna Kea, that instead of just removing that decrepit 88-inch telescope—as we promised the community—we're replacing it with the Big Eye." He peered into the general's dark brown eyes. "Nor did we consider that Senator Inouye would die before construction got underway."

A shadow passed over General Todt's stony face. "He was a good friend to the military . . . so what's your political cover now?"

"Maybe you are. Air Force involvement—even just the public asteroid component—makes it possible to ask our congressional contacts for special federal legislation to go around our opponents, like the University of Arizona did to win Mount Graham—a masterful collaboration with Senator John McCain."

"Ah . . . McCain," Todt said with reverence for another faithful Department of Defense ally.

"Yes," Jacob continued. "He drafted legislation to exempt that mountain from federal environmental and cultural laws . . . and shrewdly got it passed on a late-night vote."

Light sparked in the adjutant's blue eyes. "Ahhh . . . I see . . . with the Air Force involved we could put together a Hawai'i version of the Senator McCain strategy—this time to ensure against an asteroid disaster—and slip the exemptions into another DOD bill."

"National security," Jacob added, his little eyes now twinkling.

"Yes," said Todt, thoughtfully rubbing his square chin. "That's an excellent fallback strategy . . . play a congressional trump card that sidelines the local politics."

Jacob leaned forward. "And use federal earmarks, like Senator Inouye did, to buy the silence of local opponents with grant money for their struggling nonprofits."

"But can we manage all of that without Senator Inouye?" the adjutant said.

"Good question," Jacob replied. "No one's really stepped into his shoes yet, and I'm told by one powerful Honolulu businessman—Henry Hashimura—that Hawai'i's congressional delegation is pretty lightweight by comparison."

The general almost smiled. "Lightweight isn't necessarily bad. That may actually give us a stronger hand. It means we at the Air Force become the pressure point the politicians would rather not deal with. Since 9/11 we've successfully done that with members of Congress all over the country . . . and that, I truly believe, has helped keep our nation secure and the New World Order intact." General Todt's usually stolid face actually flushed with those last words, and Jacob noticed it.

Huh, a true patriot, Jacob thought. *That's a handy vulnerability I might take advantage of later.*

"Dr. Jacob," said the adjutant, "will the activists make an issue of Air Force involvement if only the asteroid component is known?"

"Probably. They make an issue of everything. But most of the public will buy it, especially the business community, who, I suspect, would love to find some way to resurrect the astronomy industry after the TMT fiasco."

General Todt paused to think, intertwining his fingers above the flaky crumbs of his torte. "Could we divert some of that local opposition to Haisley's bizarre desire to be buried under the telescope? In my experience, the initial point of controversy has the most sticking power, often overshadowing the other issues. Why not make Haisley and his eccentricities the target?" A placid smile stood on the general's smooth face, his eyes as cold as a snake's.

Men of the same cloth, he and I, thought Jacob with his characteristic smirk. *In it to win.*

"And if the politics fail," added the general, standing up with his aide, "we'll employ the McCain strategy. We should start lining up legislators now, in case we need to launch that weapon."

"Yes, sir," said his adjutant with a tone that sounded like a salute.

The general's eyes flashed with animus. "And the activists can cry all the Hawaiian tears they want."

CHAPTER 10

First Sign of Trouble

November winds whipped Mauna Kea with soggy Pacific air that reached all the way to the summit. Dense fog swirled about the cinder peaks, and the observatories shook with gusts forewarning winter storms that would soon bring monsoons to the coast and blizzards to the volcano's heights. At least the hurricane season was almost over. Five thousand feet below the domes, Erik Peterson sipped another coffee, marveling at the heaviest downpour to hit the base camp since his arrival a year earlier. Gusts rattled the dining room's big windows and wind thudded under the eaves, leaving the impression that phantoms walked the roof.

A few astronomers still hung out at the tables, waiting impatiently for the cold air mass above Mauna Kea to push the shroud of summit clouds down the mountain so they could work. One oldtimer who'd observed there for decades looked spooked, and Erik recalled Freddie's story about the night that astronomer came down early after seeing "weird twirling lights" on the north plateau from the UH 88-inch catwalk.

Bet there's plenty of water filling Lake Waiau tonight, Erik thought, yet again pondering the mysterious young woman he'd met there last summer. *What would she think of this wild night? Does weather like this call her up here . . . or keep her away?*

Outside, cinder ravines churned red with wet ash, and deep gullies rutted the cinder road leading up top. Protected inside the tiny guard shack, Ranger Jill Kualono read the latest detective novel about Sergeant Tita Carvalho and her futile war with the "ice" dealers of Waikiki. Bundled up in a pile jacket, the Hawaiian had felt poorly all afternoon, her stomach unsettled and a distinct chill in her bones. She eagerly awaited her shift's end at 7:30 p.m. By then any astronomers crazy enough to have gone up would be secure in their domes, waiting for the weather to ease so they could start observing. The telescope day crews and the last tourists would also be off the mountain. Jill settled in for the hour-and-a-half wait.

Bang! Bang! Bang! A bony fist pounded her rain-streaked window. She instinctively palmed the baton on her duty belt, then recognized the narrow face of Ernesto Dela Cruz, an electrician with the Gemini telescope. Droplets stood on his graying eyebrows and he trembled inside a yellow rain slicker too big for his slender Filipino frame.

"Git room in dere fo' me?" he asked, pointing through the window.

"Don't know," she replied, eyeing the rain running off his body. "I like keep my office dry," dropping into her native pidgin to match Ernesto's.

"C'mon, tita. Le'me in!"

She opened the door and went back to her novel.

Ernesto shook off the rain and stepped inside. "You seen Kyle O'okala come back down?" he asked with the islanders' singsong cadence that gives every question an apologetic tone.

Eyes still on the page, she shook her head. "Why?"

"He nevah wen' come to dinner."

"He stay sleeping, dat's why."

"Not. I wen' call his room. No one dere. He way late . . . like two hours."

She looked up from her novel. "Where's he working today?" she asked, quickly shifting back to haole ranger tongue.

"Smithsonian array. I wen' call da observatory office, but da day crew all gone now."

"You try his cell?"

He nodded. "No more nothing."

"Out of range, maybe?"

"Naw, we always git."

"There's fifty-five-mile-an-hour winds up there—and fog. That's what's making him late." She turned back to her book.

Ernesto, still dripping, leaned over her desk. "I git one bad feelin', sistah. Kyle been up dere on his own since noon. He wen' told me he had fo' check some electrical on dat far antenna, da one pas' da old TMT road."

"Way out on the north plateau?" Jill pictured the barren volcanic landscape a half mile from the main cluster of summit observatories where the Smithsonian Institution had recently moved the eighth dish of their sprawling array of submillimeter radio telescopes. She looked up at the sky, now dark with rain and imminent nightfall and remembered that nightly wind chills had already begun dropping below freezing.

"Da SMA crew said Kyle wen' leave da main building at 3:30 fo' fix some *kine* relay or somet'ing. Dey t'ought Kyle wen' come down too, but no more Kyle fo' dinner."

Jill's face darkened.

"Kyle been in weird moods lately . . . always grumbling . . . and went out dere by hisself."

Jill closed her novel.

"You like go up wit' me?" Ernesto's eyes pleading.

Jill stood up, yanking her duty belt high onto her ample hips. "C'mon," she commanded with an officious edge bespeaking the Portuguese half of her heritage accustomed to bossing Asians on sugar farms.

Locking the door, she hesitated, wondering if she should grab the Glock stowed in her locker. *Unnecessary*, she concluded, recalling Moses' cultural admonition to avoid carrying a weapon above the base camp if she could help it. *It's just weather.*

Jill and Ernesto dashed through the downpour to the bright red F-250 pickup behind the guard shack, its Mauna Kea Ranger shield gleaming with rain. Jill popped it into four-low.

"I'm heading up the mountain for a personal assist," she radioed the visitor center guide. "You get any tourists crazy enough to go up in this soup, tell them to self-register."

"Copy that. What's up?"

"Probably nothing," she said, but her na'au—those instinctive feelings in her gut—said otherwise. "We may have a stranded observatory worker, vehicle trouble, or some such. Will call you back in thirty to forty."

"Copy. Good luck."

Jill smiled wryly. She hadn't had much good luck in her life, but she never let it bother her, having chosen instead to escape her turbulent past with work. Law enforcement gave her daily license to submerge whatever sweetness remained inside the Hawaiian half of her heart beneath the hard-edged demeanor she believed the job required, a manner well learned from her bitter, abusive Portuguese father.

"I tired o' dis mountain," Ernesto said as Jill's Ford struggled up the gullied road. "It's cold, empty, and I no more sleep good when I'm up here at night." She didn't respond, just stared out the windshield, the sour feeling in her gut growing stronger.

Two thousand feet up the mountain, past the first two switchbacks, the truck entered the dark clouds that had poured rain on the base camp all afternoon. That meant fog as well as rain, and the ambient light from the just-set sun quickly dissolved into darkness. The rough thoroughfare was especially rutted above 11,000 feet, where astronomers' vehicles had earlier struggled up the wet road. Another thousand feet and she'd be back on pavement, laid down for dust control near the observatories.

Jill cranked up the heater. *Let's hope there's no rain on top*, she thought. She mentally checked the rescue gear on board—jumper cables, shovel, winch, gas can, first aid kit, wool blankets, two "C collars," and a litter. *What might have happened to that electrical engineer?* He could be lying unconscious after a fall, injured, or dead from an electrical shock, or freezing in a stalled vehicle. On the other hand, he might just be fast asleep on a control room couch.

"And it's weird too," Ernesto said, continuing his own private vein of thought.

"What's weird?"

"Dis mountain," Ernesto's eyes bigger than usual. "I wen' hear plenty stories during my twenty-t'ree years up here—most o' dem from Kyle."

Ranger Kualono wasn't keen on having him repeat them just then, not with fog, darkness, and windblown rain obscuring her view out the windshield. "Yeah, well," she shrugged.

"If da money wasn't so good, I woulda left long time ago."

Jill understood but didn't feel the same. She loved Mauna Kea, even if it was mysterious and the altitude made working on it taxing.

Ernesto grabbed her arm, "I tell you Jill, I git one bad feeling about dis. Jus' yesterday, Kyle w'en tell me he getting worried up dere, said somet'ing goin' happen."

She shook loose his grip. "What are you talking about?"

"Kyle told me he seen too much bad stuffs happen on da mountain, all adding up now." He shook his head, reluctant to speak and yet compelled to do so. "Kyle told me he git dis strange feeling lately, dat he 'fraid fo' some kine . . . 'payback.'"

"From who?" Jill's tone sharper than ever. The activists were sometimes a pain in the ass, she thought, but even during the TMT fight they were peaceful.

"No, no, Jill, from *what*, not who." Ernesto eyed the ranger closely, wondering if the half of her heritage that she shared with Kyle O'okala would understand what he was telling her. "'Consequences,' Kyle wen say, 'For all dose years messin' wit' whatevah's up dere.'"

Jill shook her head, but it was only for show.

Ernesto clutched her arm again, and this time she let him. "I not Hawaiian," he said, eyes shimmering, "but I tell you somet'ing. Even *I* seen t'ings, but nevah sure, ya know. Kyle, *he* sure. Told me dey nevah shoulda built way out on dat north plateau—Smithsonian or da TMT site. Old kine stuff out dere—shrines and I don't know what."

Jill flashed on rumors that had circulated at the camp for years, about construction crews unearthing bones while bulldozing the summit cones for telescopes. Speculation was that to avoid notifying the state, foremen had ordered workers to hide the bones somewhere down along the road to the old "13 North" research station, where decades later TMT had hoped to build. And then there were all those nighttime sightings of ghostly lights out there.

"Ancient t'ings nobody, even da archeologists, understand," the distraught Filipino continued. "Jus' yesterday Kyle wen' told me somet'ing bad gonna happen . . . now he missing!"

Jill pointed her finger at the trembling man. "You, shut up. Just keep your eyes out for Kyle or his truck."

But there was nothing to see in the headlights, save for swirls of rainy fog crossing the road. When they finally reached the upper pavement, its reflective yellow centerline helped Jill stay on track. She scanned the ditches and giant cones with the truck's spotlight, but all they saw was wet cinder, lava, and ash.

Ten minutes later and a thousand feet higher—still well below the summit—they entered the cloud tops. The rain was now below them but the fog was thicker than ever, and Jill almost missed her left turn to the submillimeter observatories. Two windows glowed through the murk outside the Smithsonian array's control room. The ugly industrial building fronted a half-mile-long array of radio dishes sprawled across the volcano's north flank.

"Gonna be a while before anybody can observe tonight," Jill commented, parking the truck as close to the building's front door as possible. "Even if the clouds drop back down the mountain, the wind's too strong to open the domes." They held tight to the door handles as they stepped outside.

Ernesto slid on the pavement. "Uh-oh! Got black ice!"

Freezing fog after sunset often plagued the mountaintop, when the dampened pavement turned treacherous with an invisible skin of ice. Jill stooped to confirm it.

"Visitor Center, this is Jill," she said into the mic of her truck's police radio.

"Go ahead," replied the guide.

"Visibility at Smithsonian Control is near zero with fog, and we've got black ice."

"Down there at 13,000 feet?"

"Affirmative."

"Suppose anyone up top even knows about the problem?"

"I doubt it. Phone the summit observatories and tell them to come down now or they'll be stranded till morning."

"Copy. What about your vehicle assist?"

"Don't know anything yet. We're checking at the control building first, but we may have to drive out to the north plateau."

"OK. Keep me posted . . . and be careful up there."

Jill joined Ernesto at the steel door. She rang the buzzer and an astronomer came over the speaker: "Pizza delivery? Couldn't you bring us some better goddamn weather instead?"

"It's Ranger Kualono."

"Oh . . . hold on. The T.O. will be there in a minute."

The two waited in the bitter cold for the telescope operator, and Jill wished again that they'd issue the rangers keys to all the buildings. The door finally buzzed and they slipped inside. Buck Johnson, the T.O., was bundled up in a red sweater and matching watch cap, and the twenty-one-year veteran of Mauna Kea observatories looked more like a lumberjack than a telescope jockey. He leaned his big frame against the door.

"Well, well, what brings you up here on such a lovely evening? Like to join us in the TV room while we wait for the astronomers to give up on the night?"

"I've got good news for you, Buck. There's black ice out there, so you can go down . . . if you can still make it. Probably can if you're careful. I don't know about your buddies on the summit."

Buck grinned. "I could use a full night's sleep, especially at thirty-two bucks an hour." He looked over at the Gemini technician. "Ernesto, what are you doing working this late?"

"Kyle stay missing," he said starkly.

"I don't understand," Buck suddenly sober.

"He's not here?" Jill asked.

"Haven't seen him. We arrived forty-five minutes ago, and I've been in every part of the building since then."

"He wen' told me he had fo' check some electrical on dat far dish."

Buck shook his head. "In weather like this? That doesn't make sense. That antenna was fixed yesterday."

"C'mon, Ernesto," Jill said, turning to the door. "We better drive out there."

"Be careful, Jill, that road's still torn up from the TMT dozers, and I won't be here to help if I can convince those eggheads it's time to skedaddle."

Jill nodded as they stepped back into the wind.

Jill eased the truck back onto the icy pavement. "How well do you know the road out there, Ernesto?"

"Nut'ing."

As she turned onto the labyrinth of cinder roads connecting the antennas, Jill felt a tingle climb her back. She dropped the tranny into four-low and started the half-mile descent to the far ridge. Fog-filled winds swept over the rutted road, rocking the truck like a boat on stormy seas. Now and again breaks in the fog revealed the towering radio dishes.

"Maybe shoulda brought Buck wit' us," Ernesto said, his face close to the windshield.

"Maybe," Jill replied, imagining what she might find at road's end in these wind chills.

"What's dat!" Ernesto hollered, rolling down his window. Fog poured in.

Jill jammed on the brakes and leapt from the truck. Ernesto watched her dash through the foggy headlight beams, baton drawn, and disappear behind what had startled him—a dozen upright stones of an ancient shrine.

Jill was gone long enough to make Ernesto start to worry. When she returned, her uniform was damp, her face flushed, and her eyes iridescent with adrenaline.

"I coulda sworn I saw someone out there," she said, struggling to catch her breath in the thin air, "a man draped in a long coat or something. Did you see him?"

"I only seen da shrine."

"Musta been fog." Jill jammed the baton back into her duty belt, and then rubbed her eyes with both hands. Her fingers trembled.

"Let's finish this job," she said, slamming the truck back into gear. They drove to the far antenna and got out. Kyle's truck was not there, but fresh tire tracks marked the ground adjacent to the giant dish and a forgotten wrench lay on its concrete base. Jill hollered into the fog but only wind howled back. They searched the rest of the array, stopping at each antenna to call out as they scanned the stark terrain with the spotlight. Finding nothing, they carefully checked along the paved roads below the summit—the upper ones too treacherous from black ice to even attempt. At ten o'clock Jill and Ernesto returned to the base camp, and immediately headed to the dining room for hot coffee. Word had already spread about the search.

"Find your man?" Erik asked, still watching the storm over cups of cocoa.

"Must o' gone straight home without stopping here for dinner," Jill said. Even so, she left a message on Kyle's home machine and reported the situation to the Hilo police, who agreed to keep trying to reach him.

Weather kept every observatory closed that night. Even after clouds dropped below the summit, sixty-mile-an-hour winds buffeted the domes, and wind chills fell to minus twenty. All the observatory teams had evacuated, including those who inched down the icy pavement from the upper domes. As the University of Hawai'i telescope operator eased his vehicle away from the highest observatory, he had noticed something shiny in his headlight beams far below the road—something metal maybe, way down inside the cinder crater of the mountain's summit cone. Nervous about the ice under his tires, and with two irate JPL astrophysicists in the back seat—having lost their last night of observing—the T.O. didn't stop to check it out. He did mention it to a base camp housekeeper watching TV in the lounge—Erik had already gone to bed—but at that point, neither the T.O. nor the housekeeper knew anyone was missing.

Eight hours later, in the cold light after dawn, the first day crew driving up the mountain noticed Kyle O'okala's pickup in the bowl of the summit cone, at the end of the gouged trail it had left as it tumbled down the slope. The electrical engineer's broken body was pinned against the crumpled dash, his last breaths frozen onto the driver's side window. He must have remained conscious for some time because he'd scratched three words into the ice: "abandon the mountain." But his message didn't explain what he was doing on the upper summit road on that godforsaken night, miles from the Smithsonian dish, or why the left front wheel of his truck had fallen off the axle, its six lug nuts missing from the wheel.

CHAPTER 11
Speculations

Two days after the incident, Moses, Jill, Erik, and Freddie gathered at a back table in the dining room to eat a late breakfast and discuss the tragedy. Braddah K, seeing the group assemble, set aside his duties in the kitchen and surprised all of them by quietly pulling up a chair.

"The coroner says Kyle died of hypothermia," Ranger Kualono said, dark bags under her eyes from two nights of agitated sleep. "He froze to death waiting for help."

Erik shook his head. "What an awful way to die."

Braddah K's big eyes moistened.

Seeing this, Jill teared up too. "I shoulda searched that upper road."

"You wouldn't have made it, Jill," Moses said, "and we'd have had to send up a search party for you and Ernesto too."

"Remember when black ice sent Archie Botelho's Suburban off the other side of that road?" hollered Jeffrey Drake, eavesdropping at the service counter. "Flattened like a pancake a thousand feet down! Good thing those idiot astronomers in the back seat thought to jump out too!"

Moses glared at the cook and waved him back into the kitchen.

"What was O'okala doing up there, anyway?" Erik asked. "Trying to warn the guys in the domes?"

"No," Jill said. "Way I figure it, he drove up there *before* ice formed on the road. It was the wheel coming off that sent him into the crater."

"And there's the real question," Moses said. "What happened to those lug nuts?"

"Maybe the guys in the garage screwed up," said Freddie, "It's happened before. Rushing too many repair jobs at once, eh?"

"Well, the police are calling it an accident," Jill said, "but I'm not ruling out sabotage."

Moses raised his eyebrows. "That's a pretty big leap."

"Maybe, but there's lots o' people pissed off about the astronomers' endless drive for scopes up here . . . and now, even after losing their Thirty Meter, they're back pushing something twice as large."

"I thought the islanders asked for the telescopes," said Erik. "That's what they say down at the visitor center."

They all laughed, except Braddah K, whose broad brow began to sweat. A long, uneasy pause ensued while they digested Jill's sabotage comment.

"For locals, it's just the latest gripe," Freddie finally said, "after they built hotels on every beach, crowded our surf spots with tourists, and put military compounds all over the place!" He cracked his knuckles. "Rumor has it one of the Army's practice drones down at PTA has some unexplained bullet holes in its wings."

Moses frowned. "Where did you hear that?"

"The Honoli'i grapevine. Some of the surfers down there work at Pohakuloa."

"Do they know who did it?" Jill asked with an ominous ranger tone.

"Coulda been anybody—a hunter, a disgruntled employee, even a PTSD soldier. There's plenty o' them around. Or maybe it was whoever shot up those two 'Daniel K. Inouye Highway' signs on the Saddle Road after they renamed it."

Moses shook his head. "There was nothing in the newspaper about the drone."

Freddie cracked his knuckles again. "O' course there wasn't."

"There's a lot o' angry Hawaiians too," Jill added, "some of 'em pretty militant."

"Eh, what would you expect, Jill?" Freddie said. "Good people can take getting kicked around only so long, and two hundred years of boots in the guts is *plenty* long. And now the Big Eye! After all their patience and aloha during the TMT fight, it's like givin' 'em da finger," he said, demonstrating it. "You t'ink your Potagee ancestors woulda taken dat shit?"

The frown on Moses' faced deepened. "Some islanders are frustrated, yes, but I don't think . . ."

"Who'd wanna hurt one nice guy like Oʻokala?" Braddah K interrupted, surprising everyone by speaking up.

Freddie nodded. "No, it doesn't make sense, does it? And why'd he go up there in dat crazy wind and fog?"

"Maybe . . . maybe somebody w'en chase 'im." Braddah K said.

Moses straightened up in his chair. "Who? Why?"

"Dunno," he replied, so softly they could barely hear him, "but, eh, it's not da first time innocents w'en die up here, is it?" He pushed away from the table and went back into the kitchen.

Jill's face flushed, but she wasn't ready to reveal to anyone but Moses what she'd told Ernesto to keep to himself—that eerie incident at the shrine.

For weeks the camp buzzed with speculation, and a few workers half seriously joked that Jeffrey Drake was "da one guy on da mountain lolo enough to put a wrench to a company truck." As for Drake, he blamed it on "that strange wahine who's always wandering around up there."

Hawaiians on the crew were oddly quiet. This was, after all, not the first Mauna Kea death attributed to violations of ancient kapus—taboos established over dozens of generations to protect the mountain's sacred power. Big Island Hawaiians remembered all too well that three men had suffocated during a 1996 construction fire at the Japanese Subaru Telescope, unable to escape in the black smoke filling the dome after a welding torch ignited its still-exposed insulation. After that accident, islanders had quietly speculated about what on the mountain had been disturbed during all those decades of construction.

Hawaiians weren't the only ones to suspect something unnatural behind the Oʻokala "accident." Construction workers had witnessed other baffling vehicle mishaps atop the mountain, and hunters, familiar with Mauna Kea's lore or having had their own strange experiences, instinctively suspected forces not easily explained with logic. Even a few old-time astronomers dared to wonder. They'd heard of strange occurrences during those first years when Americans began carving up the mountain for roads and dome sites.

All of this disturbed Erik, even as it fascinated him. He knew from his South Seas voyages and his explorations among the Mississippi's backwater islands that the world was more inexplicable than the Western mind conveniently assumed. The base camp and the domes, like the boats he'd manned on the river and the sea, were but specks of familiarity in a larger reality whose mysteries are not easily fathomed by modern man. Being reminded of all that again—and by such a perplexing tragedy—only added to Erik's growing disquiet.

PART TWO

CHAPTER 12
Nightmare

❧ July 19, 1974

Mauna Kea erupted in Joel Kuamoʻo's dream as his wife's Datsun station wagon exploded in the open carport of their old plantation house above Hilo. In his dream, fiery cinder and ash spewed from the volcano's summit as he raced down the mountain in an Oshiro Construction Company dump truck.

Joel didn't wake from the dream until oily smoke poured into his bedroom. By then flames engulfed the back half of the house and the jungle pulsed with an orange glow. When he finally realized his bedroom—not a truck—was on fire, he sprang to his feet and faced the blaze, already bubbling paint off the walls. The Zenith TV had melted into the dresser, and the hallway was a vortex of flame.

"Leilani! Keola!" he screamed, his thick beard curling in the heat. "Run outta da house! Now!" Joel's mind reeled. Thank God, Eve was visiting her sister in Honolulu, but now he alone must save the children!

Joel dashed toward the hallway but the inferno pushed him back. "Wake up! Get out!" he screamed through the pulsing orange smoke. He flew to the bedroom window, frying his fingers trying to remove the glass jalousies. He lunged under the bed to grab his birding shotgun. Choking, he smashed out the louvers with the butt end, drawing the smoke and flames farther into the room, the heat intolerable against his back. Joel dove through the window onto the damp grass and inhaled the cold night air.

"Dad! Dad!" A lone boy stood on the lawn screaming toward the burning house, the eight-year-old unaware his father had escaped.

"Ovah heah!" Joel hollered as he leaped up from the ground. "Where's Leilani!"

"Don't know!" Tears gushed from the boy's eyes. "T'ought she was right behind me!"

Joel, shotgun still in hand, bolted around the corner, his son at his heels. The front door, through which the boy had escaped, now roared with flame. Half the roof already slumped into the house, and glowing embers poured into the star-studded sky.

"Where'd you last see 'er!" father shouted to son.

"In da living room!"

Joel raced to the picture window. Black smoke swirled against the glass. He pressed his ear to the warm window and listened for his five-year-old daughter, but only the whistle of searing flame issued from inside. Manic, Joel swung his gun to shatter the glass. He was halfway through the sash when the roof fell in, knocking him back out onto the lawn. He wiped the blood away from his eyes and watched the walls collapse into the blaze.

Grief surged into his chest. He stood up on the lawn and stared, powerless, at the inferno. His son trembled next to the row of ti plants that fronted the house, his face, like his father's, iced in disbelief.

An arson investigation confirmed that a gas-soaked rag stuffed in the tank of Eve's Datsun had turned it into a Molotov cocktail, instantly igniting the dry-rotted walls of the old house. Joel thought of three possible reasons for the torching, only two of which he acknowledged to police—a random act of rage by drunken teenagers who'd been torching abandoned plantation buildings all fall, or Frankie Hakalau's way of settling a cockfight debt he claimed Joel still owed Hakalau's illicit clan. But Joel's gut told him neither of those things had taken his sweet daughter's life. He and Eve gave no serious thought to pursuing the truth with the authorities, because in

1974 the refurbished—and already entrenched—colonial establishment was just too powerful. Despite their anguish, and Joel's desire for payback, they knew that trying to avenge Leilani's death would only lead to more violence.

Joel quit his welding job on Mauna Kea and quietly moved Eve and his son to the mainland, vowing never again to speak with anyone about what he'd seen that fateful day on the mountain. Given that offense, and all that was at stake if it was fully exposed, Joel believed their lives might still be in danger. Only a few trusted family members knew where they'd gone.

As years passed and the mountain of Joel's ancestors was mentioned in the national news each time another, bigger telescope was built there, he wondered if it was safe yet to return to the island, but Eve would hear none of it. The pain of their loss seemed easier to handle from afar.

CHAPTER 13

Moses and the Astronomer

Though nearing retirement age, Moses Kawaʻaloa was still fit and carried himself like the sturdy older captains Erik had sailed with in the South Seas. Even visiting astronomers sensed something compelling in the veteran camp manager. He possessed what Hawaiians call mana—a personal authority derived from spiritual strength—and he carried out his camp duties with quiet command. Although only five foot eight, Moses had thick shoulders inherited from a long line of sailors, and muscles bulged beneath his rolled-up flannel sleeves. His hands were so brawny that once when the kitchen was shorthanded and Moses pitched in to mix up omelets, Erik marveled that he didn't crush the eggs when plucking them from the cartons. The Hawaiian's face contributed to his commanding presence, with its solid jaw, deep-set nostrils, and large luminescent eyes. Age had turned his great crop of hair snow white, but the elder's face was still youthfully smooth, save for wrinkles around his eyes from decades squinting in the high-elevation sun. His steely posture also belied his age, and when camp newcomers spotted Moses behind the garbage shack tossing meat scraps to the feral cats, they often mistook him for a man still in his forties.

Moses had worked on Mauna Kea twenty-five years, first with the kitchen crew and later as chief cook. When given a chance to run the camp, ten years back, he did, and expected to do so until retirement. Moses was a no-nonsense manager, judiciously reprimanding his crew when their work failed to meet his standards, but he also allowed for people's frailties, even appreciated their idiosyncrasies. Like the wise skippers Erik had known, Moses ran the camp firmly but fairly, a vital quality for the chief of a remote outpost like Hale Pohaku.

Erik's broader perspective on the man came late one December night after attending the stargazing program. It was cold and clear, and the Milky Way seemed to loom right above the base camp. Moses and an astronomer some years younger than he chatted at a table in the billiard room where the scientist's gangly graduate student practiced pool shots while listening via earbuds to the Royal Astronomical Society's latest *Supermassive Podcast*. The astronomer was one of those late-middle-aged men whose youthful appearance and demeanor make it difficult to pinpoint their age. Only the temples of his sun-bleached hair were gray, and his wrinkled denim shirt and baggy khakis gave his fit body a sprightly flair. He spoke with spirited gestures, and even from the dining room Erik noticed his brilliant sky-blue eyes. Several empty beer bottles stood between the two men, and the astronomer puffed relaxedly on a great burl pipe, a breach of the camp's no-smoking rule that on that night Moses ignored.

Erik, not wanting to intrude, took his Pop-Tarts and milk to an overstuffed chair near the fireplace and began perusing a copy of *Sky and Telescope*, but he couldn't help overhearing what he soon realized was a reunion of two old friends.

"Lots more telescopes since I last observed here," said the astronomer, clouding the billiard room with smoke.

"And another one planned, Jedediah."

"So I hear . . . and not without controversy."

"Yes."

The astronomer leaned back, fingers entwined behind his head. "The mountain's mood seems changed."

"So you've noticed?"

"She used to have a pure, wild feeling before the Kecks and Smithsonian, before they widened and paved the upper road. Back when I first observed, there were only four big domes on the mountain, and she felt utterly ancient, so pristine we wondered if we mere mortals should be here."

Moses nodded.

"My professor was on the new NASA Infrared Telescope, doing follow-up observations after *Voyager 1*'s Jupiter flyby. That was before they built the new base camp, and we slept in a cold, drafty dorm trailer and ate in a crude mess hall next door."

Moses chuckled. "That was even before *my* time."

"I remember when you showed up." He thrust a finger at the Hawaiian. "You had jet-black hair in those days!"

Moses grinned. "You should talk, Jedediah! You got gray coming in now too!"

They both laughed, and Moses retrieved two more beers from the little ice chest near his seat. He opened them and handed one to his friend. "You're right, Jedediah. The mood around here is different . . . from all the new buildings, yes, but all that pilikia from TMT too."

The graduate student pocketed his last ball. "I'm going upstairs to the library, Dr. Clarke," he said, putting away the cue stick, "and go over last night's data. Nothin' else to do till midnight."

"I'll come get you when it's time to head up to Keck."

The young man nodded, replugged his earbuds, and disappeared.

"Most astronomers seem to take the place for granted now," Moses continued, "and complain about every little inconvenience. They're too young to remember what it took to build the camp and the observatories." Moses pointed the neck of his bottle toward his friend. "And they don't respect the mountain like you early guys did."

The scientist sighed. "Scholarship's not the adventure it once was, back before remote observing, when astronomers had to climb a mountain to see the stars. The discoveries are more exciting but, frankly, it's just not as fun." He paused to puff his pipe. "And there's way too much competition for grants, telescope time, and tenure now . . . and fierce rivalries for professional accolades. It's a dour lot compared to the spirited astronomers of the past."

"A few of the old-timers still come up, Jedediah. You remember that cranky British astronomer who drank martinis at breakfast so he could sleep during the day?"

"How could I not?"

"But mostly a different breed now. I don't know when I last spent an hour talking story with one of 'em."

"It was inevitable." The scientist's face flushed. "Got the world's biggest telescopes? Here come astronomy's biggest egos, scientists more interested in prestige and headlines than taking chances. Few Einsteins or Feynmans now."

The astronomer got up to pace around the pool table, absently spinning its balls against the cushions. "And what about the mountain, Moses?"

Moses paused to deeply consider the question. "Changed too . . . did you hear about our recent accident?"

"The Smithsonian technician who ran off the road?"

"Yes."

"A Caltech colleague emailed me."

"It was odd, Jedediah . . . a godforsaken night."

The astronomer cocked his head. "What are you saying?"

"Kyle's wheel fell off . . ."

The astronomer stopped pacing. "I didn't know that."

"The lug nuts were gone. What with the storm, the ice, and those sharp curves up there, the driver must not have realized his wheel was wobbling off."

The astronomer rubbed his stubbly chin. "Peculiar . . ."

"The police wondered if it was sabotage, but in the end they decided it was shoddy vehicle maintenance combined with bad weather and black ice. But the ranger and technician who went up to search for him saw strange things that night . . . out on the north plateau . . . by one of the old shrines."

"The north plateau . . . ," Jedediah muttered in recognition. "Even astronomers got spooked by those mystifying light displays we'd sometimes see out there from the domes' catwalks." He reloaded his pipe. "Was anyone else on the summit that night?"

"A handful of dome crew and astronomers. The cops took down their names. Visitors sign in at the guard shack now, unless they're Hawaiians going up for cultural reasons. But I wonder, Jedediah, was it a *person* that pulled those lug nuts?"

"We've all heard the stories, haven't we?" the astronomer said, lighting up his bowl. "Going all the way back to the first telescopes—tools missing, parking brakes mysteriously disengaged, those weird incidents near the lake. As a scientist, it's impossible for me to comprehend all that, but as a blue-water sailor, I know people experience things in wild places that are difficult to explain."

Moses nodded, and the two fell silent for a moment. Moses got up and joined his friend at the pool table. "I'm glad I decided to stay over tonight, but I have an early start in the morning so I better hit the hay. It's good to see you back on the mountain, Jedediah."

"It's awfully good to be up here, but this'll probably be my last time."

"You retiring already?"

"Well . . . let's just say they gave me a golden handshake. This observing run is a leftover from an old Caltech project. I'm no longer there, but I'm not done working . . . just shifted my research to some old questions—and baffling thoughts—brought to my attention during my earliest visits to Hawai'i."

Moses nodded. "We're gonna miss you around here," he said, hugging his old friend. Erik couldn't be sure at that distance, but both men's eyes seemed to glisten with tears.

On his way out of the building, Moses made a point to acknowledge Erik with an affectionate wave.

CHAPTER 14
Celebrating Poliʻahu

The morning the pipe-smoking astronomer and his Caltech graduate student finished their four-night observing run on Keck II, a low-pressure system developed over the ʻAlenuihaha Channel. Within hours—as the two scientists slept in their dormitory rooms—the first clouds of the developing storm reached Hale Pohaku. When the pair got up to catch a late lunch before leaving for their flight home, rain was already falling over the base camp and flakes of snow began covering the summit. By the start of dinner all the day crews had come down, having secured their domes for a fierce blizzard that the mountain's meteorologist said would likely keep the observatories closed for at least twelve hours.

Most astronomers were scheduled to observe remotely that night, at control rooms in Hilo and Waimea or via teleconference hookups to their universities across the globe, so they'd learned the bad news from the observatories' Weather Center website. The few astronomers who still preferred being on the summit during their precious telescope time (to the chagrin of the telescope operators assigned to go up with them) ate their dinners with their T.O.s in the drafty base camp dining room, anxiously watching the storm develop outside its wall of windows.

Erik barely slept that night, what with howling winds, thunder and lightning, and downpours so heavy their drumming atop the roof created a roar akin to the Mississippi pouring over Saint Anthony Falls at flood stage. Each time he awoke, adrenalin from all the excitement inhibited his falling back to sleep.

The prospect of seeing the fruits of a Minnesota-class blizzard thrilled Erik, overpowering his fatigue during the next morning's shift. The road crew's burly band of locals had arrived early, barely giving Erik time to replace the previous night's sludge with fresh coffee. Boisterous with anticipation, the crew fortified themselves with omelets, pancakes, fried potatoes, and multiple cups of hot coffee, the whole time swapping stories of other great snowstorms. By 6:00 a.m. they headed up the mountain with Hawai'i's only snowplow and snowblower, followed by the Komatsu grader that smoothed out the usual washboards and ruts of the unpaved road, made rougher by erosion from the storm's deluge.

The first private vehicle, from Waimea, arrived at Hale Pohaku about nine o'clock, a Tacoma pickup with four laughing teenagers in its bed, stoked that snow had arrived during their school's Christmas break. One ranch kid had brought a grain shovel to fill the truck with snow. Others were on their way from all across the island.

"It's gonna be a madhouse here today," griped an astronomer from Berkeley. "All those people tearing up the road we have to use tonight!"

His telescope operator, a local Japanese, sighed.

"I don't know why we have to put up with it," the astrophysicist continued. "It's our goddamn road!"

"Actually," said the T.O., sipping his tea, "it's not. Hawai'i taxpayers built it."

"Huh?"

"Same taxpayers that installed those low-pressure sodium lights all across the island," added a grizzled NASA Infrared T.O. at the other end of the table, without looking up from his Spam and eggs, "to keep your skies dark."

The scientist frowned, but the T.O.s' rebukes kept his mouth shut for the rest the meal.

At 10:00 a.m. the clouds over the base camp finally cleared. Erik gasped when Mauna Loa's distant summit appeared through the dining room windows, its fresh blanket of snow sparkling under a bright-blue sky. An hour later, the road crew came back down, reporting that the road was now clear and that two feet of snow had covered the summit, with drifts twice as deep in spots. Jill Kualono opened the gate to let up what by then were dozens of pickups and SUVs. Moses and Braddah K watched the parade of vehicles from the cement landing outside the kitchen's back door.

"Poli'ahu was busy last night," Moses said, his brown eyes gleaming.

Braddah K smiled. "And look at all the people answering her call."

"Whether they know it or not," Moses replied. He gripped the younger Hawaiian's thick shoulder. "It's good when people connect with the mountain . . . even if it's just to play in the snow."

Just then the steel door opened and Erik peeked out. "Wow, this is great!" he said. "I can't wait to go up and see it myself!"

Moses smiled. "You can take the boy out of Minnesota, but you can't take the cold country out of the boy."

Erik laughed, but the homesick tug of renounced belonging made the Hawaiian's comment bittersweet, and Moses sensed it. "Look," he said, "after you deliver the day crews' summit lunch, take your time up top. We can handle things down here . . . yeah, K?"

The big cook nodded.

Erik ascended the mountain with his window open to take in the fresh, moist air following the storm. A flashy red pickup coming down passed his Explorer, its bed heaped high with snow. A pair of red-faced, grinning young men in tank tops and stocking caps sat on the icy heap, two garden shovels sticking out on either side of them.

"Eh, brah!" they hollered at Erik, flashing *shakas* with all four hands. "We takin' dis to Honoli'i! Gonna build one big snowman wit' one surfboard undah 'is arm!"

"Right on!" Erik replied as they passed.

After the second switchback, he reached the first snow-covered cinder cones, where two SUVs had parked along the road. Each family had a picnic laid out over the snow on plastic tablecloths printed with tropical foliage. Two teenagers flew down the nearest cone on boogie boards, while a young girl built a snowman with the help of her little blue beach bucket. As Erik slowed to pass the parked vehicles, the girl turned and smiled at him.

"This is the first time I ever saw snow!" she declared proudly. She bent over to grab a handful, already icy from the sun, and stuffed it in her mouth, little chunks spilling down her pink jacket. "Or ate it!" she cried.

"Good for you!" Erik replied as a raft of winter river memories floated into his mind. He hadn't built any snowmen on the islands along the river, but he'd eaten lots of snow out there during his snow-shoeing explorations.

When he reached the lower summit road below the upper cones, Erik was surprised to find dozens of vehicles parked along its plowed pavement, several with window stickers displaying the native symbol of nationhood—a royal *kahili* flanked by two canoe paddles. Muscular young men from several pickups shoveled snow into their trucks, and a blushing coquette on break from UH-Hilo tossed a giant snowball at her grinning boyfriend. Shouts and laughter filled the air as throngs of young people slid down the upper slopes on boogie boards, hunks of cardboard, and the plastic lids of garbage cans. Three teenage boys and a middle-aged couple took turns swooping down the steep grade on skis, throwing up hails of ice in their wake.

Incredibly, one haole family trudged up the blanketed cinder hill with a wooden toboggan just like the one Erik and his brother had used on Sweeny's Hill when they were boys. A wave of small-kid memories poured into Erik's mind, of family outings to sled, ski, and skate together—Peterson clan traditions from a time before cell phones and apps, when only his dad had internet (at the newspaper) and cancer hadn't sickened his mother yet. Erik flashed on how he'd help her clean up her painting studio so she could prepare the family's supper in time to eat it together watching *Nova* or the History Channel.

His eyes watered and he started to choke up. Damn! he thought. What is it about this place that brings up all these tears!

Erik was so overwhelmed with nostalgia that the reason for his ascent—to deliver hot soup and sandwiches stowed in the Cambro food carrier behind the back seat—flew out of his mind. Instead of turning right up the steep road to the summit he veered left toward the happy crowd playing off the lower road near the James Clerk Maxwell observatory. His eyes were so clouded that he had to slow the Explorer, but he didn't stop. He wanted to get away, well beyond the crowd, to be alone with his memories. With his free hand he wiped his eyes, but the tears kept blurring his vision. When he passed the Smithsonian control building, he took a sharp left into the dead end at the base of Pu'u Poli'ahu.

Unsettled, Erik stumbled out of the truck, and in the glittered view through his moist eyes he gazed up at the giant snow-covered cone. *I can be alone up there*, he thought. He began to trudge up its steep slope, breathing hard but climbing steadily, following what he soon realized was a trail of deep footprints left by someone else that morning. Ten minutes up—at about noon—he reached a small level area on the cone's snowy shoulder that overlooked the whole summit. He lay down on his back spread-eagle, gazing skyward like a kid poised to make an angel in the snow.

Breathless and woozy, but exhilarated, his mind drifted from Mauna Kea back to Minnesota. "We were happy then," he muttered as a distinct patch of iridescent shimmer formed in the clear blue sky, but his mind, muddled with emotion and lack of oxygen, missed it.

"*O Poli'ahu i ke kualono o Mauna Kea,*" came the undulating sounds of a chant from some place above him.

Again, his mind failed to grasp it, just as it failed to notice the heightened cold of the wind descending from the cone. The robust voice seemed part and parcel of the whole scene—the snowy peaks, the children playing on the mountain, the chill wind embracing this wintery child from Minnesota.

"*Noho ana i ka lau o ke kuahiwi . . .*"

It was not the words but the deep emotion expressed within them that caused Erik's mind to finally focus on the sounds that he now realized emanated from the top of the cone a hundred yards away. But he still hadn't noticed the shimmer in the blue sky.

"Wahine noho anu o uka o Lihu'e . . ."

He pushed himself up off the snow and spotted a young native woman atop the peak. She was bundled up in a parka, over which she'd draped a *kihei* dyed pink—the summit cones' color at dawn—and wore a *maile lei* around her neck, its green leaves rustling in the cold wind. Squinting against the bright, snowy cone, Erik recognized Hoku Holokai.

"E ku ana iluna o ke ki'eki'e . . . ," she continued, her arms outstretched toward the summit and her face to the heavens. *"Ho'anoano wale ana i Pali-uli e."**

Hoku dropped her arms and, catching her breath, turned south to look toward Lake Waiau, its frozen surface covered with snow. "Mahalo, Poli'ahu," she said in words too soft for Erik to hear.

Suddenly self-conscious, he got to his feet. Again he was in the wrong place at the wrong time, inadvertently encroaching on the young cultural practitioner. He strode back to the trail of footprints and hurried down the cone, never looking back until he reached the Explorer. By then the young woman was gone. *Had she noticed me?* he wondered. *And why again were we both here?*

When he got back into the truck, he noticed a text from Moses on the Explorer's cell phone:

Where are you? Crews are still waiting for lunch. Did you have vehicle trouble?

"Oh my God!" Erik said, looking at his watch. It was 12:30, making his lunch delivery already half an hour late. He quickly typed a response:

On my way. Sorry for the delay. Lots of people up here—got hung up.

He quickly drove past the Smithsonian antennas and headed up the "escape road" behind the Keck and Subaru observatories, a rough cinder track overlooking the north plateau that provided another way down when black ice rendered the paved upper roads too slick to drive. Five minutes later, Erik reached the tiny windowless summit

---

* Poli'ahu is on the mountaintop of Mauna Kea
  Dwelling on the expanse of the mountain.
  Woman who dwells in the cold above Lihu'e (on the Waimea plain)
  Standing atop the heights
  Awe-inspiring [as seen from] Pali-uli.
  (Chant by Tutu Mary Kawena Pukui)

lunch building—formerly the generator room for the UH88 tele-scope—where several observatory vehicles were parked, their staffs having been assured by Moses that hot soup was on its way.

Most of the waiting crew were old-timers—and mostly local—habituated to the tradition of having a prepared hot lunch at the summit. They were unflustered by the delay, especially on a day when their routine was already broken by the earlier road closure, their slowed ascent due to traffic and vehicles parked every which way along the road, as well as scores of giddy islanders playing on the mountain. Indeed, even before Erik had arrived, the lunchroom was filled with lively conversation stimulated by the season's first big snowfall and the buoyant vibe of the spontaneous community festival outside. So Erik was startled when, after cleaning up the lunchroom, he stepped outside to find two men squared off in threatening poses.

"We can't enjoy jus' one frickin' day on our mountain wit'out you people butt in?" shouted a brawny Chinese-Samoan, pointing his finger at Jill Kualono's youngest ranger—a small, tough haole in a clean, pressed uniform. The islander's two teenage sons stood nearby, wide-eyed with boogie boards under their arms. Their father's brand-new pickup—a big, black F-150 Raptor—was angled haphazardly across the lunchroom's parking area, blocking the last observatory vehicle still there, an old blue CFHT Suburban.

"Hey! These guys gotta go back to work!" declared the ranger, gesturing toward two observatory technicians, both local Asians, who'd just finished their summit lunch. Erik recognized the ranger's bossy tone as feigned, covering a youthful lack of confidence that Erik had observed in him before.

The flushed father pointed at the CFHT emblem on the tech-nicians' vehicle. "Tough shit! We've let dese foreign countries rule our mountain way too long! One day—dat's all I asking! One day fo' take my sons up here to appreciate da snow . . . da air . . . the pu'u . . . wit'out you guys, wit'out yer fancy uniforms and hot-shit attitude, telling us fo' 'move along.'"

"We're just ensuring public safety . . ."

"Bull! You're here fo' lay claim to our mountain for dose t'ings," he said, jabbing his finger at each and every telescope within view. "I not so young I can't remember when dere was no rangers, no guardhouse by da road, no one fo' boddah us when we come up to play in da snow! Evah since da Hawaiians say no to TMT, you guys in our face!"

"That's not true!"

The red-faced man stepped forward and banged his fist on the hood of the ranger's four-wheel-drive. "Pilau!" Stinking rotten! "Dat's wot's true!"

The ranger unsnapped the holster on his radio.

The islander leaned forward and grasped the ranger's arm, but his face and body relaxed. "Eh, try wait one second, brah," he said in a more conciliatory tone. "Lemme just drop dees kids off so dey can slide down dis pu'u. Den I go for pick dem up down below—and dees observatory guys can get back to work."

The ranger refastened his holster and crossed his arms, glaring at the man.

The islander turned around and put an arm around each of his sons, then walked them to the edge of the downhill slope. "OK, boys," he said, shifting to a kinder tone. "Now's yer chance to fly on Mauna Kea! Watch out fo' dose folks ovah dere—you don't wanna get in dere way—and meet me ovah by that big white dome dat looks like one giant coffee can." He pointed at the JCMT observatory.

The boys leaped onto their boogie boards and vanished downslope with peals of joy. The young ranger dropped his arms and, without looking back, walked stiffly to his truck. He got inside, started the engine, and continued his patrol of the upper summit ridge.

"Smart move," said the older CFHT technician to Erik, who by that time had joined the two employees. "Hard telling what dat guy woulda said to da ranger wit' 'is boys outa earshot, eh?"

"Or done to 'im," added the younger technician.

Erik nodded, but distress still showed in his face. His cheeks were also bright red, and not from the cold.

"There's a lot o' history here . . . and bad blood," the older man said, opening the passenger door of the Suburban and sliding inside. His coworker hopped into the driver's seat while the other man rolled down his window. "Don't worry about it, kid," he said to Erik. "Ain't smart to let one guy's anger ruin a nice day."

Just then the irate man reached their vehicle. "Eh, guys, sorry for da pilikia," he said. "I woulda moved my truck right away if dat ranger hadn't showed up. Nut'ing 'gainst you guys—I know just one job fo' you—but dose rangers, brah, dey get undah my skin. I want my boys to learn not fo' chicken out against phony authority—like da way I was raised."

The older technician nodded thoughtfully. "Let's just hope dese guys nevah completely close da road to us locals," he said, "like dey did in takin' away most o' our goats and mouflon."

The islander nodded back. "T'anks, eh? Sorry fo' make you late." He climbed into his big truck, spun back onto the road with panache—icy bits flying off his tires—and rumbled down the mountain.

"Gosh," Erik said, his adrenalin still pumping.

"See ya," the old technician said, and the two crew drove back to their observatory.

Erik stood on the summit ridge for many minutes, trying to reconcile all he'd seen that afternoon—island-style joy, native reverence, and cultural conflict.

The new year brought additional snow flurries to Mauna Kea but nothing as dramatic as that brief Christmas-week storm. The disturbing confrontation Erik had witnessed that day faded as the memory of Hoku Holokai chanting to her goddess atop Poli'ahu's namesake cone grew ever more vivid in his mind.

CHAPTER 15
Sunny Boy's Secret

"Hey, guys," Sam said, stretched out on the wide rail of Sunny Boy
Rocha's seaside lanai, his back against a corner 'ohia post that blocked
the cool air coming off Mauna Kea that March evening. He raised
his glass of 'okolehau, a local whiskey distilled from the root of the
Hawaiian ti plant. "Here's to Prince Kuhio!"

They all stood—Sam, Freddie, Erik, and the old DJ—and instinctively turned toward the mountain to toast the rebel prince who had
joined the armed rebellion to restore Queen Lili'uokalani to her rightful
throne. Thwarted by spies, the 1895 revolt had failed, and the sugar plant-
ers (descendants of Christian missionaries) sentenced the "treasonous"
Hawaiians to death. Christian mercy—or political savvy—exempted
the popular prince and he was sentenced instead to a year in prison.

"Kuhio!" they cried in unison, then downed their drinks.

"Perfect place fo' celebrate his birthday," Freddie said, turning to
Sunny Boy. "T'anks, eh?" He refilled their glasses with the last of
the bottle.

"Mahalo you guys fo' comin' ovah!" Sunny Boy said with his big,
garish smile.

"And t'anks, Freddie, fo' bringin' da 'okolehau," said Sam, his
grinning face flushed from the oke. "Whoa, dis stuff *mean*. I like fly
to da mountaintop."

"Yeah," Erik said, swaying gently. "Somewhere over the rainbow, where clouds are far behind me . . . an island in the sky."

"Dat's yer Bali Hai, eh?" Sunny Boy said, strumming a few bars of the famous *South Pacific* song. "'Your special island,'" he sang in a sweet, if raspy, falsetto.

"Let's toast to da greatest mountain on Earth," Sam said. "Mauna Kea!"

Again the glasses rose toward the mountain, a purple silhouette backlit by the setting sun.

"Mahalo, Mauna Kea," Erik murmured, but not so softly the others hadn't heard. Suddenly aware they were looking at him, he blushed.

"Dere he goes again," Freddie teased, pointing at Erik's pink cheeks. "Mus' be one Minnesota trait," which only deepened their flush.

"Well, without the mountain, I'd never have met you guys . . ."

They all nodded, raising their glasses yet again, this time facing Erik.

"To da t'ree Muskrateers!" Sunny Boy said.

"And Sunny Boy!' the trio declared.

"To all of us," said Erik, "and our benefactor . . . grand mountain of our dreams."

"Eh, I no can keep up wit' all dees toasts," Freddie protested. "Suck 'em up!"

They did, and when they'd settled back into their seats—Erik and Sam on the lanai rail, Freddie in one of the old koa chairs, and Sunny Boy in his ratty rocket recliner—Freddie launched into Keola Beamer's classic anthem: "My friends and we have often walked the trails of Mauna Kea . . ."

The others joined in, and Sunny boy, strumming his 'ukulele, belted out the lyrics with great emotion, his voice quivering in spots. But by the third verse, he'd grown visibly agitated—his eyes glistening and lips trembling—as if some dormant irritation was rising to the surface. When the song was over, it erupted. "Those damn mainland haoles wanna take over da whole mountaintop!"

All eyes fell on the disc jockey, and Erik's jaw dropped. He had never seen such ire in Sunny Boy, whose very name honored his unwavering affability.

They didn't realize that more than liquor had set off the DJ's outburst. Two stories he'd broadcast that morning during the hourly CBS news brief were to blame. The first reported a climate study showing that Hawai'i waters were warming so fast that by mid-century the archipelago would get slammed by hurricanes as often as the storm-plagued Caribbean. This had rekindled Sunny Boy's longstanding gripe about his homeland being victimized by "greedy mainlanders"—in this case from their unbridled fossil fuel consumption. Then, to make matters worse, the CBS announcer broadcast the latest Haisley Big Eye update from Pasadena. In it Caltech's Dr. Adam Jacob had said, "Thus far we've prioritized our siting studies on locations in Chile, but I think we should seriously reconsider Mauna Kea . . . and give islanders a chance to crown their already first-rate astronomy complex with the finest telescope on Earth. If Hawai'i's last king, Kalakaua, was here today I'm sure he'd make it happen!" Hearing the Californian presume for the islanders—and on Prince Kuhio Day!—had stuck in Sunny Boy's craw, but he'd refrained from saying so over the air. He spit it out that evening, his gullet warmed by a little 'okolehau and lots of sentimental camaraderie.

"Bastards *already* took over da whole mountain!" Freddie added, also tipsy.

"Dey w'en promise us years ago to keep it to eleven big scopes," Sam said. "We got twice dat many now!"

Freddie, scowling, cracked his knuckles. "I guess dose PhDs w'en nevah learn to do math!"

Erik was puzzled. No one at the camp had said Haisley's telescope was coming to Hawai'i. "The Big Eye's going to the Andes mountains in Chile," he said, lighting a Marlboro, "where it's high, dry, and maybe even darker than Mauna Kea."

"Dat's not what *I* heard," Sunny Boy replied, his anger now mixed with gossipy pride. "I hear da beer guy what gave da money *demanded* his telescope come Mauna Kea or no more donation."

"Who tol' you dat?" Sam said, his smooth brow suddenly furrowed.

The DJ shook his head, his eyes glazed from the 'okolehau. "Top secret."

"C'mon, Sunny Boy!" said Freddie. "Spill!"

The DJ motioned everyone to lean closer and dropped his voice. "Las' week, Nohea Nahiku was on my call-in show fo' talk 'bout next month's Merrie Monarch Festival. After we sign off, he w'en tell me Henry Hashimura was in town and invited Nohea to a dinner at the yacht club with a few select business leaders . . ."

"Ah . . . da token Hawaiian, eh?" Freddie snickered, raising his eyebrows for emphasis.

"Come join da Hilo elite," Sam added, "at da only 'yacht club' in America wit' no more harbor and no more boats!"

Freddie shook his head. "Da haoles always 'tink if dey invite a few token kanakas into dere schemes dat'll change da way we feel about dere shenanigans!"

"Yeah. Like when da gov'nor appoint dose two Mauna Kea protectors to da mountain's management authority to put a Hawaiian face on dat uddawise pro-development gang. Pilau!"

"Listen, guys!" Sunny Boy said, holding up a reproving finger to get the boys back on track. "Dat night Nohea having one smoke outside, and tru da restroom window, he hear Hashimura talkin' to dat pasty-faced spy o' his . . . what's his name?"

"Miles Millhoff," Sam said, "the real estate developer."

"Yeah . . . tellin' Millhoff to let Oshiro know dey gonna bring da Big Eye here and 'he should get his company dozers tied in right away.'"

"Bastards!" Freddie said, helping himself to one of Erik's cigarettes. "Where dey gonna put one huge telescope li'dat? Mountain's already built out!"

"Of course . . . ," Sam said, suddenly sober. "On da vanquished TMT site . . . out on da north plateau."

"Nope. And dat's da really nasty part!" Sunny Boy whispered, forgetting in his drunken ire Nohea's admonition to keep the rumor under his hat until he could confirm it. "Remember da university's promise for finally tear down dat old 88-inch telescope? Well, guess wot? Oh, dey gonna tear 'em down alright—dat and its old generator building—only put da Big Eye in dere place! 'Recycling' da site, dey call it!"

"Retaliation is more like it!" Sam growled. "Dat's it! Retaliation for all the pilikia over TMT!"

"But it doesn't make sense. The consensus up top is Chile," Erik said, but it was more to convince himself than his friends. "Your info's *gotta* be wrong."

"Maybe," the DJ shrugged, thrilled that he'd struck on something even his mountain friends didn't know. That night he went to bed almost as self-satisfied as he was angry.

Erik returned to the base camp the next day. After the dinner shift, he went upstairs to the library with a big mug of coffee and plopped down at its Mac Pro to search the Big Eye on the web. He found ample information—the telescope's history, design, and a long profile on Alfred Haisley. "Seeing conditions" had been studied on Mauna Kea and in Chile's high-elevation Atacama Desert, but Chile, already slated for even more state-of-the-art telescopes, dominated the newspaper and magazine stories. A few sadly mentioned Hawaiians' thwarting Caltech's last Mauna Kea project, the Thirty Meter Telescope.

I'll ask some astronomers up here, Erik thought. Maybe they can shed light on this.

As his search deepened, Erik stumbled upon a political scientist's doctoral thesis and learned that TMT had been more unpopular than he'd realized. Local opposition had mushroomed during a decade of stormy hearings. Elders wept trying to explain the meaning of their mountain to astronomers. Young activists alleged bias in TMT's environmental impact statement and dubious mitigation plans. Islanders howled when the state's hired planners declared that the 18-story dome—taller than any building on the island—would have "no significant impact" on the mountaintop or the native cultural practices conducted there.

Erik got up and paced the library. He wanted to stop reading. He wanted to smoke. He wanted to forget that injustice finds a home everywhere. *It's only when you close your eyes to it that it disappears*, he thought. *Dad would never do that.* He sat back down in front of the screen.

And then he read that Sam—his lighthearted fellow Muskrateer —had provided key research to the pro bono lawyer handling the Hawaiians' case against the state's five-member land board, gubernatorial appointees who ran the Department of Land and Natural

Resources, an agency notorious for siding with developers. *Why didn't Sam and Freddie tell me about this history? Did they think I couldn't handle it?*

"Damn," he muttered and resumed reading. Despite overwhelming public opposition, even the two Hawaiians on the board had gone along, apparently intimidated by US Senator Daniel Inouye's outspoken TMT support and that of other formidable political and business leaders. The thesis noted that Hawaiians had refrained from openly criticizing their turncoat brethren, fully aware that standing up against colonialism can be costly, especially to those who've found a niche in the political establishment.

As Erik perused the thesis and read various news stories and social media accounts, his jaw tightened. *No wonder that guy vented at the ranger that day*, he thought. *I would too if I was born here.*

It all reminded him of the Cattail Creek Plaza controversy back in Cottonwood, a California project to build a 75-store shopping mall atop a wildlife-rich wetland that locals had long used for duck hunting, canoeing, and high school biology classes. Those hearings were also stormy. Mall advocates touted the hundreds of jobs the project would inject into the "underdeveloped" Cottonwood economy and assured the public that CCP (as it became known) would be an "Earth-friendly" mall built with solar panels, LED lights, and designer landscaping to offset "inadvertent" damage to the wetland (i.e., bulldozing all but a narrow strip of it behind CCP's vast parking lot). The *Cottonwood Weekly* had reported the yearlong story, and when the county board approved the project Erik's father lambasted them in a rare front-page editorial.

Unlike CCP opponents, islanders hadn't given up, appealing TMT's approval in court, then disrupting its groundbreaking celebration. Dramatic online videos of the 2014 ceremony showed a cadre of Hawaiians—some in traditional garb, others with protest placards—marching onto the staked-out site, while elders and kahunas led a prayer vigil at a towering stone altar near the Saddle Road, praying that no violence would occur up top. The group's impassioned young leader, in bare feet and a tapa cloth robe, jabbed his finger at the gathered dignitaries, declaring that the impending penetration of the sacred mountain with their spades would be "*hewa loa*"—a grave sin. He pleaded with the native minister, hired by astronomers to sanctify their telescope with a Christian prayer, not to bless the project. Others reminded the Japanese and Indian representatives of the TMT partnership of their own reverential mountain traditions. All this had shocked the dignitaries and unsettled the minister. At that moment, more Hawaiians poured out of their trucks, preventing Gordon Moore and the other dignitaries from breaking ground.

Later videos showed protest encampments, first near the visitor center and eventually near the stone altar on the Saddle Road—a much larger compound at the base of a giant cinder cone, Puʻu Huluhulu, directly across from the summit access road. Repeated blockades kept construction vehicles from ascending the mountain, with hundreds and then thousands of islanders massing on and along the road. Police—many in full riot gear—arrested dozens, mostly Hawaiians, including thirty-four elders during one tense foray. Sam appeared in some of the videos, huddling with the other leaders, and Erik thought he spotted Freddie in drone footage of the crowd. Erik sat transfixed as he watched Hawaiians exchange their breath with the armed police officers about to arrest them. In one video, a clutch of young children stood on tiptoes to put ti-leaf leis around the officers' necks, some of the shaken cops weeping.

All this happened when I was running away from the world, Erik thought, *when I was drifting about in the South Seas. No wonder I hadn't heard about it.*

Halfway through the years-long turmoil, Hawaiʻi's supreme court had voided the TMT's permit, ruling that the land board had violated the public's due process with a predetermined outcome that reflected political power rather than environmental and cultural sensitivity. A second phase of land board actions and more Hawaiian litigation followed, but as political pressure to build TMT grew, the supreme court buckled, granting the permit despite a strong, agitated dissent by one appalled justice. It was then that the largest protests ensued, with the Ku Kiaʻi Mauna—"Guardians of the Mountain"—blocking the access road for months and paralyzing the political establishment.

Erik went down to the sundeck to smoke a cigarette. High above the mamane trees stars filled the March sky, and the mountain road and visitor center, dimly lit by the orange streetlamps, were empty. "Hard to imagine this was once a battleground," he muttered, but the scene's present calm provided little solace for the agitation he felt.

As he smoked his cigarette, an odd thought entered Erik's mind—of the Marquesan harpooner Queequeg in *Moby Dick*, and how Melville had made the tattooed native and Ismael unbidden bedmates at the inn and bosom buddies aboard the *Pequod*. Then he thought of Moses and Sam, and of the mysterious young woman he'd encountered at the lake and on Pu'u Poli'ahu.

"Melville backed the beleaguered Hawaiians," Erik muttered, parroting the captain's wry, whiskeyed comment the night before *Albatross* set sail from Pago Pago for Hawai'i. "But I had to read the *original* London edition of *Typee* to know that!" the old sailor had growled. "Melville's spineless New York publisher expunged every damn thing in the novel that might offend Americans, including the Honolulu missionaries' shabby treatment of the natives!"

With Erik's bubble of innocence now burst, he wanted to know more, and the next night he stayed up well past midnight searching the history of other Hawaiian protests—against other telescopes, the Pohakuloa Training Area, Maui's military surveillance compound atop Haleakala, the Navy's bombing of the former ranching island of Kaho'olawe, and its leaking Red Hill fuel tanks at Pearl Harbor. He read about countless other battles to save culturally significant valleys, mountaintops, and beaches from hotels, subdivisions, military compounds, and astronomical observatories. Year after year in the decades following World War II and statehood, opponents had fought—and usually lost—to commercial developers, military planners, and astronomers.

I guess escapism can distort your view, Erik mused, *and create a need not to know that there's trouble in your paradise.*

While Erik was researching this history, Sunny Boy suddenly found himself in the middle of it. Two days after their Prince Kuhio Day celebration on the disc jockey's lanai, an anxious Nohea Nahiku phoned to warn Sunny Boy not to say a word over the air about the astronomers' plans to put the Big Eye right on the summit—"or mention it anywhere else in Hilo for that matter! I don't want that news traced back to me . . . especially if there's pilikia from the Hawaiians!"

Sunny Boy immediately recognized the handiwork of the "old boys" who'd run Hawaiʻi for more than half a century. They'd stop at nothing to keep that telescope gold mine here—and building in Chile was a real threat. He also knew when to sit on something considered by the powers to be kapu—off limits. A nasty episode decades earlier had taught him that painful lesson!

Sunny Boy's stomach churned for an hour after the call, and he wasn't just worried about Nohea Nahiku. He knew that possessing dangerous information could be as risky as actually revealing it, and he didn't want to cross swords with the likes of Henry Hashimura. He loved his mic at KAAO too much to risk losing it.

As soon as Erik returned from his four-day shift that next Tuesday night, Sunny Boy dashed over to the Airstream. Erik was inside, changing out of his mountain clothes.

"Guess what?" the old disc jockey said cheerily through the screen door. "Dat crazy rumor 'bout da Big Eye? You were right—one shibai." A sham.

"Oh yeah?" Erik said, putting on his lavalava, and in no mood to discuss that topic with Sunny Boy yet.

"Yeah. Hashimura was just yankin' Millhoff's chain." Sunny Boy feigned a laugh. "And takin' a little jab at fat-cat Oshiro too."

"What about that Caltech astronomer on the radio?"

"Wishful thinking."

"Well . . . that's good news then," said Erik, unconvinced.

"So you and da boys just forget what I told you . . . OK?"

"Don't worry," Erik said, taking a beer out of the refrigerator. "Your reputation is safe. I didn't tell anyone that I heard it from you."

"What?" The blood drained from the old man's face.

"I talked with some of the people I know up there. They all think the Big Eye's gonna end up with the other giant telescopes in Chile's Atacama Desert, the 88-inch crew too . . . especially them."

Erik stepped out into the twilight. Sunny Boy looked pale.

"You catch the flu or something?"

The older man steadied himself against the trailer wall. "How many people you talk to?"

"Maybe half a dozen."

CHAPTER 16

The Vagabond's Wake

The night Sunny Boy tried to recant his rumor, Erik dreamt he stood on the banks of the Mississippi watching himself drown. The high water churned black and gusts howled through the cottonwoods. Lightning bolts shattered the sodden sky above the river valley, illuminating the limestone cliff on the opposite shore—and the black-crowned night heron watching Erik from a cottonwood limb. Drenched in icy rain, hailstones pelting his yellow slicker, Erik trembled above the torrent, powerless to lend himself a hand. "Let go!" he hollered to the drowning boy. "Let go!"

He awoke in the Airstream, the damp sheets askew beneath him, and stared at the jungle outside his window. A stalk of bananas sagged close to the screen and a humid breeze sated with plumeria blossoms blew across his face. *I'm a long ways from home*, he thought, picturing himself pulling up to the sandbar in his canoe, a weather-beaten Old Town handed down by his father.

The *feel* of the bar was what had made it special, as if it had been there for a thousand years (though in fact the mighty river had changed its shorelines many times). Sitting across from Bergman's Bluff, where the great muddy stream piled up against the limestone cliff carved by the river, Erik had often imagined fleets of birch bark canoes gliding over the swirling eddies of the bend.

Townsfolk along that stretch of river recited its lore, the bluff named to honor Joseph Bergman, who from 1890 to 1918 grew wheat in fields behind its precipitous edge. Ten thousand nights he (or his sons, when they were old enough) climbed down a dangling rope ladder to a narrow ledge halfway down the cliff, where they replaced the blazing candle of a lantern left there to keep paddle-wheelers from breaching their hulls, the unforgiving precipice the cause of half a dozen wrecks on moonless nights or when storm rains obscured the pilots' landmarks. From an old library copy of *Mississippi River Indian Tales*, Erik had once read that young braves leaped from that same ledge to prove their manhood. After experiencing the intense fear and joy of the sixty-foot plunge and the powerful grab of the dark, swirling current, the young men were ready to face adult life.

Atop the bluff stood several ancient burial mounds built by prehistoric Woodland Indians, mysterious monuments of the river's earliest settlers. Farther downstream, in Iowa and below, stood even larger mounds built by later Hopewell and Mississippian people. Some were huge effigies of their clans' animal spirits—bears, birds, and lizards—and others were colossal cones or terraced platforms used for religious ceremonies, elite burials, or astronomy. The deepest meanings of those places had perished with the ancient clans that built them after germs of Spanish explorers far to the south sickened villagers along the river and were carried upstream unwittingly by infected native traders. Other traditional peoples—Ojibwe and Dakota—later inhabited the lands of the mound builders, but they were eventually run off, killed, or put on reservations by white colonizers. Erik had never thought to ask the old half-Ojibwe farmer Marcel Labathe about the tribal name for the bluff, but plying the river in his canoe, the young man believed he could sense native spirits alive in the valley.

Despite one hundred fifty years of American development along the river, a primal wildness still resided there in Erik's youth. On countless nights he'd sat on the sandbar opposite the bluff and revered the moon-washed limestone as if it were a monument to his own gods of the universe. Upriver, through the rustling leaves of mammoth cottonwoods, Erik could spot the yard light of his parent's rustic riverfront home and the distant glow of the town named for those backwater trees with their thick, twisted bark. Sometimes he'd haul his 4.5-inch telescope in the canoe, and from the bar ponder the heavens' celestial objects and admire their ethereal beauty. Usually he'd just watch the currents roll by or review the passing towboats as they navigated the wide channel with long barges of oil, grain, lumber, and ore. He'd overhear the deckhands' voices, replete with accents and slang from places far to the south with exotic names like Natchez, Baton Rouge, and New Orleans. Those voices gave Erik a tangible sense that the river connected him to the rest of the world, that his canoe—at least in theory—could reach Paris, Patagonia, or Polynesia. Seeing the brawny crewmen move skillfully about the decks, a wanderlust would overtake him, despite his rootedness to Cottonwood—or perhaps because of it.

Erik's love for the river was part of a long family tradition, rein-forced whenever he popped into the *Cottonwood Weekly* to chat with his father, the paper's editor in chief. His father's devotion to the town and valley fueled his tireless passion to report and comment on the news. Erik admired his political guts, reflected in his inves-tigative assignments and hard-hitting editorials. Indeed, townsfolk deeply respected his father, just as they had his grandfather who started the paper after coming home from World War II. Erik was as independent thinking as his forebears, but his tendency to run from conflict—whether in his family or at school—kindled a submerged anger that would flare up suddenly and shame him.

Erik inherited his artistic nature from his Irish American mother, who'd given up a promising painting career to support her husband and family at home. And from her also came an affable generosity. When conflicts arose in the family, she'd give a hug, tell a joke, or spin a yarn that eased the tension. Rarely had she lashed out, and only as a last resort and in a torrent of emotion. When breast cancer took her away—Erik was still at the university—the three Peterson men were left without the wise and gentle influence she provided the serious, hardworking household.

Erik's photographic eye grew keener in his university art classes, but he knew that unless he worked for his dad at the *Weekly* he'd have to learn practical skills necessary to run his own commercial photography business. He persevered through business classes, and did surprisingly well, but his professors hadn't divulged that America's economy had undergone a revolution in which giant corporations by the end of the century had all but destroyed the old entrepreneurial free market system. After graduation, his more practical lawyer brother urged him to find a position in one of Minnesota's Fortune 500 companies. "Be realistic, Erik," he had said as they gazed out over the river from their father's back porch. "Build your business inside *Dilbert*'s world and a guy with your creative eye will rise quickly," an idea Becky, Erik's college sweetheart, quickly endorsed.

Influenced by his mother's motto, "Always match your dreams with reality," Erik tried the *Dilbert* approach and took a job with 3M. But the long commute to the Twin Cities and working in a corporate culture that demanded dutiful conformity drove him out after two years.

Living with his widowed dad helped him save enough of his high corporate wages to launch Peterson Pictures in an old building in downtown Cottonwood, and within a year he could afford to hire a part-time receptionist/bookkeeper. He also purchased an acre of old man Fenster's bottomland across from the bluff, a short canoe ride to the sandbar. On a flat, grassy rise twelve feet above the river Erik poured a concrete foundation on which he set a vintage 1950 houseboat that he'd saved from moldering away in a Cottonwood alley. He spent more than the boat's purchase price to restore and winterize its beautiful antique rooms, but from its windowed pilot-house—converted into an airy master bedroom—Erik could look across the river and watch the moon kiss the bluff below the old native mounds.

Getting commercial contracts had always been a challenge, despite Erik's growing reputation for stunning images and high-quality production—to say nothing of his tireless work ethic. To keep his business afloat during lean times he shot a few weddings and occasional advertising spreads for the *Weekly*. Meanwhile, his millennial college friends toiled at high-pressure jobs in those Fortune

500 companies, and even the dullest of them rose to phenomenal prosperity. The ones who'd grown up in the river valley and other rural areas seemed especially tense, and Erik wondered if they were as happy as they let on.

"How many iPhone apps, video games, or chic espresso bars does it take to wean someone from the river?" Erik once asked Jack Alvarson as they glided down the channel in his Grumman canoe.

"Some fish just won't bite on plastic worms," Jack replied, his characteristic Marlboro wagging between his teeth.

Jack had been Erik's best friend since grade school, a childhood fixture at the Peterson family home, so when he got back from his years at the Iowa Writers' Workshop, Erik's father hired him as a spot news reporter. That summer Jack moved in with Erik to help both young men cover expenses, and the idyllic setting stimulated the long-aspiring novelist to revise his epic story about the river that had thus far attracted only rejection slips from New York literary agents. Each rejection seemed to renew Jack's commitment to the novel, and he labored to deepen the story and hone its words.

Only once did Jack speak openly about the growing despair he actually felt. "'The Mississippi River Valley is as reposeful as a dreamland, nothing worldly about it, nothing to fret or worry upon,'" Jack had mused, quoting his idol Mark Twain as moon-washed waters flowed past the houseboat. "Sure, Twain could say that. *He* was able to get *his* river novels published."

"And you will too," Erik had replied, almost cavalierly, failing to apprehend the depth of Jack's worry. "And your story will help salve the confused and broken souls of our generation and renew their faith in people."

Jack took a long draw on his Marlboro and squinted at the great wall of limestone across the channel. "Bullshit! Face it, Erik, soul is a diminishing force in millennials. They think they can do without it 'cause they got no river or mountain to remind 'em . . . no bigger vision to warm their hearts in the wintery weather blowing across our country."

Indeed, the two young men spent many nights on the sandbar ruminating about whether their artistic dreams could survive the

"Some fish just won't bite on plastic worms."

corporate economy, discussions fueled mostly by Jack's struggle to get noticed in an East Coast–centered industry dominated by a handful of giant corporations that published 80 percent of America's books. The rejections he'd received were usually half-page form letters, on a few of which some compassionate intern had handwritten "Mr. Alvarson" or "Jack" over the typed "Dear Writer." All admonished him about the "difficult market publishers face these days," and some of the notes ended with "Good luck." Only one slush pile reader had bravely scrawled "Don't give up!" As the rejections—and subsequent revisions—piled up, Jack began drinking, first just a few beers at day's end, then one or two while he was writing, but eventually a tumbler of Jack Daniels was his constant companion at the keyboard.

Becky, by then a nurse at a big Twin Cities hospital, joined the two young men on weekends to canoe, barbecue, sunbathe, or enjoy recreational lovemaking with Erik, but as the years passed and the two "river rats" grew more passionate about their artistic quests— and frustrated at realizing them—tensions developed between Erik and Becky. That's when Erik started bumming cigarettes from Jack, who like many deep feelers had long used smoking to keep depression at bay.

Then Jack drowned in the river, leaving Erik to pursue his artistic dream alone. Erik grew sullen, then angry, leaning evermore on Becky for solace, and she drifted away.

The Twin Cities had continued to grow like Topsy in the new millennium, and new suburbs spread into rural communities far south of the metropolitan area. Erik noticed larger pleasure craft plying the river—and more trash washed up on the bar. As commuters moved into Cottonwood, fewer townsfolk knew each other and local kids gradually ceased waving at neighbors' passing cars. The influx of development might have been an economic plus for Cottonwood merchants, but as soon as the demographics changed, a Walmart and a Safeway moved into town to suck up all the newly arrived dollars and export them to Arkansas and California. Erik gained a few additional wedding clients from the influx, but the regular ad photography he'd long done for two longtime downtown merchants vanished when both went bankrupt, almost overnight. A few homeless people—men Erik had known in high school—wandered Cottonwood's streets, sleeping at night in the woods behind Walmart's parking lot.

During those last six years, Erik watched the *Weekly* struggle to stay profitable as newspaper readership declined and big corporate media companies bought up small papers all across the Midwest. Finally even the august *Weekly* got absorbed into a media franchise headquartered in Minneapolis. The new publisher—also an investor in the Cattail Creek Plaza—imposed editorial policies that constrained Erik's father's twenty-five-year-old column.

The timing couldn't have been worse. The turbulent new century had begun with the disputed election of George W. Bush, resolved by a split Supreme Court decision that polarized the nation. The September 11 attacks on New York and Washington a year later awakened a deep-seated insecurity that had incubated in the American empire for decades. In the paranoid days that followed, when George Bush and Dick Cheney's rhetoric and actions called to mind the darkest times of twentieth-century Europe, Paul Wellstone, a rare brave voice in the Senate who was being urged to run for president, died in a mysterious plane crash. His death turned control of a divided Senate over to Republicans, and many Minnesotans wondered aloud if their progressive senator had been assassinated by the Bush administration. Later came news of American troops torturing prisoners in the Middle East and of widespread domestic surveillance, once repugnant practices in democratic societies and now supported by Democrats and Republicans alike. And out of all that came more war, terrorism, fear, and anger.

Erik admired how his father had tried to illuminate all this in his column, believing that offering citizens "the editorial voice of a journalist rooted in their own community" was as important as his newspaper's coverage of city council meetings, restaurant openings, and Little League games. Much as those editorials had made Erik proud of his father, they also fueled his growing dismay about his country's decline.

Before long the *Cottonwood Weekly* had changed into a ubiquitous suburban newspaper with more ads and less news copy, and the civic-minded editor in chief had become an anachronism. Indeed, the Minneapolis publisher, billionaire Murdock Kemp, eventually began phasing out local editorials, putting syndicated columns—usually conservative—in their place. After a year of frustrating battles with Kemp and his minions, the resolute journalist's heart quit beating one evening as he labored to salvage yet another redlined editorial. When his two sons cleared out his office, Erik's brother gave him the bronze plaque his father had mounted above his desk, a quote from Thomas Jefferson: "Enlighten the people and tyranny and oppressions will vanish like spirits at the dawn of day."

Feeling adrift, with Jack and Becky gone and no parents to guide him, Erik had sought solace from his father's old friend and ally, retired US representative Amos Anderson, who lived in a riverfront mansion built by a nineteenth-century French Canadian fur trader. On lonely evenings, Erik appreciated the old congressman's fatherly companionship, the snowy-haired widower ensconced in the once plush, now worn leather chair that for almost three decades had occupied his Washington office, the pair sipping whiskeys in front of the mansion's huge fireplace made of river stones. At first the old politician's war stories—full of humor and bravado and lessons about "standing on the right side of history"—inspired the young man, but as Congressman Anderson's intimacy with Erik grew, he let his true feelings emerge, revealing the gloomy cynicism of a man worn down by battle.

"Your father's kind used to widely inhabit America," he'd said, a little tipsy and melancholic one bitter cold night during Donald Trump's second year as president, "back when *everyone* read newspapers as a matter of civic duty, and newspapers existed for more than the ads."

"You mean, in your generation."

"No . . . *definitely* not my generation!" Congressman Anderson had said with a belly laugh, his thick, white eyebrows flying upward. "You see, your father was the throwback of our crowd, and you can thank your New Deal grandfather for that."

The old politician, Swedish by ancestry, stared into the crackling fire, his blue eyes gleaming in its amber glow. "No, it was our generation who created this mess, the baby boomers, that narcissistic bunch who confused consumerism with citizenship."

"But wasn't that what they were *expected* to do? Pursue their own American dream? Go to work, raise their kids, pay their mortgage . . . keep up with the Joneses?"

Anderson's face flushed. "A convenient excuse . . . while that very dream fell out of reach for everyone else. You're probably too young to remember the novelist Tom Wolfe, but he nailed it when he named us the 'Me Generation.' Me, me, me . . . mine, mine, mine. We even had a T-shirt—'He who dies with the most toys wins!'"

"I've seen that. You can still buy it on the internet."

"What so many boomers failed to realize, Erik, were the costs of that frivolous creed—extracting every last mineral and lump of coal, exporting jobs to cut labor costs, leveraging capital beyond all reasonable judgment, and worst of all, warring to keep our hands on overseas oil. We became dupes for the burgeoning oligarchy and its powerful one percent!"

"Well, we can't all be Vikings," Erik quipped.

"Hogwash! We were cowards!"

"But you fought, like Dad did."

"Up to a point, son . . . only up to a point . . . and too late." The old Swede took a long, slow drink from his crystal glass. "People have no idea the pressures politicians face, not just from the generals and the tycoons—always whining in public no matter what you give them in private—but *every* goddamn interest group. Hell, it's a frickin' orgy, where money, influence, and celebrity trump truth and the public good.

"'*The public good*!'" he chortled, almost choking. "No one uses that term anymore! Naw, the players now are rich, well educated, and ruthless, but most act like they've had a bad upbringing."

"I haven't heard people talk like this since I was a kid," Erik said, holding up his own glass. "It's so . . . well . . . Old Minnesota."

"When the idea of a wholesome upbringing still existed," Anderson mused, a tear crowding his eye, "when parenting was about more than just stuffing your kids' heads full of greedy aspirations! And 'justice for all' was a *community* creed that *all* parents were supposed to teach!" He shook his head and downed the last of his whiskey. Erik noticed the old man's hand tremble as he lifted the glass to his lips.

"I tried, Erik . . . at first . . . but getting legislation passed was like slogging through a bog with slimy weights of accommodation on your boots. We followed the unwritten congressional code to never quite tell the public the truth, never even hint that the whole damn thing was rotting right before our eyes. After Bush and 9/11 . . . it seemed hopeless . . . and now frickin' Trump!"

He poured another drink from the crystal decanter on the hearth. "God, I trusted your dad. He was the one person I could count on to tell me the truth, even when I didn't want to know it." He looked into Erik's face with bloodshot eyes and shuddered. "When Wellstone died, my gumption died with him. Truth be told, I just warmed the chair from then on." He rubbed its tattered armrests, his eyes glistening with tears.

"Who said it—Hubert Humphrey? One of those old-timers anyway." He held up his glass as if in salute. "'Social progress depends on each generation building on the foundations left by the last one, and that means fighting the battles all over again!'" His voice fell to a whisper. "My generation failed to do that . . . and now, I fear, all is lost."

That night was the only time Erik had departed the mansion without Congressman Anderson's usual gentlemanly escort to the door. Instead, he'd left the old politician slumped in his grand, worn chair, staring into the embers of a dying fire.

Erik endured his losses for another year. Then, one Friday evening after delivering some ad photos to the *Weekly*—for a flashy spread on Cattail Creek Plaza—Erik launched his canoe into the channel, hoping that a paddle on the river would improve his blue mood. Drifting downstream, smoking one Marlboro after another, he grew more agitated. *Jack's dead, Mom and Dad are gone, Becky hates me, and my photography studio will never be viable . . . no matter how hard I work.*

As evening light began to fade and his canoe reached the far islands well below the river's bend, he understood that his grief was even bigger than that. "It's *all* gone," he muttered. "They've replaced anything real and good with what's not." He'd choked on his next words: "It's time to get outta here . . . if only . . . if only to survive."

A dreadful shiver of yet another realization passed through him like a bolt of lightning and he peered through the dusky light to examine the passing riverbank. The river had carried him back to that same fallen cottonwood on that same reedy bank where he'd found Jack's body hung up in its limbs.

The next day Erik called his part-time employee to tell her he was "closing up shop for a while" and apologized for having to lay her off. A month later he locked his canoe in the woods, boarded up his houseboat, and headed west on a vagabond trail that led to the South Seas and eventually Mauna Kea. But not before expressing his rage. He lashed out at the closest target he could find that symbolized all the unjust forces destroying the life he and Jack and his forebears had cherished—a clandestine act of revenge that fortunately the Cottonwood police never traced to him.

Erik walked to the lagoon at Four Mile Beach to wash away these memories and his terrifying dream of drowning in his beloved river, but the cleansing didn't last. Sunny Boy's news of Caltech's plan to build the Big Eye on the summit, and the startling anger of his friends that night on the DJ's lanai, flooded into Erik's psyche, washing away the fragile solace upon which he'd built his new life in Hawai'i. Old trash from his previous disappointments littered his next shifts on Mauna Kea, ugly distractions from the beauty and wonder that usually marked his four days on the mountain. Memories of his father's courage made him ever more disgusted with Sunny Boy's cowardly decision to keep his mouth shut about what he knew was true. Erik grew testy and morose as he interrogated visiting Caltech astronomers about their *real* plans for the Big Eye. Moses noticed the change in Erik's mood but said nothing.

Then Erik's father began showing up in his dreams, always clear-eyed and strong, encouraging his son to "just stick to your principles and live your life." Drained and muddled after each dream, Erik wondered if he possessed the courage to do what his father was asking—or was it time to "pack up his canoe and shove off" yet again? And in his darkest hours he let that poisonous old rage rise within him, privately relishing the revenge he'd once taken "against the bastards that ruined my world."

Three weeks later, an observatory vehicle went missing from Keck, its disappearance discovered when astronomers emerged from the dome that morning. A construction worker found it two days later, scuttled way out on the north plateau. It had been driven off a lava ridge below the TMT's abandoned site.

CHAPTER 17

The Mountain Hunters

The sun was still below the sea when Johnny Mattos' black pickup reached the sprawling cinder cone called Pu'u Kanakaleonui, "the hill of the man with the big voice." Johnny stopped the truck in the middle of the road and got out to stretch his muscles. They were tight from three hours climbing the dark roads between the ranch town of Waimea and Mauna Kea's 11,000-foot east face, the last hour picking his way along the badly eroded hunter's road that circled the mountain. This was the toughest route up, but the one Johnny had first traveled with his father five decades earlier. It was also high enough to reach a part of the mountain that his native wife called *wao akua*—a realm of the gods.

Before him, visible in predawn light, lay a moonscape of russet cinder disgorged from Pu'u Kanakaleonui during some prehistoric epoch when the volcano was more restless than today. A line of other once fiery cones towered above the road, Goliaths flanking an ancient trail to Mauna Kea's summit, where even larger cones presided over the Pacific.

Johnny inhaled the crisp alpine air that always energized his spirit on these hunting trips. The inkling of a new day and old familiar vistas dissipated subliminal strains he always carried with him—from watching Waimea's once vital cowboy life wane, decades married to a sad Hawaiian who'd long ago lost her desire for him, and vague sorrows left from Vietnam during the bitter end of that war.

Johnny uncorked the stopper of his old Thermos and filled the ceramic cup he kept in the glove box. White, with a cracked rim of faded gold, the antique ranch cup had been given to him by his father on the day Johnny felled his first mouflon, a bold ram with horns that Johnny hung in his garage after his wife tired of them in the living room. It was early April and still below freezing as he sipped the strong black brew, warm steam caressing his flushed, windblown cheeks. *Where's Josh?* he wondered, his twenty-six-year-old son running late as usual.

The sun emerged from the clouds above the eastern horizon and the cinder rim of Kanakaleonui turned red with the first kiss of light. Johnny turned to look at the giant cones farther up slope. They, too, had been blessed, their somber countenance quickly fading in the sharp light of a Mauna Kea morning.

Johnny's father first took him up the mountain in 1965, when the Humu'ula sheep station and a few hunting shelters were the only things above the military training camp in the saddle. They had slept overnight in the stone bunkhouse called Hale Pohaku, built by President Franklin Roosevelt's Civilian Conservation Corps. The next morning they trekked 4,000 feet up the old Humu'ula Trail, all the way to the snow line at 13,000 feet. Johnny could still picture his handsome Portuguese father marching through drifts in tall lace-up boots, his husky body layered in red and brown sweaters. It was one of the few times he had set aside his Stetson for a Navy watch cap, which he pulled down over ebony curls, his face flushed from the cold and his beautiful teeth glistening with delight. Johnny was only ten at the time, but after growing up with the volcano in his backyard outside Waimea, he was thrilled to experience its austere wonders close up. It was on that trip that they huddled in one of the Hawaiians' habitation caves where in ancient times, wrapped in tapa cloth or thick capes of layered ti leaves, native toolmakers had peered into warming fires while winds howled across their isolated stone quarries.

A year later Johnny's dad started taking him along on Mauna Kea hunting expeditions—for pigs and birds at lower elevations and sheep and goats near the summit. Sometimes they went with other cowboys, but usually they hunted alone because with others, "there's too much talkin', drinkin,' and foolin' around," his dad would say. Years later, Johnny realized that his father mostly just wanted to be alone with his mountain, to relish a solitude beyond even what he'd experienced riding the sprawling pastures of Parker Ranch. Now and again, while they crouched among cinder cones waiting for game, Johnny's father would point out a Native Hawaiian moving along a distant ridge on some mysterious quest. He always told Johnny to "respect those folks."

"They know things about Mauna Kea that we will never understand," he once said. "Your mother knows secrets we can't even imagine."

Johnny was one of the few contemporary islanders who had walked on the mountaintop before a single observatory was built there. Back then, when the only traces of humanity were rock cairns along ancient trails, mysterious stone shrines, and the adze quarry, the mountain's voice was distinct—a bold, clean shout of joy. That voice seemed different now, a forlorn moan carried on oceanic winds that whirled about the giant cones. Johnny heard it most times he went up now, but he wasn't sure if it was the mountain's real voice or just the way it sounded to his jaded ears.

Johnny's reverie broke when he noticed a cloud of dust rise above the southern ridge—a vehicle moving along the rough road. No doubt that was Josh, Johnny's youngest son, late for their sunrise rendezvous. Judging by the dust, it would be another ten minutes before Josh reached Kanakaleonui, so Johnny opened the bag of *malasadas* he'd cooked up the night before and started eating one. Taking these Portuguese doughnuts up the mountain was another tradition from Johnny's father, but starting in on them without Josh was a practice he'd begun a decade earlier when his son turned sixteen and began paying less attention to what his father had to say.

Although annoyed that they would now start late on the trail, Johnny had grown accustomed to his son's obstinacy. It seemed like everybody's kids had gotten a little that way—from exposure to mainland TV and internet, all those irreverent Generation Z and millennial values crowding in on island ways. And something else had crept into his son after joining the Army—the pride they'd drilled into him had turned into haughtiness during two deployments in Afghanistan. Even though veterans' preference had landed Josh a good island job after his discharge (to the envy of his siblings stuck on the mainland), the boy still hadn't mellowed. Johnny hoped this hunting trip, their first in five years, might help restore Josh's once vibrant spirit, as mountain trips always had for Johnny.

Johnny got back into the cab with a fresh cup of coffee, cranked opened both windows so the warming trades could blow through them, and switched on the radio to catch the opening minutes of Sunny Boy Rocha's morning program. Sunny Boy was another fixture of his past, the aging disc jockey having just started at KAAO when Johnny was attending Honoka'a High. Opinionated and overblown at times, Sunny Boy was a leftover from when AM dominated Big Island airwaves. Among the older set—those at least sixty—KAAO, now on FM, was still their station, and thousands tuned in to hear their favorite Hawaiian standards, catch the news, and listen to Sunny Boy reveal the latest "scoops" from around the island. His island accent and frequent pidgin made hearing even world news palatable.

That morning, after reading the day's headlines straight off the front pages of the islands' morning papers, Sunny Boy launched into a tirade about the new timing of some downtown Hilo stoplights, a pattern that interrupted his usual cruise through town at 5:00 a.m. Johnny chuckled at the monologue, recognizing from his own heritage the bombastic indignation of a frustrated "Potagee."

A shiny new Chevy Silverado with "Combat Veteran" plates roared up alongside Johnny's classic 1992 Ford Ranger, marring the soft shoulders of the road. Johnny got out to greet his son. He spotted Josh's old Winchester 270 rifle in the rack behind the seat and noticed a newly affixed "AINOKEA" sticker on the back window, pidgin word play to express defiant apathy. Josh's window whirred open and the driving beat of *Destiny's Child* poured out. The young man behind the wheel flashed a toothy grin that belied the dark cast of his eyes, an aspect Johnny had only seen on world-weary old men.

"Hey, Dad," he said, stepping down from the massive truck to give his father a hug. He dropped his youthful pidgin whenever he spoke to his father, who having never worked the plantations, used pidgin sparingly compared with Asian Americans of his generation.

Josh had his father's Mediterranean good looks but was taller and brawnier from his mother's Hawaiian blood. The Army had cut away the boyish curls that softened his sharp features in youth, and he still sported a soldier's shaved head. That Saturday morning Josh was sleepy, still adjusting to working at high altitude as an electronics technician on the US government's Gemini telescope. He was also less than excited about driving up from Hilo for a sixth time that week, just to go hunting with his father.

"Hello, son," Johnny replied. "Ready to shoot some ram?"

Josh frowned. "Better go get 'em before the state does!"

That next Monday sharpshooters from the Department of Land and Natural Resources would begin a three-day sweep of the mountain to kill sheep and goats from helicopters. The seasonal court-ordered slaughter was meant to keep the animals from destroying the habitat of a bird on the federal endangered species list—the native palila. It was one of Johnny's many beefs about what had happened to the mountain, but this blessed day that anger was tucked away. At Johnny's insistence, they took the elder Mattos' truck. Josh threw his gear into the bed of the old Ranger and Johnny drove them two miles farther up, on a remote track that dead-ended two thousand feet below the summit. With packs on their backs and .270-caliber rifles slung over their shoulders, the hunters set out for a broad wash between several cones where sheep and goats often browsed on mosses found in stony pockets where moisture collected. Josh hadn't carried a gun since Afghanistan, and the rifle seemed especially heavy, his steps across the soft cinder slow and oddly tentative.

They were both breathing hard by the time they reached their destination, a squat cone where decades earlier Johnny had constructed a stone hunting blind overlooking the wash. From there, animals crossing the wash would be three hundred yards upwind from the hunters' scents and easy marks in the open. Johnny suggested they sit together rather than spread out because that day sharing companionship seemed as important as bringing home game.

"Looks like parts of Kunar Province up here," Josh mused, but his father changed the subject.

"I remember sitting in this blind with Kawika Nanakula, long before the days of the helicopters," he whispered to Josh, who sipped a can of Red Bull. "We spotted a cloud o' dust behind that cone over there that was so big I thought a bunch of trucks musta found a way up the other side. Kawika knew better, and sure enough, a few minutes later a hundred mouflon come running out from behind that cone."

"Radical," Josh said, though he'd heard the story before.

"Craziest thing, Josh," said Johnny, shaking his head. "We were both so amazed at the herd's magnificence that neither of us fired a shot. We just watched 'em prance by, heads up high, galloping down that wash together. A minute later, their dust blew over us like a desert storm."

Josh's face darkened. "Now you're lucky if you even see half a dozen!"

The two sat on the sunbaked cone watching for game, quietly taking in the beautiful morning. At about 8:30 the cloud layer started climbing the mountain, but the sea of cumulus still lay two thousand feet below them. About midmorning two goats appeared at the rim of the tall cone opposite their lookout.

"We after mouflon today?" Josh asked. "Or are we willing to take home goat?"

"It's still early," Johnny said, knowing gunshots would spook any other animals from meandering down the wash. "Let's wait for sheep, at least a while longer."

The goats moseyed down the slope then disappeared around the cone's backside. A short while later, a lone mouflon nibbled his way up the wash from below. Both raised their weapons, but Johnny held back for his son.

"You go," he whispered, poised to fire on the off chance Josh missed.

Kewhoom! The report echoing among the cones.

Cinders flew up in front of the mouflon, and the stunned animal bolted.

Johnny pulled his trigger, then glanced at his son. Josh's hands were trembling.

The mouflon stumbled, gushing a spray of blood, then fell, sending up a cloud of ash. Not a clear hit.

The two men raced down the sandy wash, but as they approached the writhing sheep, Josh, his face pale, slowed.

A lone mouflon nibbled his way up the wash.

"She's a beauty!" Johnny declared, eyeing its perfectly shaped horns. "Come look at our trophy!"

Josh stared at the hole in the animal's chest and the swirl of blood draining into the cinder. Nausea seeped into his stomach. Only pride got the young man's boots moving again, but he swayed as he stood over the panting beast. Jaw clenching, he pulled his bone-handled knife out of its sheath and knelt down.

Johnny, seeing his son's distress, gently pressed his hand on Josh's shoulder. "I'll do it," he said softly.

Josh stepped back, and his father cut the mouflon's throat.

When the animal stopped twitching, the elder Mattos knelt beside it. "Mahalo, fine animal, for giving us your life. With your flesh we will nourish our families, and with that strength we will try to do good things that benefit all."

Josh had almost forgotten this ritual from their hunts, a benediction he knew by heart. He fought the tears rising within him. He used to admire his father for uttering those words, but now he was skeptical that anyone—*except* maybe his father—did much of anything for the benefit of all. Yet he still admired his father for holding fast to his antiquated beliefs. He just didn't think it mattered anymore.

"OK, Dad?" Josh asked, poised to sink his knife into the animal's belly.

"Want me to handle this part, son?"

"I got it," Josh said firmly, shifting his body to block his father's view of his anguished face as he gutted and dressed the mouflon. His stomach turned again at the sight and feel of warm blood on his hands, the first since Afghanistan.

Within minutes he had stowed the parcels of thick red meat inside his backpack. It was a shame not to tote the well-formed head back with them. Uncle Chris, a taxidermist, would have mounted a fine display, but Josh didn't need any more reminders of his participation in the death of innocents. "Won't have a place to put a mount in the new house, Dad," he said.

Josh lugged the remains to the back of some boulders and rejoined his father at the stone blind. There they ate a lunch of smoked marlin and poi and chatted quietly about nothing in particular while feigning to keep an eye out for animals.

Shortly after lunch the two goats they'd seen earlier reappeared from behind the cone, this time dashing madly across the wash. Before either man could grab his rifle, the roar of engines that had spooked the goats resounded over the stark terrain. Two ATVs shot out from behind the cone, stopping in the middle of the wash. The men driving them hopped off and began taking measurements, unaware of the two hunters sitting behind the low stone wall above them. They affixed a large X-shaped target to the ground, driving long stakes into each corner, then drove farther up the wash to take more measurements.

"What's that about?" Johnny wondered aloud.

"Those are for taking satellite photos," Josh replied. "They're doing it all over the upper slopes."

"Why?"

"They're surveying for a possible telescope site."

"What!" Johnny peered at the distant cones of the mountain's upper ridge. Six of the huge metal domes were visible from the blind, including the Gemini observatory where Josh worked. Johnny's face tensed with anger. "They already have at least a dozen up there—plus all those damn antennas! How many more do they need?"

Josh shrugged.

"I thought they were *finally* done damaging the mountain," Johnny moaned, "after the big protests sent 'em packing to those Spanish islands. Dammit, back in the '80s they promised us! They said they'd build only so many, and leave the rest of it alone."

"That was years ago, Dad. They never learn anything. Now they got the state and feds supporting whatever they want . . . here and on Haleakala. That old goat Hashimura's behind a lot of it, picking up where Senator Inouye left off."

Johnny got up from the ground and walked slowly to the cone's rim. A flood of memories rushed through him, so full and fast they left him awash in a melancholy that made his tall frame droop. "It wasn't enough they took over every damn beach and coastline . . . they want our mountains too."

"Look, Dad," said Josh, joining his father on the rim, "I know it's hard to take, but at least I got a job up there. A few other guys from Hilo too. Might as well get something back, eh?"

Johnny, tears blurring his eyes, turned to look at his son. He thought of Josh's new truck, the dishwasher he'd given Betty for Christmas, and the house he hoped to build in the newest Hilo subdivision, all made possible by the observatories' mainland-rate wages. "But this is our mountain, Josh, *yours* and mine." And then he thought of his own father; it was his mountain too.

Josh threw up his hands and started pacing the cone. "You want for me to find something in Hilo at half the wage?" he shouted, his face reddening. "How will I explain that to *my* boys when they're ready to go to college? Eh? Better I be poor and have the pretty mountain to look out? Is that what you want for me, Dad!"

Johnny raised his finger against the barrage of words. "Stop! You have no cause to talk to me that way. You know how I love this mountain."

The two men stared fiercely at each other until their glares subsided. Finally Josh walked over to his father and threw his arm across his shoulder. "Yeah, Dad, I know. It's like your own flesh and blood."

Johnny nodded. Tears finally spilled from his eyes, dotting his canvas field jacket. "I know that job's been good for you, Josh. I struggled when I was your age and it was hard on the family. I don't wish that on you, but they're ruining the mountain. Won't they ever stop?"

"No," Josh replied truthfully, but he hesitated to tell his father the current rumor circulating on the mountain, that Californians were planning yet another telescope—with a mirror six times the size of the Kecks. Difficult as it was for Josh to acknowledge his father's old-fashioned sentiments—and frustrating as his father's self-righteousness could be—Josh loved him devotedly, even as his own inner turmoil kept him from showing it.

"Dad, I'm pissed off to have to tell you this, but the talk up top is that they're gonna put something really big up there, bigger even than the TMT was gonna be. They're surveying down here, but word is they wanna build it up on the summit ridge." He pointed at the white dome of the UH88. "Gonna replace that one with a dome three times that size. Right there next to the summit cone."

Johnny gasped, so shocked his mouth hung open.

"Yeah, some big shot from California already gave 'em the money."

Johnny pulled away from his son and began pacing the cinder. He grabbed his rifle off the stone wall and shook it by the barrel. "It's not gonna happen!" he said, his face so contorted with rage that his son scarcely recognized him. "Over my dead body!" he said, shaking the rifle at the mountaintop.

At that moment a whirlwind spun across the wash, stirring up a tall cloud of ancient ash. It danced and skipped across the broad volcanic slope, then raced right up and over the summit cone.

CHAPTER 18

What Would Tita Carvalho Do?

Ranger Kualono ate her Sunday lunch near the windows of the base camp dining room, forgoing the gravy-smothered hot beef sandwich for pork adobo on rice. Jill could also dine down in the construction camp mess hall, her preference on weekdays when the muscled hunks replacing the CFHT dome's wind-damaged siding offered better "eye candy" than these paunchy, bookish astronomers. Eating late in the empty room, Jill hunched over an early Tita Carvalho mystery she was rereading that weekend, but her eyes kept drifting off the page to Mauna Loa, absent the snow that had rimmed its caldera that previous winter. April's radiant light had brightened everyone's mood—except hers. The recent scuttling of the Keck vehicle added to her ongoing dismay over the unsolved mystery of Kyle O'okala's death five months earlier, that and the information she'd just obtained on her days off, thanks to an old romantic imbroglio.

In the days after the November "accident" the police found only three of the missing lug nuts, each at separate locations along the observatory roads between the Smithsonian's far antenna and the upper summit ridge of observatories. Despite the police conclusion that there was no foul play, talk persisted about sabotage, especially after Kona's reactionary newspaper editor speculated in his column that the incident might have been an "act of terrorism" perpetrated by "retrograde C.A.V.E. people (Citizens Against Virtually Everything)," the developers' nickname for anyone opposing new projects on the economically depressed island. He implied that an "errant participant" in earlier protests against TMT might have done "the dirty work," despite the remarkably peaceful demonstrations of singing, hula dancing, conch blowing, and prayer. County police stood by their less sinister conclusion: months earlier, when the truck's tires were changed, some Hilo service station mechanic failed to finish the job he'd started, installing three lug nuts on that last tire but forgetting to wrench them down, and he completely forgot the other three before returning the vehicle to the Smithsonian. The remaining three slowly worked their way off the wheel in the many weeks that followed. Why all three came off on that same night police rationalized as "pure dumb luck."

Ranger Kualono never bought the official line, not only because she may have seen someone in the fog that night, but also because her gut told her otherwise. She couldn't free her mind of Kyle's last words—"abandon the mountain." The cops said it was the despondent message of a shivering, hypoxic man who knew he was going to die. Hypoxic themselves after rushing to the summit without acclimating, the police failed to carefully examine the scrawl—or even take a picture of it—having assumed with everyone else that the words were in Kyle's own hand.

Jill was skeptical, and she later—secretly—dusted the window with fingerprint powder left over from her stint at the Honolulu Police Department, but the few clear prints she'd found matched those on the employment records of three Smithsonian crew who always drove that pickup. In truth, the crude fingernail scrawl on that icy window could have been made by anyone reaching in through the cab's broken back pane.

For years "rangers" on the mountain were little more than property supervisors with fancy uniforms and radios. That changed after the TMT protests, when the Mauna Kea Cooperative eventually hired one real ranger with police training—Jill. As chief ranger she was authorized to carry a gun, but her power to respond to anything more serious than vandalism, trespass, illegal camping, or theft was limited, so the county police had controlled every aspect of the so-called "lug nut inquiry." They allowed Jill to assist only as much as they had to, an unhappy concession to her in-their-face personality. Even that ended abruptly after two lunching cops overheard Jill tell Braddah K, "Don't forget that Big Island cops have a long-standing reputation for incompetence."

After the police had reached their conclusion, Jill launched her own secret investigation—without informing her bosses at the cooperative or the other rangers. She reexamined everything—the Smithsonian dish and the wrench that she'd found there (and pocketed); the roads and ditches between the antenna and the summit ridge; the accident site; and the smashed vehicle (which fortunately had been stored for half a week behind the road crew's snowplows). But she was stymied, with no good leads, until the previous Thursday, when she'd tapped a former boyfriend working at Honolulu police headquarters. By virtue of a drunken infidelity back when the two lived together, he owed Jill a debt that he would probably pay back until the day he died. She'd found him in bed with the handsome twenty-year-old son of a Maui judge, so whenever she wanted the official scoops on someone who made it into the police reports, she blackmailed her ex.

As part of her investigation Jill had unearthed early lists of base camp and observatory employees long forgotten in a dead storage space behind the camp's workout room. She wanted to see if anyone might have had reason to hold a grudge against Kyle Oʻokala, the Smithsonian Observatory, or the NASA Infrared Telescope, where Kyle had worked for many years before taking the better-paying job at the Smithsonian. She stumbled upon the file of Joel Kuamoʻo, a handyman at the fledgling base camp from January 1970 to August 1974. The name caught her eye because the Hawaiian side of her own sprawling extended family included a few Kuamoʻos. According to the file, Joel had earlier worked as a backhoe operator for Oshiro Construction and helped build the UH88 telescope dome back in the late sixties. On instinct she asked her ex-boyfriend to check the police records for Kuamoʻo's name, along with several others. What he discovered was that Kuamoʻo's young daughter had died in a tragic house fire in 1974, later determined by authorities to have been deliberately set. Checking her uncles and aunts, she found out that Kuamo'o and the remainder of his family had moved to Las Vegas that summer, never to return to the islands. And the arsonist had never been identified.

Jill wondered what her fictional hero, Sergeant Tita Carvalho, would do with such information, but that was the Portuguese in her talking. Her Hawaiian side, inherited from her mother, sifted through a whirlwind of visceral feelings from her experiences that night, when she failed to save the technician's life because black ice kept her and Ernesto Dela Cruz from reaching the summit. She didn't know if what she'd seen near the old shrine was real or from the spirit realm, but she remembered that her gut had registered portent that whole afternoon—which she dismissed as flu. Troubled that she might bear some responsibility for Kyle O'okala's death, she was determined to clear that guilt from her conscience.

Moses Kawa'aloa noticed Jill sitting alone by the window, a blade of sunlight splashed across her face. He walked up to the table with his own lunch tray. "A little company OK?"

"Suit yourself." That was as much of an invitation as one could ever expect from Jill—unless you were one of those muscled hulks and she was in the mood for flirting or intimidation.

Unlike most Americans, Hawaiians usually felt no social obligation to converse, so Moses just sat down and began eating. But he soon received a message from his gut: "There's a reason you two are seated alone in here today."

"How was the adobo?" he asked, forking up a chunk himself.

"Pretty 'ono, Moses." Delicious. "Who made it?"

"Erik."

"Not bad for one haole."

"He's a quick study, very conscientious."

"Different kind of haole," she said. "Actually likes being up here. I was surprised you hired him, but I guess I see why."

Moses nodded. "He grew up on a river, surrounded by woods and water."

"Huh," she said absently, turning back toward the window.

"You seem somewhere else, Jill."

"Just thinking things over." She looked into Moses' kind face, a countenance of aloha that she wished she could project more often.

"The mountain's a good place to do that," Moses said.

She held her gaze on the older Hawaiian. "I'm still trying to figure out what happened to Kyle Oʻokala."

"Is that a ranger talking . . . or the Hawaiian?"

"Both. Put it this way, Moses, if I wasn't feeling something in my naʻau, I probably wouldn't be asking the ranger questions."

"And what questions are those?"

"Like what *really* happened up there that night . . . and what happened to Joel Kuamoʻo back in 1974."

A tingle of goose bumps traveled up Moses' back, all the way to the top of his head. "I haven't heard that name in years."

"You know what happened?"

"He was from before my time on the mountain."

"But you know about the fire."

Moses nodded.

Jill leaned forward over the table. "It was arson."

Moses studied her face. The furrowed brow and rigid jaw harked back to her tough plantation ancestors—and the unresolved pains of her own life—but the soft eyes were Hawaiian. He spoke to those. "Some of the old-timers in Hilo, from early construction crews, told me Kuamoʻo saw something he wasn't supposed to . . . and made the mistake of talking about it."

"And . . . ?"

"They were building three telescopes then—NASA's infrared, the Canada-France-Hawaiʻi Telescope, and the British infrared. When the D9s and backhoes leveled the cones of the summit ridge, they uncovered iwi." Bones.

"Auwe!" Oh no! Anyone with Hawaiian blood knew that the mana in human bones must be allowed to return to the land and remain there undisturbed.

Again, Jill turned to gaze out the window. After a long pause she said, "So the claim made by the TMT protesters *was* true, there are burials up there."

Moses nodded.

"I don't know why I didn't believe that . . . wishful thinking, I guess."

"Even back then ancient burials were protected by law, but few on construction crews dared breathe a word of it for fear of losing their jobs."

"Or worse," Jill added.

"'Ae." Yes.

"That happened all along the coast on O'ahu," Jill recalled. "My mother told me they'd send the crew home for a couple of days while they supposedly 'checked it out.' When the crew came back they were told, 'Oh, it was just pig bones' and started right up again. By then the iwi had been hauled off to some secret location."

"Of course, some Hawaiians quit," Moses said.

"If they could afford to. Good work is hard to find, particularly if you're Hawaiian."

"Even so . . . some dared not face the spiritual consequences."

"Moses, what d'you mean when you say Kuamo'o 'made the mistake of talking about it'?"

"It's a small community up here—especially back then—and Kuamo'o heard a rumor about the disturbed iwi at lunch. That afternoon he drove to the summit to investigate. I don't know what he saw up there, but he came back so upset he felt compelled to do something. Maybe he figured his job wasn't in danger since he worked for the base camp, not Oshiro Construction. So he talked to a Hilo guy he knew in the media—he thought confidentially—hoping that guy might tip off one of the newspaper reporters. Instead, the guy blabbed it over the radio . . . as a 'disturbing rumor.' What Kuamo'o didn't realize was that the company, or maybe a construction worker fearing a work stoppage, would try to shut up a whistleblower before things got out of hand. After the fire killed his daughter, Kuamo'o split town, and the rumor never became anything more than that."

"He broadcast Kuamo'o's name over the radio?"

"Didn't have to. Since the Oshiro crew had all kept their mouths shut, it was easy to assume it was Kuamo'o, who'd gone up there and probably made a scene."

Jill scowled. "Who was the bastard on the radio!"

"Sunny Boy Rocha."

"Figures! What a gossip! Dat guy is so niele!" Nosy.

Jill gazed out the window, sifting through what she'd heard. Unfortunately, it all made sense, except one thing. "Moses, how is it you know about all this when you weren't even up here yet?"

"Don't you have some Kuamoʻo's in your family, Jill?"

She nodded, only mildly surprised that Moses—well tied into the Hawaiians' "coconut wireless"—might have encountered that connection.

"Well, you have a distant cousin who works here in the kitchen, but you know him as Braddah K . . . Keola Kuamoʻo. It was his little sister who died in the fire."

CHAPTER 19

The Academic Rules of Engagement

"Dr. Jacob, how do you think people will react when the first direct image of a planet like ours—Goldilocks in the flesh, so to speak—is televised across the globe?" A blaze danced in the fireplace behind the young male student sitting cross-legged at the foot of the famous astronomer, the gas lit more for effect than the May nighttime chill above Pasadena. He and the three other PhD candidates watched the face of "The Bishop" of Caltech astronomy. Dr. Adam Jacob fortunately did not play poker, for his reactions were usually obvious, including his standing disregard for those he deemed of "lesser intellect" or "burdened with inferior notions." His bright little eyes and constant smirk reflected his general state of condescension, and his delicate eyebrows leaped up in mock astonishment whenever a student or colleague expressed a contestable idea.

Dr. Jacob chuckled. "It should force us to look at our species in a whole new way." He set his tumbler of Chivas on the coffee table next to his thronelike chair of dark cobalt leather, the color of the night sky. "Common folk don't like to do that."

The young man leaned close to Jacob's knee. "So you think there'll be trouble?"

"Most assuredly." His eyes twinkled.

"But few *outside* the science community were bowled over by the last decade of exoplanet discoveries—including the thousands identified with the Kepler space telescope!" asserted the British student in the room, his back to the fire. "Even finding Kepler 452b—the most promising Goldilocks to date—created little more than a yawn outside our own circles."

The professor nodded. "That's because no one could actually see details of the planets, and for the man on the street, seeing is believing. The rest—evidence by inference, theory, mathematics, or spectrographic measurement—is, to the lay mind, mere conjecture."

"But imagine," the third young man of the group uttered in staid tones, "when we directly image an Earth-size planet so like our own that even Joe Sixpack will be startled."

"Exactly!" The astronomer's face lit up with delight. "Then the revolution begins, kiddies, because one of those—and all we need is one—will resemble our own planet enough to create quite a stir on Earth."

"We've been talking about *that* for decades," said the only woman in the group and the one student to have chosen a chair rather than the Persian rug for her place in the conversation. She was neatly attired in a crisp white blouse, short blue skirt, and a coral necklace from Hawai'i. This was Dr. Jacob's first encounter with the department's newest PhD candidate and he had no idea she was the daughter of Berkeley's premier planet hunter, Dr. Willy McCrea.

Andromeda ran her fingers through her blond Dutch Boy bangs and fixed her green eyes on the astronomer. "Dr. Jacob, do you really think we can achieve that with a *ground-based* telescope?"

"Indeed I do," he replied, staring back at her, "Miss—"

"McCrea. While the direct images of giant Jupiter-like exoplanets using Keck and Gemini were exciting achievements, they also demonstrated just how limited those Earth-bound telescopes are for imaging a Goldilocks planet."

The professor frowned, his eyes no longer twinkling.

"With all due respect, Dr. Jacob," her inquiring mind now fully engaged, "recent improvements in ground-based telescope imaging are marginal compared with those of a decade ago. I believe the discoveries you're hoping for will have to be made from space. Even with adaptive optics and bigger Keck-like mirrors—ELT, Giant Magellan, and TMT—we're going to need to look through less turbulent atmosphere than Earth's to actually image a Goldilocks and then do the spectroscopy to really understand it. The Webb telescope's spectacular images are just beginning to prove that."

The other students, more familiar with the haughty Dr. Jacob, spotted his lips curl.

"Young lady, you seem to have dismissed the Haisley project with its 60-meter mirror."

"As a matter of fact, Dr. Jacob, I have," she replied eagerly. "Frankly, I think it's a case of scientific ambition exceeding the physics involved."

The astronomer's eyebrows leapt upward. "Well," he said, smiling into the faces of the three male students in the room, "Let's hear your considered thoughts on the matter, Miss McCrea. The National Academy of Sciences has adopted the Big Eye as the decade's prime project in ground-based astronomy, but what do *they* know?"

The young men chuckled, but Andromeda was oblivious; she was engaging the esteemed Dr. Jacob and enjoying it. "I read all the technical reports during an independent study project for Dr. Franklin, and I think—"

"As project consultant, so have I," Jacob interrupted, but too abruptly for Andromeda to stem the rest of her comment.

"—there's a lot of wishful thinking in them," she finished.

"Go on, Miss McCrea," sarcasm in the professor's voice.

"Well, I . . . ," she stumbled, puzzled by his changed tone. *Surely a senior faculty of such accomplishment couldn't have that fragile an ego,* she thought. *My adviser would never have asked Jacob to sit on my dissertation committee were he that rigid a scholar.* She proceeded.

"Those reports assert that past mirror manufacturing triumphs, of the Kecks' multimirrors and the Subaru and Gemini eight meters, suggest that the Big Eye's molded segmented mirror—*six* times larger!—can be made light enough that its parabolic curve can be maintained through computer-managed compensations." She leaned forward for emphasis. "Fine in theory, and sure, that may even succeed for the 30- to 40-meter mirrors now being built, but to do it at a 60-meter scale? They've assumed availability of a new generation of thin-mirror technology that hasn't been developed yet, to say nothing about computer software hundreds of times more complex than any before."

"And you don't think science will find a way to surpass those barriers?" interjected the British student, sensing some personal advantage in the professor's rebuke of Andromeda.

The other men joined the offensive.

"Who'd have believed in the 1980s that something as large as Keck's mirrors would have worked?" blurted one.

"And who's to say the Haisley won't surprise us too?" said another.

Dr. Jacob leaned back in his big chair and sipped his Chivas. "Damn fortunate that private money was available to build that first, unproven Keck." He fixed his eyes on Andromeda. "Otherwise skeptics would have won out there too, and Caltech would not today possess the world's two finest telescopes . . . performing superbly, I might add. Fortunately, the Haisley telescope has also garnered a big pot of private money, so doomsayers won't hold up the science!"

The twenty-eight-year-old PhD candidate finally realized she'd made a big mistake. She had challenged the master—not just sparred with him like the British student. Such challenges can be risky in a prestigious college like Caltech, and heresy merited punishment, in this case the intellectual shun. Andromeda's punishment wouldn't *necessarily* be long-lived but was uncomfortable nonetheless, especially for a young, strong-willed astronomer who'd inherited a pure love of science from her idealistic father and his same desire to play a part in discovering sentient life beyond Earth.

Andromeda felt a sourness in her stomach that as a dynamic woman she'd experienced before. She had inadvertently pushed the older man too far. Had one of the young men done the same he might have been forgiven, perhaps even encouraged as an "aggressive scholar." Andromeda had thus allowed herself to be cast up as a troublemaker, not because of her vigorous intellectual skepticism, but for challenging "The Bishop." Part of her wanted to boot the pompous professor in the groin, and the other regretted having drawn attention to herself.

Andromeda was striking, with large probing eyes the color of clover and an intellect as sharp as any at Caltech—traits that intrigued some men and intimidated others. That she'd traveled a year after earning her BS in physics and possessed a worldly maturity that most of her nerdy cohorts lacked added to this two-edged reaction. What saddened her most was that Dr. Jacob's attitude seemed beneath Caltech; if she couldn't stray from the department's current focus on expanding its ground-based telescopes, how would her ideas about extraterrestrial exploration strategies, the focus of her dissertation, be received? The younger men in the room weren't really threatened by Andromeda's ideas or her person; they just saw an opportunity to propel their careers by staying in league with Jacob. She recalled Professor Jedediah Clarke's famous admonition to a Caltech audience: "Dreamers beware; the quest for knowledge is fraught with difficulties—clawing brawls to get tenure and intellectual sabotage being just two common ones." It was just as well that Jacob hadn't yet connected Andromeda's last name to her father, with whom "The Bishop" had also sparred.

Thankfully, the topic of new telescope technology was soon abandoned and Andromeda gracefully excused herself from the gathering, feigning the need for a good night's sleep before a long Saturday in the library. Confused and ticked off, Andromeda hopped into her fifteen-year-old Celica ("The Red Shift"), switched on an L.A. jazz station, and drove forty-two miles down to the coast. Her mind free-floated on the two glasses of wine she'd sipped at Jacob's and a miscellany of offbeat thoughts typical of her imagination.

At midnight she found herself on a moonlit pullout near Malibu, within eyeshot of Dr. Jedediah Clarke's seaside bungalow, legendary abode of the notorious "Madman of Caltech." Some months earlier, for reasons Andromeda didn't know, the fifty-eight-year-old physicist had ostracized himself from his Caltech colleagues, but *his* banishment was long term—premature retirement. The department thought they'd forced out the iconoclastic professor, but the way Dr. Clarke saw it, he'd negotiated a "golden handshake" lucrative enough to escape a "research society sated with zealous competitors vying for lucrative projects with military spin-offs."

Andromeda stared at the ex-professor's little cliff-top cottage, perched above a beach where Pacific swells washed up creamy in the moonlight. A window glowed from some interior lamp's illumination.

Do you suppose he ever felt the way I do tonight? she wondered, not realizing that he had felt that way *many* times. Not so much in his youth when odd-ball scientists were still in vogue, but later, when Caltech's post–Vietnam era prestige had risen to an all-time high and anyone as quirky as their own Mr. Feynman was unlikely to gain full acceptance.

Andromeda's reverie broke when a shadow passed across the lighted window, the Madman stirring among his books.

"What do you suppose he's working on tonight?" she muttered, glancing at her pink Apple Watch SE. 12:45 a.m. Two more times he paced in front of the window, raising her curiosity to an unbearable level. "The genius is birthing something," she said to the night.

She reached through the Celica's window to retrieve her binoculars, 9x50 image-stabilized Nikons she kept in the coupe for impromptu stargazing. Some irrational instinct took hold of her, as if by observing his pacing figure she could obtain some hint of his preoccupation, in the same manner one observes a meteor shower or a comet.

In fact, no one knew what Jedediah Clarke was up to. He had ceased publishing articles, and yet rumors of a private research project circulated among his former colleagues, sparked one afternoon when a cosmologist dropped by to return several books he'd borrowed years earlier. Dr. Clarke had refused to invite the good professor in, "feigning illness," so the story went. While the two chatted in the bungalow's doorway, the cosmologist noticed research texts piled high in various parts of the living room. Clarke's MacBook Pro displayed some kind of multidimensional chart, and a great heap of typewritten pages was stacked on the table. The content of such a work was anyone's guess, but it made everyone nervous, since Jedediah Clarke—whose theories of life formation on other planets had given him a permanent place in the textbooks—was

He is working on something!

acknowledged by everyone, even Adam Jacob, to be brilliant and unique.

Andromeda lifted the binoculars to her eyes. Through the bungalow window she could make out floor-to-ceiling bookshelves on the far wall and a cluttered table partially in view. Yellow curtains, drawn open to let in the sea breeze, trembled on either side of the sash, and a smoky haze caught the lamplight. Again Dr. Clarke passed before the window, and Andromeda recognized his thick, sun-bleached hair (as usual, uncombed), large Roman nose, and bushy eyebrows that shadowed his sky-blue eyes. Leading his march across the room was his signature burl pipe, trailing tobacco smoke that lingered in his path. He had a notebook in his hand.

He is working on something! she thought. A moment later he reappeared, this time stopping at the table. For several minutes, he scanned the open books and papers strewn across it, occasionally penciling something into his notebook. Then, picking up a leather pouch from the table, he disappeared from view.

Andromeda waited, thrilled to be secretly watching the master at work on some new theory or idea. That she had resorted to voyeurism to do so further titillated the young woman, and the pace of her breathing increased. Drops of sweat rolled down her forehead in the muggy Malibu air and her damp blouse stuck to her back. Out the corner of her eye she noticed movement on the bungalow's beachfront side and shifted her binoculars to catch it. What came into view so startled her that she nearly dropped the glasses. There was the Madman on the bungalow's deck, staring straight at her with binoculars of his own!

CHAPTER 20

The Madman's Lair

"I don't imagine this is the first time I've been window-peeped from the highway," Jedediah Clarke said, standing on his doorstep looking into the crimson face of Andromeda McCrea. She was still in her smart outfit and heels from Jacob's party, while the astronomer wore stretched-out khakis, a denim shirt burned in two places by hot tobacco, and bare feet. "But surely I've never been peeped by a Caltech graduate student."

"No," she replied, looking at the ground.

"Least of all, someone I've met."

Andromeda shook her head in total embarrassment, wishing that she'd just raced home in her Celica on the chance that he hadn't seen her face. Instead, she'd marched right over to his bungalow, an act fueled not only by the need to "come clean" after being discovered, but by a perverse hope she might actually get inside the Madman's lair.

"Would you care to come in and explain yourself?"

She nodded, then strode past the astronomer with renewed determination to make things right between them.

"You attended that series of lectures I gave last spring on 'Space-Based Strategies for Discovering Extraterrestrial Life,'" he said with a blend of accusatory whimsy.

She was shocked—and flattered. "You remember my question then?" she said assertively.

"Uh-huh," he nodded. How could he *not* remember? What red-blooded man wouldn't have noticed the tall young beauty rise from her seat to ask one of the key contentious questions of all three seminars: "Why is the science community only lukewarm in their support of space-based observatories when the chance of finding a living planet with an Earth-bound telescope is unlikely at best—especially now that skies are deteriorating yearly with increased air and light pollution?"

"To put it simply," he had replied, "the competition for observing time on only a handful of space telescopes would be too unbearable. You can build a lot of ground-based telescopes for the price of a single eye in space, and each one on the ground yields many more research grants, PhD theses, and academic accomplishments than a lone space-based instrument, even one that could answer the timeless question of whether we're out here all alone."

His candid reply had made her laugh with delight, blushing her youthful skin and sparking her green eyes with a twinkle visible across the lecture hall. Jedediah was not the only one to notice this, and after the talk a gaggle of male students had gathered around Andromeda in animated intercourse.

"Your seminar," she continued, almost forgetting the humiliating circumstances of their current encounter, "very much affected the topic and approach of my thesis—"

"Before we leap into the depths of your own research," he interrupted, "might we entertain a more customary introduction than peeps through pairs of binoculars?"

Andromeda blushed again, but quickly recovered by offering her hand. He took it and squeezed it warmly.

"I'm Andy McCrea," using her nickname, "and while I admit tonight's circumstances are a bit unusual, I'm delighted to finally meet you, Professor . . . I mean Doctor . . . Clarke," she stumbled, remembering his defrocking several months earlier.

"Ah yes, they've put me out to pasture, haven't they?" he replied, folding his arms across his chest.

"Their loss . . . ," she began, but he held up a hand to hush her defense of him.

"They think I'm just out here grazing over old ground, chewing my cud, but I'm as active as ever." He smiled broadly, revealing a bold set of teeth. "Come into my living room and sit for a moment."

He led Andromeda past his cluttered table to a rattan couch near the room's sea-facing windows. The air was musty, a blend of pungent Latakia tobacco and mildewed books. Paintings and photographs hung on the walls, three of which drew her particular attention. One was a Hubble Space Telescope image of a planetary disk, a ring of interstellar dust and gas revolving around a star, inside which orbited unseen planets. The two others hung side by side on an opposite wall. First, a painting of NASA's proposed but never funded Terrestrial Planet Finder—five telescope-bearing spacecraft flying in formation above Earth, their huge mirrors pointing at a nearby star in hopes of gathering enough infrared radiation to detect Earth-sized planets that might yield life. Next to it hung a large seascape of a Polynesian voyaging canoe filled with awestruck explorers approaching the Big Island at night, with Mauna Loa erupting and snowcapped Mauna Kea haloed with stars.

"Can you talk about your project?" Andromeda asked, dropping into the couch while Jedediah sat down in the ruby Barcalounger next to the wall.

"As I said earlier, I think before we discuss our research inquiries, a prior question must first be answered. What compelling interest caused you to spy on me in the middle of the night?" He plucked his pipe from a pottery ashtray on the armrest and knocked out the old char. "Did one of your professors put you up to it?"

"Oh, no!" she replied, leaning so far forward her comely contours became apparent. "I would never do that!"

"Then what *did* you have in mind?" he asked, consciously keeping his eyes on her face. "Was it a prurient motivation?"

Andromeda's jaw dropped.

Jedediah nonchalantly repacked his pipe. "It does seem rather peculiar that an attractive young woman with obvious brains and a more-than-trivial education would waste her time peeping on an old professor of less-than-sterling looks while he shuffles his papers in the dark of the night." He probed his khakis for a lighter.

"No, no, you have this all wrong . . . I mean, you have it only partly right. No, that's not what I mean . . ."

"Well, what do you mean?" he replied, igniting his pipe.

Andromeda sat upright in the couch and willfully regained her composure. "First, I was over on that pullout not to window peep, but because I was full of wine and the humiliation that comes from having inadvertently alienated a member of my thesis committee at my first introductory party at his house."

"Oh my," he said, shaking his head.

"Second, when you saw me, I had only just then begun 'spying' on you, as you say. But I was motivated by pure curiosity, not by your looks—good heavens, no!—but because I've always been intrigued by your crazy ideas."

"I suppose it should ease my mind that you were window peeping because of an interest in my crazy ideas rather than my physical characteristics, but that's not much consolation for an aging bachelor who also holds some pride for his ideas."

"No! No! No! Dr. Clarke, there's nothing wrong with your looks or your ideas. Quite the contrary!"

They both blushed.

"Tell me, young lady, do you always keep binoculars in your car?"

"I'm an astronomer. I go no place without them."

Jedediah stopped puffing and leaned forward, for the first time addressing her seriously. "Good for you. Too many astrophysicists couldn't recognize a star if it came up and bit them—unless it was an image on a computer screen with its radiation crunched down into a mathematical formula." He pointed his pipe at her. "I keep a pair in my car too."

They both smiled and Andromeda finally started to relax.

"To be perfectly honest, Dr. Clarke, I was flustered after Dr. Jacob's party. I guess I put my foot in my mouth by challenging him on the Haisley project. I thought we were just having a lively discussion, and I got confused when he turned snide."

"Jacob, eh? Well, Andy, welcome to the sorry side of our profession." He puffed on his pipe, and for the first time she noticed that his broad cheeks were coarse with gray stubble from several days untouched by a razor. "Ego, turf, and competition can cause people to lose track of what we should be about!"

"But I expected to have a *real* debate. I mean Dr. Jacob's famous! He should be above ego! I felt humiliated *and* disappointed." Andromeda's moistening eyes gleamed. "So I drove out to the coast and ended up at that turnoff."

"You had to drive quite some distance north to reach that particular turnoff."

"I don't doubt that subconsciously I drove to *that* turnoff because I wanted to put myself near one of my intellectual heroes—someone who might understand my predicament. Picturing you working on your ideas was helping me regain my resolve. So when I noticed your light I got carried away."

He smiled warmly. "Good thing I wasn't having one of my wild bachelor parties."

Andromeda wiped her eyes and smiled back.

Jedediah took a deep breath and exhaled. "I'm surprised you didn't realize Jacob's stake in the Haisley project, given your own connection to its history."

"What do you mean by that?"

"Aren't you the daughter of the Berkeley astronomer who got the money out of Haisley? I'm thinking that Andy is a nickname and that your dad is Willy."

Andromeda found herself blushing again.

"Your father hasn't told you that he and Jacob have tussled over control of that telescope ever since the day Willy secured the money?"

"I knew something was bothering Dad, but he never said a word. That usually means he can't face it."

"Well, your father strikes me as an idealist rather than an infighter. He wants to find life-sustaining planets. That's why they're talking about a 60-meter mirror. With something that size they think they may actually see those babies from Earth—*if* that big mirror really works and *if* they can continue to improve visibility through our messy atmosphere."

"That's exactly what I told Jacob at the party!"

Jedediah's lips lifted into a smile. Here was a student so independent she was willing to challenge even her father's pet project. "Adam Jacob missed the chance to lead the Terrestrial Planet Finder—Congress killed the funding—so he's putting all of his eggs in Haisley's basket. He intends to oversee the Big Eye science program . . . at the expense of Willy McCrea if necessary."

"I didn't realize . . ."

"And that's not all . . . He's a stuck-up snob as well."

They both laughed. Jedediah leaned forward and squeezed her knee. "Care for a midnight snack?"

"Sure." Andromeda rose to follow him into the kitchen but stopped when she noticed the little moonlit bay below the bungalow's windows.

"Is that *your* sailboat?"

"Uh-huh . . . salmon and crackers OK?"

"Sounds great."

He disappeared into the kitchen. Andromeda turned from the window and wandered to the big table covered with books and papers.

"I've got some Chardonnay," he called down the hall, "but the bottle's been open a few days."

"I'm not particular," she replied, leaning over his materials.

"What's this?" she muttered to herself, surprised to find the astronomer's heap topped with an enormous map of the Pacific Islands heavily marked in pencil. His scribblings—of words, numbers, and phrases in Hawaiian—were difficult to decipher. She lifted the corner of the map to peek at the papers beneath it just as Jedediah returned with her glass of wine.

"Is there no end to your spying?" he asked, touching her shoulder with his hand.

"What's this all about?" she said, undaunted.

He turned the map backside up and put the glass in her hand. "I'm studying some very old astronomy problems from a freshly inspired view."

CHAPTER 21
The Crazy Woman
of Keaukaha

June and July were especially hot that year, and Erik used vacation time accrued during his year and a half at the base camp to hang out in Keaukaha—swimming, fishing, and kayaking with Freddie and Sam. All that enchanting water time made him nostalgic for the river and his backwater canoe trips with Jack. As summer sped by, Erik grew ever more curious about the squatters village behind his trailer, but each time he asked Freddie about it, his buddy changed the subject. Meanwhile, the old woman picking ti in her banana-leaf hat continued to smile whenever she caught his eye.

Then one August night, sitting on lawn chairs in front of the Airstream, the Three Muskrateers held a drunken bull session, lubricated with 'okolehau again. Erik, well in his cups, waxed eloquent about his beloved bend in the river, telling poignant stories he'd never shared with his Hawai'i friends. Patches of red rose on his cheeks when he finally revealed that he'd been "run out of town" by a flood of change that washed away everything he valued. "I felt like I was drowning," he confessed.

Tears glittered in all their eyes. Freddie tried to stem Erik's melancholy with a joke about "a freshwater fish with mittens donning a hula shirt," but it made no dent in Erik's mood.

Sam caught Freddie's eye and nodded his head toward the ferns behind the trailer. "I gotta take one leak," he said. The two got up and disappeared around the corner.

"I t'ink time for braddah to see da aunty," Sam said as they watered the plants. "He ready."

"Ya t'ink?"

"Useta be angry, now he sad, so I t'ink his heart open enough, brah."

"And she da expert on wounded souls. She know what to tell 'im."

"I like stay ovah tonight," Freddie told Erik when the two returned. "Avoid dose drunk-hunting cops on da Hamakua Coast road. OK I sleep on your built-in sofa? I got one sleeping bag in my truck."

The next morning, as the two wolfed down breakfast in the trailer, Freddie brought up the Hawaiians next door. "You ready to meet your neighbors?" He asked, tossing his fork onto his empty plate, earlier heaped with Portuguese sausage, eggs, and rice. His heavy pidgin from last night's bull session with Sam was gone.

"You mean the homeless squatters?" Erik replied, refilling their cups from his stovetop espresso pot.

Freddie lit a Kool and stretched his legs across the tiny sitting area. "They may be homeless, but they definitely don't see themselves as squatters. That land next door, and this parcel you and Sunny Boy are on, used to be Hawaiian Crown Lands, 'ceded' to the Territory of Hawai'i after America overthrew the islands."

"Overthrew?"

"Yep. 1893. Military coup d'état by US marines. No more queen, no more nation, no more constitution, the beginning of the real land grab. Hawai'i as they knew it pau!" Finished!

Freddie and Sam had often talked about the Hawaiians' vibrant cultural movement, and Erik had heard sovereignty songs on the radio, but neither friend had yet mentioned an overthrow. Then he remembered a video interview he'd watched that night in the base camp library, an activist linking the "theft" of Mauna Kea to the "theft of our nation."

"I thought there'd been some sort of vote," Erik said feebly, lighting a Marlboro.

Freddie laughed. "Only with guns, and the guns won. The Hawaiians sent petitions to Congress opposing annexation . . . signed by almost every native man, woman, and child. The lead insurgent Lorrin Thurston camped out in DC lobbying Congress and planting fake news in the papers—a myth Americans still believe to this day. Racists like Teddy Roosevelt ate it up."

"But why did anyone in the US care?"

"They wanted Pearl Harbor for a Navy coaling station to expand their new empire into the Pacific . . . America's first regime change. Anyhow, those folks next door may live in poverty, but they're also laying claim to their ancestral lands and the right to live their traditions. Wanna go see?"

"Hmm . . . OK." Still despondent from last night's journey down memory lane, did he really want to know the truth about his idyllic coastal escape?

"Eh, no worry. What they've put together next door is pretty cool. You'll see."

While Erik dawdled washing the dishes, Freddie wandered through Sunny Boy's yard, gathering flowers for a small bouquet.

"I have a special friend over there," he said, guiding Erik through the ti patch behind the shower house to a dirt lane that bisected the settlement.

Close up the camp looked less slip-shod than it had through the jungle. Behind the Walmart camping tents near Keaukaha's main road stood two dozen shelters crafted of blue plastic tarp nailed to two-by-fours, with roofs of unpainted plywood. They were tidy structures with screened areas and plank lanais, all facing the sea. Inside were refrigerators and stoves fueled by propane and lamps and TVs run off solar panels or gasoline generators. A communal shower house and three port-a-potties stood in the jungle at the settlement's far edge. In the narrow clearings between shelters were vegetable gardens, taro patches, and banana trees. Ti plants and lava rock walls lined most of the shacks, and traditional thatched roofs covered a third of them. Old fishnet decorated several lanai, adorned with glass floats that had washed up on the beach. Most homes had fishing gear stowed nearby. Curious upright stones similar to ones Erik had seen on Mauna Kea stood in front of many dwellings, some placed atop the rock walls.

"Those and the ti are for protection," Freddie explained. "The first Polynesians brought ti plants in their double-hulled canoes, and to Hawaiians stones—pohaku—possess mana, or even the spirits of ancestors."

Erik was surprised at how many people greeted Freddie, with a wave, an "aloha, braddah," or that quick uplift of eyebrows so typical of Polynesians. The pair walked through the village onto a stone path leading to the beach, a small arch of black-and-white sand washed up between ridges of lava that extended seaward as reefs, now exposed by low tide.

A grizzled Hawaiian with a mesh net slung over his shoulder stalked a rocky outcrop, his keen eyes watching for flashes of color in the transparent water. His yellow trunks stood out against skin maroon from the sun, and he wore green *tabi* on his feet—knit boots with felt soles that cling to wet lava. A younger man, dive knife and bucket in hand, dipped in and out of the surf along the exposed reef, searching for little conical shells of 'opihi—a tasty limpet prized by Hawaiians. Two young mothers chatted on the sand, watching their toddlers cavort in the gentle waves.

"This reminds me of the south islands," Erik said, his mood lifting.

In a tiny protected cove at the waterfront's far edge, a broad-faced old woman sat in the water up to her neck, her long white hair splayed on the surface like another fishing net. It was that odd woman who always smiled at Erik from the ti patch. She was gazing out to sea with a peculiar smile, talking on and on as if in conversation with some unseen companion, her words obscured by the *shush* of breaking waves and the rattle of coco palms behind the beach. The radiance of her enormous round eyes in the low eastern light shone even across the cove.

"She's probably talking with Kanaloa," Freddie said cheerfully, "one of her favorites, the great sea god revered by Hawaiian sailors. Kanaloa was a legendary navigator of old, who over time they deified as the power of winds, waves, and tides."

Suddenly, as if struck by insight, the old woman halted her chatter, dropped her smile, and turned to peer directly at the two young men. Freddie waved and the smile reappeared. She turned back to the sea and began talking again.

Freddie chuckled. "Some people say Aunty Moana is pupule—crazy—but they don't know her . . . Like many things in Hawai'i, the reality is not what it seems."

"She's probably talking with Kanaloa."

Freddie walked Erik to a cluster of three flat stones under the shade of a *kamani* tree, its fallen red leaves and oval nuts littering the ground. He gestured for Erik to sit on the stone closest to the water, and he sat opposite his friend. Erik was surprised at the comfortable feel of the stones, made smooth by generations of just this use, the reason the community had brought them there.

"Moses is not all he seems either," Freddie added, watching for Erik's reaction.

"No."

"That's right. He's the kahu—the guardian—of the base camp, but he's also one of the mountain kahu. At important places—beaches, community centers, old temples—kahu quietly, sometimes secretly, watch the place and tend to its needs. It's one way Hawaiians malama the 'aina—take care of the land."

"I've noticed that Moses knows a lot more than he lets on," Erik added.

"Yep. Months before anyone else, he knew they were planning more cabins at the construction camp, for TMT crews. I don't think even his boss at the cooperative had been told. That's part of the kahu's job. People feel his mana so they tell him things they wouldn't utter to another soul. Me included." Freddie cracked his knuckles, which by then Erik had learned meant he was a bit self-conscious. "Moses is soft-spoken," Freddie continued, "but he tells you exactly what's on his mind—sometimes in so few words it's easy to miss the message."

Aunty Moana stepped out of the water, her yellow-and-black *pareu* clinging to her rotund body. She bent sideways and squeezed the water out of her hair with sturdy fingers as she had done countless times during her seventy-two years. She moved up the shore with an almost youthful gait, but as she neared the pair, her age became apparent—by her feet. Wide and callused, they were like those Erik had seen on South Sea islanders who preferred bare feet to rubber flip-flops. She strolled up to the two young men, who stood.

"No, no," she said, motioning with her plump arms for them to remain seated. Freddie ignored this and stepped forward to throw his arms around her.

"Aloha, Freddie." She reached over to accept his hug, and placing her forehead on his, tips of their noses touching, exchanged breath in the old Hawaiian way.

"Aloha, Aunty."

After sharing their *honi*, but still clasping each other, Freddie said, "Sam Chun sends his aloha. He can't join us today because he's getting ready for a case—that hassle over the diesel leak at the wharf."

"Maikaʻi," she said, nodding thoughtfully. Very good.

"Aunty, this is Erik."

"Aloha, Erik," she said, leaning forward to encourage his hug. He responded, stiffly, surprised when she placed a soft kiss on his cheek. Although she had just stepped out of the cool water Aunty Moana's body was warm.

"Well," she said, peering into Erik's dark-blue eyes, "you've finally come to see me." Erik flushed and beads of sweat welled up on his brow.

Aunty Moana sat down on the largest of the three smooth stones, her visitors taking the others flanking her. Freddie was about to offer the flowers he'd picked, but she immediately asked a question. "How are things on the mountain, Freddie?"

"Cold in the mornings and *really* cold at night. Unusual for August."

"Sometimes what's routine is anything but . . . when larger forces are involved." She gazed up at the sky, her eyes narrow as if focused on something visible only to her. A sudden gust of wind tugged her damp hair. "Who but the gods can predict the weather?" She giggled. "The season of hurricanes is still upon us. Remember Wanana last year? Whirling by so close?" Aunty Moana smiled as if this was all good news, and Erik again noticed her missing teeth.

"What are you doing up there these days?" she asked Freddie.

"The usual repairs and painting. But I'm also gonna be putting up security fence around the snowplows."

"Hmmm," she mused in a deep baritone voice.

"Another change after the big protests. At least I'll get to work outdoors."

She patted Freddie on the hand and, addressing Erik with shining eyes, said, "Oh, this youngster, he so loves our mountain . . . and the mountain loves him too."

Freddie, pleased, cracked his knuckles.

"And what are *you* doing on Mauna Kea?" she asked Erik. Something in the way she said it immediately brought to mind that day at the lake when the mysterious young woman had asked a similar question.

"I'm a cook at the base camp."

"Moses hired him," Freddie added.

"Ahhhh," she said thoughtfully. "So you're from the islands?"

"No, from Minnesota. I grew up on the Mississippi River."

Aunty Moana beamed. "I saw your mighty Mississippi once, south of the Twin Cities, on my way to Pipestone." She glanced out to the sea, remembering. "That river was . . . impressive."

"Pipestone! What were you doing there?"

"I was on assignment," she giggled. "Secret stuff, you know, for Ke Akua." God. She winked at Freddie.

Erik wiped his increasingly damp brow.

"It's too hot out here," Aunty Moana said. "Let's sit in my hale." Her home.

They followed the old woman through the coconut trees to a blue tarp shack at the farthest edge of the cove, its sea-facing lanai flanked by numerous ti plants and a large upright stone of the same dense basalt Erik had seen in the adze quarry. The shack's front wall was all screen, and a beautiful thatched roof extended well out over the lanai to shield Aunty Moana and her guests from sun and rain. A pair of wicker armchairs and a rusty card table and two plastic chairs furnished the lanai, all shabby as if salvaged from a dump. On the table were an egg-smeared plate from breakfast and the Hilo library's copy of Alexandra David-Neel's 1932 memoir *Magic and Mystery in Tibet*. Nearby, on the floor, was the current *Astronomical Almanac*, numerous of its pages flagged with Post-it notes and *Moana Keali'i Kuahiwi* scrawled in bold strokes across its cover.

"I brought you some flowers from Erik's place," Freddie said, finally handing her the bouquet.

"Oh, mahalo! I'll put these in some water. Come with me, Freddie. I want to show you something new inside the hale. Bring your friend."

Aunty Moana stepped inside to the small cupboard, hot plate, and tiny sink that made up her kitchen and put the bouquet in a plastic vase, while Erik scanned the single-room home. An unmade daybed lined one wall, and a stout little desk—cluttered with notebooks, articles, and an old rehabbed MacBook—protruded from the other, affording its user a sea view out the screen wall. A tattered loveseat and rusty floor lamp also faced the ocean. Two bookshelves overflowed with a wide variety of volumes, including thick tomes on Hawaiian history and culture, a row of mystery and science fiction paperbacks, and an old Time-Life series on world religions. Atop the bookshelves were several sea-smoothed stones draped with ti-leaf or nut leis, two huge 'opihi shells, and, facing the sea, a ceramic statue of an octopus, symbol of Kanaloa. Pinned on a two-by-four above her desk was a reproduction of a 1965 newspaper photo of Martin Luther King and his comrades wearing flower leis during their march from Selma to Montgomery.

Hung above the bed was the most striking furnishing of all, a large expressionist painting rendered in bold oils with a palette knife. A shimmering silver lake lined with maroon cinder—it could only be Waiau—floated on wispy clouds beneath a splash of opalescent blue. Out of the tiny lake poured reticulated waves of light. Far away, rendered as if out of focus, stood a white mountain, its peak encircled with creamy swirls. Slabs of driftwood embedded with bits of coral framed the painting.

Aunty Moana smiled proudly. "A friend of mine gave this to me."

Freddie stepped back from the painting to get a better view.

"Have you ever seen the lake?" Aunty Moana asked Erik.

"Lake Waiau? Twice."

"Really . . ." Her curious gaze compelled him to say more.

"I went there because I dreamt about drinking from it."

"And so . . . did you?"

"Drink from it? Yes."

"Hmmm," she murmured again in her deep voice, then gazed up at the painting. "The sacred waters of Kane . . . pure . . . healing." She spun around on her toes. "Let's go back outside now. I'll join you two in a moment."

Freddie and Erik returned to the lanai while Aunty Moana rinsed off a hand of fresh bananas in her sink and placed them in a wooden bowl.

"Please help yourself," she said, setting the fruit and Freddie's flowers on the card table. She eased her big frame into the wicker chair. "Come sit next to me, Erik," she said, patting the other wicker. "Freddie, you don't mind sitting at the table."

The brief tour inside her home had filled Erik's mind with questions, for which he felt grateful. Asking this strange elder questions would be easier than answering any she seemed poised to ask. "Are *you* from this island, Aunty Moana?" he said before even sitting down.

"Well . . . hmm . . . yes," she replied, her lower lip forming a slight pout. "I grew up at the foot of the Kohala Mountains, in a little town you've never heard of. My grandmother raised me."

"But you spent years in Honolulu, right, Aunty?" Freddie said.

"Yes. I went back to live with Mom and Dad when I was eighteen and spent most of my life in the city. But, finally, I made it home."

"So you've been living here for a while then?" Erik said.

"In Hilo for seven years, and two here in Hoʻololi, our little 'avant-garde' village." Aunty Moana paused to probe Erik's face, sensing his apprehension. "So you want to know about me?" she said. "Well, I was a schoolteacher for almost thirty years. I had to wear haole clothes every day, even nylon stockings! I married a haole and had two children. Both still live in Honolulu, but my husband ran off years ago. I have no idea where he is." She looked up at the young man. "Are you taking notes?"

"Sorry, I didn't mean to . . ."

"Erik, why are you so nervous?" she asked, patting the back of his hand. "I won't bite."

"I'm not nervous," he said, moisture gathering in his armpits.

"Forget it, Erik," Freddie laughed. "You can't keep anything from Aunty Moana."

"I'm a sensitive, you see," she said, leaning close to him, a disconcerting shimmer in her eyes. "I see most things with my heart. In fact, I feel much more in people than I'd like to." Her face darkened. "What makes you run, Erik?"

"What do you mean?"

"You're a long way from your river."

His eyes watered.

"Give her the scoops, man," Freddie said, lighting a Kool. "Aunty'll understand."

"Um . . . disillusion, I guess."

"Ahhhh," she replied, leaning back in her chair, the wicker squeaking. "One of life's most difficult hurdles."

He nodded, a tear crowding his eye, but he wasn't sweating anymore.

"So, Erik, where are you running *to*?"

He shrugged, and his cheeks pinkened.

"Freddie," she said, "would you go over to Aunty Audrey's hale and see if she's made haupia today? If so, buy a few pieces, would you?" She reached into the woven *lauhala* bag next to her chair and handed him three dollars. Freddie took the bills and walked away.

Aunty Moana bent forward, the gleam in her eyes so intense that Erik actually leaned back.

"Freddie tells me you lived in the south islands for a while."

"Three years . . . crewing on sailboats."

Aunty Moana placed a big palm on her cheek and smiled. "Sailing . . . wonderful!"

"It was. I could have stayed forever."

"How is it you came here?"

"I ran out of money in Samoa. I came to Hawai'i to find work."

"And you got a job on our mountain. Wonderful!"

He nodded warily. The old woman leaned even closer, almost whispering. "One night in Honolulu, years ago, just after my husband left, my grandmother came to visit in a dream. I woke wide awake. I went out into my yard and stared up at the heavens and saw a light moving across the sky. I was sure this light was for me, so the very next day I told my principal that the doctors thought I was dying.

Could I take a leave of absence to try and find a cure?" She chuckled mischievously. "Of course, they had to agree. I found a guide, also from Kohala, an old man who'd known my grandmother. Even when I was a child he seemed ancient. He took me into the deepest, most remote valley on this island, a place created when half the volcano slid into the sea. He left me alone there for . . . well . . . I don't know. Days? Weeks? Longer?" She shook her head. "Eventually, I came back out, and I knew what I must do."

"You left your job?"

"Not immediately. I couldn't. I had two children and no husband. But when at last I retired, I came back to my real home—my 'aina— and began my real work. That's what I do now. That's why I'm here . . . in this . . . Hawaiian village."

Erik didn't know why she was telling him all this, or what he should say, but when Aunty Moana took his hand in hers, he was glad and squeezed it. She was very warm.

"I think you have found the right place for the next part of your journey, Erik. When you come back down on Tuesdays please don't worry when I smile at you from the ti patch." And then she smiled, her face full of love.

When at last he got up to leave, Aunty Moana rose too. "One more question, Erik. When you were in Samoa, did you get to the island of Upolu?"

"Yes."

Her eyes lit up. "And did you climb Mount Vaea? Did you see the grave of Tusitala, the storyteller Robert Louis Stevenson?"

"I was only passing through on a boat delivery."

"Ahhh . . . too bad. Tusitala was a good friend of our last king, Kalakaua, and he wrote about our plight, and that of the Samoans too. If I ever get there, I'll do a chant for him."

"When I get back to Samoa, I'll try to visit the grave . . . and say a word for you."

"Oh, mahalo!" she said and hugged him warmly.

In the twilight after sunset, Erik strolled down to the shore below Sunny Boy's bungalow to ponder his meeting with Aunty Moana. Smoking on a slab of rock at water's edge, he heard a soft splash nearby. He turned to look and spotted the same ghostly face with sheeny eyes that he had encountered sailing across the 'Alenuihaha Channel. Now much closer to the creature, Erik could clearly tell it was a seal, with a broad whiskered snout, a gently upturned mouth, and probing black eyes.

The words, *you're still in the South Seas* surfaced unbidden in Erik's mind, *don't mistake this for the other world and miss what awaits you here.*

Erik watched the seal glide leisurely about the surface, its face fixed on the sailor sitting on shore. Its silvery coat shimmered like pearl.

"Aloha," Erik finally greeted, then smiled in private embarrassment. He glanced back at Sunny Boy's lanai, relieved to see his landlord rattling around inside the lit-up bungalow. When Erik turned back, the seal was gone. Getting up to leave, he noticed a night heron perched on the limb of a kamani tree just down the shore, its squat profile exactly the same as the red-eyed herons that had watched him on the river. Goose bumps rose on his back.

*Its squat profile was exactly the same as the herons
that had watched Erik on the river.*

CHAPTER 22

Planetary Passions

Three months had passed since Andromeda McCrea's embarrassing binoculars encounter, and the prospect of seeing Dr. Jedediah Clarke so excited her that she speeded on her way up California Highway 1. More than intellectual curiosity fueled her impatience. That first night Jedediah, recognizing that her spunk and brains might get her into trouble at Caltech, had offered to serve as her "unofficial" PhD adviser over the summer. Their passion for finding life on other planets, and their mutual preference to search with space telescopes, had generated a discussion that lasted until dawn. Driving home in the first light, Andromeda had pondered the eccentric man with whom she'd spent the night talking, and realized that she'd become smitten with the defrocked professor.

Since then she'd met him three times for coffee at Io's Fire café in Pasadena, where they'd discussed planetary evolution, accretion disk detection, and the latest scientific debates about the prevalence of life in the universe. She'd also explained her thesis in detail, each session worried she might betray the flush she felt across the table.

Jedediah was more striking than handsome. His blue eyes were so dazzling she grew convinced that some starlight had lodged inside them during his nights observing the heavens. In truth, it was his brilliance that shone, which while *akin* to starlight, actually reflected his uncanny ability for insight. He was not the kind of scientist who doggedly accumulates fact upon fact in a staid ritual of step-by-step deductions and conclusions. While he could readily discern any logical mistakes in such analyses and could masterfully execute the same ritual when required, Dr. Clarke's greatest insights swept into his mind like meteors across the sky, ideas whose validity was later grudgingly verified by the dogged efforts of his colleagues, men who tried mightily to disprove the mystical conclusions of the "Madman."

Why wouldn't a robust young intellect be attracted to a man whose brain seemed as primordial—and intemperate—as the very forces of nature they had both dedicated their lives to study? But Andromeda feared that if Dr. Clarke knew what a terrible crush she had on him, he'd dismiss her as "foolish," so she masked these rising feelings during their coffee shop discussions with her own displays of brilliance.

She didn't realize this would only increase his interest in her. During even their first encounter, he had noticed much more than her attractive shell. He had recognized her potent intelligence and wondered whether he had finally found in this young woman a mind open enough to share the ideas of his current project.

When the first hint of dawn had become apparent, he'd urged her to step out onto his porch to catch a last glimpse of the fading stars over the sea. Four especially bright ones were still visible in the southern sky, which Andromeda immediately recognized as Procyon, Sirius, Betelgeuse, and Rigel.

"Puana, A'a, Kauluakoko, and Puanakau"—said Jedediah, throwing his hand up to the sky—"to Polynesian navigators, four beacons guiding their way across the Pacific."

"Did they really know the sky that well?" Andromeda had asked, moving close to the scholar, their shoulders touching. She was by then infused with sweet euphoria from all the Chardonnay, the probing conversations, and her budding attraction to the man.

"Oh yes!" he had replied, grasping the porch rail as if standing on the deck of his sailboat. A sudden sea wind tossed the mass of sun-bleached hair off his forehead—fully exposing his striking silver temples—and he pushed his face forward as if accepting a caress. "The Pacific Islanders understood them much earlier and far better than did their Western counterparts. Only the Chinese were up to their speed."

"I didn't realize that," she had said, studying his face, serene after their night of kindred discourse.

"This is what you're studying, isn't it, Dr. Clarke? Your *next* project?"

"Yes, the wayfinders . . . oceanic stargazers guided by mental maps of the heavens. I believe that once they learned to navigate successfully among the Pacific isles, they went on to other seas throughout the world."

"What an exciting thought!" she had declared, as if the idea had been uttered for the very first time right there on that Malibu porch. "One that might upset a few historians."

"That's why it's so significant that they sailed their famous voyaging canoe *Hokule'a* on a worldwide journey across all those same seas, after decades proving their ancient methods throughout the Pacific. That finally debunked Thor Heyerdahl's *Kon-Tiki* myth that they merely drifted to the islands from South America. By the time *Hokule'a* finished that global voyage in 2017, the whole world understood better—maybe even appreciated—the islanders' extraordinary sky knowledge and navigation skills, and the underlying Polynesian wisdom that guided their quest.

"We Westerners eventually learned much more about the stars than Polynesians ever could—their distances, ages, heat, and evolution—but they really *knew* them, and trusted them in an intimate way that today is rare even among astronomers. And the philosophy and metaphysics behind it all . . ."

Jedediah had turned to face Andromeda. She peered back, her mouth open slightly in anticipation of his words. Her youthful vulnerability had suddenly struck him. While comfortably drawn to Andromeda's candor and intellectual strength, this added appeal was too much for him. He stepped back and leaned on the rail.

"But that," he continued, "is for another time."

Although confused by sensations he had not felt in a long time, Jedediah was glad he'd offered to advise her—and pleased she had accepted.

Andromeda pulled into the bungalow's little driveway fifteen minutes before their appointment. The ex-professor bounded up his beach stair and greeted her in swim trunks still dripping from a late afternoon dip in the Pacific. Above his slight paunch bloomed a chest of graying hair still drizzled with sea, upon which rested a spiral seashell hung from a leather thong around his neck. The shell reminded her of a galaxy whose innermost regions had been pulled upward by a powerful gravitational force.

"Come in, Andy!" he said brightly, scraping his sandy feet on the doormat. She hadn't noticed on her earlier embarrassed visit that the mat read "Get Lost!" and in her pleasantly disoriented state of mind wondered if it might have a double meaning.

The bungalow's atmosphere was fresher that afternoon, and the sun shone through the wide-open windows.

"I'll be with you in a moment," he said, slipping into the bedroom to change. "Make yourself at home."

Andromeda's eyes wandered about the living room. The papers and texts on his table were now neatly stacked to one side with the Pacific Islands chart rolled up against the heap. His bookshelves held numerous volumes from many fields, including history and anthropology as well as astronomy and physics. Among the titles were several about Caltech and she pulled one, a photographic history, from the shelf. She sat down at the table and thumbed through it.

Andromeda felt lucky to be a student at one of America's most prestigious training grounds for research scientists, where Nobel Prize winners were a Caltech tradition. Only the Massachusetts Institute of Technology dared compare itself with the West Coast wonder, and like MIT, Caltech had military and industrial connections to keep its coffers full of research grants and contracts, despite the Great Recession and the pandemic. It was the home of the famous Jet Propulsion Laboratory, whose lunar and planetary space missions were legendary. Having also built the world's largest telescopes—the Hale 200-inch on Mount Palomar in 1948 and the two Keck 10-meters on Mauna Kea in the 1990s—Caltech was one of the most sought-after schools for those astronomically inclined. Besides all that, Andromeda's father had also studied there.

With straight As in physics, chemistry, and math from UCLA, Andromeda had placed high on the admissions list. She had hoped to study under Dr. Jedediah Clarke, but he was on the way out by the time she arrived, for reasons that were widely debated. Some thought he had crossed swords with Caltech's president over a JPL proposal that involved several nights of military observation on the Keck Telescope. Others wondered if it was because he had successfully—and intemperately—challenged the quantum mechanics equations of two colleagues in front of their students (during one of Jedediah's famous impromptu visits to other professors' lectures). Others assumed his eccentric habits were the culprit, not the least of which were his nighttime pilgrimages to the rooftop of Caltech's tallest building, the Robert Millikan Library. The nine-story tower— called "Millikan's Last Erection" by students—was built by city variance to loom over Pasadena as a memorial to a school founder whose research on the photoelectric effect underlay modern particle physics (a tribute bestowed despite Millikan's notorious involvement in California's eugenics movement). On clear nights when rare big rains washed away L.A.'s smog and fresh alpine air swept down the San Gabriel mountains, Jedediah (binoculars in tow) would obtain access to the roof from the library janitor, there sitting night after night contemplating some problem or idea that had hitherto vexed him. Loyal students left food and drink by the locked door, and sometimes, according to school legend, an occasional joint or mushroom to facilitate the professor's contemplations.

Whatever the real reasons for his early retirement, no one claimed his scholarship was the cause; indeed some believed that had he not stirred up trouble during that eighteenth year on the faculty, Jedediah Clarke's picture would also be hanging in the school's hallway of Nobel laureates. The consensus, however, was that a school like Caltech can afford but one Mr. Feynman per century, especially after that legendary professor had shamed one of Caltech's most important contractors, NASA, by ferreting out the real reason for the 1986 *Challenger* Space Shuttle disaster. So Jedediah had never become a national celebrity, but his theories drew international attention, and the moral and academic support he gave his students stirred great loyalty among them. Yet, when he disappeared from Caltech, he cut himself off from them too.

Andromeda heard Jedediah heating coffee water in the kitchen and looked up from her book. He had changed into khakis and a faded T-shirt printed with the project emblem of the *Cassini* Saturn probe.

"Dr. Clarke, do you swim every day?" she called toward the kitchen.

"Just about," he hollered back, inserting a filter into the ceramic holder. "I find it stimulates my imagination."

"As if you need more of *that*!"

Jedediah laughed. "That's the hardest part. The thinking is easy."

Andromeda got up from the couch and wandered into the kitchen. "Can I ask you a personal question?"

Jedediah's grizzled brows jumped upward. "I may not answer it, but go ahead."

"Why did you leave Caltech?"

By that time he was accustomed to Andromeda's upfront questions. He paused a moment, loading the filter with coffee from a jar labeled SYNAPSE STIMULANT. "You mean why was I *encouraged* to go? I suppose some of my colleagues thought I'd lost my mind."

"Since when is that a reason to give an astronomer the boot?" Her eyes twinkled and he smiled back.

"Point well taken. Despite Caltech's legendary 'honor code,' our rumor mill can really grind up a person's reputation. I made the mistake of opposing the department's decision to build the Big Eye. In point of fact, I urged them in a key meeting with Haisley to give the kind donor his money back."

"What!" Andromeda was astonished, perhaps even unconsciously protective of her father. With astronomy research money increasingly hard to get, how could any astronomer—even one favoring space telescopes—turn away $1.5 billion for the finest telescope ever? Maybe Dr. Clarke really was mad.

"Well," he added, "unless they build it in Chile. But Haisley doesn't want it there. He insists it go to Mauna Kea or he won't hand over the money."

"And you said, 'Keep the money'?"

He nodded, handing her a steaming cup of coffee. "Cream?"

"Yes." She stirred as he poured, and her mind whirled.

"Sit down, Andy, and I'll tell you the whole story . . . if you want to hear it."

She did and she didn't, worried she might learn something about him—or her father—that she'd rather not know. Back in the living room, they faced each other on the couch.

"You see, to Native Hawaiians Mauna Kea is sacred. In fact, according to my own research . . ." He probed her face, then thought better of it and started over.

"Three decades had passed since a Caltech professor had opposed a private contribution, or any substantial research grant for that matter, the last being during the Cold War debate over weapons research. In those days society was divided on that issue so the school made allowances. But scientists aren't all that divided on how to treat native people—unfortunately. It's more an external cultural clash, you see . . . us versus them. Happily driven by the idea that any means to more knowledge in their field *must* be good, scientists can easily become myopic. Even after all the protests and litigation and media coverage sparked by TMT, few American scientists are able to truly comprehend, let alone appreciate, the depth of the local outcry. Proof of that was the National Academy of Sciences' 2021 decision to try to salvage the besieged telescope with NSF money."

Jedediah's expression darkened as he returned to the details of his defrocking.

"Anyway, my opposition to the Big Eye grant was based on what I had learned from Hawaiians on the mountain, information I'd verified—well, that which I could verify about a culture that assiduously protects its secrets—by examining historical records and written native lore. But my colleagues on the committee reacted just as you—incredulous. Here was the research opportunity of the century, a chance for Caltech to stay ahead in the race for giant telescopes. It wouldn't have been so bad had I not approached Haisley, later in private, to explain my reasoning and urge him to move the project to Chile. That's when I found out the real reason for his insistence on Mauna Kea."

"Which was?"

Jedediah looked at Andromeda with compassion for the innocence of youth. "Andy, you must remember that all people—no matter how bright, rich, or powerful—have human frailties. In Haisley's case, I suspect it's a mix of ego, insecurity, and some New Agey gobbledygook about past lives or some such. But the man wants to be buried on the highest point in the Pacific, and he has the money to make it happen by putting his crypt under the Big Eye."

Andromeda burst out laughing, her face flushing with the absurdity of it.

Her mentor gently grasped her arm. "It's not funny, Andy. It was your father who actually struck that deal, and the Caltech committee agreed to those terms. They also decided to keep that part of the arrangement secret for as long as they can."

Andromeda got up and wandered the room, the professor's story percolating through her mind.

"Well, what difference does it really make?" she finally said, facing Jedediah from the seaward windows. "I mean, the land baron who forked over the money for UC's Lick Observatory rests in peace under his namesake telescope on Mount Hamilton."

"In 1887 the native Ohlone of that area might have objected had anyone bothered to ask."

Andromeda just stared at him, befuddled.

"Anyway, that committee had some influential faculty on it," Jedediah continued, "not the least of which was Adam Jacob. You already know what a prima donna he is, but he's also the kind of in-fighter I wasn't used to. Almost in spite, he went after me, badmouthing me in physics circles for a set of public lectures I'd done at Berkeley on the Polynesians' use of stars. He called them 'romantic drivel beneath the stature of a Caltech astrophysicist.'"

"I heard about those lectures," Andromeda said, her face filled with consternation. "They were just light public presentations, weren't they? How could Jacob object to that?"

Pain crossed Jedediah's face—which Andromeda noticed.

"Apparently you didn't attend," he said, rising from the couch, "Jacob set out to assassinate me with my colleagues, using that and anything else his devilish mind could conspire." Jedediah opened the screen to the porch and stepped outside to witness the sunset, only minutes away. Andromeda followed, placing herself a few feet down the rail.

"It was true, of course," he said, amber light of the dying sun in his face. "I hadn't done any real Caltech research for three years. I'd devoted all my waking hours—save for my teaching and advising—to the study of an old astronomy left too much in the hands of anthropologists."

"The wayfinder stuff."

"Yes. 'The wayfinder stuff,'" he parroted. His face was drawn, and for the first time since she'd met him, Dr. Clarke seemed as old as his years.

He spun toward her, his dazzling eyes locked on hers. "There are *secrets* there, Andy. Old astronomical knowledge mixed with a complex understanding of *meta*physics," both of which he planned to further explore on an upcoming trip to Hawai'i. Jedediah turned back to watch the sea turn steel in the shadow of Earth's disappearing star.

"So now they think I've lost my bearings." He laughed uproariously, his youthful verve returning. "Truth is," he muttered to the sea, "I've actually just found them."

Andromeda, unsure what to make of all that, retreated to the corner of the porch. Neither said a word until twilight was well upon them and Jupiter and Saturn heralded the imminent appearance of the stars.

"Much as I love astronomy and would give my right arm to use a 60-meter telescope," he said, "I'm afraid I've adopted the Hawaiian view of the Big Eye."

Andromeda was startled all over again. "C'mon, do you really think the Hawaiians have a point of view on this, beyond a few noisy activists?"

He paused, searching her face for a sign that she might actually understand. He was convinced of her intellect, but still unsure of her heart, so he ignored her question. Instead, he looked out at his sloop, *Wayfinder*, its little hull gently rising and falling on the swell. "Well, all that is water under the bridge . . . or should I say a matter of rising and falling tides, effects of forces we cannot see, forces well beyond *our* Western horizons . . . forces we cannot control."

He turned again to face his puzzled student, and smiled with a mixture of warmth and resignation. "Anyway, you came here not to learn the dark side of our profession but to gain access to its wonders. Let's have a look at your latest work, shall we?"

He stepped inside and without a word sat down at the table and turned on the light. Andromeda joined him. She pulled her thesis outline from her backpack and placed it in front of the astronomer, but she was still thinking about the earlier conversation.

"Your defiance was admirable," she said, "but I wonder, Dr. Clarke, if we can afford the loss of such a phenomenal research opportunity. Just imagine what the Big Eye will see from the top of that tall mountain."

With those words, they each recognized the first reef of division between them. Jedediah then knew just how isolated he had become.

CHAPTER 23
Unexpected Visitors

A week after his conversation with Aunty Moana, Erik, fast asleep in the Airstream, dreamt of his own little "*hale*" on the river. In evening twilight, he sat on the deck of his vintage houseboat, gazing down on the currents swirling along the bank. A towboat groaned as it pushed its heavy barges up the channel, and a night heron flapped stealthily along the shore, glancing at the young man as it passed. A lone man in a distant canoe also moved up the valley, his paddle strokes laboring against the turbulent current. Erik recognized the lanky silhouette of old man Labathe, the half-French, half-Ojibwe farmer who lived downstream. The ninety-year-old descendent of Lake Superior voyageurs had lived on the Mississippi his whole life, eking out a subsistence on five acres of rich bottomland below the bend. Erik knew the old voyageur was coming for another of his evening deck chats over cigarettes and beer.

"Some of my ancestors dwell in this valley," he told Erik in the dream. "I asked 'em to watch over you too, *mon ami*." A Marlboro between his ruddy lips, Labathe inhaled deeply, his fleshy cheeks warping inward as the cigarette's ash curled in the muggy air. "You ain't of the blood o' course," he said in the dream as he once did on Erik's deck, "but you've the kindred heart of the oldest rivermen— the natives who heed the Great Spirit's will, pay attention to the rocks and trees and birds, and seek direction in the waters of our great river."

Labathe pressed a bony finger into Erik's chest, right above his heart, "On my land and in other places along the channel lie some of our bones. From your little 'hale,' Erik, can you keep an eye on those burials after I'm gone? Protect 'em against anything that threatens our valley, eh?"

Erik awoke sweaty in a muddle of emotions—sadness from missing the old man who'd died a year after Erik left home; anxiety for abandoning his responsibility to protect the river; and fear that he was beginning to care too much for another beautiful place on the verge of peril.

But he was also strangely excited. His visit to the Hawaiian village next door so reminded him of the south islands that he pulled his mildewed copy of Frederick O'Brien's 1919 memoir *White Shadows of the South Seas* off the shelf and went outside to reread it. Every now and then he'd pause to let his own South Seas memories float by—net fishing with the old men on Niue, those bright-eyed children on Aitutaki, the wise old man from Mangareva, and that sassy girl with the shining moon face who wept when Erik finally left Savai'i.

Two hours had passed in happy remembrance of the Polynesians' natural way of life when he glanced up through the foliage to notice Aunty Moana on the sitting stones above the distant cove, talking with a haole man. Something in the man's bold gestures seemed familiar, and Erik went inside the trailer to fetch his sailing binoculars. Peering through the galley window, he recognized the khaki pants, blousy shirt, and unkempt hair of the Caltech astronomer he'd seen talking with Moses eight months earlier at the base camp. Puffing on the same big pipe, the astronomer gestured excitedly over a thin sheaf of papers on the elder's lap. Some minutes later, he put the documents back in a large manila envelope and handed them to Aunty Moana. They rose and embraced, exchanging their breaths as Aunty Moana had done with Freddie, and the astronomer left. Aunty Moana sat back down on the rock, reading the documents, pausing now and again to stare at the sea. Eventually she, too, left the beach and disappeared inside her hale.

Over breakfast Erik recalled the uncommon name Moses had used to address his friend—Jedediah—and pondered how it was that the mainland astronomer would know both elders. He went back outside to his book and eventually got lost in more South Seas memories. Two hours later, his attention was again drawn to the village when Aunty Moana stepped back onto the beach, this time to take a swim. She eventually emerged from the water, squeezed the sea out of her magnificent white hair, and sat down on the rock. A few minutes later, a young Hawaiian woman stepped out from the shade of the coconuts, exchanged breath with the elder, and sat down beside her.

Erik couldn't help but peek through his binoculars, and what he saw added to his puzzlement. The Hawaiian who'd come to see Aunty Moana was the same young woman who'd appeared out of the mist at Lake Waiau and whom he'd seen chanting atop Puʻu Poliʻahu, the woman Moses said was a painter named Hoku Holokai. The women's exchange was animated, even agitated, and at one point the young woman got up and paced the shore between the elder and the beach. Aunty Moana reached into her lauhala bag to retrieve the envelope she'd received from the astronomer and handed it to Hoku. Then, as if struck by the same thought, they halted their conversation and looked over toward Erik.

Heart pounding, he dropped the binoculars, snatched up his book, and feigned reading. When he finally glanced back toward the beach, both had left. *What could that astronomer possibly have in common with those two Hawaiians . . . and with Moses?* he thought. *And why am I now being pulled into that same current as well?*

Four days later, during his next shift, the camp was astir with talk about an article that morning in Sunday's *Honolulu Star-Advertiser.* Quoting leaked Caltech documents from "anonymous sources," the reporter revealed that astronomers had all but decided to build the Haisley Big Eye on Mauna Kea's summit ridge, rather than in Chile, by "recycling" the sites of the old 88-inch telescope and its former generator building now used as a summit lunchroom. Even more shocking was the story's allusion to "rumors circulating among astronomers" that Alfred Haisley had donated his money in exchange for a promise to rest for eternity under the telescope. Dr. Adam Jacob acknowledged that "some astronomers want to keep this latest mirror marvel in America," but he downplayed the commitment to Mauna Kea as "premature speculation" created by "advocates for the Hawai'i site," not mentioning that he was one of them. As for Haisley's "burial request," Jacob confirmed the fact and said, "We'll deal with that detail after we solve the technological and environmental issues engendered by such a huge telescope and dome. Yes," he added, following General Todt's advice, "I dare say some astronomers will urge Haisley to reconsider that rather, well, curious request."

The story also quoted Erik's buddy Sam Chun, Island Defenders attorney: "Astronomers' latest false promise—to remove that old telescope from the summit—has been broken by California astronomers so desperate for Hawai'i's unpolluted skies that they've already forgotten the community's outcry over TMT." A Hawaiian elder expressed sadness at the "continuing intrusion of industrial technology on a summit reserved for gods," and was so offended by the burial idea that he refused to comment on it. Koa Makali'i, a hot-headed community college professor transplanted from Honolulu, fumed. "Who the hell does Haisley think he is, demanding to be buried on our sacred peak!" quoted the reporter. "How many times do haoles have to break our hearts and abuse our lands before we draw the line against them? We were warriors once and can be again!"

The camp crew responses were a little different. Jeffrey Drake told anyone who would listen that "Haisley's ego is bigger even than the mountain" and asserted that he, for one, "would never again drink that bastard's piss-water beer!" For his part, Braddah K refused to engage the irascible cook, all morning having been uncharacteristically sour, even blue, thought Erik, projecting his own mood. "Is there no respite for these islanders?" Erik muttered to Freddie when he handed him the newspaper. Freddie just shook his head. Moses was nowhere to be found, but Erik could imagine his reaction.

This latest news so agitated Ranger Jill Kualono that she hid out in her guard shack reading another Tita Carvalho detective novel. Having had no further retaliatory episodes since the scuttled Keck vehicle in April, and stymied by a worry that the quiet cook and distant cousin Braddah K might actually be a suspect, she'd let her secret investigation go dormant. *Now what else might happen?* she thought as her eyes glazed over the pages.

The next day at breakfast, Jill Kualono received radio traffic that compelled the ranger's abrupt departure to the summit. "Must be astounding news," quipped Drake. "In all the years I've been imprisoned here, Ranger Bitch has never abandoned a Portuguese sausage omelet for *any* reason!" A rumor of possible vandalism to a dome leaked back to the camp, carried by a solemn telescope operator returning to sleep. Two county police officers stopped at the base camp for a few minutes to acclimate and Drake quizzed one of them in the men's room, who refused to say anything.

Jill returned to camp after lunch had finished. Erik was still in the kitchen, wiping counters and chatting with Freddie. Knowing Jill had missed breakfast, Erik made her a hoagie on a half loaf of Portuguese sweetbread, and the three of them sat down at a table.

"Well?" Freddie asked.

"I'm only gonna tell you two . . . and for three reasons. One, I think I can trust you to keep your pie holes shut. Two, because those weak-kneed Hilo cops buckled under some kind of pressure and agreed to keep the incident under wraps. And three, I want somebody besides me to know what's up in case things get sticky." A fourth reason, that she didn't share, was that the pair were the only souls in the common building when she'd returned and her gut told her to let them in on the secret.

"Maybe you two should talk," Erik said, starting to rise from his chair.

"Sit down!" Jill commanded.

Erik did, his cheeks turning red as two tomatoes.

"A sniper tried to off the Keck I mirror last night," she said.

"Jesus," Freddie replied.

"Used a rifle, I think, around midnight, if our one eyewitness is correct."

"Those mirrors are worth, like, millions," Freddie added.

"Basically irreplaceable," said Jill.

"Who saw it?" Erik asked, his eyes dark as cobalt.

"Heard is more like it. The T.O. up on the 88-inch was out on the catwalk having a smoke when he heard a loud 'clap' coming from the west side of the summit. The Mauna Kea weather page shows 40-knot north winds at midnight, so who knows how sounds were bouncing off the cones."

Erik leaned forward. "He didn't see anything?"

"Says not. Fortunately, the bullet missed the mirror—so say the cops—but just barely. I didn't see it myself. They wouldn't bring me along—bastards!"

"I don't get that," Freddie said, stepping over to the coffee urn.

"That's the other interesting part. Since there was no serious damage, the cops are keeping the incident hush-hush."

Erik cocked his head. "I don't get that at all."

"'Too soon to tell if it was an errant bullet from some mouflon hunter,' the sergeant told me, 'Don't want to panic anyone.'"

Freddie poured cups for all of them. "A hunter? At midnight?"

"What about the T.O. who heard it?" Erik asked.

"Just windblown sounds in the night, as far as the T.O. knows. No one's told him about the bullet hole in the mirror frame, and no one's gonna tell him—including you two—until I can gather more information. Someone's put a muzzle on the men in blue, and that means holding information could be dangerous at the moment."

"Gee, thanks," Freddie said, rubbing the back of his neck.

"Look, I intend to get to the bottom of this—big boys and cops be damned!—but I need help, and I'm recruiting you two. This isn't the first time someone sent a message to the astronomers. You guys remember what happened to Kyle O'okala? Well, that was no accident, and a message was left there too."

"What do you mean?" Freddie said.

"'Abandon the mountain' scratched inside the icy truck window— maybe by Kyle, maybe not." Jill's eyes watered. "I intend to get to the bottom of that too."

"What about Moses?" Erik asked. "Certainly he won't go along with any cover-up."

"Moses isn't around to know anything about it. He called in sick this morning. By the time they talk with him they'll have their whitewashed story all cleaned up."

Erik shoved his fingers into his blond bangs. "I don't understand any of this. Why wouldn't they let *everyone* know what's happened? I mean . . . this is . . . terrible."

Jill and Freddie eyed Erik with the same "poor thing" look on their faces.

"This ain't the Midwest, Erik," Freddie said. "With the biggest telescope in the world slated for Mauna Kea, the powers that be—especially the Hawai'i construction companies that'll build it—aren't gonna want anyone else to get big ideas about damaging the telescopes. You saw what that activist Koa Makali'i said in the paper yesterday."

"Exactly!" said Jill. "That's why they called O'okala's death an accident."

Freddie got up from the table and paced in front of the windows. "None of dis makes sense—da potshot or da paranoia," he said, his rising worry evident in the pidgin infiltrating his words. "Not once in all dose years of TMT protests was dere any violence—except from da cops who got kinda rough during da arrests."

"And a couple of mentally ill haoles," Jill corrected. "That lolo guy who chased those two VLBA technicians in his pickup and the hippie that rammed a ranger vehicle with her car—both lone wolves condemned by the protesters."

"Dat's right. Even da most militant Hawaiians did their damnedest to follow da Kapu Aloha protocol. Christ! Da protesters w'en even aloha-ed da cops! Gave 'em hugs and leis!"

Jill's eyes narrowed and her jaw clenched. "And what's da astronomers' reply to all dat, Freddie? Eh? Hana hou wit' one even biggah telescope!"

"Relentless!" Freddie said, "Endlessly relentless! Americans w'en pride demselves on dat, Jill. You know dat? Dey no realize da rest o' us 'tink dat's one o' dere least civilized traits."

"Poor 'tings," Jill said.

The meatballs Erik had eaten for lunch moved inside his stomach.

CHAPTER 24
Recognizing Clues

The next morning, Moses arrived at the camp early and headed straight for Erik in the kitchen. He looked haggard, bags under his eyes as if he hadn't slept in days.

"Are you OK?" Erik asked. "Should you have stayed home to rest another day?"

Moses shook his head. "Have you seen Freddie yet?"

"He's working on the new security fence over by the snowplow."

Moses set his burly hand on Erik's shoulder. "Let's go see him. Braddah K can get things underway for breakfast."

They crossed the camp parking lot and found Freddie already shirtless on the cinder slope behind the road crew's workshop. Freddie put his tools aside.

"Moses! You feeling better?"

"No."

Freddie glanced at Erik, and Erik shrugged.

"What's up?" the muscled handyman said.

Moses motioned the two young men to sit with him on the slope. "Listen boys," he said, dropping his voice in case any of the road crew was still in the shop, "there's something I wanna share with you . . . about this terrible thing that happened on the mountain."

Erik's cheeks flushed at the mention of it, and Freddie cracked his knuckles.

"The three of us are the only ones Jill told about the shooting. I'm glad she told me because it helps explain the dream I had that night . . . just after midnight.

"It was vivid . . . like real life. I was sitting in my office, tallying the monthly room bill for the Caltech observers, when my grandfather strode into the common building, red cinder dust on his boots like he'd just hiked down from the summit. He stood in my doorway, peering at me until I finally looked up from my roster.

"'Tutu!' I said. 'What are you doing here?' He just kept staring, like he was gonna give me scoldings or something. 'Tutu, what's wrong?' I said.

"'*A'ohe wa'a ho'ohoa o ka la 'ino,*' he said. That's one of the ancient proverbs he taught me as a kid . . . 'No canoe is defiant on a stormy day.' '*A'ohe wa'a ho'ohoa o ka la 'ino,*' Tutu said again. As I reached out to him, I woke up.

I had this unshakable feeling that something really bad was about to happen. I looked over at Carol, but she was sleeping peacefully. Then I realized Grandpa's warning was not about her or our family. It was about the mountain.

"No canoe is defiant on a stormy day," Moses repeated, gazing into the faces of each young man. "Put another way, 'It doesn't pay to venture into the face of danger.' I took this to mean Tutu was warning me not to go to work that day—so I called in sick. Then yesterday Jill phoned. I was beside myself. Violence has no place on Mauna Kea. The mountain is a place of love and healing, not for conflict."

Moses turned and pointed a brawny finger toward the treeless slope just above the base camp. "From here up is a wao akua, a domain of our gods. Even in ancient times, warriors were not allowed up there!"

"Ah," Freddie nodded, "so that explains the feeling."

"And why Jill leaves her gun down here if she can possibly help it," Moses added.

"I was agitated the rest of the day," Moses continued, "and last night I couldn't get to sleep. When I finally did, Tutu came again. This time I was in the kitchen talking with you two and Jill. Grandpa appeared just as before—with dusty boots and that severe gaze—but now he seemed sad too. He said to all four of us, '*I ho'olulu, ho'ohulei 'ia e ka makani'*—'There was a lull . . . and then the wind began to blow about.' That's a warning that 'the peace we thought was coming has again been disturbed.' When I woke up I realized our quiet life on the mountain is about to change, that we must now prepare for trouble." He shook his head. "And I thought our troubles were over after TMT."

He then said, "I also knew that you two and Jill will play a role in whatever's ahead, and that we must put our faith in the greatest power humans possess—love."

Erik and Freddie looked at each other, not knowing what to say.

"I know that what I've told you may sound weird or heavy, especially to you, Erik, but I'm compelled to share it because all of you were in the dream."

Erik flashed on his own portentous dreams—the river storm, his inability to save himself from drowning, the assignment from the old voyageur Labathe, and his father's urgings to be strong. A wave of anxiety washed over him.

Moses put a hand on each of their shoulders. "I'm counting on you guys to keep all this to yourselves."

"Sure," they replied in unison, but not without trepidation.

That evening, after the crew had finished cleaning the kitchen, Erik was in his dorm room packing his duffle to leave for his days off. He was so agitated that he kept forgetting items he'd hung in the closet or tucked into his dresser, making his departure much later than usual. A knock on the door startled him. With everyone working different schedules, visits to the sleeping rooms were rare. Erik was all the more surprised to discover it was Jill Kualono on the other side of the door.

"Good," she said in her serious ranger tone. "You're still here. I need your help. Did you bring your camera up this shift?"

His heart dropped and anxiety rushed into his chest. Why had it had taken him so damn long to pack up and leave? "Yes," he replied.

She strode past him and shut the door.

Forty-five minutes later, they stood alone outside the double-domed Keck observatory, still closed because of the shooting. She had parked well away from the building and in starlight guided them on a circuitous route away from the ever-vigilant eyes of the weather-monitoring webcams. The August winds whistled through the metal braces of the entrance roof.

"The bastards finally gave me keys." She grinned mischievously, slipping one of them into the lock, "to improve security." The observatory building was dark, save for the amber glow of emergency lights here and there. Jill pulled her Blackhawk LED light from her duty belt and switched it on. Walking through the locked rooms and corridors of the giant industrial edifice unnerved Erik, a feeling amplified when they finally reached the inside of the dome, its formidable shutter closed to the stars outside. Jill found the light switch and turned on the fluorescents.

By order of the police, the giant telescope still pointed as it had been at the time of the Sunday night shooting, the steel frame holding its mirror elevated high to point low into a young Southern Hemisphere galaxy 12 billion light-years away.

Jill and Erik crossed the dome's refrigerated floor and climbed the steel staircase leading up the side of the telescope. From a platform at the Nasmyth focus, they gazed down on the world's most famous mirror—thirty-six hexagonal segments of aluminized glass operated simultaneously with a sophisticated system of software-driven pistons. Erik's knees quaked at the dizzying view below.

"Look! There!" Jill said, using her flashlight to better illuminate the area. "See that dent in the frame? Just above the top of the mirror?"

Erik spotted the gouge, less than an inch from the glass. Horrified, he nodded.

"The bastard's aim wasn't half bad considering the dome was pitch dark that night and his sniper's perch was a quarter-mile away . . . if I've got it figured right. You think you can get a clear picture of the damage with your camera?"

Erik set the flash of his Canon Rebel T6 on its highest setting and snapped a dozen pictures at various focal lengths and exposures. "Got it," he said after examining every shot on the LCD monitor.

"Lemme see," Jill said, checking them for herself.

Satisfied, they retraced their steps from the telescope, careful to leave no trace of their visit and to lock every door they'd opened. Flashlight off, they returned to Jill's truck following the same indirect route they'd used to reach the observatory.

"Now comes the hard part," she said, closing the truck door, "the hike to the sniper's perch. How good are your lungs, Erik, after all those cigs—and god knows what else you and Freddie smoke?"

Aware that two of the observatories' webcams—at Subaru and JCMT—caught portions of Puʻu Poliʻahu, they climbed the zigzag trail up the thousand-foot cone in the dark.

It was nearly midnight when, breathless, they finally reached the top of the cone named for the mountain's goddess of ice and snow. The exposed peak howled with bone-chilling winds, and Erik was glad Jill had remembered to throw two camp parkas into her truck for the trek. A rising moon turned the eight domes on the summit ridge into stark silhouettes a quarter mile away. It also began to illuminate this cone, but they'd still have to use Jill's light to locate what she believed would be there.

"My theory is that the bullet came from here. Whether it was a premeditated plan or just some yahoo pissed off at the moment, this seems the most likely place to stand undetected and hit that close to the mirror with the telescope positioned as we saw it tonight.

"We'll have to work fast and hope that when we use my light and your flash the webcams are between their staggered exposures—and that no one inside the domes steps out on a catwalk." Jill directed the search for the shooter's position on the cone, systematically examining the rounded peak from one edge to the other. Whenever she used the light, she cupped her hand over its summit-facing side. The pair treaded lightly to avoid disturbing any trace of the crime in the loose cinder. Jill had hoped at best to find footprints, but to her surprise Erik discovered a single spent shell from a .270 caliber bullet.

"This is the ammo hunters use to kill mouflon sheep and goats," she said, "but it coulda sat here for years, something a forensic lab can tell us." She crouched to examine the cinder with her light. "These footprints could be old too."

"Why didn't he pocket the shell after he fired?"

"That's the kind of oversight that's easy to do with an oxygen-starved brain," Jill said, sliding the flashlight back into her duty belt. "I once left my thousand-dollar binoculars on a summit guardrail and didn't even realize they were missing until the next day."

Erik took flash pictures of the footprints and the shell's location, along with a moonlit time exposure of Jill pointing toward the Keck observatory. Jill pocketed the shell, marking its location with a triangular stone. Their work done, they stood for a few minutes on the windy cone. Jill pulled the unlit light out of her belt and trained it at the shutter of the Keck I dome.

"Yeah, he coulda done it from here, 'specially if he was a good shot." She swung the flashlight toward the mountaintop and pointed at the ridge below the United Kingdom Infrared Telescope. "Woulda been easier from the south side of Keck—a much closer perch—but the Lockheed guys inside UKIRT's dome woulda heard the report, making an undetected escape a lot more difficult."

Jill grasped Erik's arm and stared into his face. "After we download the pictures at the camp, I want you to go home and forget what happened here tonight . . . I'm counting on you."

Erik, wishing he didn't know any of it, nodded.

Jill's face softened. "And mahalo, Erik, for coming up here to take these pictures."

Jill fell silent, thinking for a long time. In the moonlight, Erik noticed her eyes moisten. "This is a sacred cone," she said, her voice suddenly different, as sad as the moaning wind blowing over the pair. "No one should carry that kind of anger up here."

The pair slowly made their way to the path.

"What's that!" Jill whispered, thrusting up her arm to halt Erik's progress.

He froze.

"Did you hear it?" she said, searching the sky. "The call of a bird."

There, high above them, a white speck in the moonlight circled the cone.

"An 'io . . . ," she muttered, ". . . our holy hawk."

CHAPTER 25

Skeletons

Erik didn't get home from his summit adventure until almost 3:00 a.m. Exhausted, he dropped into bed and fell sound asleep, but his rest was short-lived. At four o'clock he woke up in a cold sweat, his heart pounding and his mind reeling from a nightmare in which he'd chased a rifle-toting man through a maze of mirrors. Erik had no idea who he was chasing or why, only that the man meant harm and that Erik had to apprehend him.

Erik's legs wouldn't run any faster than slow motion, as if some gravitational force held him back, and he constantly lost ground on the assailant. Dread rose within him as he struggled through the intricate passages and abrupt dead ends of the mirrored maze. The reflections added a macabre aspect to the chase, creating illusory hallways, startling glimpses of the distant gunman, and flashes of Erik's own anxious face. Just when he though he'd drop from exhaustion, Erik turned a corner and collided with the assailant. The gunman spun around and pressed the rifle barrel against Erik's heart. Erik looked up from the gun to peer into the man's face . . . and it was himself.

Erik awoke at the sound of the blast—a ripe avocado fallen on the Airstream's steel roof—and stared into the darkness. "What the fuck was all that about?" he muttered, kicking off the sheet knotted around his feet. Then a picture of *Voyageur*, Murdock Kemp's 1955 antique cabin cruiser, flashed into his mind. There it was, moored just where Erik had last seen it, at the far end of the dock built for boaters dining at the Riverboat Captain's Inn, a mile above Cottonwood. The priceless 37-foot Chris Craft Corvette, with its teak decks and classy midhull bridge, was Kemp's pride and joy. To Erik, nothing could be more incongruous—and disgusting—than for that "cheesy corporate newspaper marauder" to have in his possession one of the most beautifully crafted boats ever to ply the river, a gem originally custom built for Congressman Anderson's father.

Erik sat up in bed. A whirling torrent of rage—and fear—coursed through him. He glanced nervously out the patched window screen above his bed and then remembered the angry gouge next to the Keck mirror.

But just one of those emotions—rage—had he felt that humid Minnesota night long ago when he'd spotted Kemp's boat moored under the only burned-out lamp above the inn's dock. *No one will notice it's gone until Kemp returns from dinner*, he'd thought, the downstream end of the long wooden pier hidden by trees and far from the restaurant's amber glow. Erik had tucked his canoe into the woods a hundred yards below the inn, then, as silent as a mole, crept along the bank until he'd reached Kemp's boat. He'd listened at a brass porthole for sounds of anyone aboard. Hearing nothing but the squawk of a night heron swooping over the river, he'd untied its two mooring lines. With strength fueled by vengeance, Erik shoved the irreplaceable cabin cruiser into the powerful currents of the main channel.

Kemp's first thought on seeing the boat missing was of thieves, a natural reaction given his own competitive outlook on life. But two days later, when the boat was found sunk at the base of Bergman's Bluff, the billionaire blamed his daffy young girlfriend—reputed to be a casual cocaine user—of failing to double-cleat the mooring lines.

Voyageur's wooden hull had breached when it drifted into the limestone wall, sinking the boat, which the gooey muck beneath the channel quickly sucked into its mire. The wreck might never have been discovered, but a barge overloaded with gravel on a night haul upstream rammed into the sunken cabin cruiser, tearing off its fancy bridge and depositing it on rocks a quarter mile away. A kid in a canoe spotted it two days later. The Cottonwood police, having overheard the owner chastise his girlfriend (who admitted she wasn't certain she'd secured *Voyageur* properly), chalked it up to human error, and for a month after the *Weekly* published an article about the incident the young woman was the brunt of jokes at Cottonwood's marina. Erik, afraid and ashamed, never told the real story to a soul.

All this and the previous night's clandestine investigation with Jill sifted through Erik's mind as he tried to fall back to sleep. At 4:30 he gave up, made a cup of coffee, and walked out to the ledge in front of Sunny Boy's place to smoke a cigarette. *Jack would've been shocked at what I did to Kemp's boat*, Erik thought, watching the dark waves roll into the shore, *and he wouldn't have approved, even if there was no other way to bring justice to the situation.*

"Kemp deserved it," Erik muttered, as if to Jack's ghost, "not that it made a damn bit of difference . . ."

And ruined a perfectly good boat, a voice rising from the breaking waves seemed to say.

"Yeah, well, what about that perfectly good novel of yours? Who sunk that?"

Not my fault.

"Hell it wasn't," and the whole ugly story of the novel's final rejection came back to him.

"He's our own Mark Twain!" Erik's father had pronounced to the boys after reading that last revision of *Valley of Dreams*. "Fine writing and deft construction," the veteran editor had added, surprised a man so young could craft at that level. "You've beautifully caught the spirit of our river and the people whose lives run with its history and currents," he wrote on the title page. None of this had surprised Erik; chapter by chapter, Jack had read the whole story to him at the sandbar and on their houseboat deck as the river rolled by.

"We're a long way from New York, Jack," Erik's father had cautioned. "Why not send this to one of our Minnesota publishers?"

But Jack would hear none of that; he'd always said he was writing the novel for a broader audience and greater impact, "to inspire all the lost souls who've become disconnected from the larger forces of nature that keep us on track."

Mr. Peterson's praise so renewed Jack's hope that he decided to submit the manuscript to the Twin Cities' most well-connected literary agent, B. J. Presley, a former Random House editor. Twenty-five years earlier she'd "left the East Coast rat race to mine these great Midwest writers long ignored by publishers on both coasts," as Presley had said during her departing—and last—interview in the *New York Times*. In actual fact, she, like dozens of editors, had been laid off after the legendary publisher was absorbed into the Bertelsmann corporate empire. To meet Bertelsmann's exorbitant stockholder-demanded profit margins, Random House downsized its staff and refocused its efforts on more predictable—less risky—fiction, mostly commercial stuff.

Watching the dark waves roll into the shore, Erik remembered how confused and disappointed Jack was when nine weeks later Presley's rejection letter arrived:

> Dear Jack:
>
> I thoroughly enjoyed *Valley of Dreams* (indeed, had a hard time putting it down). It's an earnest novel with a stirring, life-affirming plot and painfully realistic—yet admirable—characters. I loved your unique insights about life's potentials in this crazy world, inspired by growing up on America's greatest river. Frankly, I was surprised that in this day and age a young male could be so cognizant and at the same time so, well, optimistic (wow, that ending!). Your powerful rendering of the Mississippi surprised me less, having long watched that great river from my downtown office window.
>
> Twenty years ago I would have taken this project in an instant, but with today's fashions and fierce competition, New York editors would likely find your novel too rural and too emotionally challenging for today's urbane young readers (i.e., "cynically savvy city people," a Bantam editor once told me).

Not that your novel wouldn't do them some good, but that's not how fiction is sold these days, at least not to major New York publishers.

I suggest you investigate small, independent houses who are less captive to today's fashions, and who might not require an agent . . .

Bolstered by a glass of whiskey, Jack had sped into St. Paul, blasting the interior of his rusty Dodge Dakota pickup with repeated plays of K'naan's millennial anthem "Wavin' Flag" and Daft Punk's techie-rouser "Harder, Better, Faster, Stronger." He parked high up the river bluff on Kellogg Boulevard, dashed over Wabasha Street, and strode into the shiny new office complex built into the limestone cliff. Presley's suite was two floors down, with spectacular views of the river valley.

"Look! A golden eagle!" Jack had said to the bespectacled receptionist, barging past her as she turned toward the window.

"Where?" she replied. "I don't see it."

Jack was inside the agent's office by the time the receptionist glanced back. Presley looked up from the galley proofs on her desk. "You're the river author," she said when Jack told her his name. Pausing only a moment, she invited him to sit in the chair beside her desk, waving away the chagrined receptionist who'd just burst through the door.

"I'm sorry about the rejection," she said when they were alone, relieved to be able to say so face to face.

"Then why?"

"My younger agents discouraged me," she said with a sigh. "I loathe admitting it, but I know they're right, given today's market . . . and stockholder profit expectations. Everyone in the industry is afraid."

Jack watched as the renowned agent seemed to grow smaller in her chair as she explained her decision.

"I called editors at two big houses and they both said, 'Why risk a new novel about the Mississippi when Twain's books still dominate the market?'"

"*Life on the Mississippi* was published more than a century ago!"
Jack said, incredulous.

"Even so, it makes more economic sense for them to market those
old novels than take a chance on a new author," she said, looking
away from his face, a trace of moisture in her eyes. "And they won't
really *get* the novel's rural, middle-of-the–country perspective." She
looked back at him. "No valiant effort on my part can change that . . .
and for that I'm doubly sorry."

Driving home along the river on Highway 61, Jack remembered
that this literary midwife of fine Midwestern writers was lately best
known for representing Lee Raymond, aka Gerald Berkowitz. The
former Pulitzer Prize–winning *Chicago Tribune* reporter had decided
midcareer to apply his writing skills to macabre and violent thrillers
that landed him on *New York Times* bestseller lists, making Presley
and him rich after Hollywood bought the movie rights.

Erik had learned all this from a long, emotional note Jack had
left on the galley table with Presley's rejection letter, discovered when
Erik returned home after work. "Gone, dear friend, to seek solace in
the River," was Jack's last line.

At first Erik assumed Jack had gone swimming below the houseboat, despite the thunderstorm that was quickly moving into the valley,
but going down there he noticed Jack's canoe gone. Dread took hold
of Erik, and despite the dimming light, rising wind, and increasingly
frequent thunder and lighting, he had launched his Old Town and
headed downriver for the sandbar. There sat Jack's Grumman canoe
but no sign of its owner. An empty quart bottle of Jack Daniels—the
kind Harvey Dubois sold at his corner gas station—and a crumpled
cigarette pack lay on the sand near remnants of a bonfire that had
consumed the rejected manuscript, charred bits of the story scattered
amid the still-warm ash. That's when Erik realized that the skilled
writer's use of the preposition "in" instead of "on" in that last line was
no accident: "Gone, dear friend, to seek solace in the River."

God, I was dumb! Erik thought, never really comprehending his
comrade's dismay, never letting in how depressed Jack actually was.

Erik called 911 on his iPhone and paddled back to the houseboat
to get his 2,000-lumen flashlight and some blankets. Heavy drops

of rain had begun to bleed from the black sky, thudding against the hull of the old wooden canoe.

Lightning flashed all about Erik as the current carried him downstream, his bright light eerily illuminating the trees, rocks, and muddy banks along the shore, as he desperately hollered out his buddy's name. The thunder, at first a series of deafening claps, became one long roar, and the shroud of low-hanging clouds unleashed their burden. It was as if the gods dwelling in the valley were raging. Even so, Erik knew he'd be OK—and his gut also told him he'd probably find Jack.

He did, early the next morning, after the storm had blown far to the east. Jack's body had hung up in the long limb of a cottonwood that had tumbled into the river after a lightning bolt severed it from the tree's massive trunk.

CHAPTER 26

Tides of Fear

Erik was still sobbing as the sun peeked above Keaukaha's eastern horizon, casting a pink glow on Mauna Kea's upper cones. He kicked off his rubber slippers, pulled off his T-shirt, and leaped from the rocks into the waves. He swam along the shoreline, stroking like a madman, determined to wash away those dark Minnesota memories. He had no sense of how far he'd swum—until he collided with something in the water.

"Good heavens!" blurted a voice from someone floating in the calmer waters of the cove fronting the Hawaiians' makeshift village. "Where did you come from!"

"From hell!" he blurted involuntarily.

"Auwe!" the person cried. "It's Erik!"

He opened his eyes and stretched his toes down to the sand.

Aunty Moana, treading water, peered into his startled face. "Dear child, what are you doing tearing through the sea with such violence!"

His face dissolved in tears.

They sat in the shade of her thatched lanai, drinking *mamaki* tea as Erik recounted Jack's disillusionment and drowning.

"Grief is part of life, Erik, a natural reaction to disappointment, loss . . . and injustice," she said. "But it's a dangerous emotion when not tended carefully. Your friend didn't allow himself time to regroup, and so the vile act spurred by his unhealed sadness spread that grief to his loved ones. It even drove you from your home, from the great river that was your mother."

"Something Jack refused to do," Erik blurted, more tears flowing. "Dad urged him to follow the advice of his Iowa professors and move to New York . . . take advantage of the connections they'd made for him . . . but he wouldn't do it. He moved back to the river instead."

"Of course he did," the elder said, a flash of puzzlement crossing her face. "How could he write without his source of inspiration? How could he live? Really, how could *you* live without your 'aina . . . especially with Jack gone? Look at the turmoil *that* decision made!"

Erik's face hardened. "There were other things, too, Aunty. Our way of life, my family's values . . . washed away! Jack's death was the last straw."

The elder gazed at him intently. "I've had ample time to observe grief among my own people. None of us have been immune to the sweeping changes that continue to alter our islands, and we now know the full extent of the colonial history that brought us here. Yes, there's much to be sad about . . . and angry. Yet the world still expects us to be 'the happy people of aloha.'" She shook her head.

"I know that kind of anger," Erik said. "I've spent years trying to get over it!" He turned away, his blue eyes fixed on the swells crashing against the reef bordering the cove. Aunty Moana could see only the back of his head but the sensitive kaula felt the dark energy he emitted.

"Erik," she said softly, "have you heard of the Vietnamese monk Thich Nhat Hanh?"

He shrugged, still watching the sea. "No."

"He was a Buddhist poet, a writer like your friend Jack. I have several of his books," she said, "gifts from one of my teachers, a priest at the Hongwanji in Hilo."

Erik slowly turned back to look at her.

"Thich Nhat Hanh worked to save the soul of his homeland, an ancient country with native, Taoist, Confucianist, and Buddhist roots. It was colonized by the French, then occupied by Japan, and again taken over by France. Eventually civil war ripped the country apart. The Americans, blinded by their own fear of communism and with little understanding of Asian cultures, assumed that Ho Chi Minh and his communists were pawns of Red China and the Soviet Union and stepped in to support the French and their puppet government in South Vietnam. It became a big mess, afire with anger, blame, and violence as the civil war escalated into a geopolitical conflict where other nations were expected to take sides. Millions died, and millions more were maimed and displaced. Moved by this suffering, dozens of Buddhist monks protested the war with the ancient practice of self-immolation . . . burning themselves alive as holy sacrifices to bring peace to those still living."

Erik cringed at the thought.

"Perhaps those suicides were Thich Nhat Hanh's last straw, I don't know, but he and others in his Buddhist community stepped out of their usual quiet practice to advocate for peace and mutual respect among the North and South Vietnamese. The monk traveled to the United States and met with its leaders—Martin Luther King was one of them—to explain how US bombs and soldiers only made resolution of the conflict more difficult. But the warring factions were in no mood for compassion and they condemned the monks, claiming they, too, were communists. Fear of reconciliation was great, and after Thich Nhat Hanh led the Buddhist delegation to the Paris peace talks, the South Vietnamese government refused to let him back into his country . . . he became an exile in France. "

"So he lost his home too," Erik said.

"Yes. Bearers of goodwill and aloha are the *real* threat to chest pounders who cloak their fear and cowardice with bravado and hoisted guns . . . polarizing everyone."

"Hmmm, " Erik said, tapping a finger against his lips. "I think I do remember that monk . . . but not from the war—I wasn't even born yet—but from 9/11. Wasn't he one of the religious leaders who urged restraint after the attack? Along with the Dalai Lama?"

"I wouldn't be surprised."

"Yes . . . my father wrote an editorial about that for his newspaper. The religious leaders had urged the US not to respond with vengeance, and Dad agreed with them. They said it would only lead to more violence . . . which is exactly what happened."

"And yet . . . it was that same Vietnamese monk who said that 'to deny your anger is to do violence upon yourself.'"

Erik's face suddenly paled. His dream's terrifying image of himself as his own assailant rose up in his mind so vividly that it obscured everything in front of him—Aunty Moana, the coastline, the squatters village behind them.

"Erik? Erik? Are you all right?" The elder's words were distant, detached as if in the ether, like Jack's voice had been in the waves.

"Yes," Erik heard himself say, gradually aware again of Aunty Moana's kind face. "Yes, I'm OK . . . but that dream . . . that dream!"

"What? What did you dream?"

He shook his head. "I'm not the good person you think I am, Aunty. I've done violence . . . not to people but . . ."

The elder's face hardened, her frown as if carved in stone. "How? When? Not here."

"No . . . a long time ago . . . back on the river. It's one reason I left."

"Oh no. Are you running from the police?"

"No, from the memories . . . all the memories . . ."

"If what you say to me is true, then you've passed your anger on to others, just as Jack passed his grief on to you. Do you not understand how potent human emotions are? That rage can be as powerful as love?" She shut her eyes and shook her head. "Hewa!" Grave sin.

Again, tears of shame overwhelmed Erik's eyes, and he shifted in the wicker chair.

Aunty Moana leaned forward and grasped his hand. "Some people vent their rage on a wall or window, or, unfortunately, at a family member. Many turn it against who or what they imagine to be their enemies—the obnoxious neighbor, those 'welfare moochers,' the 'greedy rich,' someone of a different color or from a 'suspect' nation . . . people not like themselves. Sometimes they create simplistic ideologies to justify aggression—Lenin and Stalin, Kissinger and Nixon, Cheney and Bush, Bannon and Trump . . . Putin. On and on, the bloodletting of the self-righteous could fill the whole Pacific Ocean!"

She shook her head fiercely, as if to cast away her disgust. "And one hewa leads to another. The Japanese attack Pearl Harbor, so the US rounds up innocent Japanese Americans and imprisons them in camps, then eventually drops atomic bombs on the people of Hiroshima and Nagasaki. And that leads to the arms race. One escalating reaction after another . . . all fueled by fear."

For the first time all morning, the shadow in Erik's face lifted. "You should have met my dad, Aunty. He'd have appreciated the way you look at things. You'd have given him hope."

But Aunty Moana would not let Erik sail her off course. "Some people internalize their rage," she continued, "letting it stew till they have ulcers, or worse, cancer. Others accept a perpetual state of depression, unable to construct a future. That's what happened to many of us. And, most tragically, some even take their own lives. They see no way out of pain and can no longer bear the despair that has seized their hearts."

"And some," Erik said, "run away."

"Hmmmm," she said, looking deeply into his dark blue eyes. "As I was telling you, the wise monk said that 'to deny your anger is do violence upon yourself.'"

"I don't get that."

"Erik, rage is a mask, a mask that covers all kinds of emotions—especially in men—sadness, disappointment, injustice, loss . . . *failure*. By lashing out we pretend that we can protect ourselves from these things or, worse, achieve revenge by inflicting pain on others. Look at the rageful despair that led to the violence at your US Capitol."

"I know that rage! I fear it! That's why I left! I could no longer trust myself."

Aunty Moana smiled softly, yet the fervor in her words intensified. "Yes, the delusion that by changing places you can put distance between you and your sadness. But the mind is too strong for that, Erik. You may think you've purged those emotions from your mind, but they will never be exorcised from your heart unless you do the long, hard work of healing those wounds, of understanding them, of knowing better what to do the next time. The antidote to any of these inflictions is not escape, Erik. It's love and the open eyes that come with it—love of life, love of self, love of others . . . indeed, love of love."

Erik shook his head as a cascade of images washed into his mind: the Cottonwood Walmart and his clients' boarded-up shops, a newspaper photo of Senator Wellstone's incinerated plane and Congressman Anderson's leather-worn chair, Murdock Kemp's mahogany cabin cruiser and his father's oak coffin, charred fragments of Jack's manuscript in the ash and his lifeless body in the bottom of the canoe on that long paddle home. "I don't know, Aunty. What about—"

"Injustice, unfairness, oppression? These are never justified, but I agree with the monk that we must sit down with our rage and ask ourselves what is really behind it, then work on those things in the light, not live our lives in dark reaction. That's what your people failed to do in Vietnam and after 9/11."

Aunty Moana squeezed Erik's hand even tighter. "Our greatest challenge is to commit to love in the face of injustice. Too few are able to do it, but we herald those who do—Martin Luther King, Mahatma Gandhi, the Dalai Lama, Desmond Tutu, and for much of her ordeal, our own queen, Lili'uokalani. These people set the example for the Mauna Kea protectors who blocked the TMT with love . . . in Kapu Aloha."

Erik recalled the video footage of children putting ti-leaf leis on the cops who then arrested their parents. "I saw a picture of Martin Luther King above your desk," Erik said.

Aunty Moana smiled. "A gift from a policeman I once knew . . . part of an apology. It's of Dr. King and his comrades on their famous march from Selma to Montgomery. 1965. Did you notice the leis they wore?"

"Yeah. How was that?"

"They were given to them by Dr. King's Hawaiian friend the Reverend Abraham Akaka, in solidarity and as a clear sign of the marchers' peaceful intent. I like to think that's why their prayers were answered. When we wear a garland of flowers, leaves, or other gifts from the Earth—our mother—we can't help but be grounded. And when we're grounded, it's easier to speak truth to power."

"I watched some videos of the telescope protests and noticed many Hawaiians wearing leis. Did those help them keep their cool?"

She nodded. "That's one reason. You see, Erik, oppression does have peaceful solutions, but they require patience and resolve to bring them to fruition—and an unflappable belief that ignorance and prejudice and greed can be overcome with aloha."

"Huh."

"You don't think so?"

"Well, frankly, what's the difference between aloha and 'happy talk'? I heard plenty of *that* back in Minnesota, the reputed land of 'nice' people."

"What you call 'happy talk' has nothing to do with love," Aunty Moana said firmly. "Happy talk is what we use to hide the ugly truth under veils of complacency and self-deception. It's what lets drunks believe it's OK to beat their wives, how CEOs talk when they exploit their workers, what generals say to themselves as they order the death of thousands. What we tell ourselves when we know it's a lie, that it's not how we really feel, not what we actually see.

"No, Erik, I'm talking about tough love . . . militant love. Why can't the truth be told with love? Why can't we take action against our adversaries without believing they are *evil*? That's why the TMT was ultimately chased away.

"Why do we always wait too long to say what our gut tells us we should say, too long before we act in the pono way that we know we should? That's the delay that allows untruth, injustice, or apathy to take root and grow stronger. It's that *wait* that allows anger to grow inside us more than we realize . . . until we're inflamed beyond our control."

Erik's eyes burned.

"Better to speak up, Erik, to take action, to *be* an honest truth. That's far more fruitful than running away to the South Seas to pretend you're not angry anymore. True healing requires a program, eyes fully open . . . and time. It involves much more than just putting salve on the surface to ease the pain."

"I agree, Aunty. I do. But staying . . ." His moist eyes glistened. "Staying became . . . intolerable for me."

"It must have been for one who loved his river so deeply," she said, her voice lowering. "But then . . . you come from a culture where fear too often overwhelms love, where fear of difficult or unpopular truths puts people in reaction." She patted him on the knee. "So it is good that the winds and tides have brought you here to heal, to learn from people who have long believed more in love than fear, more in truth than illusion. And they do that despite all that's been done to them . . . by the conquering Tahitians, the zealous missionaries, the ethnocentric Americans."

"But it doesn't make sense, Aunty."

"Oh, yes it does." The elder smiled broadly, her missing teeth visible inside her beautiful lips. "Five thousand years sailing in small canoes and living on small islands. That's a lot of ancestral memory. Somewhere along that watery road, we learned that you cannot go it alone, that we need one another, that we cannot afford to foster enemies. Good God, you'd be drowning everyone!"

When Erik finally got up to leave, he gave Aunty Moana a long, quizzical look. "Aunty, how do you know all that about the monk and Vietnam? From reading books?"

"Some of it, yes, but I've also had wonderful teachers. Our islands are full of them, men and women with deep roots in ancient cultures that honed their philosophies of life for five thousand years—Buddhists, Taoists, Pacific Islanders. My Hilo Buddhist friend says Hawai'i is an example of what they call 'the pure land,' a perfect place to flower spiritually. I have immersed myself in all that those teachers have to offer."

"What made you study all this—these philosophies and religions, the terrible conflicts of the past. It seems like ancient history."

"You mean what got me started?"

He nodded.

"One of *my* beloved also never came home. My brother Lalea went missing in action, probably in Cambodia or Laos. The narrative of 'brave boys doing their duty' brought me no comfort at the grave. I had to know whether losing my brother—and all the other carnage of that war—was worth it."

"And?"

"No. It would have been better to speak up, like the monk did."

CHAPTER 27

The Mountain Responds

In early September, a huge tropical depression moved over the island, bringing a week of rain to the mountain. The weather matched Erik's mood, and he started smoking his Marlboros even during his summit lunch deliveries, suicidally inhaling the near pure carbon monoxide they produced at 14,000 feet. Despite the wise perspectives Aunty Moana had offered him—and her admonition that escape was delusional—Erik still wondered if it was time to return to the South Seas. Almost two years had passed since his unwanted voyage to Honolulu, and his bank account was almost fat enough to do that.

Tipsy and melancholic, he'd broached the idea with Freddie over beers. "No place will stay a happy fantasy forever," Freddie replied. "Once you put down roots your eyes open to anything that threatens the place, and you can't help but give a damn."

Erik's funk grew, and despite the cloudy skies, he arranged with Moses to finish the last day of his shift early so he could make an evening "pilgrimage" to Lake Waiau before heading down the mountain. After ten minutes on the trail, he already felt calmer. The thick clouds above the saddle had begun to break up, and a shaft of evening light turned Pu'u Poli'ahu's cone golden yellow. Lovely against the dark clouds, it compelled Erik to dig into his backpack for his camera. He also took pictures of a thick raft of clouds passing over distant Mauna Loa and was reminded that nature—including elements pulsing within him—was more powerful than prestige, money, or human ambition, that he must learn not just to appreciate nature's power, but to channel it for personal strength in adversity. That's what his father had done all those years, drawing on his own bond to the river and to the human community that had sprung up along its banks.

All this circulated through Erik's mind as he crested Waiau's cone, and he was well down its inner slope before he noticed that the lake looked strange. The water level was so low that a third of the lake bottom was exposed. Astonished, he walked all along the right side of the lake, studying the change, then stepped out into the ashen mud that only weeks earlier lay under sparkling water. It made no sense, particularly in light of the past week of rain. He stood ankle-deep in the mud, puzzled.

During his earlier visit, he hadn't even considered taking pictures of the sacred lake, especially after his mystical encounter with the young Hawaiian woman, but now he felt compelled to document the change, knowing instinctively that Aunty Moana would want to see it. No sooner had he begun snapping pictures did he hear far behind him what sounded like a gasp. Turning to look, he spotted that same woman marching down into the cone with such vigor that her long hair trailed behind her.

Uh-oh, he thought. I'm in trouble again.

As before, she wore a garland of green leaves atop her head and a pink tapa wrap over her black leather jacket. As she approached the lake, Erik noticed that she carried a green parcel in her hands, a gift wrapped in ti leaves that Hawaiians call a ho'okupu.

"Aunty Moana needs to know the lake is draining!" he blurted to explain himself, his voice echoing inside the cone.

The Hawaiian stopped in her tracks, shifting her intense gaze from the exposed lake bottom to the man standing in the muck down the shore who'd just uttered her mentor's name. She strode over to Erik, her face full of storm and her eyes, tears.

"This is bad," she said, "really bad. I was here a week ago and the banks were full."

"But how is it possible? It's been raining cats and dogs."

She looked at him with the same intensity that had marked their first meeting—as if she was peering past his eyes and right into him.

"Your pictures are for Aunty Moana?" she said finally.

"Yes."

"How do you know Aunty?"

"She's my neighbor. Freddie introduced us."

"Freddie Hartwig? 'Tank top Freddie'?"

Erik laughed, and embarrassed, she did too. Her face transformed, and for the first time he saw her broad, toothy smile.

"Now I get it," she said, nodding her head. "Wait a minute. OK?"

"Sure."

Hoku, with ho'okupu cradled in her hands, walked over to the water and began to chant. Erik stepped back onto the shore to give her ample space. Goose bumps rose on his skin as she uttered the names of the goddesses he'd read about in the base camp library—Poli'ahu, Lilinoe, Waiau, and Mo'oinanea, the giant protectorate lizard who dwelt in the lake. After her chant, Hoku knelt in the mud and gingerly set her gift where the lake's tiny waves lapped its waxy leaves. She leaned forward, and with cupped hands, drew water from the lake and drank it.

"Sorry I was so abrupt the last time we met," Hoku said when she rejoined Erik. "I can't stand it when people come up here and treat the lake like it's just another destination on the tour—throwing rocks in the water, leaving trash, sunbathing, even swimming."

"I don't view it that way at all. I came today to get centered after all the trouble on the mountain."

"What trouble do you mean?"

Oops, he thought. He had promised Jill and Moses not to tell a soul about the Keck shooting. *Must be the damn thin air.*

"What trouble?" she repeated, her tone as somber as the ashen hue of the mud lining the lake.

Erik's na'au overrode his promise. "A week and a half ago someone took a potshot at the Keck Telescope mirror."

Her eyes narrowed. "I've heard nothing about this."

"The police are keeping it under wraps . . . I guess to avoid an uproar, or encourage a copycat. I promised Moses not to say anything until we find out more. "

Her face darkened. "No wonder I felt unsettled all week. That's why I came up today." She turned and slowly walked back to the lapping waves where she stood staring into the water. "A sniper . . . ," she muttered to herself, ". . . and on top of everything else."

She strode back to him. "You say you're taking pictures for Aunty?"

He nodded. "My shift's done, so I'm going off the mountain tonight. I think she'll want to see these pictures right away."

Hoku thought for a long moment, eying the young man. "Yes . . . that's right. She'll know what this means. What's your name, anyway?"

"Erik. Erik Peterson."

"OK, Erik. We'll meet Aunty together. I'm Hoku Holokai. Let's see what you've taken to make sure they show Aunty what she needs to see."

They walked over to a large rock on which they could sit side by side. There, Erik showed her the three pictures he'd already taken. She suggested several more, from different angles. "Make sure you get the clouds above the lake in at least one of them," she said.

After their final look at all the pictures, Hoku grasped Erik arm and said, "Don't worry about breaking that promise to Moses. Telling me was the pono thing to do. Aunty needs to know . . . and so do I."

They agreed to meet Aunty Moana the next morning at the "village" in Keaukaha. Before they parted, they exchanged phone numbers in case Hoku was unable to reach the elder. The intimacy of that act, and of having strategized the pictures together, made Erik feel differently about the young woman, as if perhaps they had more in common than either might imagine. The beautiful, flowing script with which she had rendered her name and number also struck him, and he looked at the scrap of paper twice more on his way back to the truck.

He used the computer and printer in the base camp library to make 8x10s of the pictures. Before driving down the mountain, Erik left a sealed envelope for Moses containing a copy of one of the photos and a note describing his latest encounter with the lady of the lake. He apologized for having spilled the beans about the shooting, explaining that Hoku—and a feeling in his gut—had compelled him to do it. He hoped the elder would understand.

PART THREE

CHAPTER 28
The Thin Veil

❧ September 1965

Two young men recuperated from the cold alpine night in a government surplus truck trailer hauled 12,000 feet up Mauna Kea as a weatherproof shelter on the gentle slope above Puʻu Waiau. Usually they chatted, read magazines, and watched the clock for their next scheduled check on the mountain's very first telescope, built atop the cone of the snow goddess. But that night strange sounds had them spooked. Both local boys from Honolulu—a Chinese and a haole—they knew the dormant volcano was veiled in mystery, and had even heard that spirits dwelt up there. They were also keenly aware that they were utterly alone.

A year earlier, the Arizona astronomer Dr. Gerard Kuiper, renowned "father of planetary astronomy," had convinced NASA that Mauna Kea's remote peaks might offer their best US alternative to the sullied skies of industrial America. Hawaiʻi's gung-ho governor, after spurring post-statehood development on Oʻahu and Maui, now had his eyes set on the Big Island and had allocated money to bulldoze a rough track from Hale Pohaku to the top of Puʻu Poliʻahu, where Kuiper planted his 12.5-inch telescope to collect data on the mountain's "seeing conditions." That same telescope, and other instruments out on the north plateau, would soon determine the site for the world's seventh-largest telescope and the first major observatory on the mountain, a NASA-funded skygazer with a whopping 88-inch mirror.

Donny Wo and Buck Hamilton, young men with tough constitutions, adventurous spirits, and technical skills learned in the Army, gladly accepted the job collecting the data. Each evening, they drove the jarring jeep trail from their crude quarters in the hunters hut at Hale Pohaku up to a nighttime base camp in the windowless truck trailer they affectionately called their "rest can." The technical challenges of the job and the prospect of being part of an ambitious science quest more than offset the lonely isolation of the dormant volcano's vast upper slopes—at least until that night.

Forty-knot gusts transformed the 40-degree temperature near the lake into wind chills well below freezing, and cold air seeped in under the trailer's door and through its air vents. Wo and Hamilton warmed up on their bunks next to the propane heater. In a half hour, at midnight, they would drive the track up Pu'u Poli'ahu and then out to "13 North" to collect their data. Wo perused the latest *Edmund Scientific* as he replenished his ashtray with one spent cigarette after another. Hamilton consumed Fig Newtons and black coffee.

"What's that scratching sound?" Hamilton said, cocking an ear toward the trailer's door.

Wo looked up from his catalog. "Sounds like a branch scraping against the trailer."

It took a moment in the oxygen-lean air to remember that the highest trees on Mauna Kea stood three thousand feet below them. They flashed each other puzzled looks.

Again the scratching. *Skreeeeeeeeeeeeeerreeeerreeee . . .*

"Maybe we should go look," Wo said indifferently, hiding back in his catalog.

"You mean maybe *I* should go."

"You're the one who seems bothered by it."

Hamilton *was* bothered. He'd worked on the mountain longer than Wo and knew that Hawaiians of old had rarely trekked as high as they were now. Hamilton was the guy who'd planted the route flags in front of the bulldozer that cut the trail. Each time the crew passed one of the mountain's many ancient stone shrines, he wondered how Hawaiians would feel had they known haoles were opening a road to their revered mountaintop. He remembered feeling "creepy" at times, glancing over his shoulder with the distinct feeling of being watched. He also knew that one man had already lost his life opening up the mountain, crushed beneath his backhoe when its brakes mysteriously gave out, sending it pell-mell down the mountain into rocks off the half-cleared road.

"Probably just wind," he suggested.

"Yeah . . . wind," replied Wo.

The scratching ceased a minute or two later, and they donned their parkas for the jeep ride up to Dr. Kuiper's instruments.

When they finally got back, predawn light dimly illuminated the trailer and the tall wooden staircase next to it. Climbing the steps, they noticed several blue-gray streaks on the trailer's wall above the staircase, the steel exposed where its white coat of paint had been scraped away.

The next night it was Wo who first heard the scratching, and although the gusts had lessened from the night before, the two debated whether the cold, dry air somehow made the old paint easier to strip off in the wind. The unnerving sounds lasted much longer that night, and the pair didn't even discuss going out to see what was happening. As they left for their midnight data check, Hamilton's Eveready flashlight revealed more paint gone.

This happened two more nights, always a little before midnight, and the unnerved technicians decided "enough was enough," and that on the next night they'd find out what was visiting them. Hamilton volunteered to open the door when the scratching began while Wo would shine their big 9-volt Ray-O-Vac spotlight onto the wall.

It started at 11: 55. *Skreeeeeeeeeeeeerreeeeeerreeee* . . .

"OK, Buck, this is it," said Wo, grabbing the spotlight. He moved into position behind the door. "What are we gonna do if there's something really weird out there?"

"Wing it," said Hamilton, grabbing the latch.

He yanked it open and Wo shone the light.

Screeeeeeeeeeeeerrrrrrrrr, the sound startlingly loud with the door wide open.

Wo and Hamilton peered out at the wall above the empty staircase. In the bright oval of Wo's light, they watched aghast as strips of
paint peeled off the wall.

Hamilton slammed the door and peered into Wo's astonished face.

"The wind," Wo pronounced, switching off the spotlight, "just
like I said that first night."

Back down at Hale Pohaku, Hamilton tossed in his bed, unable
to get his usual seven-hour sleep during the day. Dead on his feet, he
asked Wo to drive them up for their nighttime shift, the howling wind
blowing cinder ash against the windshield. The two spent much of the
jarring journey reassuring each other that their unnerving mystery was
solved. Even so, both grew wary as midnight approached.

The hour came and went without any scratching. If ever winds
could peel paint, the ones that night certainly would. Yet in the
remaining months of the project, no scratching was heard and no
more paint disappeared. Eventually, as normal job routines diluted
their alarming memories of those nights, they allowed themselves to
tell a few people about how the mountain winds once "played tricks
on them."

But their intrigues weren't over.

Several weeks after the peeling-paint incidents, the two chatted
outside the trailer drinking their coffees under the brilliant Milky
Way. So silent was the windless night that Hamilton said he could
hear blood pumping through his brain—until splashes echoed out of
Pu'u Waiau.

Wo turned his head toward the cone's rim, two hundred yards
away. "What the hell is that?"

"Sounds like waves, Donny."

Miffed, and not a little uneasy, they shared one of Wo's cigarettes, listening.

"There's no way we could hear the ocean way up here," Wo said,
"yet that's exactly what it sounds like."

"I guess we better go see," said Hamilton, again aware of how
much he and Wo were like explorers, the first non-Hawaiians to
spend so much intimate time on Mauna Kea, to them a cultural
wilderness charged with mystery.

Wo grabbed the Ray-O-Vac from the trailer, and the two trekked in starlight down the ancient trail leading to the lake. As they approached the cone's rim, farther and farther from their steel sanctuary, the austere remoteness of the mountain began weighing on them. Hamilton felt suddenly out of place, as he had in those first days guiding the bulldozer. On the horizon below were the caves and stone workings of a once bustling adze quarry littered with stone tools, garment fragments, and decayed offerings to native deities. Above them towered the summit ridge, where ancient oracles on nights like this had conversed with the gods.

They crested the rim and proceeded down the steep path to the shore. Now well inside the cone, the waves boomed like *pahu* drums.

"I don't get it, Buck," Wo said, hesitating on the trail. "There's not a breath of wind down here either."

"Turn on the spotlight, Donny," Hamilton said. "I'll bet we can see it from up here."

Wo flipped the switch and pointed the Ray-O-Vac toward the distant pond. Its beam just reached the cindery shoreline, where two-foot waves curled into the light.

"This mountain is weird," said Hamilton, instantly thinking of other Hawaiian places where the ancient past intruded on the modern present, and recalling what an old Hawaiian had once told him, that "the veil between the spirit realm and the physical world is thinner in Hawai'i."

"I'm outa here!" said Wo, and Hamilton agreed. When they finally reached their familiar "rest can," they were running—out of breath but greatly relieved. Neither man had a place in his mind to file the experience, and each independently decided he would prefer not to discuss it. Both hoped to forget the whole thing.

Despite their rationalizations and self-imposed amnesia, Hamilton and Wo were not unaffected by these bizarre incidents. Two years later, when they watched the fiercest winter in memory defy construction of the NASA telescope that Dr. Kuiper had advocated, they began to wonder all over again. To optimize seeing conditions, NASA and the University of Hawai'i had decided to build the mammoth observatory on Kukahau'ula, the towering complex of cones that formed the mountain's upper ridge, rather than out on the north plateau. The summit peak itself was declared off limits as a gesture to the island community. In September 1967, just after the last Lunar Orbiter finished mapping the moon for the upcoming Apollo missions, dignitaries in suits and ties braved Mauna Kea's cold, thin air to break ground for NASA's UH 88-inch telescope. The chilly winds lashing them as they jabbed their gold-painted spades into the cone were nothing compared with what arrived when the big shovels and backhoes started leveling the site—months of storms that brought frigid gales, swirling snow, and gear-coating ice. Old-timers called that winter the most severe in memory.

Hamilton and Wo watched the excavation attempt out the window of a base camp jeep.

"The cinder's froze solid!" shouted the power shovel operator to the burly Hawaiian spotting for him on the ground, only the red faces of each man visible inside their parkas. "I can't make a dent in her!"

The spotter shrugged as the shovel operator again futilely banged the teeth of his bucket against the ground. "Poli'ahu," they heard the Hawaiian say into the frigid wind. "You don't want to give it up, do you?"

After weeks of frustration, and little progress, the construction company hauled up huge steam machines shipped in from Alaska's oil fields to melt the frozen cinder. Only then could the shovel's bucket and dozer's blades penetrate the mountain. The winds, blizzards, and arctic temperatures grew even fiercer, blanketing the cones with snows deeper than the men were tall. The storms, along with the hardships of thin air, ultimately set the project back an entire year—disappointing NASA officials who had planned to use the telescope during their 1969 Apollo moon landing.

When the telescope's mirror finally did see first light, on May 26, 1970, astronomers managed to take only one photograph—a spectrographic image of Jupiter—before snow began falling on the summit, forcing them to close the dome. Weeks of mechanical problems followed, delaying observations right up until the telescope's dedication in late June.

Before the 88-inch began operating in 1970, two tiny unheated domes had also appeared on the summit ridge. In 1968 the Air Force built a 24-inch telescope to distinguish man-made satellites from heavenly bodies, making the first observatory on the mountain a military one. A year later, the Lowell Observatory of Flagstaff built one of their six International Planetary Patrol telescopes higher up the ridge, in part to study Mars dust storms. Astronomers from the prestigious observatory—founded by the man whose theory of Martian canals popularized the idea of life there—had fiercely advocated crowning the summit peak with their dome, but Hawai'i astronomers demurred.

Data from the 88-inch telescope eventually exceeded even Dr. Kuiper's expectations and astronomers began talking about building three, much bigger telescopes. Alarmed islanders strongly objected, mustering enough opposition to nearly kill the next round of world-class observatories—the Canada-France-Hawai'i Telescope, United Kingdom Infrared Telescope, and NASA Infrared Telescope.

Families with ancestral ties to Mauna Kea grew worried that all this construction might disturb bones placed there centuries ago to help guide the island's future. Native priests had already received dreams, signs, and gut feelings that some burials had been harmed. When word got out that several Hawaiians on the construction crews had quit, rumors that bones had been removed spread islandwide via the coconut wireless.

Hamilton and Wo, by then working as technicians on the UH 88-inch telescope, shrugged off the rumors when their Hilo friends asked, but inwardly they were less certain, remembering their inexplicable experiences during those early days on the mountain.

Hamilton even began pondering where uncovered bones might have been taken. *Probably dumped somewhere close*, he thought, *maybe off the old 13 North road down on the north plateau.*

CHAPTER 29

Meeting with the Oracle

Erik walked briskly down the path to Aunty Moana's hale by the sea, glancing apprehensively at every upright stone or ti plant guarding the shacks he passed along the way. Following Freddie's example, he carried a bouquet of flowers for the elder, picked that morning from Sunny Boy's backyard. Strong September trades rattled the fronds of the village coconuts and huge swells pounded the cove, leftovers from the distant Pacific storm that had brought rain to Mauna Kea the week before. Erik was relieved to see that Hoku Holokai had already arrived, the two Hawaiians talking intensely on Aunty Moana's lanai. They rose as he approached, the young woman behind the elder.

"Aloha," they said almost in unison.

"Good morning," he replied, handing Aunty Moana the flowers.

"Oh, mahalo!" she said warmly.

Hoku nodded thoughtfully, surprised that Erik had followed the island tradition of bringing a gift when visiting.

Aunty Moana leaned forward to accept a hug and gave Erik a buss on the cheek. Hoku also hugged Erik, stiffly, and without the kiss.

Both women looked as if they'd been crying. *Hoku must have told Aunty Moana about the Keck shooting too*, he thought. After all the elder had said during Erik's last visit—about fear and violence, and maintaining love in the face of injustice—he could imagine how that news would add to her distress about the draining lake.

"Hoku, would you mind going inside to get us some ice water?" Aunty Moana said, motioning Erik to sit down in the wicker chair next to her. The young woman obliged.

Aunty Moana eased her large body into the other wicker and pressed her hand atop Erik's. "Mahalo for alerting me to this change in our lake. You did the right thing taking pictures."

"Here they are," he said, handing her an envelope containing seven 8x10s. She pulled out the photos and looked at the first in the stack.

"Oh, no!" she sobbed, her lovely moon face eclipsed by dread. "Auwe! Auwe!"

Erik wanted to avert his eyes but he couldn't bring himself not to stay present with the grieving woman. Hoku noticed the elder weeping when she stepped back through the screen door, and her face contorted with concern. She set a glass by each of them and sat down at the card table, quietly observing the pair with keen, almost defensive interest.

Aunty Moana's deluge finally stopped, and catching her breath, she wiped her soaked face with a tissue. One by one, she studied the pictures on her lap, now and again pausing to sip from her glass. With each image, Aunty Moana's convulsions returned, and Erik fought back his own tears.

"Lake Waiau holds the sacred waters of Kane," the oracle murmured, referring to Hawaiians' procreation deity, the god of pure water and sunlight. "That Kane is taking them away means something is terribly wrong on the mountain."

"No surprise," Hoku said darkly. "The Big Eye, the donor's plans to be buried on the mountain, and now this shooting."

"The hewa goes back long before that," the kaula said dolefully, "to when they removed the tops of the summit cones . . ."

"Desecration!" Hoku snarled under her breath.

"Worse . . . they disrupted our connection to the higher realm." Aunty Moana looked up at Hoku with piercing eyes. "That's why so many of us get confused."

She let her eyes drift back to the photo atop the stack. "The lake departing is certainly a warning . . . and yet . . ." She ran her finger across the top of the picture, tracing a puff of white cloud that hung over the far side of the lake, ". . .there is still time to do something about it."

Hearing this kind of talk was a challenge for Erik, and it made him perspire. He knew Polynesians put great stock in signs from nature, and he'd heard stories of shaman who could interpret them, but he'd never met one of these mystics.

"I need to pray on this," the elder announced, gingerly sliding the pictures back into the envelope. She took a long drink of water and gazed at the sea. Eventually turning to Erik, she pressed her hand atop the envelope. "May I keep these a while?"

"They're yours. I don't need them back."

Her face brightened a bit. "You know, the moment I saw you, many months ago now, I had a good feeling. I knew we would become friends, but I didn't know it would be like this."

Blood rose in Erik's cheeks. "I have . . . a confession to make, Aunty Moana."

"Oh?"

"So many times you smiled at me with such warm aloha, but I didn't accept it. Instead, I wondered why. You didn't know me from Adam."

"Ah, but you see I did. Your heart may be wounded but it's still open, as the hearts of all nature's lovers are open. I sensed that immediately and recognized a kindred spirit."

Erik's eyes misted over and though he tried to speak was unable to get out his words.

Aunty Moana brushed the back of her hand over his damp cheek exactly as Erik's long dead mother had. "Tears reveal your deepest truths," she said. "Trust them, young man. They're signs of strength."

Hoku nodded, but her face remained unchanged—watchful, protective of her mentor.

Erik, embarrassed, quickly composed himself. "Anyway . . . and I feel guilty about this . . . every time you smiled I wondered 'What does she want from me?'"

"And now you realize we have been thrown together, all *three* of us"—she said, glancing at Hoku—"by forces none of us control."

Erik nodded, so full of feelings that even his fingertips seemed to tingle. Old man Labathe's leathery face popped into his mind and his Ojibwe stories about "the mysterious ways the world really works," as the old voyageur had put it.

"I don't know why all this seems strange to me," Erik replied. "I certainly paid attention to uncanny coincidences when I lived on the river. But here in Hawai'i they come so often, and they always seem to make sense . . . afterwards anyway." Numerous touchstones flashed through Erik's mind—the want ads at Waikiki, his hiring by Moses, seeing Hoku on his first trip up the mountain, moving into the Airstream next to the village, encountering Hoku again on Pu'u Poli'ahu and then at Waiau yesterday. Perhaps even his appendicitis on Samoa was a part of it—forcing him back to Hawai'i and to the island of the magical mountain. And what about that strange light he saw on Mauna Kea as he approached from the sea?

"There are no coincidences," Aunty Moana said, laughing with delight.

"That's because our islands still operate the way most of the world *used* to," Hoku said, a bitter tinge in her voice.

"But why is that?" Erik said.

The elder gently slapped his knee. "Because, Erik, here in Hawai'i synergy is not so dissipated by the will of men. You know what I'm talking about—people so fixed on chasing desires that they ignore the currents around them. Most islanders, the Hawaiians and many of our Asian cousins, strive to live in harmony with the energies that drive the universe, instead of fighting them. Islanders here follow ancient wisdoms, truths deciphered long ago by alert observers."

"I see," he said, but his slumped body and crossed arms suggested he still didn't get it.

"Consult the Taoist and Buddhist teachings of Asia, the mythologies of native peoples across the globe, the physics of Western science—all contemplations on the rules of the universe and the nature of energy. But too many people, especially in the eager, impatient West, misunderstand the role of human will in all that. We must act, or 'not act' as our Asian cousins say, when our intuition—what we Hawaiians call na'au—tells us to, not when we independently choose to act out our desires and expectations . . . or our greed. In Hawai'i, enough of us still follow those wise teachings . . ." She chuckled. ". . . even when we don't realize we're doing it. And that allows our human activities to synergize with other forces of nature, the akua—our gods."

Erik was taken aback by the potent ideas flowing from the old Hawaiian's mouth, as he had been during his last visit. He glanced through the screen at her shelves stuffed with books and remembered that she had been a teacher in the "other world."

"And our mountain—in fact, Erik, all high mountains on our planet—gather and concentrate these energies in mysterious ways that make it possible for those who go there, or even just gaze up at them, to feel their power and gain knowledge."

"Yes," Hoku said, "I use the mountain that way all the time."

Aunty Moana smiled knowingly at the young woman. "Some, those especially in tune, actually see this energy as light or color."

Erik again thought of the beacon he'd seen approaching the island. *Am I "in tune"?* he wondered. *And if so, what is my na'au trying to tell me?* A perilous feeling of standing on the edge of a chasm between two worlds rose within him and he stirred in his chair, wondering whether he could contrive a convenient reason to leave.

"You must forgive us, Erik," said the kaula, "if we speak our truths with concepts that may be foreign to you. But I would not share these if I did not believe you had the ability to understand. Never underestimate the impact of a life at sea or on one of Earth's mightiest rivers."

"We mountain people understand," Hoku ventured with pride.

"Yes," the elder said, a hint of rebuke in her voice, "if we're paying attention."

"How can astronomers work on Mauna Kea for decades and still not get it!" Hoku interjected, her words pregnant with barely restrained irritation.

Aunty Moana frowned. "Yes, I'm afraid they're so focused on the data they gather with their instruments that they miss the lessons of the heavens they observe, let alone what they could learn from Mauna Kea . . . and it doesn't help that some of them still feel vengeful after losing their TMT to the Canary Islands. What's your excuse, Hoku?"

Erik's eyes flashed with surprise, and then he wondered, *How much of that comment was meant for me too?*

"Have you seen Hoku's paintings, Erik?"

"Only the one in your hale," he said, glancing through the screen.

"Hoku caught the true spirit of Waiau with her brush," she said, beaming, "don't you think?"

"Yes . . . but you both know the lake better than I."

"I don't agree," Aunty Moana said. "We have known it longer, but you were the one chosen to see the message of its disappearing water first."

"That was just coincidence."

They all laughed, even Hoku.

"Hoku," Aunty Moana said, rising to indicate the meeting was over. "I think you should show Erik your other paintings. This Mississippi . . . 'river rat' . . . if I'm remembering the right term, will appreciate them, I'm sure."

Hoku sighed warily, but she agreed to follow her mentor's instructions. Besides, she was curious about the mountain newcomer she'd encountered at the lake and had seen on the snowy cone named for Poli'ahu—even if he was a haole from the mainland. The two agreed to meet the next day at her studio, farther down the road in Keaukaha.

"Call me after you've had a chance to show him your paintings," the elder said.

"OK," Hoku replied as she stepped off the lanai onto the sand.

"Aunty Moana," Erik said, lingering after Hoku left, "may I ask another question?"

"Of course, if the question demands to be asked." She motioned him to sit.

"Do you have seals in Hawai'i?"

She beamed. "Oh yes, our dear little monk seals, but they rarely show themselves."

"Why's that?"

"How often does one see an angel?" she chuckled.

Erik's eyes narrowed. After all they'd discussed, why would she toy with him now? "Well, I saw one."

"An angel?"

"No. A monk seal."

Her eyes lit up and she leaned forward in her chair. "Where?"

"Crossing the 'Alenuihaha Channel when we were sailing to Honolulu, and again right out there." He pointed to the waters off the reef in front of Sunny Boy's bungalow. "The night after Freddie introduced me to you."

She sat up straight and eyed Erik for a full half-minute. "You are a very fortunate man, indeed. You must tell me when you next see our little kupua."

Erik, miffed by her riddle—and feeling overwhelmed by all they had shared—found his feet without even realizing he'd gotten up out of the chair. The chasm he'd sensed earlier was suddenly below him.

"Mahalo for coming, Erik." She reached up to hug him, and as he bent his tall frame forward, she gently placed her forehead atop his and shared her breath. "Aloha no!" she said. Warmest aloha!

His whole body tingled as he ambled back up the village's dirt road. There's obviously more to this "crazy" elder, and to the young lady of the lake, than meets the eye, he thought, but how much of what they said is actually true?

When he reached the ti patch at the edge of Sunny Boy's property, Erik glanced back at Aunty Moana. She was sitting on her rock under the big kamani tree, wagging her finger at two mynah birds on the sand. The offshore breeze carried her muted voice. "I spoke with both of you yesterday about this!" she babbled to the usually raucous birds who stood silently looking at her. Erik shook his head and stepped back onto what he hoped was more familiar territory.

At eleven o'clock that night, he woke up dreaming that the ivory seal was lounging under the plumeria tree outside the Airstream. Erik got up and walked to the sea, but there was nothing in the water except whitecaps catching the milky light of the crescent moon. On the way back, he noticed that Sunny Boy was still up, watching TV. Erik knocked on his lanai screen door.

"Erik! Come in!" said the aging disc jockey, shirtless in blue jean shorts. "Wanna beer? I'm watching reruns of da original *Hawaii Five-O.*"

"No thanks," he said, standing in the threshold.

Sunny Boy's huge mouth frowned

"Do you have a Hawaiian dictionary?"

"Yes, I do . . . somewhere in here. Hold on a minute." The old DJ lumbered over to a small bookshelf containing sheet music, two cookbooks, a phone directory, and a worn copy of the Bible. "Here it is!"

He returned to the door and handed the musty dictionary to Erik. "Sure ya don't wanna come in and watch? Dis is da episode where one terrorist plants a bomb to trigger an eruption on Mauna Loa . . ."

"No thanks, I gotta hit the hay. Can I return this to you tomorrow?"

"Sure," and a moment later Sunny Boy lay sprawled on his sofa, blue in TV glow.

Back in the Airstream, reclined in his built-in sofa, Erik read the definition for the word the oracle had used for the monk seal—"our little *kupua.*"

kupua, noun. Demigod or cultural hero, especially a supernatural being possessing several forms.

CHAPTER 30

Bunkmates and Pirates

While Erik met with Aunty Moana and Hoku that morning, another group discussed Mauna Kea on a sea cliff across town, at the headquarters of Williams & Company Shipping. Tom Williams Jr. sat alongside his son, Tommy, and scanned the chamber of commerce members sitting at the big table under the painting of his great-grandfather's ship. Tom was not entirely pleased. Those gathered had responded to his son's invitation to discuss "high-tech solutions to the Big Island's economic slump," but the real agenda—hatched as a father-son compromise to their earlier land sale disagreement—was to garner local support for the Haisley Big Eye. Recent news stories revealing Caltech's plan to build the telescope on the old 88-inch site with Haisley's tomb underneath now complicated their task.

The unexpressed anxiety in the room was that telescope opponents were already organizing and that the theft and scuttling of a Keck vehicle the previous winter could mark the beginning of an ugly confrontation. (News of the recent mirror shooting hadn't yet reached the island's coconut wireless.) Even the pair of usually complacent Hilo politicians—a county councilman and a state senator—fidgeted at the table.

They're gun-shy, Tom thought, *from the Thirty Meter Telescope fiasco. I'll bet some of these weak knees actually hope astronomers take the Big Eye to Chile.*

During that decade-long fight, the island's elderly mayor, Richard ("Dicky") Yamamoto—a man with ancestral ties to Mount Fuji—was one of a handful of politicians to finally side with TMT opponents, and the only one not of Hawaiian ancestry. To make up for years of earlier cowardice, he called the existing domes "ugly pimples marring the mountain I've gazed up at all my life." Younger Tommy regretted having had to invite the turncoat to this meeting, and both Toms wished Yamamoto had chosen instead to attend that day's ribbon cutting for a new county road in Kona.

Tommy's announcement that the mayor would arrive shortly only added to the discomfort of the businesspeople at the table. Battered by the death of sugar, two US recessions, and tourism's slowdown, they would do almost anything to bring more dollars to the Big Island, particularly if some of the greenbacks found a way into their own companies. Even so, they were wary of another fight between the local community and mainland astronomers, especially because, as far as they knew, the last $500 million needed for the $2.5 billion telescope had yet to be found. Had they known Tommy planned to secure their political commitments to Haisley's telescope that morning, they might all have gone to the ribbon cutting.

The senior Williams' biggest disappointment was that Henry Hashimura—to him, Noburo—would not attend. Certainly the aging kingpin of the "old boys" could force the group's resolve. Tom had looked forward to seeing him again. He had even rehearsed with Marilyn how he would thank Noburo for arranging the Stryker and drone transport contract, Hashimura's part of the deal they'd struck that led to this meeting. Instead, the Honolulu real estate developer Miles Millhoff sat at the far corner, Hashimura's usual spy at meetings run by haoles.

Many strategy sessions had been held in this room over the years, but at those meetings Tom had known intimately the others at the table (even if he had not always trusted them). That morning he personally knew less than half the attendees, the rest only by reputation—and that also worried him. The old-timers who'd previously gathered there had motivations easier to respect than those of these younger business leaders, who seemed more committed to making money for themselves than building a future for the island. In the past, even the "money grabbers," as Tom had called them, had some sense of destiny, or at least gratitude, for having personally escaped the poverty and repression of the plantations.

As the current elected president of the island's chamber of commerce, Tommy presided at the table's head. Middle-sized and middle-aged, the lean, good-looking Tommy was immaculately dressed in a Sig Zane aloha shirt tucked into gray slacks. As usual, Tommy carried himself like the "winner" he imagined he was, with steely posture and a forward gaze that showed off those lagoon-turquoise eyes he'd inherited from his father.

Watching Tommy assume the chamber's leadership role had once stirred Tom's familial pride, but a world of difference now stood between the two. Tommy, who'd grown up in prosperity—indeed felt entitled to it—did not appreciate the pioneering challenges faced by previous generations of Williams & Company executives. A product of Punahou School in Honolulu and the Stanford Business School in California, Tommy had upper-class values when it came to investment return rates and community obligations (high in the first case, low in the latter), despite his father's admonition that just keeping a business alive in the islands was a worthy accomplishment if it also contributed to the community. But like many island offspring trained at American schools, Tommy had acquired mainland expectations for his own prosperity and the twenty-first-century ethic of meeting those expectations at any cost.

The short, plump man sitting on Tommy's left was Herbert Oshiro, one of only two attendees from the same generation as his seventy-year-old father. While the elder Tom had shared rounds of golf with Oshiro, those were rare and strictly professional events, because Tom disdained Oshiro's former use of bagmen and bribes to obtain county approvals, state appropriations, and juicy federal earmarks for his projects. To Tom, those unseemly methods were also counterproductive because in those days most islanders respected the business community and supported their projects. But Oshiro, whose Okinawan ancestry had inhibited his full acceptance into the inner circle of Hilo's "full-blooded" Japanese, relished the power those political connections gave him. "I own those men," he once boasted to Tom, pointing his golf club at two state legislators on the next green.

On the other side of Tommy was the other septuagenarian Tom knew well, C. Lyman Harris, president and CEO of Brower Brothers. His old *kama'aina* company owned vast acres of now idle sugar fields, as well as urban real estate ventures meant to offset their annual losses. Four generations earlier, Harris' Congregational clan had come from New England to "save the native savages with the Lord's divine word." One of those ancestors married an ali'i chiefess to bring Hawaiian (if pagan) blood into the family—along with ten thousand acres of prime agricultural land. Harris' missionary ancestors had helped persuade the American foreign secretary to send in Marines to overthrow the queen's constitutional monarchy and make possible better US prices for sugar. But as the Bible says, the sins of the fathers are visited upon the sons, or in this case great-great grandsons; after displacing the Hawaiians, felling their forests, and depleting their once fertile soils, the century of sugar came to a close. C. Lyman Harris now desperately looked for any alternative for his land, high tech or otherwise.

Sitting next to Harris was the astronomer in the room, Dr. James Bushmill, director of the University of Hawai'i's Department of Astronomy and Astrophysics, whose faculty received observing time on every new telescope in exchange for supporting it against local opposition—and in lieu of millions in rental fees the law required for use of state land. The elder Williams had interacted with Bushmill at observatory ground breakings (including the one for TMT halted by angry Hawaiians). The former New Yorker was incessantly enthusiastic, but his inability to look a man in the eye and his propensity to fudge facts made Tom leery. Tom's son tried to get Willy McCrea to make the meeting's astronomy pitch, but the idealistic Berkeley scholar used "tight scheduling" as an excuse to skip hobnobbing with any more power brokers.

The next two on Tommy's right were small-time businessmen—a shopping mall clothier and the owner of Hilo's last family-owned hardware store—both of whom clung to the belief that *any* island development would benefit their ventures too. The heads of the local carpenters and electricians unions also sat at the table, but by their choice, opposite the men at the front.

Near them was the charismatic Namaka Hee, a potential Republican mayoral candidate and owner of Paradise Studios, a modeling agency that trained handsome young islanders to market themselves to television and film companies, advertising firms, and tourist magazines. Although fifteen years had passed since Hee won the Miss Aloha Hawai'i Pageant, she still turned men's heads, which may explain why Walter (Pano) Kamalu had taken the chair next to her. The two Chinese-Hawaiians made a striking pair, she with her huge brown eyes, sexy mouth, and copious black hair piled atop her head, and he with his glossy black eyes and ruggedly handsome, pockmarked face.

The fifty-six-year-old Kamalu was the eldest son of a notorious underworld assassin and the successor to Haku Kane, the deceased chief of the Hui, an underworld syndicate made rich on vice, money laundering, and labor and construction contract kickbacks. Kamalu often attended meetings like this under his presumed occupation, owner of Pano's Polynesian Plate restaurant in Kona's King Kamehameha Hotel. As soon as the new Hui chief sat down, Tommy felt pressure to get the meeting underway, and commented apologetically that the mayor had not yet arrived.

"I wouldn't worry about that," Kamalu said with a smirk. "Busy Dicky will be along at some point. He's an important man, after all."

To Tommy's relief, the mayor hobbled in while the last two guests getting coffee and malasadas sat down. Dicky was the unlucky 13th.

"Thank you all for coming," Tommy said, then introduced the economic benefits of high tech, touching on GMOs, geothermal energy, supercomputer applications, and military R&D. He then focused on "the most promising" of the various science applications, Mauna Kea astronomy. "We're fortunate today that Dr. James Bushmill has come over from Honolulu to give us an overview of what he thinks lies ahead for astronomy and, hopefully, Mauna Kea. Thank you, Dr. Bushmill."

"Please call me Jim," the fifty-year-old astronomer said, jumping up as Marilyn, standing near the door, dimmed the lights. While he mentioned future "astounding upgrades" of several existing telescopes, 90 percent of his PowerPoint presentation focused on the Haisley Big Eye and astronomers' current search for a suitable site. As he moved through the spectacular show—complete with cosmic animations, space music, and video clips—Bushmill grew ever more excited, his trembling hands shaking the red laser to the point of distraction.

"From the beginning, UH astronomers favored the Mona Kea site," Bushmill said, as usual mispronouncing the mountain's name with his thick New York accent.

Of course you did, you egghead, the younger Williams thought with a poker face. *You squeezed Caltech's nuts to extract 10 percent of the Big Eye's observing time in exchange for the old 88-inch site and for fronting the project with a UH face.*

"To this day we remain loyal to the mountain," Bushmill continued, pounding the table, "even though Chile's desert peaks are now in vogue."

The two politicians began to applaud, but held back when the rest of the room didn't respond.

"But now it will be *an uphill climb* to get the Haisley built here," confessed the astronomer, winking at the pun that only he, among the grimly serious group, appreciated. "For some time now, the international astronomy community has shifted its aspirations to Chile's high-elevation Atacama Desert, and two twenty-first-century titans—Europe's Extra Large Telescope and Carnegie's Giant Magellan Telescope—are now being added to Chile's amazing astronomical arsenal." Bushmill made sure to mention the Atacama Large Millimeter Array, "a 66-antenna behemoth nearly ten times the size of our Smithsonian array," he said, painfully reminding the group that chamber complacency in the face of local opposition had helped derail the Mauna Kea site for that project, just as the four Keck outriggers and TMT had later been thwarted.

Atta boy, Bushmill, the elder Tom thought, having advised the director just before the meeting started to "say whatever you need to fire up these people."

"We at the university still believe the Big Eye should be here in Hawai'i," which he pronounced "Hah-why." "Some astronomers in California do too." The biggest understatement of the meeting. "However, there are formidable advocates pushing to build the Big Eye in Chile . . . and, candidly, credible scientific reasons to do so."

To say nothing about the likely protests here, thought Tommy.

"Only visible support from the Hawai'i community will bring this cutting-edge project here . . . some sense of groundswell to reverse the Chile momentum." The astronomer glanced around the dark-ened table, pausing dramatically at each face. "Had caution prevailed during competition with Arizona for the Kecks, the whole history of astronomy—and its economic impact on the Big Island—would be very different now. But the chamber rose to the occasion, and the two Keck giants came home. That we haven't succeeded with TMT is all the more reason to fight vigorously for the Big Eye!" Bushmill's hazel eyes shimmered with practiced emotion.

Herbert Oshiro raised his chubby little hand. "Jim," he asked with a familiarity born of the two men's long association, "have you done an estimate of the Big Eye's economic impact on the Big Island?"

"We have," the professor replied, his tone now *very* serious. "During the eight-year construction phase alone, the Haisley Big Eye will bring at least $700 million to the local economy."

There was an audible inhalation of breath among the group, and the eyes of Oshiro Construction's president began to water. Bushmill didn't tell them that the "study" from which he drew that dubious number was done by a Honolulu PR firm hired by his department.

"Already the observatories on Mona Kea contribute—directly or indirectly—over $100 million to this island's economy every year. With the addition of the Big Eye, we see that figure increasing by at least 25 percent."

"And jobs?" said the head of the carpenters union.

"We anticipate the creation of at least four hundred jobs during the construction phase, with about one-third that number retained over the instrument's long-term operation."

The mayor, always polite, raised his hand.

"Yes, Dicky?" said the senior Tom, signaling his son that he would handle the old-timer.

The mayor removed his eyeglasses and set them on the table, as he often did when poised to utter a personal truth. His placid oval face, still smooth at sixty-five, and the emerging gray at his temples gave him the look of a Japanese patrician.

"As you all know, I'm on record opposed to any more telescopes on the mountain. I prefer to pursue the other high-tech opportunities Tommy mentioned. For years, Big Islanders have told me their anxieties about the never-ending expansions on Mauna Kea. We need to bring a halt to it, once and for all. I intend to do that for as long as I'm mayor."

Thank God that won't be long, several at the table thought, Dicky Yamamoto having decided to retire at the end of this, his second term.

"We have plenty of other opportunities," he continued, "if we trust our creativity. Take aquaculture for example—"

"Not many jobs in that," interrupted the electrician. His union cohort chuckled.

"Gentlemen," Hee said with her sultry voice. "I hear the same thing around town that Dicky does," choosing to highlight the public uproar rather than expose her own Native Hawaiian view. "Politically, the Big Eye is already in trouble, because when it comes to Mauna Kea, the natives are more than restless," her ironic quip meant to further veil her true sentiments. "That's the reality we all must face after the TMT fiasco, no matter how much we might want more telescopes."

The councilman and legislator, glancing apologetically at the astronomer, nodded their heads.

"I agree with Namaka," said the clothier. "I hear it all the time at the mall."

The elder Williams pointed his fat finger at the mayor and ignited the old fire that had seen him through many a struggle. "You bear some of the blame for that, Dicky. Your opposition has given reactionaries in this community a credibility they never had before."

Mayor Yamamoto raised his eyebrows. "I dare say the astronomers themselves have done more damage than any position I've taken, what with pressuring state officials to look the other way on environmental regulations, cultural protections, and public oversight that our people fought to set in place a generation ago. Take, for example, the original lease of those Hawaiian ceded lands on the mountaintop—"

"Don't go there, Dicky," the underworld chief said in a low, formidable voice. Displeased with the meeting's tenor, Kamalu decided to turn it around. And with the absence of Henry Hashimura—also Noburo to him—he knew he was the one to do it.

"You've done your share of fudging those requirements over the years, Dicky, on the county council and as mayor. You want me to bring up Lanakila Street Shopping Center?"

The apprehension that had permeated the room before the meeting now amplified to fear. Everyone at the table knew the Hui's political and economic reach extended further than any of them dared acknowledge. Most disturbed was the old kama'aina, C. Lyman Harris, whose missionary temperament was repulsed by power politics played so crudely.

The Hui chief pressed both palms on the dark koa table and leaned forward, an intimidating gesture he'd learned from his criminal father. "I've looked at this Big Eye issue with considerable care," he said in a deadly serious tone, "and I've concluded that I'm for it."

Even the mayor said nothing, and an awkward silence stifled the room. It was almost a relief when Sam Chun burst through the door in a shaft of light from the outer office, followed by Marilyn, who glanced apologetically at Tom for having failed to prevent the environmentalist's entry with her claim of a "private company meeting."

"Well, well," Sam declared. "The gang's all here!"

An irate Hawaiian woman marched past Marilyn, her wild hair bouncing with her stride. "We're here to speak for the people and against that goddamn atrocity you people call GOD," referring to the astronomers' unfortunate acronym for Giant Optical Device.

Sam flushed with embarrassment. He had only meant to give Koa Makali'i a heads up that he was going over "to talk some sense into the group" after the mayor had alerted him to the meeting. He hadn't intended for the raging professor to show up too.

"You S.O.B.s are always meeting in the dark," she shouted, flipping on the lights, "and we're tired of it!"

Marilyn pushed past her and switched them back off, then wondered if she'd done the right thing. But in those moments of illumination Koa had spotted the Hui chief sitting next to the ex–beauty queen. A lump in her throat blocked the rest of the speech she had screamed at her dashboard on the way over.

"Look," said Sam, stepping to the table, his eyes now on the two Toms. "There are legitimate environmental and cultural concerns about this telescope that must be addressed before something of its magnitude is seriously considered. You know the issues—impact on mountain views from the coastline, wekiu bug and ua'u bird habitats, ancient burials and shrines, hazardous waste from aluminizing mirrors, and assurance that no telescopes are used for warfare. As we've done in the past, we can, and must, discuss all of these concerns . . . *calmly*." Sam flashed an admonishing glance at Koa Makali'i, and was struck by her oddly subdued expression. Puzzled, he scanned the room until he, too, found the grim, pockmarked face of Pano Kamalu. Ire rose in Sam's chest.

"Oh, I see," Sam said, externally still calm. He peered over at Tom Williams. "So that's how it's gonna be," he said with a tone Tom recognized as a veiled pledge to battle.

CHAPTER 31

Sins against Fathers Visited upon Sons

That same morning—as the chamber conspired and Erik met with the Hawaiians—Johnny Mattos peered up at Mauna Kea through the picture window of his living room in a modest old house on Hawaiian Home Lands outside Waimea. He slurped his second black coffee of the morning, made bitter overheating in the pot. The more he imagined the mountain's new profile with the twenty-five-story Big Eye lording over all the other monstrosities up there, the greater his angst and ire.

He recalled that same vista when he was a young ranch hand, looking up from the sweaty back of his eager Palomino, how the ever-present mountain fed his spirit as it had his father's. Tall, grounded, capped with bold cinder peaks that turned pure white each winter, even when Waimea was hot and dusty. Looking up in those days had made him feel strong and clean.

He remembered that relentless winter of 1968 when the rain and wind blustered for weeks, flooding the valleys, shattering the cane, and making cattle herding miserable. After the clouds had finally cleared, he was astonished that Mauna Kea's snowline stretched to Pu'u Kemole, almost halfway down to Waimea. For weeks, dozens of the mountain's cones wore robes of white, and old-timers agreed that "Poliʻahu is either overjoyed or pissed as hell!" Johnny's mentor, Uncle Bill Moamoa, an old *paniolo* who taught him how to rope mean bulls without bloodshed, once told him how he got caught near Lake Waiau in the worst of it. He had said it was "the fiercest weather I ever endured on Mauna Kea, like she was gonna seal the whole mauna in a rock-hard crown of ice. Cold as it was, I stayed warm with my aloha for the mountain."

The mud in Johnny's cup was almost too harsh even for him. He considered watering it down, but his despondency kept him ensconced in his ratty old La-Z-Boy. He recalled his confusion when scaffolding appeared on the summit ridge that winter—onset of the 88-inch telescope's construction—and wondered *what in hell was giving Kukahauʻula that ugly new profile?* Months later, a dome started taking shape, and the newspapers explained that NASA had decided Mauna Kea was the best place on Earth to study the heavens. Johnny's native wife, Nani, told him an old kahuna in the family had prayed on it. "Hawaiian astronomers have made pilgrimages up that holy mountain for centuries," the kahuna had said. "Maybe Ke Akua figured it was time to get some modern, high-tech stargazers up there to learn something from Wakea and Papa" (Sky Father and Earth Mother), "from the mauna, and from us, the Hawaiians." That idea hadn't comforted Johnny any more than it had his father.

"Hey, Dad . . . you home?" Josh's voice at the kitchen screen door broke Johnny's reverie.

"In the front room!" he yelled back, an unusual edge in his big voice.

Walking into the kitchen, Josh immediately sensed his father's mood.

"Got some fresh poi from Uncle Chris," Josh announced, peeking into the living room to show off the big bowl of taro mash.

"My brother makes the best," Johnny replied, his eyes still fixed on the mountain.

Josh placed the poi bowl in the center of the kitchen table and joined his father in the living room.

Johnny turned to look at him. "Day off, today?" he said, surprised to see his son in Waimea on a Wednesday.

Josh plopped into the saggy old couch that also faced the window. "Called in sick," he said.

"You look beat."

"Been stayin' up too late. Sleepin' like shit. Betty's mad at me, says I'm in a lousy mood ever since you and me went huntin'."

"What?"

"Don't get me wrong, Dad. I'm glad we went up together. I kinda forgot those old days, the good times, but carrying a gun threw me. Coming back after Afghanistan—to the island, to the family—hasn't been easy. I can't explain it. It's like all that heat and dust and blood confuses your bearings, makes you unsteady like. Hard to talk about . . . easier to just go to the job every day, drink after work with the guys . . . until that day you and me hit the slopes lookin' for mouflon."

Johnny knew well what Josh was talking about. He'd felt that way after Vietnam, but his Portuguese bravado had kept it hidden. Even Nani never realized how hard that time had been; she only knew that Johnny's sweetness had soured a bit.

"I just couldn't face drivin' up to Gemini this morning, so I figured I'd come see you." Josh had hoped the trip from Hilo would calm him, but big swells along the Hamakua Coast—left from the earlier rainstorms—only fueled his turmoil, as if his own distant storm from the war was just now washing up on his shore.

"Glad you came," his father said, looking back toward the mountain. "But I'm in a horseshit mood myself."

"How come?"

"Sonsobitches!" he blurted. "I can't face watching 'em build out the summit all over again! No amount o' talk makes any difference to those damn haoles. Nothin' stops 'em—hearings full of shouting residents, the Hawaiians bawling their eyes out, protesters blocking the road to stop the bulldozers, even all the lawsuits! I don't get it."

"They don't care, Dad. I know. I work for 'em. Oh, they'll tell ya how they 'just love' livin' here, how they 'appreciate' the Hawaiian culture, but ask 'em to give something up for it, it won't happen."

Johnny leaned toward his son, his swarthy face turning burgundy. "I'm glad somebody took a potshot at that goddamn Keck mirror!"

"What!" His father's news slammed into Josh's chest like an AK-47 round.

"Yep, about ten days ago. Heard about it at the café this morning. They can't keep something like that under wraps for long on this island."

"Jesus Christ." Josh paused a long moment, sweat forming under his T-shirt. "Somebody workin' up there coulda got hurt . . ."

Flames flashed across Johnny's moistening eyes. "Haven't *we* been hurt, Josh? Over and over and over again!"

Josh grimaced seeing the pain in his father's face, and his own suppressed ire rose again. "I feel shame workin' for 'em, but what can I do, Dad?"

His father looked away, remembering all the compromises his siblings had made to become middle class in a colony dominated by "ignorant haoles" and "kowtowing Asians," while he chose the harder, more traditional path of the cowboy. There was no money in it—God knows Nani made him pay a price for that—but he stayed mostly independent his whole life. Without Nani's Home Lands lot, they'd never have made it.

"Everybody's gotta make choices, son, and they're no easier now than when I was a boy. Your mother will tell you that."

That comment only added to Josh's distress, stirring memories of his parents' bitter quarrels. He needed to quiet the anxiety pouring into his chest. "Wanna beer, Dad?"

"This early?"

"You're right," he answered promptly, but it wasn't early for Josh. Since Afghanistan, he'd been drinking earlier in the day and later at night—and quietly taking the pills his doctor prescribed.

"Hey, Dad, the ranch still letting you use the horses now and again?"

Johnny nodded, but his mind and gaze still clung to the mountain.

"We could go ridin' this morning." Anything to disperse his torrent of anxiety before it shook him apart, before he exploded, as he had last night at Betty.

"That'd be nice," Johnny said after a moment. *Been a long time since I rode with my son*, he thought, *not since before Afghanistan*. Johnny looked deep into his son's face, seeing again how his features now drooped oddly to the right, how his eyes, once steady and bright, always looked away in conversation. Even a simple, straightforward man like Johnny could see the damage done. First his mountain, now his son.

"Oh God," he moaned, "Oh God!"

His unbidden howl of anguish surprised both men. Johnny tried to squelch it, but his durable heart had just then broken, and out of it poured a river of tears as unstoppable as the floods that carved Mauna Kea's gulches when the glaciers thawed.

Josh was so stunned he couldn't think what to do—but his heart knew. He leaped from the couch and threw his brawny arms around his father, squeezing him so tight that even a prideful male like Johnny Mattos couldn't resist the brazen affection. It was as if Josh was instinctively trying to hold those broken pieces of his dad's heart together.

Johnny felt Josh's tears on his cheek. "I'm sorry, son," the words gurgling out like the death rattles Josh had heard too many times from bomb-maimed Afghans.

"They've broken my spirit, son. Oh God, they've broken my spirit!"

Josh couldn't believe his ears. Everyone knew Johnny Mattos was a paniolo as strong and unfettered as the wild longhorn cattle that once roamed Mauna Kea. No one—nothing—could break that old man's spirit. And yet here he was, convulsing in front of his son.

Josh let go of him and stood up, facing the mountain.

"No, Dad," he said with that bold Portuguese certainty that ran in their family. "They're not gonna take the mountaintop. They're not gonna win. You'll see."

Josh felt like Kilauea, the volcanic pressure inside him so close to bursting that he knew he had to get out of there. He leaned over and hugged his father. "Don't worry, Dad. We'll protect your mountain."

Johnny didn't even hear him. All he could think of is how the Army had stolen his son. "I'm sorry, Josh," he muttered. "I'm so sorry."

Before dashing out of the room, Josh knelt down to kiss his father's stubbly cheek, as he had when he was a kid. "I love you, Dad."

Then he vanished like a ghost, but the anguish of both men haunted the Mattos house the rest of the day.

CHAPTER 32

Sea Change

"Ponder this question, Andromeda," offered Dr. Jedediah Clarke to his unofficial advisee, the two astronomers sitting on the sand against a driftwood log below Clarke's Malibu bungalow. Earth's star had already dropped into the Pacific and Venus had just emerged in the purple twilight. "What is the most important skill Polynesians had to possess to make the long journeys between islands?"

Andromeda tilted her pretty face sideways, lips pursed in thought, and watched the white froth of the breaking waves sink into the sand. "To get along, I suppose."

"Exactly!" Jedediah said, raising his glass of Chardonnay, delighted again with the acuity of her mind. He reached deep into the pocket of his khaki pants to retrieve a lighter and fired up a pipeful of fresh shag.

She watched the handsome lines of his face as he puffed the tobacco aflame, his tangle of hair a wild halo in the pipe's glow.

"You're wonderful, Andy!" He squeezed her knee, sending a little thrill through her body. "One of the quickest students I've ever had."

Her heart dropped. *Silly*, she thought, this stirring that had grown over months of thesis discussion with a man so different from her father—save for their cosmological passion. She had even submerged her earlier skepticism about his Polynesian "wayfinding" obsession and a worry that he was now more committed to Hawaiians than the astronomical quest that had put his discoveries in textbooks. Yet in the intimacy of all those lively discussions, he had never once shown anything other an intellectual interest in the young woman.

That evening, affected by the wine he had sipped during their afternoon consult, Jedediah waxed romantic about his deepest loves— the heavens, the sea, sailing, and the Polynesians. Andromeda had consumed less, but her young heart made up for it, and she found herself terribly aroused.

"The Hawaiians' ability to love their fellow man has survived," Jedediah continued, his blue eyes sapphire in the faint light. "I see it in them even now, ingrained by generations of survival on tiny boats and small islands. I know of few other cultures where when a stranger shows up on their shore, they don't bash in his head."

Andromeda, not really listening, looked up at Venus.

"That's where their greeting 'aloha' comes from," he continued, blowing a smoke ring. "Most still offer it, even to the crass tourist, despite the logical lessons of their tragic colonial history. Yet that's who they are, so they persist with it." He shook his head. "Indeed, aloha propelled them to brave the seas again, circling the globe on their *Hokule'a* canoe to share that wisdom with a world steeped in tribal, sectarian fear . . . to remind people who've forgotten the power of love." He turned to face Andromeda, who still gazed at the sky. "Running off at the mouth, I am . . . too much wine."

"I don't mind, Dr. Clarke," she said. "I find everything you say interesting."

He placed his hand on Andromeda's shoulder and studied her face, searching for the green hue of her eyes in the dark. "Well, I can say the same of you. I've really enjoyed helping you with your thesis."

The words struck him as idiotically flat compared to his real feelings about the comradeship he'd experienced with this freethinking young woman. How often in recent weeks had he wondered how much richer his life would've been had he met someone like her when *he* was a student at Caltech? He sighed.

Noticing, Andromeda cocked her head, an endearing gesture he now recognized as "Yes?" Despite the wine, he knew it prudent to change the subject.

"Venus is bright tonight," he commented, reaching for his binoculars. "Sea winds must have blown L.A.'s smog south. Want a closer look?"

She took the Nikons. "I love it when Venus is up," she said, noticing the planet catching the sun's light in a three-quarter phase.

"Is it the cosmology or the Roman ideal that captures your imagination?" he asked, taunting himself to step on ground he knew was dangerous. He finished his Chardonnay and poured another.

Andromeda pulled her eyes from the glasses and smiled at him. "The ideal, of course."

"Thinking of your boyfriend?" he dared.

"Yes," she said.

Jedediah puffed his pipe and pondered the odd sensation her reply created, a relief one feels when given a last chance to opt out of a harrowing—but compelling—challenge.

Andromeda put her eyes back to the binoculars. "Actually . . . I don't have a boyfriend . . . just a foolish picture in my mind."

"Uranus is the mythic idea that intrigues me," he said as if not hearing her comment, "the Greeks' sky deity. Uranus mated with Gaia, the earth goddess, and thus were born the Titans. Though the Western tale is more turbulent than the Hawaiians' creation myth, there are similarities. Their sky father is Wakea and the earth mother, Papa. In fact, in some oral traditions, Mauna Kea is named after Wakea . . . Mauna a Wakea."

"I don't know much about Uranus."

"He's here tonight, you know." Jedediah pointed his pipe stem at the sky. "Over there, to the right of Pleiades, about five degrees above the horizon, maybe ten to the left of the Trapezium. You'll recognize the distinct blue orb in the star field."

She shifted the glasses to the right. "Wow! I'm impressed. You must have good eyes to see it naked," by which she meant without binos.

"No, I consulted my stargazing software before we came out."

They both laughed.

"I can see its beautiful blue color," she said, "similar to your eyes actually."

His face flushed, but the darkness and his deep tan masked it. He knocked the char out of his pipe. "Too bad we have no green planet, to match *your* beautiful eyes."

She set the binoculars on the log and placed her hand on his. "It was you I was thinking of, Dr. Clarke . . . that foolish picture in my mind."

Jedediah reached over and took her in his arms.

❧

Seagull cries issuing through the bedroom window woke Andromeda at dawn. Jedediah, his arms wrapped tightly around her, felt warm against her skin, a remnant ember of the fire that had consumed both of them the night before. Smiling, she gently slid out of his grasp and stepped to the window. The cool breeze felt refreshing on her naked skin after so much passion, and the sea vista enlarged her distinct sensation that life was truly grand. Jedediah, instantly aware of her absence, opened his eyes. He looked up from the disarrayed sheets and saw her willowy silhouette framed by the picture window as if in a painting. *An Impressionist work*, he thought, defocusing his eyes to accentuate the shimmering light surrounding her body. "Though ill defined, full of emotion," he muttered to himself. "A picture certainly worth hanging in the living room."

She slowly turned to face him. "Did my sleepy lover say something?"

"Just musing about what ought to be a fantasy but is right here before my eyes."

Andromeda lazily stretched her limbs, then ambled back to the bed. Jedediah pulled her down beside him.

"I can't quite believe it myself," she said, snuggling, "after imagining it for so long."

"So you *did* have a prurient interest when you window-peeped me way back when."

She sat up with mock offense, folded her fingers into a fist, and punched his shoulder.

Jedediah sat up next to her. "I wish I'd met you years ago."

"My dad wouldn't have allowed it."

"Snot-nosed kid, I suppose not. But the long wait has rendered me pretty damn old."

"Not on the inside, Jedediah. In that way you're young, much younger than most of the guys at school. Your ideas are fresh, yet timeless . . . and you certainly haven't forgotten how to make love," she said, smiling.

Propped up now on pillows, they stared contentedly out the window, the sea bright blue under cloudless sky.

"Speaking of fantasies," she said, "I had an unusual dream this morning, of stars and planets . . . and even a beautiful goddess." She tucked a fingertip under her lip. "I wish I could piece together the details—that's what I was doing at the window—but I'm afraid they've slipped way. Whatever that dream was made me wake up happy."

"I used to dream of a goddess, and now she's right here next to me."

"Oh god." She curled her lip. "Talk about corny."

"No, really, Andromeda, you've no doubt heard about my notorious sojourns to the roof of the Millikan tower?"

"Who hasn't? 'The Madman's nighttime contemplations' are part of Caltech lore. Who were you cavorting with up there? The ghost of Mr. Feynman?"

Andromeda had never heard such a boisterous belly laugh pop out of the professor, and like his newly unveiled romanticism, it delighted her.

"No, it wasn't Feynman, though I wouldn't have minded, especially had he shown up with his bongos *and* his blackboard. It was Urania, the Greek muse of astronomy, always urging me on . . . which was crucial in those early days before my big discoveries. In fact, without her guidance up there on the roof none of those achievements could have been possible." He winked to cover the risk he took sharing his mysticism, and for good measure said, "Of course, the herbal contributions smuggled up by my loyal students may also have helped."

She assumed Jedediah was joking, and was relieved to think so. And yet, she also knew his eccentric history may well have justified his other nickname, "the crazy guru of Millikan's roof."

"How do you know it was she?" Andromeda teased.

"I recognized her cloak of embroidered stars and the globe in her left hand."

Andromeda leaped out of the bed, pillow in hand, and instinctively covered herself. "What are you? A mind reader too! That's the woman I saw this morning!"

He peered up at her, her face twisted with disbelief.

"You're not kidding me, are you, Andy?"

Her childlike surprise and trembling Dutch Boy hair made the twenty-eight-year-old seem much younger.

"Consider it a gift, Andy," he replied firmly, deciding in that instant to step onto even more dangerous ground. "Those she chooses to visit, from the Greek cosmologists on, have always forwarded our science, a field blessed by men and women unafraid of their imagination, fearlessly connected to their sources of discovery."

She let the pillow slip and cocked her head, struggling to process Jedediah's words with the logical circuitry of her brain.

"Don't try to understand it, Andromeda. You won't be able to. But please never ignore what comes in your imagination, treasures yielded by the deeper intuitive part of your mind. Dreams are part of that. Carl Jung was right when he said, 'Who looks outside, dreams; who looks inside, awakes.'" Jedediah's face took on a somber, inquisitive look that she had seen many times before. "May I ask, when you stood at the window, deciding you were happy about the dream, what you thought the goddess was trying to tell you?"

Tears she did not understand filled her eyes.

"'This man . . . ,'" Andromeda muttered, struggling to recall the exact words, "'. . . is old in spirit but young in outlook. Together you will make great discoveries.'" What she didn't repeat were Urania's next words, just coming to her after recounting the others: "The journey with him . . . however brief it may be . . . will forever change your life and our understanding of the universe."

What Jedediah didn't tell Andromeda was that Urania wasn't the only muse to visit him in his dreams. In recent years, when Mauna Kea's Poli'ahu came, she wore a snow-white cloak, without stars but luminescent, and her messages were much more puzzling for him to decipher.

CHAPTER 33

The Dark and the Light

The morning after Erik's meeting with the oracle and the young Hawaiian practitioner, he sipped a dark cup of espresso in his lawn chair next to the Airstream, pondering his imminent afternoon visit with Hoku. The early September winds off the sea carried a crisp hint of fall. "Transitions . . . ," he muttered, "and the changes that come with them." He lit a Marlboro.

When he went back inside to refill his cup, Erik recalled Hoku's description of her studio and realized that he'd often passed the tiny red cottage with saffron trim while walking to the black-sand beach near the end of the road. Once he'd even paused to ponder the weathered tiki in the yard and listen to the hollow *bong! bong! bong!* of the bamboo wind chimes under the eave. Indeed, each time he'd passed that funky oceanfront cottage, it reminded him of his own sanctuary on the river. Even so, knowing he would be there soon, Erik felt unsettled. "What's in store now?" he said to himself.

His apprehension continued all morning, so after lunch he sought distraction by picking some flowers for his afternoon host from Sunny Boy's yard. But as he assembled the bouquet, second thoughts entered his mind and he left it in the galley. To center himself, Erik decided to walk to Hoku's cottage, and intending to swim afterward, he wore trunks, flip-flops, and a T-shirt.

Hoku's four-foot statue of Kanaloa peeked out from a thicket of ti plants so old that they now towered over the cottage. Two banana trees flanked its bright yellow door. Only as he walked up the path did Erik recognize the vehicle in the driveway. He'd seen that dusty white RAV4 parked at various places on the mountain, though he'd never noticed its bumper sticker—the word "EARTH" with the letters ART emblazoned in red.

"Aloha, come in," Hoku greeted without embracing him.

Inside, the cottage was just as intriguing as its exterior—a living space only twice the size of his Airstream, with a kitchen on one wall, a sleeping cubby on another, and the rest of the room set up as a painting studio. A large casement window with numerous panes, some with stained glass, opened out to the sea, and a double French door led to a small freshwater pond bounded by lava. An easel held a cloth-covered painting in the center of the room near a worktable, and a stack of canvases faced a wall. A tall, sea-smoothed stone draped with a fresh garland of ti leaves stood atop a low bookshelf containing neatly organized volumes on art and Hawaiian culture. Two photographs shared the stone's shelf, a small snapshot of Hoku with Aunty Moana and a larger picture of a man in a military uniform, which Erik took to be her father.

"Great house!" Erik said, the bohemian setting easing his apprehension. "There's nothing like living on the water, is there?"

"I'm very fortunate," she agreed. "Even a little cottage like this is now out of reach for most islanders," a tinge of dismay in her voice. "My family on O'ahu built this for my great-grandmother after the '46 tsunami. After finishing my MFA, they asked if I wanted to caretake it for our 'ohana." Our family.

"I'm looking forward to seeing your paintings, Hoku, if you're still willing. I know Aunty Moana kind of pressured you into this."

"If she hadn't asked, I wouldn't."

Erik's cheeks flushed.

"But Aunty has something in mind, I think, and I usually trust her instincts. She's one of those elders who like to give you riddles to solve . . . so let's do it."

"You sure? As a photographer, I know showing your art can feel pretty intimate."

She nodded, motioning Erik to sit in a sagging overstuffed chair in the corner of her workspace.

"Iced tea?" she offered, stepping to her miniature refrigerator. "It's mamaki."

"Sure, thanks," he said, noticing the pleasant splash of waves issuing through the window and the open French doors. "Keaukaha's a great neighborhood, isn't it?"

"A special community." She handed him the glass. "You're lucky to live here, you know."

Hoku took her work in progress off the easel and leaned it, still draped, against the worktable. She replaced it with one of the canvases stacked against the wall.

Erik's reaction to the abstract stunned him. Its murky purples, blues, and blacks made him feel as if death brooded in the foggy swirls daubed throughout the canvas by her brush, the sorrow evoked by the oil disturbingly raw with no representational forms to diffuse it. Even an impressionistic rock or tree would have helped.

Hoku studied Erik's face as he examined the painting. "I call this *Life in the Real World*," she said finally.

"Interesting," he muttered as a substitute for saying nothing.

Inwardly she smiled at his reaction, and then replaced that canvas with another.

Erik felt relieved—until she stepped away from the easel. Splotches of blood red splattered a dark field of the same somber hues as in the first painting, some violently smeared into jagged ridges with her palette knife.

Three images flashed through Erik's mind—that iconic 9/11 photograph of the fireball blowing apart the South Tower, the bullet's gash beside the Keck mirror, and Murdock Kemp's cabin cruiser drifting downriver in the starlight after Erik had freed its mooring lines. Erik needed to smoke a cigarette but dared not ask.

"Well?" she said, crossing her arms. "What's your reaction to this one?"

"Your paintings are intense," he said truthfully. "So much so, they're a little hard to look at."

Now she smiled openly, and Erik saw it.

"Frankly, I think the one you did for Aunty Moana is better," he said tersely. "You have any others of the lake?"

"No," she replied, reaching for another canvas. "The lake is too sacred to paint, like saying the word 'God'—a feeble substitute for the real thing."

"Yet you painted it for Aunty Moana."

"Yes," she said. "That was different. One day chanting at the lake, my naʻau said, 'Aunty needs to experience this.'" She didn't tell him that with that insight a white ʻio soared in from Puʻu Poliʻahu and circled high above the lake. "Aunty's heart is not strong and her doctor won't let her travel above 10,000 feet. So I made the painting. Yesterday at Aunty's I realized why I'd been instructed to break the kapu. With the lake draining, Aunty needs that painting so she can pray at its shore without risking going up."

Hoku shuffled through the paintings leaning against the wall and set her next selection on the easel. The sallow face of a haole man, ripped in half by a jagged brown line, nearly filled the canvas. His eye sockets were empty, and his gaping mouth spewed dark hues all over the canary yellow around him. Pinned to the lapel of his business suit were three symbols—a crucifix, an American flag, and a dollar sign.

"This is *Lack of Faith*," Hoku said, staring at Erik with taunting eyes.

He leaped to his feet. "Listen, Hoku! You can't shock me! Why do you think I bolted for the South Seas! I've had a belly full of *that* America! I know it better than you ever can!"

Hoku, startled, stepped back.

"I don't know what you call that second painting—the one full of rage—but I know those feelings all too well! They're what takes hold of you when you've had too much of that sad fog you painted in the first canvas." His face was bright red.

"And see that?" He thrust a finger toward the regurgitating face on the easel. "He's like the men that ruined the river with their sewage and suburbs and stole my freedom with their corporate greed!" Another, unbidden thought came to his mind: *And broke my father's heart and the spirit of my best friend!*

Tears crowded his eyes, and it pissed him off. *Why can't I just be angry? Why does it always come with grief!*

Hoku stepped closer to him. "E kala mai, Erik . . . I'm sorry."

"Yeah, sure."

"Aunty told me you weren't a typical haole, but . . . I've been disappointed before."

Erik pushed his face forward and ran a finger across the flushed skin of his cheek. "It's not about this, Hoku." He brashly tapped his forehead. "It's about this. The problem is the stupid ideas people have in their heads!"

No wonder Aunty can relate to this haole, she thought, *he's not racist.* The elder had tried to teach Hoku that it wasn't a person's skin color that mattered or even their ideas—stupid or otherwise—but the *heart* they held open to others. And on that score, Hoku had failed miserably that afternoon.

"I'm really sorry, Erik. Aunty would be very upset with me." Hoku walked back to the easel and turned the canvas over. "Truth be told, I was mad at her for setting up this 'show and tell' . . . and I took it out on you. Will you accept my apology?"

"OK," he muttered, but it was just politeness.

Hoku surprised him with a repentant hug, and for the first time Erik felt her true aloha. A wan smile softened his face. "I guess I still haven't figured out how to cope with the kinds of emotions you portray so brutally with your paints . . . except to put a distance between them and me."

"And that's why the South Seas?"

He nodded. "But I've never been able to forget the river."

"Of course not. Why would you want to?"

Erik walked to the open window. "Hoku, imagine that everything out there vanished except the sea itself—the way people live, the things people believe, the environment along the coast—all irrevocably changed. That's what happened back home. And then Dad died, fighting to the last with his damn newspaper." Erik couldn't bear to bring up the worst—Jack.

"Why didn't you fight too?"

"With what? All I had was my camera. Besides, I'd be damned if I'd waste my life fighting a losing battle against a dysfunctional, neurotic society where all you can do is complain or cry . . . and with no effect. Or worse, become a goddamn cynic, like all those malcontents posting their opinions on Instagram and Twitter! Sure, my dad was a hero, but it cost him his heart, and then his life . . . and what difference did that make?" Again Jack pressed in on his mind.

Tears welled up in Hoku's eyes. "What you experienced on your river Hawaiians have dealt with for generations . . . with one major difference. We have no place else to go. This is our last island."

Erik finally let his own tears flow.

"Look at us," Hoku said. "Some hard-bitten misanthropes, eh?"

Wiping their eyes, they both laughed.

"Erik, can I show you one more painting?"

"Oh God."

"No, really. It's the one I'm working on now." She exchanged the painting on the easel with the cloaked one leaning against the worktable. "I started this after Aunty urged me to spend more time on Mauna Kea."

It was a larger, even more flamboyant painting than the others. A shimmering white peak rose out of turbulent seas under a starless void mottled with weird purples, blacks, and burgundies. A golden meteor with a human face flamed toward the mountain. Tranquil, sea-green eyes and a blue, anguished mouth stood out among its androgynous features. The details in the mountain were left undone.

"Whoa . . . I can feel your conflicts in this one."

Hoku stepped back from the oil, tilting her head one way and then the other. "Conflicts? Huh. I would have said contrasts."

"But that moody sky, the weird mouth . . ."

"Aunty says the dark and light—both creations of nature—exist to give definition to one another. Without the dark, we would not recognize or appreciate the light, and vice versa. She says to wish that ignorance and cruelty did not exist is to misunderstand the nature of life and our responsibilities."

"Sounds like a rationalization to me," he said impulsively, then remembered Aunty Moana's story about the Vietnamese monk.

"It's ancient thinking, Erik. The part I can't figure out—and that's why the painting isn't finished yet—is, What's the solid ground we're supposed to stand on? If we live in our pain, or cynically accept it as the way life is, we're lost. Morally, I mean. If we pretend there's no pain, we're ignorant—or mad—and that won't work either. So how do we live in such a world and still keep aloha?"

"I guess when you figure that out, you'll fill in the mountain."

She nodded. "You're a sailor. What's your reaction to that sea? I didn't consciously paint it that way. It's just how it turned out."

Erik stepped close to the painting. "Those waves could sink a ship."

"Yet the mountain—like our island—rose out of that turmoil and now stands tall and strong above it."

"I don't know, but I'd like to see this painting when you're finished. May I?"

"It may take me a while."

Erik glanced over at the stack of canvases she hadn't shown yet. "What's in the other paintings?"

"You'd be surprised, I think. They're mostly things I did when I was younger, pretty pictures without much substance—palm trees, flowers, and seascapes—all representational, not an abstract or expressionist among them."

"Really?"

"I did those before my father died . . . in Iraq."

She passed her hand through the air, as if to swish all that away. "Are you getting hungry? I've got some fresh poke and poi . . . and cold beer. We could sit by the pond and watch the sunset."

"That'd be nice. Let's do it."

Erik and Hoku dangled their feet in the cool water, savoring Hoku's own blend of raw fish chunks with seaweed and her cousin's taro mash. They said little as their bodies turned to gold in the evening light and they watched the distant mountain they both loved become a purple silhouette above the Hamakua Coast.

"I'm glad we followed Aunty's advice." Erik said, raising his bottle of Heineken. "Thank you."

Hoku smiled with a warmth he had not seen before, or even imagined she was capable of. The formidable countenance of her chiseled native face, while still bold, softened, and the luminescence he'd seen in her eyes on the mountain returned.

CHAPTER 34

South Seas Protection

As the sun dropped close to Mauna Kea, Hoku suggested they take a dip in the pond, and Erik readily agreed. "Hop in," she said. "I'll be right back."

Hoku stepped into the cottage to don a pair of surfer shorts and a jog bra while Erik gathered up their dishes and set them near the door. When Hoku returned he was already swimming about in the small but deep pool.

"This is great!" he said. "Bracing!"

"The freshwater in this pond flows all the way down from Mauna Kea," Hoku said, easing her body off the smooth lava lining the pond. "That's why it's so cold."

It was the first time Hoku had seen Erik without a shirt and she immediately noticed his tiki of urchin spine dangling below the surface.

"Where did you get that?" she asked.

"On Mangareva in the Gambiers." He lifted it out of the water to give her a better view.

"May I touch it?"

"Sure."

She held the carved urchin spine in her hand, and chicken skin rose on her arms. "This is an image of Kanaloa . . . and it's old. How did you get it?"

"My third year in the islands. I was on Mangareva for two months, waiting out the hurricane season between boats. Mangareva's a tiny island, and I got to know the people pretty well, including a Parisian expat and an old fisherman who'd taken him under his wing, Papa Kai. I spent my last month on the beach helping those two refinish Papa Kai's old plywood outrigger."

Erik's face, ruby in the last light, took on a wistful look, and his eyes smoldered. "Mangareva . . . 'the floating mountain' . . . what's left of a long-dead volcano that you see far offshore when you approach the island. The ocean side of that mountain looks like a high citadel wall. Papa Kai lived inland near its base, and from his weathered plank house you could see the lagoon where they dive for pearls. On his neck, as a talisman, the old man wore a beautiful medallion of mother-of-pearl shell."

Hoku's eyes brightened with surprise, as if the cloth covering an oil painting of Erik had just been removed.

"Papa Kai had traveled in his youth and knew a little broken English, and my vagabond friend René could translate the combinations of French, Tahitian, and English that we used. While we scraped and repainted his outrigger, the old Mangarevan shared stories about his life in the Gambiers, Marquesas, and Tuamotos— his fishing grounds. He asked me through René about my South Seas travels and my life on the Mississippi, as we ate smoked fish, oysters, and popoi, their fermented breadfruit mash." Contentment washed over Erik's face. "Lots of smiles and laughs, occasionally a bit too much beer. Those months on Mangareva reminded me of the happy, innocent world I grew up in on the river. Anyhow, when we finished the outrigger—a few days before I caught a packet boat back to Tahiti—Papa Kai took me out in his canoe alone, which that day he had rigged with its mast and sail instead of using the 20-horse.

"'No fishing today,' Papa Kai said with one of the few English phrases he knew. René translated the rest as he helped us push the canoe into the turquoise lagoon. Papa Kai said, 'We honor our weeks of work with a debut voyage, and show our sailor friend Erik what a Mangareva canoe can do.'"

"'A joy ride!' I said, and René translated.

"'No!' Papa Kai replied sternly in English. Then in French he said, 'No matter how peaceful the day, sailing is *never* a joy ride! The sea is too powerful—too alive!—to carry frivolous sailors. No!' he said again in English.

"His sudden harshness threw me. *'Ah oui, je comprends,'* I said with the little French I'd learned. 'Yes, I understand.'

"'*N'oublie pas!*' he said. 'Don't forget!'

"That was my first time in an outrigger. Papa Kai sailed the canoe across the lagoon and beyond the reef into the open sea. Watching that eighty-five-year-old man deftly handle this small, speedy, and sometimes temperamental craft was impressive. *'Fantastique!'* I declared, which Papa Kai acknowledged only with a contented smile.

"It sailed low in the water, the rolling swells just inches away. Schools of fish passed beneath us, and a big turtle popped its head up to see who glided overhead. At that moment a shadow passed over the outrigger.

"'The bird . . . you know?' Papa Kai said, pointing at the silhouette soaring above us in the blue sky. I recognized the angular contours of its six-foot wingspan. 'Frigatebird,' I said.

"'Iwa!' he said in Tahitian. We watched the frigatebird as it circled us three times, then headed back out to sea. 'A sailor . . . *ancêtre—à moi et la vôtre.*'

"It took me a moment to piece together from René's lessons what the old man had said, that the bird was a sailor ancestor of both him and me.

"'Maururu,' I replied softly in his island language. 'Thank you.'

"Papa Kai smiled, then pointed at his seat in the stern. 'Next time, you here!'

"I did sail the outrigger, the next day, with calm, wordless guidance from him. Again we saw an 'iwa, this time far out to sea. When we returned to the beach that evening, he gave me this urchin spine talisman, an heirloom he'd intended to give to his son. He said it would protect me on future voyages."

"Did he tell you why he didn't give it to his son?"

"No, but René did. His young son died of leukemia, like others in that part of the Pacific after the 1974 nuclear test on Mururoa when much of the South Seas was showered with plutonium fallout."

Hoku's eyes overflowed. "Mahalo for sharing that story with me," she said.

In silence they watched the sun drop below the mountain, leaving the Keaukaha coastline in muted light reflected off the sky.

"Shall we?" Hoku said, placing her hands on the pool's lava ledge.

"Good idea," and the two climbed out of the water. Hoku stepped inside to get towels and two more Heinekens.

"Would you tell me about the river?" Hoku asked when they were settled back on the pond's stone bank.

"Ah, the Mighty Mississippi." Erik gazed at the sea beyond the pool. "The 'Great Waters,' as the Ojibwe say, both titles well deserved. The Mississippi has a power akin to your volcanoes or even the sea. With all its tributaries, that river drains half the continent, and nothing stands in its way when it floods . . . trees, buildings, levies. Even its own limestone banks give way. To live beside such a river is a privilege."

"I'd like to see it. Do you have photographs?"

"Many. I'd love to show them to you but I left them with my brother back in Minneapolis."

"Maybe someday I'll be able to see your river in person. I know Aunty never forgot it."

"Do you know why she went to Minnesota?"

Hoku paused, checking in with her na'au. "Yes. I can share that. Do you know a place called Pipestone?"

Erik nodded. "Where Plains Indians quarry the reddish claystone used in their sacred pipes."

"Their *peace* pipes," she said, "smoked as prayer. A Dakota woman took Aunty there, part of their vision quest . . . but seeing your Mississippi River was also a significant event on that trip. Her friend took her to the river first, driving along the bluffs to a special place where they spent time in the water."

"Wow," Erik said, taking a long, thoughtful sip from his Heineken. "Another coincidence."

As the beer loosened his tongue, Erik shared more about his once contented life on the river and his "half home, half studio" houseboat on its bank. Hoku's luminescent eyes, now absent any skepticism, showed a kindness that compelled Erik to share with her even more deeply than he had with Freddie and Sam. She learned of the old voyageur Labathe, of the ancient burials atop the bluff and the great effigy mounds downstream, and of Erik's personal totems, the beaver and the elusive night heron.

"You almost sound like one of us," she said.

He smiled. "Aunty Moana told me that the spirit of the land and those who have walked it comes up through your feet . . . if you pay attention. As a child, I did that naturally. That's why old man Labathe used to call me a 'river rat,' referring to the muskrats who make the river their home. To him it was a honorific term. You don't get that title just living near the river. 'You have to live the river,' as Labathe used to say."

"A wise man . . . ," she said ponderously. "When I was a UH student in Honolulu, I was oblivious to the real wonders around me. I craved the fast lane, the cool clothes, the jewelry. I saw myself as an avant-garde artist babe, hustling the brawn down at Rumours nightclub and drinking too much at Ginza. I made good money at a Waikiki gallery. My paintings were gorgeously shallow back then, beautiful in technique but empty . . . just like me. The tourists loved them! I even got some Honolulu notoriety . . . because of the money.

"All that changed when Dad died in the war. Like a lot of local guys, Dad was one of those National Guard 'weekend warriors' that helped during storms, floods, and tsunamis, including on the mainland. We never imagined him going to war overseas. And for what? Anyway, I came to the Big Island to heal. I met Aunty Moana in the sea one day and she took this damaged city chick under her wing. Her teachings changed my life. Of course, at first I didn't know what to think of her. She's kinda out there."

Erik laughed. "Yeah."

"You would never know that she once lived a pretty conventional Honolulu life. But then . . . so did I."

"I was kinda spooked by her," Erik admitted. "She was always eyeing me from that ti patch next door, smiling with those missing teeth. Now that I know her, I'm ashamed at my reaction. She has a huge heart, even if she is a little 'out there' . . . as you say."

"Did Aunty ever tell you how she lost her teeth?"

Erik shook his head.

"During a protest vigil, right here in Keaukaha. Hawaiians had gathered at Puhi Bay to pray for the Home Lands Commission to finally give six local elders the lots they were entitled to by federal law. They'd waited on the list for over thirty years while the commission leased acres and acres to business and government—for Walmarts, Home Depots, even the observatories' offices and planetarium in Hilo. The county council was about to hand over even more land for a Walmart superstore."

"You're kidding."

"Fed up, and worried the elders would die before they got their lots, Hawaiians organized a protest. Aunty convinced them it should be a prayer vigil *for* the elders, not a protest *against* the politicians and developers. She supervised the building of a beautiful stone altar above the bay where people could make offerings. And the first prayer that day asked Ke Akua to give those commission members the strength to do the right thing . . . to be pono.

"There'd been a lot of protests, peaceful but increasingly militant—about GMOs, geothermal development, expansion of the Pohakuloa military training area, sovereignty, and of course, the endless push by astronomers to build more telescopes. So when the Hawaiians showed up, so did the police and an FBI SWAT team, riot gear and assault rifles in tow. They started arresting everyone. Two of the protesters, hotheaded Iraq War vets, lost their cool and started punching back. Everything went wrong, and in the process a cop shoved Aunty Moana face-first into the altar."

"Christ! I had no idea there was so much trouble in Hawai'i."

"It seldom made the mainland news . . . until the TMT blockades . . . but Hawai'i has become a tinderbox, with decades of volatile fuel waiting for the right spark. People like Aunty, people who've seen too much violence in their personal lives, are working hard to keep that from happening. Anytime I let my frustrations leak out, oh brah, is she on my case!"

"Why doesn't she fix her teeth? She's so beautiful otherwise. Is it the money?"

"No. Aunty says that after that cop smashed her face—you'll also see scars on her forehead if you look close—she fell into despair, mired in her own sorrow and the woe of her ancestors. Ugly thoughts poured into her mind, and she got scared, worried her damaged heart would never be free to love again. She's been trying to find compassion ever since, because she believes that when Hawaiians lose their aloha they are no longer Hawaiian. She says she won't replace those teeth until every bit of rage inside her is gone. She says that the gaps in her smile remind her every day that a person in anger is not whole."

"Wow, that's commitment. By her standard, I'd have no teeth."

"I wouldn't have many either."

The picture of repression and the prospect of violence shook Erik all over again, but the story of Aunty Moana's commitment put it in a different light. He thought of his father's courage to defend his ideals without entertaining despair—or running away.

"Can you see now why Aunty was so upset about the Keck mirror shooting? It may seem small compared to the terrorist acts inflicted on—and by—your people, but it's a sign of danger . . . that things might someday get out of hand. Has she talked to you about Captain Cook?"

"No, she hasn't. Of course, I read about Cook in South Seas tourist magazines, and in high school they taught us about his three Pacific voyages . . . and his death in Hawai'i."

"I can just imagine *their* rendering of that history. You should ask Aunty about it. Cook was killed on this island, along with other crew and many Hawaiians. It happened when a toxic mixture of fear, pride, and cultural ignorance got outta hand. Aunty says there were warnings—ho'ailona—and missed opportunities to defuse the conflict . . . all ignored." Hoku paused to sip her beer. "And so England's greatest explorer perished and our ancient tradition of aloha was forsaken in reaction, during a regressive period when warfare was already playing too big a role in our lives."

Hoku watched a dark wave break against the lava reef below them. "It was a good thing you joined us yesterday *after* I'd broken the news to her about the shooting. She was beside herself and had barely recovered by the time you showed up. What you didn't see was the leftover anger still inside her from all the injustice . . . anger that surfaces even in her when the locals respond in kind."

Erik and Hoku talked into the night, each realizing they had more in common than either would ever have imagined. When the moon rose at midnight, Erik snubbed his cigarette on the rocky ledge and got up to go. "I guess now we know why Aunty Moana wanted us to get together today," he said.

Hoku, her face full of moonlight, beamed. "I think so."

Just then an owl passed over the pond, the whoosh of its wings startling them.

"A pueo!" Hoku exclaimed. "One of Aunty's 'aumakua!"

"'Aumakua?"

"A spirit form of her ancestors. It's come to acknowledge us."

They watched the bird move up the shoreline and alight on the limb of a kamani tree.

Without a word, Hoku dropped the towel she'd wrapped over her shoulders and slipped back into the water. She gently pushed off the lava and drifted to the other side of the pond, then motioned Erik to join her.

They floated on the surface in silence, their faces moonlit. After a few minutes, Hoku climbed out of the pool, and Erik watched her towel off. Despite the icy water, a warmth rose in his body. *If I had had a sister*, he thought, *she would have been like Hoku*, and he felt grateful that Aunty had put them together.

Another, less pleasant thought washed into his mind too. "There's something I need to tell you, Hoku," he said, climbing up onto the ledge. "You remember that newspaper story about the astronomers wanting to put the Big Eye on the summit ridge?"

Her face darkened, as surely as if a cloud had shrouded the moon. "Yes."

"Well, that very night is when the Keck mirror nearly took that bullet."

"Oh my god!"

"And it wasn't the first incident that's been kept under wraps. There was a vehicle theft at the Keck dome in March and some people believe Kyle Oʻokala's truck wreck last year was sabotage."

"Sabotage? I'd read about that old accident but I had no idea . . ."

"I think the police are afraid that if news of the shooting gets out, we might have that spark you talked about earlier."

"Does Aunty know any of this?"

Erik shook his head. "I don't think so."

"This is a small island. It's only a matter of time before people find out. And then . . ." Hoku put her hands over her mouth, her eyes watering.

"What?"

"We didn't expect anything like that when we leaked the Big Eye story."

"You?"

"An insider gives us information. I was the one who insisted we leak it. Aunty wasn't sure, but she reluctantly agreed that we should follow my naʻau. To be honest, it was my anger that made me do it. And now . . ." Hoku crumpled to the ground and wept.

Erik knelt beside her and took her hands. "Hoku, what?"

"The spark," she choked. "That newspaper story was the spark . . . and now the lake is draining!"

CHAPTER 35

Ignition

"Rifle Bullet Strikes Keck I Telescope," read a small headline on page 3 of the next morning's Hilo *Tribune-Herald*. The one-column story described the two-week-old shooting in words so vague Erik wondered if the county police chief who was interviewed actually knew what had happened. The article left the impression that the incident was probably a hunting mishap that "only nicked the telescope's frame," and made no mention of the bullet almost hitting the mirror. Despite the chief's downplay of the incident, its import was lost on no one. Indeed, with more than a hundred employees on the mountain, word of the near miss had already reached the island's coconut wireless and the dominant interpretation was "this was no 'mishap.'"

"The astronomy community is astonished by this news," said Dr. James Bushmill in a story posted a few hours later on the *Honolulu Star-Advertiser* website, the UH astronomy director parsing his statement to leave the impression he'd only just learned the news. Dr. Adam Jacob, tweeting from Caltech, went further: "If this wasn't a hunting accident, we can only assume some unhinged lone wolf got stirred up by Hilo's anti-astronomy fringe who never understood the importance of our work."

Officials from Keck immediately decided to install security cameras inside and outside their buildings, and several other facilities, including the Smithsonian array, followed suit. Hawaiian elders on the observatories' longtime cultural advisory committee strenuously objected, worried that cameras would make it impossible for Native Hawaiians to conduct traditional ceremonies at their sacred sites in private. Observatory administrators, caught up in reaction, rejected the elders' plea.

Back in California, Dr. Jacob set up a teleconference with Air Force General Michael Todt to discuss whether the shooting might foreshadow things to come if they chose Mauna Kea's summit for the Big Eye. "We have effective means to control that sort of thing," said the general, his eyes as cold as stone, "especially since 9/11. I'll organize the surveillance."

The elder Tom Williams was less surprised at the news than his son, Tommy. Tom's generation knew well that ugly things happen when people's emotions run rampant. They'd lived through three years of martial law imposed on Hawai'i after Pearl Harbor, Roosevelt's order to arrest their innocent Japanese neighbors, and Truman's annihilation of Hiroshima and Nagasaki. But to Tommy those events were just paragraphs in history books. His ideas of conflict were formed by watching TV episodes of *Magnum PI*, *Hawaii Five-O* reruns, and NFL football. The horror of 9/11 and subsequent terrorism, and the anti-Muslim prejudice that followed, injected some cruel reality into the younger Tom's perspective, but all that seemed far away from Hawai'i.

As soon as Tommy grasped what had happened—"a goddamned terrorist taking a potshot at million-dollar mirrors"—he was outraged. Unlike his father, who held some ancestral guilt about how his missionary ancestors had treated the islanders, Tommy felt abused by the incident. It was as if the shooting was a personal assault on progress, which Tommy, like most of the chamber, equated with economic prosperity.

The only businessman who smiled at the news was Pano Kamalu, not because the Hui chief wanted any mischief to disrupt the next "golden egg atop the mountain," but because as a second-generation crook whose father taught him to "reserve aloha for your own tribe," he could viscerally appreciate the audacious violence of the act.

It took all of Sam Chun's seasoned diplomatic skill to keep Koa Makaliʻi from endorsing the shooting on Honolulu's KITV news that evening. Sam was all too familiar with the hot-headed community college professor's outbursts, having fought other environmental battles with her, including the Army's expansion of its firing range at Pohakuloa Training Area (and he'd privately worried that Koa's tirades against PTA might have incited the drone shooting that only he and a few others had yet caught wind of). Sam believed Koa's incessant ire was caused by what he called "activist PTSD" from all her battles against endless assaults on the islands. He also knew that most Hawaiian activists were uncomfortable with Koa's rages but, like Sam, they put up with her because they sensed the deeper pain she carried.

Willy McRae chose to believe the telescope's marring was caused by a hunter's wayward bullet. It was simply inconceivable to him that anyone would attack an astronomical instrument of such wonder. His millennial daughter, on the other hand, readily believed the worst when informed by another Caltech student. Andromeda may have inherited Willy's optimism, but her generation had grown up in a polarized America, puzzling over their parents' passive "happy talk," so she valued frankness to a fault. She was offended by the sniper's act but not incredulous and immediately called Jedediah Clarke at his Malibu bungalow. Knowing he opposed more telescopes on Mauna Kea, the intensity of Jedediah's reaction confused her.

"This is terrible!" he blurted into her cell phone. "Terrible! What kind of nut would do that! Jesus!"

After she hung up, Jedediah paced the bungalow, wondering what kind of nut *he* was for leaking Caltech's plans to build the Big Eye on the summit and Haisley's idiotic scheme to inter his carcass underneath it. Jedediah had hoped the real facts of the matter would kill the project early and avoid the kind of long, bitter conflict—akin to the TMT fight—that he knew would happen once the usual bullshit hearings started. Instead—unlike the TMT clash—violence had already raised its hideous head and would aggravate long-standing schisms between islanders and outside exploiters. Now everyone would be forced to take sides. Black and white.

"Imagine if I'd leaked the stuff about the military connection!" he muttered to himself, shaking his shaggy head. That bit of explosive news would soon come out anyway, without his help. It had to. The astronomers and the Air Force were already playing a dangerous game in delaying the announcement, hoping to build business and community support for the "wondrous" Big Eye before people found out it would play a surveillance role in America's continuing "war on terror." Jedediah scrounged through his freezer until he found an old stash of pot long ago left by a student. He grabbed a bottle of Chardonnay and a jar of peanuts and headed down to his sailboat.

At the base camp, speculation about the shooting was the hot topic. Freddie figured an inebriated hunter had probably done it, more pissed off about the "mass extermination of mouflon and goats from state helicopters than the mass building of observatories." (He'd long believed the drone sniper was a hunter upset at PTA for taking over more and more prime hunting grounds.)

Moses shook his head when he saw the *Tribune-Herald* article, and he moved around the camp with grave lines on his usually placid face. Jeffrey Drake's oddly calm pronouncement—"What else would you expect?"—puzzled Moses, especially after noticing Drake's fidgety demeanor and marijuana on his breath, two things that normally fired up the cook's harangues.

An even more peculiar reaction that morning came from the reserved Braddah K. The news had so upset K that Moses stepped in to take his place in the kitchen. "I've told K to sit out this shift," he told the crew. When K showed up later to prepare lunch, he was jittery and inept, confusing recipes, dropping a saltshaker into a pot of split pea soup, and frequently stepping outside to get air. Moses pulled him aside.

"Keola, you better go home to Hilo," advised the elder, probing the cook's sweaty face.

"I no 'tink so, Uncle. I stay so funky I no can drive."

"What's wrong? Can I help?"

K just shook his head and went back to his dormitory room.

Only Moses and Jill knew that no one at the camp had more justification to applaud the retribution than the quiet, affable cook who'd lost his sister to observatory transgressions. But Moses couldn't believe that he was involved, even knowing that K's father had given his son one of his hunting rifles. More likely, the attack on the telescope had brought back Keola's memories of the arson that long ago killed his sister. Or the cook, like many other Hawaiians, was upset that violence had again touched their sacred mountaintop.

Erik tried several times to reach Hoku, but she wasn't at home. Kicking himself for not getting her cell number, he finally left a terse message on her home voicemail: "Hoku, this is Erik. I'm afraid we have ignition. Call me when you get a chance."

Late that afternoon, a call came into the base camp for "da mountain rangah." A housekeeper forwarded the call to the guard shack where Jill Kualono was commiserating with Freddie.

"Mauna Kea ranger."

"Dis da wahine rangah wen' work up dere?"

"Yeah."

"Eh! Try listen close, you," the voice muffled, as if speaking through thick cloth. "Dis da guy wit' da rifle. Newspaper get 'em wrong. Was no accident, ya know."

"What? Who is this?" Jill pulled a notepad out of her breast pocket.

"Dat night jus' da beginning, sistah. I t'ink maybe I goin' really wreck somet'ing . . . know what I mean? For all wot's happened . . . all da shit! I jus' might, ya know . . ."

"Freddie," Jill whispered, her hand over the mouthpiece. "It's the sniper. Go to the office and call the police. See if they can track it. Sounds like a cell—junk reception." Freddie was off on winged feet.

". . . or maybe blow away one truck. I wen' cry why I say dis, sistah. Can you hear dat?"

"I do," she replied in a focused ranger voice, scribbling his words on the pad.

"But, eh, what can I do? Dey no listen! Dey wen' nevah listen! Dat 'Eye' telescope dey wanna build on da mountain? No can! NO CAN!"

Sweat formed inside Jill's uniform, but outwardly she remained calm.

"Bad, ya know, fo' me talk like dis . . . but WHAT CAN WE DO?"

"Braddah, dat won't work," Jill replied, consciously dropping into pidgin but still speaking as evenly as her personality allowed.

The caller was sobbing now. "Gotta. Dey wen' took da queen. Dey wen' took da land. Dey wen' even took da iwi o' da kupuna!" Ancestors' bones.

Chicken skin erupted on Jill's back and her na'au shifted into full gear. "What iwi you talkin' 'bout, cuz? Mauna Kea bones?"

"Mauna Kea, Kalihi, Hilo, Honolulu, Kaupule, Makena, Maku'u, all ovah. C'mon, sistah! You know I wen' tell da truth! Dees guys, dey no care. Dey build dat t'ing up top, dey jes' gonna disturb *more* bones!"

"Dat's not goin' happen, cuz. Big Eye goin' Chile, dat's why. Too much pilikia. No need worry."

"Bullshit, you! I know dat bullshit! You talk li' dem! I goin' now."

"Wait, braddah! We all gonna fight dat stupid t'ing! You see."

A long pause, then crying.

He's stoned, Jill thought, *or really drunk*. "Braddah, you called me," she said. "What can I do fo' help you?"

Sniffles, then the dial tone.

Was that fo' real? Jill wondered, staring hard at the phone. *Or some lolo blowhard jes' makin' trouble?* She looked out her windows at the cinder cones lining the road. "Den why he cry?" she said in reply.

Aunty Moana was napping in her hale when that call came in to Jill. She snapped awake as if struck by a bolt of lightning. Soaked in sweat, her chest tightening, she felt certain she was having another heart attack. She reached over to the crate that served as her bedside table and fumbled through its clutter. Her fingers finally found her vial of nitro. She snapped it open, shook out the bitter pills and pushed one under her tongue. She fell back on the daybed, breathless, and stared up at the thatch. Images invaded her dizzied brain, and she closed her eyes to concentrate until distinct pictures passed across her eyelids like frames of a movie across a screen.

Dark wisps of cloud swirled about the mountain's cinder cones, out of which darted shadowy figures across the stark terrain. They were sort of like people, but not. Then the crack of a rifle's report! Everything stopped—the swirls, the shadowy figures, even the howling wind that seemed to be rising. And then . . . only the wind was there, so strong and wild that the mountain's cones and moraine disappeared in an amber cloud of ash.

Then . . . people gathered around the exposed lakebed, muddy cracks where the lake's water had drained away. They chanted, summoning the gods and the ancestors. At first, the people cried and cried, the mountain above them still veiled in swirling dark clouds. Gradually the cinder peaks cleared and everyone smiled, then laughed, then hugged each other and exchanged breath. A luminescent shimmer opened up in the sky above the gathering—Poli'ahu watching, affirming. As water bubbled up from the cracks, hope brightened everyone's face. Wisps of dark energy—like elongated black birds—flew up out of the rising lake and vanished far away.

Aunty Moana opened her eyes. She breathed normally now, and the sweat was gone. She sat up against her pillow and gazed out the window. *Spared again,* she thought, *to carry out a mission for Poli'ahu.*

CHAPTER 36
Possible Suspects

Nothing more was heard from the caller, and the police had been unable to trace his call. A special agent from the Honolulu FBI office, Muku Makau, joined the county's police investigation, and because Jill Kualono had taken the call (and had once had a fling with Agent Makau at a Waikiki law enforcement conference), he suggested she be brought in on the case. Jill was delighted to get into the action. She also liked Makau, a former Oakland cop, now back in his hometown with 'the agency.' He was straightforward like her, and even more candid. Makau wasn't as smart as Jill, but she figured his zeal for solving crime—and his brawny good looks—made up for that.

"It was a .270 Magnum rifle that pelted that steel," she said to Makau, pointing up at the scar on the giant telescope, her words echoing in the cavernous dome. She reached into her jacket and pulled out the shell. "Here's the casing."

He rolled it between his beefy fingers. "You always withhold evidence?" flashing his watery brown eyes.

"I gave the cops almost twenty-four hours before I started my own investigation. It's not my fault they're so frickin' dumb."

"You'll have to show me where you found this."

"Bumbye." By and by.

"I think the police found the smashed bullet in the dome. We'll check your shell against that."

Back at the base camp, sitting at a table in a vacant observatory office, Jill briefed Agent Makau on all she'd discovered, even showed him the pictures taken on Puʻu Poliʻahu (without mentioning Erik). Makau, more familiar with police and military weaponry, made a note to check the range of a .270 Magnum hunting rifle. Jill also told him about the stolen Keck vehicle scuttled out on the north plateau in April and the missing lug nuts on Kyle Oʻokala's pickup that eerie November night almost a year ago. Makau was a fully urbanized Hawaiian, and part haole, so Jill omitted the mystical aspects of those events and the naʻau messages she'd received. Jill's rugged face flushed as she recounted each occurrence.

"I wanna get that son of a bitch!" she blustered. "This shit doesn't happen on the mountain! Not on my watch!"

Her outburst reminded Makau of Jill's volatile nature. He'd read her detailed account of the would-be sniper's conversation, and given the tense situation, he was all the more impressed by Jill's empathetic handling of the caller. *She may be in a cush job now*, he thought, *but she's still a pro.*

"Tactics, brah," she replied when he asked about it, her bravado stirring his old attraction.

"You say the caller sobbed over the phone. What did you make of that, Jill?"

"Probably was on some shit—dope or booze—something that brought out his real distress."

"Ice?"

"No way, Muku. This guy was sane, and meth woulda made him mean and lolo."

"Sounds like he was pretty pissed off though."

"Yeah, but sad . . . and full of guilt too."

"So you think the caller was legit? The real sniper?"

"I wondered about that, but my gut said yes. Otherwise, why blubber like he did?"

"Hmmm."

"Fact is, Muku, I think this guy may have done more than just take a potshot at a telescope . . . either that or he's got a lot more ugly shit planned."

Agent Makau stuck the end of his pencil under his lip and gazed out the window at distant Mauna Loa. "This kinda thing is usually done by someone tied into the place somehow, like a disgruntled employee—past or present. Could also be a ticked off construction worker or a regular visitor to the mountain who's nuts."

She nodded.

"So who is he, Jill?"

"You tell me. The FBI has experience with terrorism. I don't."

"Terrorism? You mean this could be political violence?"

"Call it what you will. This guy recited all the injustices, even mentioned the queen. And Oʻokala's truck carried a message too—'abandon the mountain.'"

"Hmm." Makau rubbed his handsome chin. "We learned about political movements in our training at FLETC," referring to the Federal Law Enforcement Training Centers on the mainland. "Civil disobedience sometimes turns violent, but the lone sniper or bomber is another thing. Even when politics is a part of their act—in this country at least—that's usually just a surface excuse for a mentally disturbed person to go off. But our FLETC instructor said that assumption's starting to change with the growing divisions in the US . . . seems like everybody's pissed off now."

Makau tapped his fingers against the tabletop. "And our shooter only fired once. Why's that if he really wanted to off the mirror?"

Jill got up and walked to the same window Makau was looking out of. She placed herself so close he could smell her green uniform. "I wonder, Muku," she said.

He stood up, narrowing the distance between them. "Why? You got suspects in mind?"

"Some who fit your typical description." She peered into his smoldering eyes and remembered looking up at them from tousled sheets. "Three insiders, all cooks. Jeffrey Drake, a loudmouthed, doped-up crank with more axes to grind than a lumberjack. A year ago a rumor passed through the camp that an Army drone at PTA got snipered, and the favored staff suspect was Drake. He's unstable, in my opinion capable of anything."

"Hmm," Makau said with stern professional skepticism on his face. "Not just a blowhard?"

Jill curled her lip and shrugged.

"Who else?"

"Keola Kuamoʻo—'Braddah K'—also a cook. A shy, mild-man-nered Hawaiian, but his baby sister was murdered years ago in an arson fire set by someone who wanted to shut up his father from telling the world that burials had been dug up when they built some of the early telescopes."

Makau whistled, jotting down details in his tiny notebook. "And your caller did mention bones . . ."

She nodded. "My third insider seems unlikely, but I'd keep him on the list. He's a new guy on the mountain, been here about two years, a drifter, Erik Peterson . . . and a friend of one of the activists, Sam Chun. Peterson's a nice guy, respected by the Hawaiians, but once in a while he flies off the handle. Says it's the Viking in him. Sometimes he gets real blue. Tries to keep it under wraps but I can see it. And he was up here that night. I'd like to know who he was in the past. Know what I mean?"

The agent nodded, recalling how she was always unnervingly acute. "Think any of those guys was the one you talked to on the phone?"

"Hard telling. The caller had a sock or something over the cell. He also spoke pidgin, but I wondered if it was just part of his cover."

"We need to investigate all those possibilities, Jill. I notice the suspects on your list are all men. Any chance the person on the cell was female?"

That hadn't even occurred to her. "Sure sounded like a man to me . . . but then, the voice *was* muffled."

"Any women suspects come to mind?"

She thought a moment, shifting her weight so her hip touched his.

"There is this strange wahine, often up on the mountain, elusive, a Hawaiian practitioner. But . . . I don't really think so."

"Name?" he asked, pen poised.

"Later. Lemme think on it."

Makau closed his notebook. "Mahalo for sharing your list, Jill. I'll check 'em out. Your suspects are real different from the ones the Keck Observatory guys gave me. They assume the sniper is totally driven by politics."

"It's possible, I suppose. The locals *are* fed up. There's always been tensions, what with different races living together, and with the latest flood of haole newcomers, who knows?"

"Things are also tense in Honolulu, Jill, a lot more than when you were on the force."

"Yeah. Plenty Big Islanders lost their homes after the '80s hotel boom jacked up all the prices, then that real estate bubble in the early 2000s, followed by the recessions. Foreclosures . . . homeless . . . like Waikiki. And now all these well-heeled retirees from the mainland jacking up prices again. We even got gated communities, like on O'ahu, filled with boomers who only interact with the locals when they order a drink at the golf course. Even the Hawaiians are getting shaky. Most of us still hope for the best, but after the 'old boys' pretty much derailed the sovereignty thing . . ."

"There's something I don't get, Jill," he said with that fleshy furrowed brow she found so endearing. "Where's Mauna Kea come into it? I mean, compared to everything else, a few telescopes doesn't seem like such a big deal."

"Most people don't realize that battle has raged on this island for like forty years, 'cause until the TMT blockades, it all happened in hearing rooms. Hawaiians showed up to complain, astronomers claimed their science was sacred too—one guy even called his dome their Sistine Chapel—construction company execs packed the hall with union guys wearing pro-telescope buttons, while the 'old boys' worked behind the scenes to get the permits approved. Enviros disillusioned, Hawaiians despondent."

"I guess I was still working on the mainland when a lot of that stuff happened."

"It was more a Big Island thing, Muku. I didn't know the details till I moved over from Honolulu. Then along comes Caltech and the University of California with their Thirty Meter Telescope—an eighteen-story dome twice as tall as the state capitol."

Makau shook his head and whistled again. For the first time, Jill sensed the native in him was shocked.

"But no more room on the summit so they tried to open up the north plateau. That straw broke the camel's back and moved the battle right to the mountaintop, starting with blocking the TMT groundbreaking in 2014. That was the beginning of civil disobedience. A new generation of Hawaiians joined the old-timers—Hawaiian Studies students, kids from immersion schools, hula halaus . . . millennials willing to become activists. And lotsa other folks too . . . locals, enviros, hunters. Over sixty thousand people signed an online petition, and then hundreds showed up to block the road at Hale Pohaku.

"The good news was that the protests were amazingly peaceful—militant, yes, but peaceful—the leaders steadfast about keeping aloha, even toward the police and us rangers. Oh, a few folks yelled at us and some guys put rocks in the road to block the bulldozers, but most of the protesters were civil, even during the arrests."

"So what happened? How did we get to those huge protests I saw on TV?"

"Things got tenser and tenser, one showdown after another—on the mountain and in the courts. Eventually, as you'd expect, the haoles won the courtroom game and the Hawaiians came back to block the road, only this time with thousands . . . including keiki and kupuna, cultural icons, and even Hollywood and sports celebrities. Thirty-four elders were arrested—us rangers had nothing to do that!—which only fortified the protesters' resolve."

"Yeah, right," Makau said. "Whose dumb idea was that?"

"Anyway, eventually the governor caved, the cops went home, and the TMT guys backed off . . . for a while. Then they adopted some culturally 'woke' rhetoric and tried to regroup with support from local politicians. Even the National Academy of Sciences tried to salvage the plagued telescope, but that didn't really go anywhere. By then something like half a million people had signed that petition—and some young astronomers had one too.

"Actually, things got relatively calm . . . until Caltech announced the next telescope, the Big Eye. Thing is, it'd been in the planning long before the big stink over TMT. The only questions were, Would it be sixty meters or a hundred? and, Where—here or in Chile? Long story short, a few days ago the newspaper revealed they want to build the Big Eye here."

"I get it," Makau said, looking up from his pad. "Here comes one whole 'nother round of pilikia."

Thousands of feet down the mountain, another briefing was underway, this one beneath coconuts in Keaukaha. Aunty Moana was uncharacteristically somber, listening to her elderly visitor, with her na'au as well as her ears.

"The energy of the mountain has been changing for some time," murmured the ninety-two-year-old woman sitting on Aunty Moana's lanai. The big wicker chair dwarfed her tiny frame, but her mana filled the whole lanai. Her face was deeply creviced from the corrosion of age and decades chain-smoking her long-stemmed pipe, handed down from her great-grandmother, the overthrown queen, Lili'uokalani. Within her wizened face, her black eyes sparkled like stars.

"Despite our best efforts, Moana, negativity grows in our islands . . . most of it turned inward. Family abuse and drug addiction fed by despair. Community discord nourished by crime, corruption, and injustice. And what's the impact on our 'aina of all these soldiers and weapons of war now present on every island?" Her shaggy white brows dropped into a furrow. "Mauna Kea rises to the very top of the whole island chain. Eventually all that negativity had to affect the mauna too."

Aunty Moana's eyes watered. She hated to hear these truths uttered aloud.

"And I wonder about all these recent arrivals from America, a land steeped in cynicism, a people besieged by fear and negativity for decades. For centuries, our akua kept the tools of war off the mountains with a barrier of purity. Have the Americans sensed that too, or have they already, secretly, violated the kapu against weaponry up there?"

The ancient woman set her skeletal hand on Aunty Moana's plump arm, the veins in her fingers as blue as the octopus tattoo on her wrist. "But it's not too late, wai puna." Sweetheart. "However, we must be diligent . . . and quick with our response. Prayer is the key, as it always has been. After all we've been through, do not lose faith now. After all *you've* been through, Moana, stay the course you set for yourself when you came home, the same route your great navigator ancestors took."

Despite her mentor's comforting words, Aunty Moana's face was flushed with anxiety, her infectious smile still lost in frown. "And what of my vision?"

"To gather at the lake? Yes, yes. I told you!" the pitch of her raspy voice suddenly higher. "That must go forward! Immediately!"

"I meant the *other* vision, Aunty."

"Oh." The ancient woman leaned back, and the wicker weave groaned. Her shimmering eyes looked out to sea, and a sigh escaped from her soul.

"I have seen it too. The winds are on their way." She held a finger up as if detecting the first breaths of the maelstrom. "But the love we have spoken about, Moana, our faith, will be all the more important after the disaster. Yes, people may die . . . even children. And much will be lost. But Kanaloa would not send the winds without purpose. We must make sure our people understand why. Perhaps even the foreigner should know. That I cannot say."

CHAPTER 37

Vision and Faith

.

A week later, a squally September sea brought showers to Keaukaha the morning Hoku and Erik were to meet with Aunty Moana on her lanai. The full moon, still up, brought an unusually high tide, and waves thundered against the reefs. Erik had not yet arrived and the two Hawaiians conversed at the card table over steaming cups of coffee. A red-eyed, black-crowned night heron flapped low over the cove, its short, hefty body sinking briefly with each stroke of its wings.

"'Auku'u!" said the elder, her puffy face and tired eyes signs of a restless night. "The ancestors are watching . . . we must do our best." She gazed at the bird as it moved down the shore, then smiled. "He'll let them know we're trying."

"Did you read the newspaper this morning, Aunty?" Hoku said, eyeing the *Tribune-Herald* on the table, her body pulsing with tension.

The elder nodded gravely.

Hoku pointed at the front-page article, with its color illustration of an asteroid plunging toward Earth and a small black-and-white photo of General Todt. "How are we supposed to respond to that?"

Aunty Moana took a deep breath and exhaled. "With love."

"With love?" Hoku got up and paced the lanai. "It's not enough they want to build another monstrosity on the summit and bury their beer maker under the telescope! Now they've invited the Air Force to join the party!"

Aunty Moana set her fingertips on the illustration. "So this is what they call a 'near-Earth object.' I feel fear in that picture . . . deceit too." She leaned forward to examine General Todt's icy features. "Appropriate name for a man with a cold face . . . the German word for death and the name of the Nazis' famous weapons minister. Hmmm . . . ," she mused. "Was that German perhaps an ancestor of this man?"

Hoku's eyes flashed. "What a clever game they play! Inciting people with fear of apocalyptic collisions! For every asteroid they look at with the Big Eye, how many enemy satellites will they take pictures of with their GOD? It's not enough they practice sea war on our ocean and land war in our valleys, launch missiles from our beaches, and track satellites from Haleakala. Now they want to spy from Mauna Kea too!"

Aunty Moana grasped Hoku's hand, interrupting her stride along the rail. "Calm your grief, child."

"I'm not sad," she blurted, her eyes rimmed with tears. "I'm mad! How could the astronomers—heaven gazers—cut a deal with the military? You said they were just ignorant, not evil. Do you still believe that, now that they've teamed up with the Air Force?" Hoku's wet eyes, fixed on the general's picture, boiled with anger. "I hate them, I hate them all!"

"Hoku!" Aunty Moana grasped the young woman's other hand and squeezed both.

Weeping and ashamed, Hoku looked away from her mentor's shattered face. "I'm sorry, Aunty, I know anger's not pono, but I feel this way because I love the mountain so much."

"Don't you understand, Hoku? Love and hate cannot occupy the same space. It's impossible. Loving hearts—and all humans are born with them—cannot stay loving once hate is allowed in. As Dr. King said, 'darkness cannot drive out darkness, only light can do that.'"

"I know, I know, but Aunty, the mountain . . ."

"Don't try to justify your anger by claiming your love made you that way. That's *your* failing. Either you're in aloha or you're not. You

can't have it both ways. This is the wisdom of our elders! This is why
we still walk the earth, why we survived—*how* we survived. Part of
our task, what we learned through all our many trials, is to guide the
ones who don't yet understand. If you forfeit this wisdom because
of personal weakness—your lack of courage—you abandon your
culture and humanity."

Hoku sat down across from her mentor and wiped her eyes.
"Over and over, we've given them our aloha, Aunty, and they always
take it as a free gift."

"Love *is* free. What some of them don't understand is that *not*
giving love has a terrible cost."

"So we're supposed to sit by and let them take everything? Destroy
us as a people?"

"We only do that, Hoku, if we give up our aloha and become
less than human. Why do you think so many in the world now hate
Americans? Because they fear America, and with good reason. To
regain their humanity, Americans will need our loving guidance,
not our fear and anger. Perhaps that is why Ke Akua keeps drawing
them to our islands, so they can learn another, more universal way
of being. Over the centuries, many people have come here, and we
have influenced them, as they have influenced us. First came the
Chinese, and we discovered those master sailors were much like us,
with similar wisdom. Then the Spanish, but like other Europeans,
they did not recognize us as human, so we knew their culture had
already strayed from the universal path of love.

"When Captain Cook arrived, he also mistook us, but it was under-
standable. By then, five hundred years of Tahitian influence had altered
our culture, and our deepest traditions were less visible, especially to
British officers interacting mostly with royal chiefs and priests."

"What do you say about the missionaries, Aunty? They preached
the love of Jesus while denigrating our culture."

Aunty Moana sighed. "Ahh, the tragic path of those courageous
people. They sailed all those many miles to honor their prophet, and
when they got here they let fear of the unknown overshadow their
love, and allowed their instilled sense of guilt—a need to purge all
sin—blind them to our deepest character. Had their book not taught

them 'original sin,' they might have recognized who we really are and learned something from us too."

"Exactly!"

"But those were *other* cultures, Hoku. Look at our own difficult history, before the Western boats arrived. What did we Hawaiians do when the Tahitians took over by force? They called us 'mana-hune'—those of lesser spirit—and even demoted our family chiefs. We showed them aloha . . . and yet they enslaved us. We tried to teach them the lessons of teamwork we'd learned in the canoes, and they sacrificed us for their altars. Some of our people lost their faith along the way, but most of us kept loving, and we survived that scourge and the European and American ones that followed."

Hoku turned to look toward the sea, her face contorted with confusion. "I want the world to be the way you say, Aunty, but I can't help feeling we've been suckers. The queen should have called up her troops and stopped the overthrow. It would have been easy against that small band of insurgents and US marines."

Aunty Moana face flushed. "So you think Lili'uokalani was a 'sucker'? That she failed her people when she kept the peace?"

Hoku turned back to face her mentor. "Oh, Aunty . . ."

"I'll tell you something, girl," plump finger pointed at Hoku's heart. "That woman had faith. Even under attack, she lived aloha. Think of the courage that took in her time—after haole diseases wiped out thousands of us, after missionaries robbed our dignity and banned our religion, even after her own brother, King Kalakaua, was poisoned. After all that, our queen kept her faith, that universal faith that Jesus, Buddha, King, and Gandhi all drew upon when they faced adversity. Against bigger odds than we face, the mahatma won his country back from the British Empire with militant nonviolence."

"And then his own people assassinated him!"

"Yes, and that's the lesson, Hoku. A fellow Hindu nationalist shot Gandhi because he wasn't anti-Muslim enough, indeed had fasted to restore Hindu-Muslim peace. The assassin couldn't accept that Muslims were fundamentally the same as himself.

"It is the mark of our people that we've sought affinity with those different from us. We married non-Hawaiians and bore children together. We tried to defend our Japanese neighbors when the Americans interned them after Pearl Harbor. And for all we have struggled against the American colonizers, we have never seen ourselves as fundamentally different from them. From a different culture, yes, but humans, and we treated them thus. We have always given them aloha and hoped that someday they would realize the wisdom of that view."

"I still say she should have called out the troops."

"Had the queen squelched the overthrow with violence, had any marines or plantation owners been killed, the Americans would have sailed back on that news and killed the few of us left. Instead, President Cleveland, an honorable man, sided with us against the revolutionaries and the Congress."

"Yeah, but Congress undid that, and even Cleveland went along."

"True, but eventually Congress did apologize in an official decree."

"Right—a hundred years later!"

Hoku looked down at the newspaper. Fat tears dropped onto the face of General Todt. "Oh, Aunty, I just can't bear it. I don't have your kind of faith. I know you've tried to teach me. I just can't do it."

Aunty Moana slid her chair next to Hoku and cradled the young woman in her arms. "You're wrong, Hoku. Having faith doesn't mean you won't stumble. God knows I have."

Both women fell silent, each gazing at the turbulent sea. Aunty Moana sighed. "When the first telescope appeared on the summit, I took it to mean that Ke Akua wanted to launch a spiritual discussion between our people and the scientists, to begin a conversation about humanity's place on Earth and in the universe. Maybe, I thought, through their noble science and amazing discoveries astronomers would contribute to the movement away from the shortsighted tribalism that had held back humanity for so long. Instead, they brought the prejudice of their ethnocentric culture and missed that opportunity. I was dismayed, then angry, for I had publicly defended them and their telescope to our own people. Eventually I realized my anger was wrong, that their madness does not mean we should become mad too. We must never lose *our* hold on reality, even when they do."

Hoku nodded slowly, absorbing the significance of her elder's admission. "I'm sorry, Aunty, for what I said about the queen."

"I know you weren't really talking about the queen, Hoku. You were talking about your father. He went to Iraq, killed for the generals, and didn't come back."

~

Erik jogged down the village trail, a spray of heart-shaped anthuriums bobbing in his hand. He noticed the elder sitting alone at the card table, deep in thought.

"Sorry, Aunty Moana," he panted, handing her the flowers. "You know Sunny Boy—he wanted to blab about that newspaper article on the Air Force and the Big Eye. When he gets started, it's impossible to get away."

Aunty Moana smiled so broadly her missing teeth showed. "He doesn't know it, but your landlord did us a big service this morning. Mahalo Ke Akua!"

Erik, accustomed to not getting it, shrugged his shoulders. He glanced into the little thatched-roofed hale and was surprised—and deflated—that the young woman was absent.

"Hoku not here yet?"

"She's in the water. She'll be back in a few minutes. Want some coffee?"

"Yes, please!" Erik said, as he followed the elder into her hale. "Coffee's comfort food for Scandinavians."

She chuckled as she loaded her old Presto percolator with Folgers.

"Hoku said I should ask you about Captain Cook."

Aunty Moana looked up from the pot, her face suddenly grave. "A sad moment in our history, heralding our troubles with Western empires."

"What happened?"

"Kealakekua Bay," she muttered ponderously, "home of my ancestors . . . 1779. For weeks we hosted Cook and his two ships of sailors with food, water, gifts, ceremony . . . our women. Then King Kalaniopu'u asked his new British friend to contribute his armed ships and marines to a naval assault on Kalaniopu'u's archrival, King Kahekili of Maui. The stoic captain refused, and relations quickly soured."

"Did the Hawaiians really think Cook was a god?"

"Ahhh . . . the European myth of Lono," she laughed. "Imperial histories are full of such canards—the foolish natives mistaking the fair-skinned colonizers as gods, then giving away their land for a mirror or a necklace." She shook her head. "Amazing those myths still persist.

"Anyway, Cook finally left the island," she continued, "but not before ordering his men to steal the wooden statues of our gods from the great temple above the bay . . . to burn as firewood aboard his ships."

"That part wasn't mentioned in my high school history class," Erik said sarcastically.

"No," she replied, handing him a hibiscus-adorned mug of steaming coffee. "There's a story in my family. An oracle living in the kahuna compound near the heiau pointed at the departing ships and declared, 'Cook is a dead man.' This was neither threat nor curse, but a premonition.

"Sure enough, within days the winds of Kanaloa shattered the mast of Cook's ship—the *Resolution*—and then nearly ran it up on the rocks as they limped back to Kealakekua, the only safe anchorage along that coast. He was not well received, and during the days it took Cook's men to repair the broken mast on the beach below the desecrated temple, some of our people grew surly. Tensions heightened—fed by both sides—and one night Hawaiians paddled out to the *Resolution* and stole one of its shore boats.

"Mind you, this happened right after Cook strung one of our people up on the ship's shrouds and lashed him with a cat-o'-nine-tails while the whole village watched from shore."

"Why?"

"Retribution for stealing a blacksmith's tongs from the ship. Notice, Erik, how gripes always escalate—a pocketed tool leads to a flogged islander, which results in a stolen boat . . . and ultimately to a murdered chief and a kidnapped king. After that, all hell broke loose, and the king's warriors rushed Cook and his musket-firing marines. Within minutes the famed explorer, several of his men, and many Hawaiians lay bloodied on the lava shore. "

"Wasn't Cook way outnumbered? What was he thinking?"

"He wasn't. It was British pride." She shook her head. "Ethnic conceit underlies most clashes. But even worse was yet to come. Grief and fear in the hearts of Cook's men turned to hatred and rage, and they torched my ancestors' compound beneath the temple. Several kahuna were bayonetted, their severed heads spiked on poles hauled back to the *Resolution*."

"Christ! That part never got into our history lesson either."

"Wasn't it Winston Churchill who said 'history is written by the victors'? *All* societies adopt their own dubious narratives, but hopefully some truth tellers persist to challenge them." Aunty Moana glanced through the screen window and spotted Hoku stepping out of the water. "Here comes Hoku. Let's take our coffee outside."

Hoku was calmer when she returned from her *hi'uwai* in the sea. The salty waves had cleansed her spirit and swept away much of her angst. Her pause in the sea had also given her an opportunity to connect with her ancestors and, with their guidance, think more constructively about her father's death and the telescope. Hoku's dark, earthen eyes glowed with tidal energy and her heart beat briskly with renewed resolve to follow the pono path. She strode up to the table and reached down to embrace the young man.

"Aloha, Erik," she said warmly, reflecting the bond they'd forged a week earlier at her seaside cottage. Then, to Aunty Moana's pleasant surprise, Hoku placed her forehead on Erik's and they exchanged their breaths.

"I showed your pictures of Lake Waiau to the other elders," said Aunty Moana. They've decided to gather at Waiau to begin the healing. We will commence at midnight and continue until dawn. The kaula—our oracles—will be there, along with healers and a kilo honua who can read signs in the earth. A very old pahu drum will be brought up, along with conches and other ceremonial tools. I'm inviting you two to participate. You were the ones who brought us the distress call from Waiau. Please come if you can."

"I'm . . . honored to be asked," Erik said, wondering if his apprehension showed.

Aunty Moana took his hand. "I truly hope you will come. I have a special task for you, if you're willing. It would be a great help to me."

"OK," he said.

Aunty Moana turned to Hoku.

"Of course, I'll be there, Aunty. Mahalo a nui." But Hoku knew that to participate in a healing she would have to work harder to soften her heart and toughen her faith. "When will it be?" she asked.

"I don't know yet . . . but soon. The date is being set by a kilo hoku and a kahuna kilo kilo—a Hawaiian astronomer, Erik, and a priest of our sky omens. We must act quickly before the lake drains and things on the mountain get worse."

A wind gust, the strongest of many that morning, blew Aunty Moana's extraordinary hair back from her head. She looked out to sea and spotted the dark, angular wings of a huge bird halfway to the horizon.

"'Iwa," she said, her eyes riveted to the frigatebird. "Are you coming ashore?" She raised her face into the wind. "Storm already on its way?"

Erik and Hoku glanced at each other like two siblings decoding the words of a parent, then looked back at their beloved elder.

CHAPTER 38

Collateral Damage

The night after the article about asteroid defense appeared in the Hilo newspaper Moses Kawaʻaloa tossed in his bed, agitated that the Air Force now openly participated in the Big Eye. After lying awake an hour, he crawled out of bed. Might as well just go up, he thought, and by 2:30 a.m.—three hours earlier than usual—he was on his way from Hilo to the base camp.

Six thousand feet up the Saddle Road—within eyeshot of the ancient cinder cone where Mauna Kea protectors had built their 2019 encampment—Moses pulled his old Bronco over and got out to look at the two mammoth volcanoes flanking the road under star-studded skies. The only lights on Mauna Kea caught his attention, the orange glow of the sodium lamps illuminating the base camp three thousand feet above him. He shuddered—and not because of the cold winds blowing through the saddle. "Gotta stay on my toes from now on," he muttered, climbing back into the truck.

Ten minutes later, as the Bronco groaned up the last steep incline below the base camp, his intuition was confirmed when a pueo crossed the road, the owl's yellow eyes flashing in the truck's headlights. "OK," Moses said, "Makaʻala." Eyes open.

Moses' feral feline friends heard him stirring in the kitchen and meowed outside its big steel door. The four ragged cats followed him down the concrete loading bay to a clump of gnarled mamane trees below the dining room where he always fed them. As the cats tore into the two bowls of table scraps, Moses noticed a pair of headlights coming up the road.

He glanced at his watch: 3:45. *Who's that at this hour?*

He was even more surprised when the vehicle pulled into the employee parking lot, and he recognized Jeffrey Drake's filthy old Isuzu Trooper. The only thing not adorned by rust or cinder dust was the shiny new sticker affixed to the center of its back window: a bold, black graphic of an AR-15 rifle flanked by the words "DEFEND HAWAI'I." It dwarfed the small, faded peace sign affixed to the rusty bumper.

Instinct took over and Moses moved swiftly through the mamane trees and down the cinder bank to the parking lot. Jeffrey stepped out of the 4x4 and jumped when he discovered Moses standing behind the Trooper.

"Moses!"

"I thought you stayed up here last night," the camp manager said to the cook.

"Had something to do in Hilo."

Moses pointed at the sticker on the back window. "Besides get that?"

Of course Moses would notice, Drake thought, but why the hell is he up here so early? "Yeah, what of it?" Drake replied.

"Kind of a contradiction for you isn't it . . . I mean the gun."

"Shit! Lay off me, Moses," he growled. "Did you read the paper yesterday?"

Moses nodded.

"Goddamn Air Force! Now *they're* gonna be up here too! It's pilau"—stinking rotten—"and I wanna make a stand!"

"Is that why you brought up a rifle too?"

Even under the orange lights, Moses noticed the blood drain from Drake's face. Drake glanced into the Trooper. The nylon rifle case he'd stashed under a blanket had slipped out on the steep, winding road, the case now lodged against the back seat.

"Fuck you, Moses!" Drake started to tremble. "Fuck you!"

"So it was you who shot at the Keck mirror."

"Is that what you believe?" His eyes watered. "You, who know my history?"

"That's why I'm surprised. I know your deeper commitments. Your protests at Pohakuloa were always nonviolent, even after the MPs started arresting you folks . . . all powerful examples of your Quaker upbringing and faith."

"Yeah, yeah, including that final arrest, the one that sent me to federal prison!"

"A badge of courage, Jeffrey—of honor—like the ones your parents earned fighting for peace against the Vietnam War."

"Yeah, they sat a day or two in a San Francisco jail, but the bastards sent *me* to Victorville Pen. No one else arrested during our blockade went to prison! Only me!"

"They knew you were the leader."

"Ha! The brainy tactician."

"No. It was because they knew you were their *spiritual* leader, the pono young man with a passion and purity that inspired people . . . and kept them peaceful during all those protests."

Drake shrugged. "Hard to imagine now."

"That's what prison can do to a man, especially one with a tender heart."

"Three years in that hellhole, Moses! Three fucking years! They didn't put me into Lompac. No! High security for this peace activist. That's the cost of opening your mouth in the weeks after 9/11!" Tears fell from his eyes.

"Jeffrey," Moses said, reaching his big hand out to comfort him, but Drake stepped back.

"You can't imagine it . . . what being in there does to you."

"It tests your faith."

"Ohhhh, how easy that is to say." Drake shuddered as an onslaught of memories blew through him like a cold wind.

"You're not the only man whose suffering tested his faith . . ."

"Don't give me that shit about Jesus. Not now. I purged all that from my soul. Three years trapped inside those gray walls. That would break even you, Moses . . . man of dual faiths . . . offspring of the lucky Hawaiians whose tradition is aloha. Even you!" He jabbed his finger at the elder's chest. "The smug generals sitting in at my trial; those sadistic guards at the Honolulu federal detention center—my limbs never recovered from their boots—and the animals inside the cage, the criminals *and* the guards. It changed how I look at humanity. It would change you, too, Moses."

Drake began pacing behind the Trooper, his breaths labored and his face reddening, giving him a complexion that under the orange lights looked demonic. "That first awful year I hid from my predicament like a monk in his cell, immersing myself in biblical study and a hundred books on faith. But by the second year bile became the flavor of my existence and payback the passion in my heart. . . I should've quit reading the newspapers . . . watching our wrath played out daily in Iraq and Afghanistan, all those civilian deaths, the bullshit from Bush and Cheney, the twaddle from Congress. . . and then someone leaked news of the torture. Even after all the other rot, I couldn't believe *that*. How could Americans do *that*? It was like we'd become barbarians . . . like the Nazis as they demolished the culture and politics of the Weimar Republic, ripping up their civilization."

Again, Moses reached out to him, but Drake veered away.

"The third year was the worst. I was despondent . . . confused . . . lost. I gave up believing in anything—God included—and put on the soiled cynic's clothes I wear today, the outfit you first saw me in."

"Even so, I recognized a good man beneath the frock, a wounded man beaten down by injustice."

"And so, despite my prison record, you hired me." He stopped pacing. "You saved my ass, Moses, and I appreciate it . . . even if it did mean blue-collar work in a kitchen, even though I had to toss my Stanford diplomas into the garbage bin with the orange peels and onion skins. Even though it provided little comfort to my parents whose humiliation in Hilo during my three years in the pen chased them back to San Francisco and hastened their aging. Christ!" Drake's eyes flared as he looked into the Hawaiian elder's face. "And yet . . . it did save me from unemployment, debt . . . gave me a chance of some facsimile of normal life."

"And you were on the mountain."

Drake nodded. "Yeah, I know you hoped Mauna Kea would heal me. Maybe it did . . . at first . . . but after a few years, it felt like prison again. I knew I was wasting my time, but I just couldn't get motivated to start my life over. It seemed . . . pointless."

"That's why Erik Peterson gets under your skin, isn't it? Why you're always needling him. He's too much like you were when you first arrived at the camp, adrift, his angst and anger just beneath the surface. But he's healing, with the help of the mountain, and that threatens your decision."

Drake's eyes flared again. "What decision?"

"To give up."

Drake's fingers clenched into a fist and he stepped forward. Moses didn't move.

Drake pivoted on the asphalt and swung his fist down on the Trooper's roof, the *BANG* echoing through the cold night air like a gun's report.

"I tried, Moses!" he said, not looking at the man but up to the heavens. "I really tried, but it all started swirling around inside me. We were on the pono side in those protests—standing firm against the destroyers of Bikini who'd irradiated innocent islanders with nuclear fallout; the live-fire despoilers of Pohakuloa, Kahoʻolawe, and dozens of other beautiful places; the mad creators of chemical weapons that still fester in secret dumps on this island; the killers of dolphins and whales driven lolo by naval sonar; and now the drone trainers at PTA who teach their young recruits how to murder from afar with no personal risk to the murderer. It's fucking obscene!"

Drake's tears came again, this time in streams that ran down his cheeks. His scraggly curls trembled as he convulsed with a rising torrent of words. "And then . . . then the mountain came under attack! First TMT and now the Big Eye. Again by the Californians! The same uber-rational . . . mainland-centric . . . hard-hearted . . . exploiters! The kind of men who reduce mountains to private ambition! Who see dissent as a sacrilege and make native cultures collateral damage in a quest for their own private vision of 'progress'!"

"Don't you see, Jeffrey?" Moses said, thrusting his hands up against the torrent. "That was your moment of truth! Why didn't you join the TMT protests and become one of the mountain protectors? You could've brought all of your experience—all that soul work—full circle. You could have helped those inexperienced young people . . . and helped yourself."

Drake wiped the moisture off his cheeks, and his face softened. "Reality works just like faith, Moses. When the revelation comes—that clear, crisp awareness that gives you chicken skin—you can't undo it, any more than you unring a bell or turn back the clock. At that point the only solace comes from escape."

"The paka lolo, the fast girls . . ."

"Being holed up on the mountain. Keeping my head down and well off their radar—until I saw that goddamn article! Here they come, I thought, the same military bastards who put me in prison, marching right up onto the mountain!"

"You're making excuses, Jeffrey. Besides, you'd already put yourself on their radar when you took that potshot at the Keck mirror."

"I told you! I didn't do that . . . but I'm glad somebody did!"

"If that's true, then what's with the rifle? You despise those things!"

Drake stopped pacing and looked long and hard at the man who'd long ago opened his heart to him, the man who hadn't cared that he'd been in Victorville. "That's for shooting down drones."

Now Moses' eyes moistened.

Just then the owl reappeared, swooping down so near the two men that the wind off its wings ruffled their collars.

Jeffrey fell to his knees, tears streaming from his eyes. "I've become my own enemy," he cried out.

Moses, his eyes welling up, crouched down to embrace the younger man.

"Forgive me," Jeffrey sobbed.

"Yes," Moses said softly, "I'm sure He will."

PART FOUR

CHAPTER 39

Stemming the Tide?

The ʻiwa is a portentous creature. In some nautical traditions, its appearance is an ominous sign, for unless one is at sea, sighting the frigatebird means it has left its ocean habitat to come ashore—and only does so to dodge storms. But for Hawaiians of voyaging ancestry the appearance of an ʻiwa indicates the spirit presence of long-dead sailors. That an ʻiwa had visited Aunty Moana on the day of the newspaper article might have suggested a storm, but the hurricane foretold in her vision had not yet emerged from the sea. To her, that particular ʻiwa, spotted with Hoku and Erik both there, marked her ancestors' presence—she thought—to bring some other warning.

She pondered that insight a week later as she ascended the mountain on a nighttime journey to Lake Waiau with Hoku and Erik. They pulled over twice in Erik's old Tacoma to allow the elder's body to acclimate, first on the Saddle Road at Puʻu Huluhulu, the towering cinder cone where the protectors' encampment had once stood. There, the chanting kaula heralded the mountain's gods and the ancestors buried on it as Hoku added their ti-leaf-wrapped bundle to the other fresh offerings placed atop the tall lava rock altar below the cone. Inside were potent items gathered by Hoku and Aunty Moana and, at Hoku's suggestion, an anthurium from Erik's last bouquet to the elder.

They acclimated for another half hour in the base camp parking lot—where Aunty Moana teased Hoku about how pleasant for the young woman to be "pressed against such a warm, handsome man"—while Erik swapped Baby Blue for the more reliable kitchen pickup that Moses had lent them for the trek. Heaped in back were a dozen camp parkas he'd also commandeered for the healing ceremony urged in the oracle's vision.

Farther up the volcano, and nearer the heavens than she'd ever gone before, Aunty Moana watched for stars out of the passenger window of the yellow Ford Ranger. Hoku, squeezed between Erik and Aunty Moana, could almost feel the elder's heart racing, but the palpitations came not from her worn-out organ but from the kaula's excitement at entering the realm of the gods visited by oracles for centuries. Wispy ancestral figures, visible only to her, flitted among the starlit cones, their faint translucence reassuring. Far ahead and behind them, headlights of the other Hawaiians making their way to Lake Waiau flashed across the cinder slopes and lava flows of the ancient volcano. The whole group had bathed at dusk at a secret beach in Keaukaha, calling on the sea to dispel any negative feelings from the participants' earthly agitations.

Erik was relieved to see Aunty Moana's contented face in the lime glow of the dash. Radiant heat from both Hawaiians gave him a snug feeling that offset his anxiety at having been asked by the elder to be her "physical guardian" at the ceremony. Had she chosen him because, like her own ancestors, he had sailed the South Seas and so felt kindred? Was it because he knew the upper roads and trails and could recognize symptoms of mountain sickness? Or had she just liked the idea of having the tall, muscular Dane as personal bodyguard, someone to keep an eye out for physical dangers while she focused on spiritual matters? Aunty Moana might have asked Hoku to assume that task, but she wanted the young woman wholly immersed in the healing ceremonies, not worrying about some old lady's heart problems.

The vehicles killed their lights at 13,000 feet to avoid drawing attention near the observatories. The starlit cinder peaks stood out against the Milky Way's stellar haze. By then Hoku had made her usual connection to the mountain, and her consciousness floated on deep currents of intuition and ancestral memory. In that condition, little would pass her notice.

"Hoku," Aunty Moana said, pointing at the thousand-foot cone ahead, its peak haloed by familiar constellations. "What puʻu is that?"

"Poliʻahu," she replied in a reverential whisper.

Tears flowed from the elder's eyes. "So many times I have dreamt that cone, but it was always white."

"It will be again," Erik said, "a little later in the season. How are you feeling, Aunty Moana?"

"Just wonderful!" she beamed. "Don't worry." She reached across Hoku to squeeze his knee. "Doctors are nervous by nature . . . much too afraid of death."

The assembly of twelve gathered in an old construction staging area below the domes, donning caps, gloves, scarves, and the blue parkas Moses had provided. Two beefy men looped a nylon sling over their shoulders and hoisted a heavy sharkskin drum between them. A young man and woman atop an outcrop blew conches to herald the trek while a heavy-set kahuna, his parka draped in a kihei of white tapa, chanted at the front of the procession. Once the Hawaiians started down the cinder trail, the full impact of the thin air and near-freezing cold tested their bodily strength and spiritual resolve. Breathing hard, everyone soon felt lightheaded. The only thing that kept Aunty Moana and another of the older kahunas, seventy-five-year-old Uncle Peʻa Morgan, from collapsing was their extraordinary ability to summon help from the gods. Even so, they fell behind, and with them Erik and Hoku.

"Let's pause a moment," Erik said, stopping the quartet. Aunty Moana's face already sagged with fatigue. "Aunty, maybe you and I should go back to the truck." Even that would be a challenge.

"I must see the lake," she panted. "How much farther is it?"

"Another half mile of trail, and the last hundred yards down to the water is steep." Even under starlight, Erik could see the anguish in her face. "I'm sorry, Aunty."

"Is there someplace closer where I can at least get a view?"

"You know, I think there is." Erik scanned the near horizon. "If I take you straight to the cone's rim instead of down the trail, you would only have to walk about three hundred yards."

"I could do that."

"So could I," said Uncle Pe'a. The tall, lanky man leaned forward atop his elaborately carved staff, his long fingers draped over a chiseled image of Kanaloa like the eight arms of an octopus.

Aunty Moana took Hoku's hand. "You go catch up with the group. Just tell them we'll do our part from on top of the rim."

"I'll go tell them, Aunty, but I'm coming back to be with you."

The trio trudged on at an ever-slower pace, Aunty Moana stumbling twice on the uneven terrain. Hoku rejoined them twenty minutes later, just as the two old priests, guided by Erik, hobbled to the edge of the cone's deep crater. By then the other eight had reached the distant shore below and began preparing for the midnight ritual. Aunty Moana and Uncle Pe'a sat down on a broad lava outcrop to catch their breath. Aunty Moana's limbs trembled from the hike, and her heartbeat felt erratic, but the mountain's loving energy seemed to replenish her spirit. She took a deep breath and gazed down into the cone.

The lake was now more than half gone, but stars shone on its jewel-like remnant. Far away, Mauna Loa stood like a giant monolith above the whole planet with white-hot Altair sparkling above its summit crater.

"Aloha e Humu," muttered Aunty Moana, greeting the southern star named for a famous navigator. She scanned the sky for other navigational beacons, and spotted many. She giggled when she saw Makali'i, "the seven little eyes" of Pleiades that had guided her ancestors to Hawai'i, now sparkling like a lei of diamonds above the eastern horizon.

A peculiar feeling came over Aunty Moana, as if ancient spirits called nearby. She turned in the direction of the feeling and noticed six upright stones arranged on a flat spot just above the rim. "Uncle!" she gasped, instinctively rising. "Those pohaku feel like family."

"Wait here," he said, leaning on his ornate staff to get up on his feet.

The three watched the old priest gingerly tread the rugged terrain to get close to the shrine.

Aunty Moana smiled. "What good fortune Uncle Pe'a decided to stay with us. He's one who understands the pohaku."

The old kahuna approached each stone in turn, bending forward with great respect, as if meeting an elder. With intense concentration, he held his palm in front of each pohaku's stony face. His companions heard the murmur of his deep voice as he spoke to the spirits within the stones. Uncle Pe'a returned five minutes later, just before midnight.

"Moana, your 'ohana left those pohaku long ago, when they were still making voyages. They're happy to see you."

"I knew it," she said, tears congealing on her cheeks.

At midnight the throaty blast of conches and the deep thump of the drum sounded through the crisp air. They echoed off the summit cones, leaving the impression that many more than three souls played the instruments. Then the chanting began, and the first offerings, followed by muted sobs of the Hawaiians gathered side by side along the shore. This was the period of *ue* that Aunty Moana had seen in her vision, a spontaneous lament inspired by the primal elements to purge from the participants' hearts whatever grief might taint the purity of their prayers or cloud the clarity of their insights. It lasted almost an hour, and the four on the rim felt an even deeper closeness to one another as they held hands, embraced, or dabbed each other's cheeks with hankies.

During the next five hours the Hawaiians chanted more prayers, made additional offerings, and unrolled a ti-leaf lei that circled the entire lake, all the time registering messages conveyed to their na'au. Each, in accordance with their individual inborn talents, recognized some sign from nature—in the water, the occasional mountain mists, or the icy gusts of wind. Some saw or felt the mountain's female deities, and Uncle Pe'a, from his perch high above the starlit lake, saw the giant lizard Mo'oinanea. This legendary protector of the mountain glided just beneath the lake's surface, then dove into its depths, the tip of her tail generating a wake that some at the shore also noticed. At one point, a distinct gust of frigid wind blew down the slopes of Pu'u Poli'ahu, embracing Aunty Moana in a crisp, clean chill that warmed her heart.

Three of the kahuna—including Aunty Moana—saw ephemeral "dark energies" emerge from the cindery terrain. Agitated, they darted about erratically, taking their leave of the mountain.

As the night unfolded, all of the pilgrims felt profound contentment in having heeded Aunty Moana's vision, and the volcano's raw beauty fortified their primal link to the land. Only time would tell whether the kahunas' efforts would restore the lake, but at least two at the shore thought they heard bubbling springs as predawn twilight glimmered in the east.

Watching the Hawaiians endure the cold, thin air and their own grave sorrows to act out their faith touched Erik deeply. Many times during the night he cried, often when a soulful blast of the conches called up his father, Jack, or the river, or when he noticed the eyes of his three companions flowing with tears. *How little faith I had*, he thought, *to abandon the river and forsake Dad's legacy of service to the river and its people. And what was I thinking when I gave up photography to run away . . . forsaking the most natural way for me to honor beauty and express love?*

For Hoku, the ceremonies were devastating. Seeing Aunty Moana standing on the remote rim of the sacred cone, risking her life to join the prayers, presented to Hoku a living example of strength born of aloha, and of the faith in people that aloha relies on as its foundation. The contrast of her loving and beloved father risking his life to "do his duty for country and freedom" was too stark to manage, and she spent much of the night crying. But her salty tears were as cleansing as Kanaloa's sea, and by morning Hoku's vision was clear. Despite the long, cold night at high altitude and the lack of sleep beforehand, Hoku felt energized, as if by purging her grief and anger, poisons had been flushed from her body.

For Aunty Moana, the night was like no other. She had finally communed with the sacred lake, felt Poli'ahu in her own domain, and reconnected with her most ancient ancestors. Only joy occupied her heart, and every tear was a testament to the love pouring out of her and into her from Ke Akua. She felt so purified that when the broad shadow of Mauna Kea rose blue-gray in the west at dawn, she decided it was time to fix her teeth.

When the stars faded with first light, observatory vehicles had begun leaving the summit. The drowsy astronomers and telescope operators hadn't noticed the kahunas' half dozen vehicles parked near the trailhead, but they scarcely believed their eyes when they encountered a fleet of twenty pickups ascending the mountain road. As they passed, the somber-faced Hawaiians behind the dusty windshields unnerved them. A Caltech astronomer, impaired by his long night of high-altitude observing, panicked. When the 911 operator got his 5:46 a.m. call, he told her "all hell is about to break lose on Mauna Kea," with "truckloads of Hawaiians rushing up to the summit." He even mistook the picket signs bouncing in the truck beds for "stacks of rifles" and the traditional tattoos on several faces as "war paint." Well aware of the recent sniping incident, and startled by the astronomer's alarming message—delivered with a scientific proficiency that made his mistaken "facts" seem believable—the operator contacted county Civil Defense. Within minutes, police in Hilo and soldiers at Pohakuloa Training Area began mobilizing.

Trudging back up from the lake, the kahunas got their first hint of the summit gathering when the distant sound of conches and chants drifted down the mountain. Aunty Moana smiled, recalling talk in the community about someday holding a mountain prayer vigil. That it would be on that same day struck her as the handiwork of Ke Akua. But when the kahunas finally got back to their trucks, they could hear the communal voices carrying not only traditional chants but protest slogans as well.

"No more telescopes! Malama 'aina! Off the mountain now! Malama 'aina!"

"Take me up there!" Aunty Moana insisted to Erik.

"That's another thousand feet," he said. "You've been up here too long as it is."

"I need to go," her face dark with concern. "I *must* go!"

"No!" Erik declared, crossing his arms. "You asked me to be your physical guardian. I'm just doing my job."

"Hoku!" she blurted, fatigue affecting her judgment, "Tell him we have to go!"

"But Aunty . . . ," Hoku glanced over her shoulder, searching for Uncle Peʻa, but the elder had lagged behind them and was too far away to help.

Aunty Moana pulled herself into the pickup's driver's seat.

"What are you doing?" Hoku said, blocking the elder's effort to close the door.

"Listen carefully," Aunty Moana replied, her face suddenly calm with resolve. "They're up there undoing all we've done this morning. I can feel their fear and anger all the way down here! Someone's got to turn this around."

Aunty Moana didn't realize that in her weakened state her sensitivities had confused the source of the anger and fear she perceived. It was not on the summit. It was heading *up* the mountain in a troop truck, Humvees, and a Stryker combat vehicle from Pohakuloa.

CHAPTER 40
Insights atop Kukahau'ula

Ten minutes later, Erik and his two passengers reached the summit's uppermost switchback. Two large picket signs flanked the road, MAUNA KEA—OUR TEMPLE and PRAYERS IN PROGRESS—PLEASE RESPECT. A moment later the crowd below the UH 88-inch dome came into view. A hundred people—Hawaiians, environmentalists, and other islanders—had gathered for sunrise on the mountain's top ridge, facing the summit cone. Adorned with leis and carrying ti-wrapped offerings, the assembly was upbeat and happy. They had long ceased chanting protest slogans. That brief, spontaneous outburst was instigated by Koa Makali'i when two Parisian astronomers, having finished a night on the Canada-France-Hawai'i Telescope, had inched their sleek Mitsubishi Outlander through the throng.

At Aunty Moana's direction, Erik nosed the kitchen's yellow Ranger right up into the main body of the group.

"It's Aunty Moana!" shouted a young woman wearing a big red hibiscus in her hair.

Sam Chun turned to look. *Thank God!* he thought. Conflicting emotions and divergent leaders had confused the prayer vigil's mood, and Sam knew that the presence of someone like Aunty Moana would ensure a purer tone. Then he spotted Erik through the dusty windshield and dashed over to the pickup. "Erik! What's happening?"

"We've been at the lake all night . . . a healing ceremony."

"Ahh . . . hush-hush no doubt . . . but what timing! Our flash-mob vigil was a last-minute inspiration from another elder. The call went out through social media yesterday, and I left a message on your Airstream phone. You really gotta get one cell, brah!"

Aunty Moana swung open the door, and she and Hoku climbed out. Those nearby, including Sam, acknowledged their arrival with "alohas," smiles, and waves. Amid this group stood a young Portuguese-Hawaiian man with a warrior's bearing and brawn. His head was shaved clean, his face handsome, and his dark, stony eyes were the first to exchange looks with Aunty Moana. It was Josh Mattos.

An odd expression crossed the elder's face. "Oh no!" she gasped, hand pressed against her chest. She collapsed to the pavement.

Josh was the first to reach her. In Afghanistan every soldier had to be a first responder, and he immediately recognized the heart attack. He assigned a bystander to comfort the unconscious elder and bolted to the Gemini dome to fetch its defibrillator. In less than two minutes he was back, and in less than three he had shocked Aunty Moana's heart back into sync. Kneeling close, he watched her carefully, and when her lids finally fluttered open, her gaze again met his eyes.

"You'll be fine now, ma'am," he said. "Someone's called 911."

"Mahalo, son," Aunty Moana replied, but the crushing turmoil she felt emanating from the young man compelled her to peer deeper into his face. Tears suddenly came to her eyes. She placed her palm on his cheek and urged him nearer, so close that he could taste her sweet breath.

She clutched his hand. "Don't," she whispered. "Please don't. It's not necessary now. We need *your* heart too."

Josh jerked back, goose bumps on his arms.

She tightened her grip. "Trust me . . . I know."

Josh gazed long and hard at Aunty Moana's loving face before extricating his fingers.

"She'll be all right now," he announced to Hoku and stood up. "Keep her comfortable until the paramedics arrive."

A young woman, cell phone in hand, stepped forward. "Nine-one-one said to drive her down the mountain and meet the ambulance halfway." As the group fell to the task, Josh repacked the defibrillator and handed it to Erik, then vanished into the crowd. Several beefy Hawaiians carefully loaded Aunty Moana into the cargo space of a big, black Ford Expedition, and a haole woman covered her with two brightly colored beach towels. Hoku knelt beside her and Erik took the passenger seat next to the driver.

As the Hawaiians shut the back door and the Expedition sped away, Josh Mattos slipped back into the Gemini observatory unnoticed.

"Hoku," Aunty Moana whispered, "come close."

Hoku leaned forward and took her trembling hand.

"A vision came to me while I was unconscious on Kukahau'ula," the oracle uttering the ancient name of the multiconed summit ridge. "A *deep* vision . . . so many things coming clear now . . ."

Aunty Moana's face was suddenly luminescent. "I saw it all, Hoku, but only now . . . unfortunately . . . and only because I finally made it to Kukahau'ula, the ultimate vantage point of my kaula ancestors . . . of those gifted to see. I must pass that vision on to you. Listen carefully."

"OK," Hoku replied, also whispering.

"This morning, during our ceremony at Waiau . . . did you see the dark entities leave the mountain?"

"No, but I felt them go."

"Good," she nodded. "Let's hope all of them are gone."

"What are they?"

"Malevolent entities that bring mischief . . . even harm. They can stick to human beings, confuse them, make them do their foul work. Now I know how that Keck vehicle ended up on the north plateau. Whoever drove it there probably doesn't even remember doing it."

"Auwe!" Hoku muttered, the sun's harsh first rays jagging about the interior of the vehicle as it bounced down the ashen road.

"But the most potent entities can inflict harm on their own. I believe they're responsible for removing the lug nuts from Kyle O'okala's wheel . . . In the vision I saw three nuts unscrewing slowly."

Diving deeper into her mind, her dark eyes glazed over. "Between each of them three empty wheel bolts, their lugs already gone . . . the others fell off . . . one by one . . ."

Hoku, mouth agape, steadied herself on the shelf below the SUV's window.

Aunty Moana closed her eyes and slowly shook her head. "Somehow they muddled Oʻokala's mind . . . planted the idea that he had to drive up that icy upper road in conditions he would never defy on such a godforsaken night."

"So *they* scratched that warning in the icy window?"

"No. Oʻokala did . . . to warn us." Her baritone voice grew weak and raspy. "Lying there freezing to death, he must have put it all together."

Hoku turned from her mentor and glanced out the windows at the passing volcanic landscape, dust billowing up from the tires. "It's a frightening thought, Aunty, about those negative entities. I'm up there all the time."

"They can't touch you, Hoku. Evil spirits can only subvert the truly faithless, those who have fully succumbed to cynicism or despair."

"I never noticed anything creepy."

"That's because the mountain's loving energy is mostly intact . . . so far. Remember what I told you long ago? *Everything* is drawn to the light, including negative energies. Just as bad people latch on to good ones—the innocent, the loving—to tap their sacred mana . . . so, too, with the mountain."

"That's why our prayers are so important."

"Exactly, Hoku. But for decades people had neglected the mauna. Occupied with their own lives . . . surviving . . . or despondent . . . they neglected to send their love. Pockets of trouble popped up here and there . . . especially after some of our oldest iwi were removed. The north plateau is one of those areas affected by all this. Perhaps that's where they hid the bones they removed from Kukahauʻula. Strange things started happening . . ." Again, her eyes grew distant. ". . . trucks moving with no one at the wheel, emergency brakes mysteriously released, a tourist car erupting in flames, astronomers seeing 'weird' phenomena that confounded their logic."

"But Aunty, how did you . . ."

"Our people have always worked on the mountain. They kept us informed."

"Oh."

"The worst was that terrible fire in the Japanese dome . . . right above the north plateau. Hawaiians died in that fire . . . no question, it was a taking."

Aunty Moana closed her eyes, and tears trickled out from under the lids. Her breathing grew labored. "We were supposed to prevent all this, Hoku," she muttered after a moment. "Some Hawaiians tried, but it's difficult against entrenched powers. The mauna's sacred taboos were ignored, and eventually all of Kukahau'ula—save for the uppermost peak—was leveled for telescopes. Our spiritual anchor was weakened . . . and I'm sure the mountain felt abandoned."

"Until the battles over Keck's 'outriggers' and TMT."

"Yes, all those protectors on the mountain—all their prayers— helped but . . ." Her eyes opened halfway. "What's that noise?"

Hoku looked out the Expedition's windshield and saw the troop truck, Humvees, and Stryker rumbling up the road. Seeing alarm in Hoku's face, Aunty Moana lifted her head to watch them pass, spewing clouds of ash that coated the windows. Again her heart skipped, but this jolt struck deeper and she went pale.

"God! Where's that ambulance!" Hoku screamed.

"It's here, Hoku!" Erik shouted, the military medics from Pohakuloa having just pulled over. "They were trailing the Stryker!"

"Hoku . . . come close," Aunty Moana muttered, struggling for breath. She took the young woman's hand, the elder's fingers trembling like leaves in a gale. "If I . . . *don't* make it . . . promise to put my ashes on the mountain . . . Uncle Pe'a will know where."

Erik opened the Expedition's back door, and the medics reached in. "Ask Erik to help too . . ."

Hoku and Erik followed Aunty Moana as the medics eased her out of the vehicle onto a gurney. "I promise, Aunty," Hoku said, her face collapsing in grief, tears falling onto the cinder. "Please don't go, Aunty. I'm not ready."

CHAPTER 41

Human Frailty

Four miles upslope, the Army convoy arrived in full riot gear—bulletproof shields, batons, and side arms. The flabbergasted Hawaiians stood transfixed as three dozen camo-clad men and women poured out of a troop truck and four Humvees—all painted in the same Middle East desert camo the soldiers wore. They flanked the crowd as the squat, green Stryker moved forward to block the road. Protruding from the open hatch atop the tank was a young female gunner posted behind its M2 machine gun.

"Everyone sit!" hollered Sam, "like we talked about last night!"

"Yes! Yes! Get on the ground!" bellowed Koa Makali'i. "Make them shoot us without provocation!"

Many did sit, but others, skittish after Koa's outburst, crouched, poised to bolt down the slopes or behind the observatories. Their fidgety manner unsettled the rookie soldiers, now also woozy from their hasty 7,000-foot climb to the summit.

"Remember George Helm! They'll have to martyr us too!" Koa blurted, referring to the trailblazing native activist lost at sea while returning from an illegal protest occupation of Kaho'olawe to halt the Navy's bombing practice on the island.

Sam, crawling through the crowd, finally reached Koa, fire in his eyes. "You're not helping the situation!" he said, struggling not to curse.

A wizened old woman rose above the throng and began chanting. *"O ke akua . . . O ʻaumakua . . ."*

Despite her age and tiny frame, her voice boomed over the summit, wavering with an eerie resonance that brought goose bumps to everyone's flesh, especially the soldiers'. Her plea to the gods and the ancestors echoed off the summit cone, amplifying its already formidable effect.

"Whoa. I'd liketa get da hell outta here," said a South Carolina infantryman to his buddy from Des Moines.

"Quiet!" ordered his nearby commander, a tall, trim lieutenant colonel with iron posture and a war-seasoned face. His jaw flexed wildly. He had already determined with his own eyes that the astronomer's 911 report was way overblown. *The only weapon these people have is this frail woman caterwauling to scare the living shit out of everybody.*

"Calm down!" he barked. "And I mean everyone! Please ma'am," he said to the chanter. "Help me out."

She finished her verse, drawing out the syllables, and stopped.

"Thank you." The lieutenant colonel seemed to grow taller as he turned to the crowd. "Now, listen up! We're gonna move all you people off the mountain, so pay attention!"

Every mouth dropped. This was their mountain, their vigil. Who was the Army to order them away? *America's sposed to be a free country,* thought Sam, but he was the only one at the vigil who still believed it.

The collective rustle of twitchy feet on cinder added to the palpable unrest, and a pasty-faced trainee vomited. Other soldiers, feeling the unsteadying effects of the thin air, began hyperventilating.

A young Hawaiian man with a ponytail rose from the crowd and broke the tension by singing "Hawaiʻi Aloha," the islands' most beloved and stirring anthem:

"E Hawaiʻi, e kuʻu one hanau e . . ." O Hawaiʻi, o sands of my birth . . .

Every Hawaiian spontaneously took to their feet to sing, and the others quickly followed.

"Kuʻu home kulaiwi ne . . ." My native home . . .

"Stop that!" snarled the lieutenant colonel, aware that he, too, was getting lightheaded. "We need to move you out! Now!"

The troops girded themselves for confrontation, despite their uneasiness about manhandling a bunch of singing Hawaiians with flowers in their hair and garlands of leaves around their necks.

"*Oli no au i na pono lani e . . .*" I rejoice in the blessings of heaven . . .

The commander's face reddened. "Attention troops! Prepare to disperse the crowd!"

The soldiers lowered their face shields, raised their riot batons, and took a collective deep breath. At that moment, two infantrymen fainted from hypoxia, but in the rising clamor no one noticed. The middle-aged sergeant helping the commander organize his troops tripped on one of the ashen-faced bodies. "Man down, Colonel!" he shouted.

"Jesus," muttered more than one jittery soldier (and the lieutenant colonel thought it).

"Someone else down over here, sir!"

"Nobody move!" roared the commander, yanking his side arm out of his holster. "And I mean nobody!" He waved his pistol to direct the medic, who dashed to the closest unconscious man.

"Jones, what's wrong with those men? Any wounds?"

The tension was too much for high-strung Koa Makali'i. She took her stainless steel mug—half-full of lukewarm coffee—and heaved it at the lieutenant colonel, the only soldier not yet wearing a face shield. Though more stunned than hurt when the projectile wacked his nose, he snapped.

PBOW! PBOW! PBOW! PBOW! firing into the air.

Sam crouched close to the ground. "This can't be," he muttered to himself, "not on the sacred mauna!"

The startled islanders bolted every which way, soldiers dashing after them. A handful of Hawaiians stood their ground and continued singing.

Sam spotted a teenage conch blower cowering nearby and tugged on the cotton kihei draped over his jacket. "Come with me!" he whispered, peering into the boy's nervous eyes. "We're gonna turn this around, you and I, with help from Ke Akua!"

"Ah, OK, Uncle," he said.

Clutching the conch blower's arm, Sam pulled him close and pointed toward the Stryker. "We're going up there," Sam said. "And get everyone to calm down—with my voice and your pu. Can you do that?"

"Yes . . . yes . . . I'll try."

"Good. See those big shackles hanging low on each side of the tank?"

The boy nodded.

"We'll use 'em as toeholds and grab the side mirrors to pull ourselves up. As soon as I start addressing the group, blow your pu with all your heart."

"Gotcha," the boy replied, his resolve strengthened by Sam's confidence. He pushed his seashell into his armpit, leaving his other hand free to climb.

"Now!" Sam said, and the pair scrambled up the front corners of the Stryker. Strong from kayaking, Sam ascended quickly, but the boy struggled. Sam grabbed his free arm and pulled him aboard, then leaped to his feet.

"STOP!" Sam bellowed to the crowd in the biggest voice he could muster from his five-foot-five frame. The conch blower, by then also standing, closed his eyes and inhaled deeply, his chest rising under his kihei. He blew the seashell in a long, deep tone, amplified by the echoing summit cone.

"Hey! Whatcha doin', brah!" the machine gunner shouted, "Get offah here!" aiming the weapon's formidable barrel at a spot between Sam's shoulder blades.

Sam turned to look, and in a flash of insight, realized she was at least part Hawaiian. He spun fully around, placing his chest in front of the barrel and dropped his arms to his sides. "Guns are not allowed up here, sistah," he said. "You know that."

She glanced over at her bewildered commander, his mouth open in astonishment. "But . . . but . . ." she stuttered.

Sam leaned forward, pressing the barrel deep into his jacket. "You wanna save lives, soldier? Den we gotta turn dis around—NOW!"

The boy blew the pu again, his breath now creating a sound that seemed equal to two or three conches. At that moment, a white hawk—an 'io—soared in from the north and hovered high above the lieutenant colonel's head. Everyone but he noticed it, and the crowd inhaled in unison.

"Mean," the Hawaiian gunner said, pushing her machine gun away.

Sam turned back to the spellbound crowd. "All right!" he hollered, folding his arms across his chest. "That's enough! Everyone calm down!"

"Exactly!" yelled the lieutenant colonel, leaping up next to Sam. "I don't know who the fuck you are, and climbing up here was a goddamn crazy idea—but it worked." He holstered his gun.

"OK, commander," Sam said, "let's do this together so no one gets hurt."

"Affirmative," the steely officer said, no longer befuddled. In that instant, he decided he'd blame the fiasco—and firing his pistol—on high-altitude confusion. For the moment, he was satisfied to clear the summit with help from Sam and, at Sam's request, the wiry old chanter.

"Somebody from 911's gonna get an earful from me," said the commander after they'd managed to get both sides back into their vehicles.

"Good!" said Sam. "By the way, at some point we're coming back up here, and when we do, we expect no interference. Agreed?"

The lieutenant colonel nodded. "Count on me to trashcan any more dumbshit orders. And thanks for helping get this mess under control." The two men shook hands as the commander's sergeant approached.

"You always bring that bird with you?" the sergeant asked Sam with sarcasm.

The lieutenant colonel's eyes narrowed. "What bird?"

Sam turned to point up at the sky, but the 'io had vanished. "Ask your soldiers. They'll fill you in," Sam said with a knowing smile.

The islanders' vehicles drove down the mountain, followed by the convoy, while Sam and the lieutenant colonel watched from the summit. The Hilo police, far below, had only just reached Hale Pohaku. As the long line of vehicles snaked down the steep road, two helicopters roared up from the saddle.

"Now what!" growled the commander, standing with Sam by the Humvee.

"You tell me."

The lieutenant colonel grabbed his combat binoculars from the dash and peered up at the choppers.

"KGMB . . . KHNL," he read off the ships. "Dammit! Looks like we're gonna be on TV too!"

Halfway down the mountain, the ambulance sped Aunty Moana toward Hilo. The diligent medic had stabilized her heart, but his grave face affirmed what the erratic blip on the monitor showed. Hoku gently stroked her mentor's snowy hair, whispering encouragements into her ear. They raced down the Saddle Road, the ambulance swinging wildly at every curve. Beneath the hissing oxygen tubes in her nose, Aunty Moana's lips quivered with indistinct syllables. Twice she squeezed Hoku's hand so hard the elder's knuckles went white.

Hoku glanced through the van's small rectangular window and saw the ocean come into view below the forested slope. "We're almost there, Aunty. Hang on. I can see the ocean now."

Aunty Moana half opened her eyes and smiled. "You can see Kanaloa?"

"Yes, Aunty, only a few minutes now."

"Let me see."

The medic nodded and Hoku gently lifted the elder's head. The blue horizon sparkled in the morning sun, and contentment illuminated Aunty Moana's face.

"Hoku . . . I think we started turning things around last night . . . I saw darkness run away in the face of prayer." She struggled to take a deep breath. "Even those soldiers can't undo that . . ."

"She shouldn't talk," the medic said. "She needs to conserve her energy."

"Ahhh . . . energy," Aunty Moana mused. "It's all around me."

"Shhhhh," the medic urged.

"Hoku, please keep an eye on the lake . . . If it's still draining . . . or doesn't come back . . . you must tell Uncle Pe'a. He'll tell the others."

"What about you, Aunty?"

"I'm going back to my ancestors," she stated calmly. "They're already smiling."

"No, Aunty, please."

"I have no say in it . . . Ke Akua is calling. Just remember . . . I love you as if you were my own daughter. Aloha no, wai puna. Malama pono." My warmest aloha, sweetheart. Take good care of your soul.

Aunty Moana smiled again, that expansive smile that showed her missing teeth, and closed her eyes one last time.

CHAPTER 42

Digging Up the Past

As soon as Josh Mattos was confident that the islanders and the convoy would be off the summit road, he raced down the mountain in his big Silverado, flinging clouds of cinder dust and jostling its struts to their limits. He white-knuckled the wheel and sweat dampened his T-shirt as a whirlwind of vexing thoughts swept through his mind.

That morning he had arrived at Gemini at 4:00 a.m. to fix a fried switch on its tracking gears after the telescope operator called him at home for help over the phone. The T.O., who usually ran the telescope remotely from its Hilo control room, was apparently too dazed from ten hours at altitude to make sense of Josh's instructions, so Josh went up in person. Losing sleep was no loss; his anxieties of the past month had made dreaming unbearable. Driving up to fix something he could actually repair provided a happy distraction.

Lost in thought as he ascended the upper road, Josh hadn't noticed the kahuna vehicles parked near the Lake Waiau trailhead. While walking from his truck to the dome, he'd glanced up at the Milky Way and thought he heard a far-off conch. Chicken skin erupted all over his body, followed by a strange sensation that streams of gnats swirled about him. He couldn't see anything, yet he clearly felt their presence. When a drum started beating, he'd bolted for the dome and took ten full minutes to calm down before telling the operator he was there.

"You see or hear anything strange up here tonight?" he'd asked the tall, scruffy T.O. as they monkeyed with the switch inside the frigid dome.

The operator nudged his spectacles farther up his nose. "Perfectly honest?"

Josh nodded, with apprehension.

"You saw that Canadian babe observing tonight?"

"Yeah?"

"A professor at the University of Toronto. Can you believe it? We hardly ever get women astronomers, and never young ones. I died and went to heaven!"

Josh's face flushed. "I said *strange!*"

"Check it out, man," the T.O. had said, reaching inside his parka to pluck out his iPhone and show him their selfie. "And she friended me on Facebook!"

Obviously, neither occupant of the observatory control room had noticed *anything* outside (no wonder the T.O. couldn't focus on Josh's repair instructions). Josh hung around until the pair left at 5:30 in case any more problems cropped up. In truth, he'd been wary of stepping outside again, worried he'd hear more drumming and conches or that "the gnats" would come back. Alone in the sealed dome, he'd put away his tools, but his fingers trembled as he stowed them in the metal cabinet. When he had finally closed all its drawers, the recollection of his father sobbing in front of his picture window immediately entered the void—and the promise Josh had made to protect the mountain. He began pacing around the giant 8-meter telescope, and was almost out of breath when the muted rumble of the islanders' vehicles issued through the dome's steel walls.

He darted through a nearby emergency exit and stepped onto the towering steel staircase that clung to the building. From there he saw more vehicles arriving in the predawn light. He slipped back inside and panted against the cold wall. "Gotta get outta here!" he'd howled into the cavernous dome.

Within minutes, he was outside and had slipped into the assembling crowd.

They're fed up like me! he thought. *Ready for action!* When the islanders shouted Koa's protest slogan at the departing French astronomers, Josh had the urge to throw a stone at their Outlander, and he bellowed along with the crowd. Indeed, he had actually felt deflated when several Hawaiians admonished the group for venting anger "up here in the realm of the gods."

Two elders had started chanting to their gods and ancestors. *What good will dat do now?* Josh had thought at the time. *Look at dere faces, so full o' love, while da mountain dies! What would dese people t'ink if dey knew one killah among 'em? One loyal soldier dat also stood by and watched his buddies murder innocent women and children . . . some as young as dere own kids? Stood by and nevah say nut'ing!*

Now, bouncing down the road, a rush of guilt coursed through him, souring his stomach. He pictured that windy night a month ago on Poli'ahu, a pu'u his mother had taught him was sacred; how, despite that, he'd slung his M16 over his shoulder before climbing up the cone. *I was jus' gonna nail da side o' one a da domes,* he recalled, *maybe even plug dat damn Gemini!* But then the amber beam of Keck's guide-star laser streamed out of the dark observatory, pointing low into the southwest heavens. He realized the famed mirror might actually be within his line of sight. *I was grinnin' when I noticed dat,* he recalled as the Silverado rounded the lowest switchback. *But I nevah meant fo' shoot . . . was jus' checkin' to see if it was possible.* Before Josh knew it, he had pulled the trigger, and an instant later, in the clear, night air, he heard the distant clang of the bullet strike the telescope's steel frame.

"Missed!" he had muttered atop the cone, and raised the M16 to shoot again. But a sickening feeling rose in his chest when it dawned on him that a ricocheting bullet inside the dome could wound one of his mountain friends out there adjusting an instrument. Oh, how he'd lain awake all that night worrying about it.

"Dumb shit!" he sputtered inside the truck.

Josh switched on the radio, set to the Hawaiian station from Kona—the Saturday morning "oldies" show. Gabby Pahinui crooned away about family life and elders with "Na Ono Na Ia Kupuna."

Den dat old woman w'en show up! he thought. *What was da name? Yes, Aunty Moana. She knew . . . like dose old Hawaiians do. She knew I did it, even knows I plan to do more. What da hell did she mean, "We need your heart too?"* *Don't she realize people who love always lose. Look at Jesus! Look at Dad! Look at da Hawaiians!* Tears streamed from his eyes, fell onto his lap. *Yeah, she knew. Would she talk . . . ? Only a matter o' time 'fore da cops track me down. Gotta work quick now! Soon!*

～

The sensationalized televised "coverage" of the Mauna Kea brouhaha sent authorities into high gear. By Saturday night, police had locked the gate just above the base camp, with Jill and other rangers checking vehicles—shadowed by FBI Special Agent Muku Makau. Only observatory staff and astronomers were allowed through. Unbeknownst to Jill, Agent Makau had mobilized two other agents to help track down the sniper and profile any activists who'd attended the Saturday summit vigil. He felt guilty not telling her, especially since they'd also partnered in bed, but the agent knew that doing a good job required his secrecy. *And better our local FBI guys take the lead than those paranoid Homeland Security transplants,* he'd rationalized.

Troops at Pohakuloa Training Area stood at the ready despite the lieutenant colonel's repeated admonitions that "the whole damn thing was overblown." After reprimanding him for his "shabby handling of the crisis," higher-ups issued a press release committing the Army to "diligently protect the several US government observatories and other astronomical facilities from civil disobedience." Their 6:00 p.m. release provoked more news coverage, and two cable networks dispatched reporters from their L.A. bureaus to arrive the following day in case more trouble ensued.

Plans to install security cameras around the summit were accelerated, and Moses was told that he had to put two at the base camp as well. Moses quietly instituted the security measures, all the while informing Hawaiians in the community of every step taken or planned.

After a hastily called meeting with Sam Chun and several Hawaiian leaders, the often-vacillating governor called for calm, but other leaders of the old Democratic establishment moved quickly to take advantage of the news coverage. They had long hoped some flashy political disruption would give them a stronger toehold against the Hawaiian-rights movement and its efforts to expand native sovereignty at the expense of the colonial economy.

"This will help clear the way for the Big Eye," said Henry Noburo Hashimura to loyalist members of Hawai'i's congressional delegation, meeting that night at his oceanfront Black Point mansion outside Honolulu. "And dampen public enthusiasm for the radical Hawaiians," he added with his trademark grin. Hashimura made no public statements, of course. That was left to the congressional delegation, who gravely parroted the usual developers' spin that "science and native culture can coexist if everyone would just learn to get along."

Native Hawaiians responded to the "police takeover" of their mountain in three distinct ways. Activists used the coconut wireless to begin secretly organizing a massive protest march from the base camp to the summit one month hence, an event they hoped would bring Hawaiians from every island, as the TMT protests had. Cultural practitioners and native elders prayed individually and in small groups to stem confrontation and preserve aloha, and to call on the gods to shield Mauna Kea from more turmoil. Hawaiians not part of the political or cultural movements—regular folks just trying to live out their lives—fell into a deep funk. They'd seen it all before, not just on Mauna Kea, but on Haleakala and Kaho'olawe, at Pohakuloa and Barking Sands, in Makua Valley, and of course at Pearl Harbor—to Teddy Roosevelt the biggest prize of the 1893 coup d'état. But now a confrontation was building yet again at their most sacred of sacred places, the legendary mountain where creation began, where Wakea had mated with Papa.

All of this greatly distressed Hoku, already overwrought by Aunty Moana's death. "I feel like a canoe that's lost its rudder," she sobbed to Erik over the phone, "just when stormy seas are coming. Aunty was one of the few who really understood our place in the world, our destiny, who always saw the bigger picture beyond her own culture. I don't know what we'll do without her."

Planning her mentor's funeral, scheduled for the following Wednesday, helped Hoku set the growing turmoil aside, at least for the moment. Moses gave Erik the whole week off so he could help with the arrangements and console Hoku. He urged the young man to keep them focused on returning the elder to Mauna Kea rather than get involved in the upcoming protest. Freddie, although deeply upset by Aunty Moana's death, kept working so he could assist Moses and help convey updates to his own contacts among Hawaiians, including Sam.

All four got consolation, however, when Aunty Moana came to each in their dreams, a misty white presence surrounded by hawks, owls, and the great seabound 'iwa. Hoku's dream even included a verbal message from the oracle: "Despite all the turmoil, things will turn out well for our mountain and our people. The confluence of light and dark, heat and cold, love and hate, will create a tempest that may finally stem the greed and anger contaminating our islands and our mountain . . . maybe even help heal the world."

Two days after the summit clash, Braddah K vanished from the base camp without a word to his coworkers. He confided only in the camp manager later that night at Moses' house up Kaiwiki Road on the slopes of Mauna Kea above Hilo. Braddah K trembled as he drove his rusty hatchback along the old road of his youth. Almost fifty years had passed since he'd seen the now overgrown lot where his sister had died that awful July night. The row of ti plants meant to guard the house from evil now towered above the weeds, and the shattered window in the half wall that had survived the blaze glinted under an orange sodium streetlight. K peered straight up the road as he drove by.

Moses' house was four lots above that ill-fated place, with an even better mountain view than from the Kuamo'os' old yard. It had been K's dad, in a phone call to Vegas, who had encouraged his old friend and former neighbor to apply for a kitchen job at Hale Pohaku. "I know dat work is jes' labor, Mose," Joel had said, "but one smart guy like you will go a long ways up dere. 'Sides, you belong on dat mountain . . . like our ancestors . . . like I did." It was the same reason why decades later Moses had urged Keola, then a chef's assistant in Vegas, to come back home, tempting him with an offer to run the camp's kitchen on weekends.

Now the two sat sipping beers under stars on Moses' chilly lanai.

"I cannot stay on the mountain no more, Uncle. I w'en feel shaky, like somet'ing terrible gonna happen. I w'en called Pop on da mainland and he agree—'Don't take no chances.'"

"But we need you there," Moses said.

"T'ank you so much, Uncle, fo' give me dat job, and mahalo fo' helping me dese past five years . . . fo' being like one second dad. But I jus' cannot."

Moses' eyes watered, but his firm jaw didn't budge. "What about our ancestors? You know they've supported you up there."

Keola nodded, even almost smiled. "Yeah, I connected now, and I plan fo' stay connected, but from down heah."

Moses knew Keola's mind was made up. Keola was like his father that way. Once his na'au told him to act, he did, and going back was not an option until a new message came to his gut. This was not impulsiveness; it was connection.

"Keola, how much do you know of what happened that night in 1974?"

K's broad face darkened. "Eventually Dad told me most of it."

"I think Joel was right to report the stolen bones," Moses said. "That was pono. They were the marrow and mana of his ancestors."

"Den why da gods take my sister?"

"I wish I knew the answer to that. Maybe your dad got their warning too late."

K's eyes narrowed. "What d'chew mean? What warning?"

"The night after Sunny Boy blabbed about those iwi over the radio, your dad and I talked, almost till midnight. We were both worried, trying to decide what to do . . . drinking too much. Had he been more together and less tired when the dream came—his ancestors' warning—I think he'd have woken up in time to get you both out of the house."

"Dream? Uncle, I w'en neveh know about one dream."

"He saw the fire . . . but in the dream it was happening on the mountain . . . and by the time your dad woke up, the house was already in flames."

Keola sipped his beer a long moment, his gaze turning inward. "I had one dream dat night too, Uncle," he said finally. "I nevah fogit it aftah all dis time . . . maybe dey was trying fo' warn me too."

"What did you see?" Moses said, leaning forward, the same question he'd asked Joel on that same lanai the morning after the tragedy.

"Dat dream was *wild* . . . way too heavy for one eight-year-old. But it did wake me up."

"And got you out of the house on your own."

Keola nodded. "Yeah." He paused again, staring into the dark forest. "Say, Uncle, did you know I w'en saw da guys dat torch us?"

Moses, rarely flustered, shuddered in his chair.

"Oh yeah, I nevah forgit dat either. After da dream I sat up and noticed somethin' out my window . . . da arsonists bolting for da trees. A big, beefy guy—one mean-lookin' Hawaiian—and a kid, one teenager barely older den me. I remember seein' dat guy slap da kid ovah by da woods. 'Stop bawling, Pano!' he w'en shout, 'or I gonna tell yer fadda!'"

"Pano? Dice Kamalu's boy?"

"Dat's how I figure it. I t'ink maybe Dad t'ought so too, but he w'en never say. I guessed it later."

Moses' eyes glazed over as he consulted his na'au. *Could it be?* he thought, shaking his head. "Auwe, they start them young in the Hui," he muttered. "Unlucky kid . . . pushed into murder before he was even grown up."

Moses flashed on all the astronomers he'd interacted with over the years. They're so naïve, he thought. They have no idea how things work here . . . or how their own esteemed observatories would probably never have been built if our politics was cleaner.

"Uncle, dere's somet'ing else," Keola said, setting his empty beer bottle on the cement next to his chair. "I always wondered 'bout our leavin' . . . if *dat* was pono."

"Your dad did the right thing taking you and your mom away. It was the only real choice he had at the time . . . especially if he thought underworld crooks were involved. But Keola, the story's not over. Don't you see that's why you came back to the mountain? And why I'm still there?"

CHAPTER 43

Burying the Past to Move Forward

Except at Hilo's Walmart—shopping center of the underclass—Erik had never seen so many Native Hawaiians in one place as he did that Wednesday evening at the Makuakane Funeral Home in Keaukaha. Two hundred people jammed into the converted seaside residence to honor Aunty Moana, including members of her extended family, former students from Honolulu, and any number of souls who at one time or another had sought advice from the oracle in her little thatched hale by the sea. A few neighbors also showed up, including Sunny Boy Rocha, 'ukulele case under his arm in the event that Moana's friends struck up some tunes during the potluck following the service. Everyone was surprised at the size of the crowd, each having assumed they were among a small group who knew and appreciated the "crazy woman of Keaukaha." Special Agent Makau and two undercover operatives also attended, mixing inconspicuously at the edges of the crowd.

Evening light through seaward windows gave a warm glow to the immense former living room now used as a chapel, and the distant *shuu-shuu* of waves beyond the grounds brought the sea's energy inside. Aunty Moana's two middle-aged sons from O'ahu sat in the front row of chairs, greeting family and friends filing past the white coffin. Both men looked like her—big, round, and affable. In the corner of the room next to the windows a trio of guitar players from the squatters village quietly strummed Hawaiian melodies.

Freddie, Sam, and Erik joined the long line of people paying their last respects, Erik clutching a small bouquet collected from Sunny Boy's yard. Aunty Moana's plump hands rested one over the other atop a kihei of ivory tapa cloth. A garland of fragrant maile leaves adorned her neck, its lush open ends extending to her waist, and a fresh banana-leaf sunhat, like those she'd worn in the ti patch, lay next to her belly. Dozens of mourners' leis draped her coffin— garlands made of yellow and white plumeria, green maile leaves, *kukui* nuts, and the large orange seeds of *hala* fruits. Tucked into the casket's corner was a coconut shell containing water from Lake Waiau, lovingly placed there by Moses.

Freddie sobbed before the body, his shoulders quivering. Inside the coffin, he set his own hala lei, strung with seeds from the hala tree behind Aunty Moana's hale. "Good-bye, Tutu," he murmured, then wiped his eyes on the flowered sleeve of his aloha shirt. Sam, solemn—worried about her absence in the struggles ahead—placed a lei of white kukui around the crown of her sunhat.

Fighting his own tears, Erik stepped up to the white coffin. The mortician, a cousin, had modeled Aunty Moana's face perfectly, and her mouth smiled at Erik as it first had two years earlier—only now it held the teeth she'd always hoped for. *She's whole again*, Erik thought, *as Dad had always been whole. The callous world had broken both their hearts, but not their spirits.* Erik glanced back at the packed room, noisy with love for this woman. *People were drawn to Aunty Moana*, he thought, *because she epitomized love, just as Dad drew people from the river community because he epitomized ethics and principles . . . and both led by example.*

Then an image of Aunty Moana giggling next to her collection of books popped into Erik's mind, and he smiled. *She fully engaged with life*, he thought. *Not like me, uncoupled and drifting, expecting trouble and finding it, perpetually disappointed and running away.*

Erik felt the line of people waiting patiently for him to finish paying his respects. Yet his feet would not move. He gazed down at

Aunty Moana's placid face, committing that final view of her to his memory.

"You now run in my soul like the river, Aunty," he said softly, tucking his bouquet under her hands. "I'll always hold your love in my heart." He leaned forward and kissed her cool cheek, leaving behind a warm tear.

The firm hand of the tall Hawaiian behind him gripped Erik's shoulder. "Maikaʻi!" he whispered into his ear. Righteous! Erik glanced over his shoulder. It was Uncle Peʻa, his stately native wife beside him. The old kahuna placed his forehead on Erik's, and the two men, hugging, exchanged breath.

Erik spotted Hoku sitting near Aunty Moana's family and walked over to sit down beside her. As he turned from the casket, Erik remembered Jack's funeral. *I wish Jack had met Aunty*, he thought. *If he had, he'd be alive today.*

The ceremony began with four pu blowers atop the sea cliff outside, bare-chested under their yellow kihei, heralding Aunty Moana's final journey with their conches. No less than five different clerics spoke during the service in accord with Aunty Moana's instructions, long ago given to Uncle Peʻa after her first heart attack: a Hawaiian kahuna to summon the gods and the ancestors, a Catholic priest to satisfy any family still struggling to reconcile their Polynesian and Western traditions, a Tibetan Buddhist monk befriended by Aunty Moana during a weeklong compassion retreat at Wood Valley Temple, along with a Jewish rabbi and a Sufi master, both of whom she had studied under while still in Honolulu. Uncle Peʻa gave the eulogy, a chronicle of her diverse life and "a tribute to her courage to remain Hawaiian."

"So today," he said, towering above the dais with his elaborately carved staff, "we honor a true Hawaiian, a woman with the courage to defend aloha at a time when fear, prejudice, and despair challenge human beings all over our planet. The last time I saw Moana Kuahiwi was on her beloved Mauna Kea, risking her very life to pray for the healing of hearts and a return to the natural order of things—to love as a way of life.

"To those of us steeped in the customs of our own little islands, Moana's wide taste in books, cultures, and philosophies may have seemed peculiar, but like all seers, she trusted her sources of insight and wisdom. In the great tradition of navigators, she looked for pathways well beyond our shores—and found them.

"One of her favorite quotes was from a wise Chinese philosopher named Lao Tzu:

> *For there to be peace in the world, there must be peace*
> *in the nations,*
> *For there to be peace in the nations, there must be peace*
> *in the cities,*
> *For there to be peace in the cities, there must be peace in*
> *the families,*
> *And for there to be peace in the families, there must be*
> *peace in the hearts of men.*

"She told me once that Lao Tzu also said, 'A journey of a thousand miles begins with one step.' She took that step, in love, and we are all the better for it. Moana knew our journey back to our Polynesian roots would be a long one, but she never lost faith that one day, perhaps generations from now, we would 'reach the mountaintop,' as she liked to say—quoting another of her heroes—and as she most certainly did. Let none of us gathered here today forget that. Take heart in her quest . . . and keep climbing."

The funeral continued for another hour as friends and family got up to speak. Few had prepared comments, instead spontaneously sharing whatever came from their hearts and na'au, and always stirring tears, laughter, or nods affirming some truth about Aunty Moana.

Again the conches blew, "Hawai'i Aloha" was sung, and as the sun dipped into the sea, the crowd gathered outside to swap more stories and share a meal prepared by the community to honor Aunty Moana.

Four "village" residents muscled an enormous wild pig from the *imu* roasting pit as friends of the Kuahiwi clan uncovered twenty foil pans of other local foods. At least two hundred fifty people feasted to Aunty Moana's life that night, including those whose jobs had kept them from attending the service.

The Hawaiian trio reassembled outside, now singing as well as strumming. They beamed with delight when Sunny Boy, a local celebrity, pulled up a chair and joined in on his grandmother's 'uku-lele. A half-dozen hula dancers in the crowd, inspired by the earnest spirit of the event, spontaneously stepped forward to gently sway in the twilight. Staff from the funeral home moved about the grounds lighting tiki torches as an orange crescent moon rose out of the sea like a mythic canoe. A pearly-gray monk seal bobbed in the waves offshore, unnoticed except by Uncle Pe'a and another, even older elder.

Erik introduced Hoku to Freddie and Sam as they joined the line to get their dinners. They took their heaping plates to a vacant picnic table near the ocean. Like the others, the long table was covered with white paper and adorned with a flower arrangement wrapped in ti leaves.

"What a funeral," Freddie said, cracking his knuckles. "Nice job, Hoku."

"And all those wonderful stories," Erik added. "I don't know when I cried so much . . . or laughed. You Hawaiians sure know how to pull our heartstrings."

Hoku smiled. "Aunty loved luaus, you know. She didn't drink much, but she sure could get silly. I hope she's smiling tonight."

Erik squeezed her hand. "I'm sure she is."

"Got room for one more?" asked a familiar face approaching the table.

Erik leaped up. "Moses! Of course you'd be here! Yes! Come join us."

Moses didn't tell the Three Muskrateers that he had come down the mountain as much to support *them* as to honor Aunty Moana. "She had a lot of friends," he said, scanning the crowd, whose mood had begun to lighten. "Moana was a deep root for many here . . . including me."

Erik squeezed the elder's shoulder. "Moses, this is our friend, Hoku."

"At last we meet," he said.

She blushed, having long evaded him on the mountain. "You're the kahu," she said, "the man who guards our mauna."

"It keeps my na'au busy."

She laughed. "I'm sorry, Uncle. I know it must seem that I've avoided you."

"Our paths do keep crossing . . . yet you always slip away."

"I wasn't sure yet."

"Wasn't sure?"

"That I was ready to talk with you. Some people might not approve of what I do on the mountain," she said, leaving unspoken that Moses, like many other Hawaiians, had Christian roots too.

"Didn't Aunty Moana teach you to trust your na'au? That's your direct line. If you are really listening, no one else should interfere with you and your kuleana." Your path and responsibility.

She nodded thoughtfully. "Mahalo, Uncle."

"I'm not huna," he said, referring to those who hold the culture's deepest secrets, "so there are some things I don't understand about the mountain. But I am one link. You should know that others are also making frequent trips to the mountain, to distance places far off the road. An effort has long been underway up there to set things right again."

"Moses!" said a hearty voice emanating from an approaching silhouette, backlit by a pair of blazing tiki torches. Clinging to one side of the silhouette was a willowy shadow with a sleek neck and bobbing bangs.

The elder squinted against the glare. "Jedediah?"

"I'm not surprised to see you here, Moses," said the retired Caltech astronomer, his wild hair trembling in the freshening breeze.

Moses stood up and hugged his old friend. "Yes, but I am surprised to see you. I always wondered how you knew so much about our islands. Now I know . . . Moana."

Jedediah pulled his burl pipe out of his khakis and pointed its stem at Moses. "She was a fascinating person. We had long talks about the energy of the universe and about how so much of modern physics fits neatly into Hawaiian thinking. She had me convinced."

Moses chuckled. "And who is this beauty on your arm?"

Andromeda blushed.

Jedediah put his arm around her. "Andy, this is Moses Kawa'aloa, the Mauna Kea base camp manager. He provided good company—and marvelous conversations—whenever I acclimated at Hale Pohaku. Moses, Andromeda McRae."

"That's quite a name."

"It's Irish," she quipped, and they all laughed.

The couple set their plates on the picnic table and sat down. Moses introduced them to the rest of the group.

"Jedediah," said Moses, "I didn't see your name on the camp reservation list."

"We're here for the funeral, staying at the Naniloa Hotel. It's Andy's first time on the island, so yesterday we did some sightseeing."

Andromeda set her fork down and locked her green eyes on Moses. "Your island is so exquisitely beautiful! Being here makes me want to read poems, maybe even write them . . . and I'm an astrophysicist!"

Moses grinned, his teeth shining.

"I'll take all you folks kayaking if you want," Sam offered. "I'm sure I can rustle up some more boats."

"Unfortunately, tomorrow we're in Honolulu, but thank you," Jedediah said, igniting his big pipe. "I've got a final bit of research to do at the Bishop Museum."

"Ahhh," Moses said. "And when is the voyage, Jedediah?"

"Within the week. *Wayfinder* is fitted out and ready to go."

"Sailing!" Erik blurted, his mouth full of kalua pork. "What's your destination?'

"The Marquesas, Samoa, and the Cook Islands."

Moses slung his arm over the vagabond's shoulder. "Erik, here, is also a sailor. Three years in the South Seas, wasn't it?"

Erik nodded. "You're in for a great trip," he said, surprised to find himself not envious of someone else going there.

"You've prepared a long time for this expedition, Jedediah," Moses said, glancing at Andromeda. "Andy, are you going too?"

With misty eyes, she shook her head. "I have to finish my PhD before I can even think about something like that."

"Despite all my efforts to convince her otherwise," said the astronomer.

"Everything in its own time," Moses said with a sympathetic warmth that reminded Erik of Aunty Moana.

Jedediah squeezed Andromeda's hand under the table.

"Hey, how about those nice new teeth of Aunty's?" Freddie said.

"Yeah!" Erik replied. "How did that happen?" They both looked at Hoku.

"I have no idea, but it's very cool."

"Jedediah found a dentist on the island," Andromeda announced. "Arranged the whole thing through the funeral home."

They all looked at the tousled-haired astronomer. He shrugged, his blue eyes twinkling.

"How did you meet Aunty?" Hoku asked.

"At the small boat harbor behind the Hilo pier. That was . . . gee . . . almost five years ago. I'd finished observing on Keck and had an afternoon to kill before my flights back to L.A., so I decided to drive down to the quay and see if any sailboats were in. As it happened, a kiwi ketch from Auckland had tied up for a few days to provision for its passage through to Honolulu. The skipper and his Maori wife invited me aboard, and I queried them about the South Sea islands they'd just finished cruising. A striking Hawaiian woman with a tress of white hair appeared on the quay—Moana. After chatting across the water for a while the skipper helped her navigate the gangway, and thus began a several-hour conversation. As you know, Maori lore has them migrating originally from Hawai'i, and the two women eventually realized they shared some common ancestors. For the rest of the afternoon the skipper and I just listened to the eye-opening cultural exchange. As I left to catch my plane, Moana invited me to visit the next time I came on-island. I've been making that pilgrimage ever since."

Jedediah looked over at Andromeda. "But it wasn't just her ideas, Andy. Moana's lifestyle intrigued me, living as she did in a squatters village below the harbor. Here was an accomplished schoolteacher—and indomitable scholar—living in poverty as an ascetic. I began to realize that her separation from the hubbub of the modern world had given her the time . . . and distance . . . to think deeply, to formulate the right questions, see the key connections, and develop a philosophy that gave her life integrity and joy—*and* obviously enabled her to influence her world. Moana lived at the margin and in so doing was a true revolutionary."

She wasn't alone, Andromeda thought, knowing Jedediah was on that same kind of quest. *Perhaps others are doing that too . . . wayfinding*

. . . looking for ideas far from the madding crowd. I wonder . . . will I, too, eventually find my way?

After more reminiscences and finishing their supper, the two astronomers got up to bid the group good-bye.

"Wait a minute," Andromeda said, reaching into her purse for her iPhone. "How about a picture of all of you with Jedediah?"

"Maikaʻi!" Moses said. Fine idea!

Andromeda snapped the picture, everyone arm in arm with Jedediah in the middle.

"Let's get one with Andy, too," suggested Erik. This time Jedediah took the shot.

"Fair winds," Moses said, hugging Jedediah after all the other embraces had been given. "Malamo pono!" He turned to Andromeda. "Good luck finishing that PhD, Andy. I'll look forward to seeing you at the base camp someday."

The couple waved as they strolled away. They drifted toward the sea cliff, hand in hand, moonlight catching the windblown clouds from Jedediah's pipe. Watching them leave, Hoku noticed an old Hawaiian woman sitting alone on a chair at the cliff's edge. Moonlit swells rolling toward shore silhouetted her tiny frame and long-stemmed pipe.

With the astronomers gone, Freddie asked Hoku the question that had troubled him for half a week. "What happened up there? Was it the altitude?"

"She was fine until we went to the summit," Erik said. "But she insisted."

"No, it wasn't that, Erik," Hoku said. "I think she sensed the violence about to happen, the soldiers on our sacred mountain . . . the guns. That's what finally broke her heart."

"The world had broken Moana's heart many times before," said Uncle Peʻa, walking up to the table with his ornate staff. The lanky kahuna sat down across from Hoku. "Apparently that was a necessary condition of her life."

"Necessary condition!"

"Moana lived aloha, Hoku, especially in her final years. Until all human beings come to understand that loving is our natural state, broken hearts are bound to happen. But hearts will heal. Close your heart and you're no longer human."

A residual of old rage rose within Hoku. "What good did that do Aunty! Her heart broke, and she died."

Like Dad, Erik thought.

Uncle Pe'a's long face darkened. "You don't understand, Hoku. It was your Aunty's heart that broke, not yours. You must not take on her sorrow. That was her kuleana. But you can call on Moana's mana, and her aloha, to help you through whatever heartbreak you experience." Uncle Pe'a turned his face toward distant Mauna Kea, its long, steep slopes blue under the sliver of moon. "Too many in the world live in the shadow of their ancestors' pain and never enjoy Ke Akua's miracle of each new day." He turned back to Hoku, her face still full of storm. "Please don't be one of them."

The group broke up a few minutes later, with hugs, kisses, and expressions of "Aloha" and "Malama pono." Most of the crowd had already departed, and the last of the feast was piled on plates for the remaining guests. Hoku sat alone at the table, thinking about what Uncle Pe'a had said, and about her beloved mentor, now gone forever. She noticed that the old woman still sat on the sea cliff, smoking her pipe.

Go see her, said her na'au. She's waited all this time for you.

"Aloha, Aunty," Hoku said, walking up. "May I join you?"

The old kahuna, mentor to Aunty Moana, removed the pipe from her wrinkled lips and smiled. "I was hoping you would."

"I'm . . ."

"Hoku," said the kahuna. "Moana told me all about you."

"How did you . . . ?"

"I was her teacher. I'm a kaula too. You know, Hoku, Moana knew that her time in the physical realm was almost complete."

Hoku's eyes glistened with tears.

"Your teacher is still here, Hoku. Do you realize that?"

A long silence ensued while Hoku stared into the old woman's dazzling eyes.

"Chant to your 'aumakua." Your ancestors. "Watch for ho'ailona." Signs. "Listen to your na'au." Messages from within. "Pay attention to your dreams. Moana will come. She will guide. And you, dear child, will carry on."

A shadow passed over the two women on the cliff, the angular wings and body of an 'iwa.

The kahuna smiled. "Aloha no!" she called to the frigatebird. Deepest aloha!

They watched the 'iwa soar away until it faded into the dark sky offshore.

"Our ancestors are here tonight, Hoku. Do you feel them?"

She nodded, the roots of her hair tingling.

The wind, which had strengthened all evening, grew blustery. The kahuna turned her wizened face to the southeast and pointed her pipe at the sea.

"Storm on its way," she said.

Driving back to her oceanfront studio, Hoku caught the midnight news brief on the radio. Among other stories, the announcer mentioned that a tropical storm had formed earlier that evening fifteen hundred miles south-southeast of the Island of Hawai'i, moving northwest at eight miles per hour. It had emerged from the sea just west of the 140th parallel, so meteorologists had given it the next name on their Hawaiian list, Alana, "the Awakening."

CHAPTER 44

Weighing Anchor

Andromeda stood on the beach below Jedediah's bungalow, still tingling from their lovemaking that morning and heartsick to see him go. The wet hull of *Wayfinder*'s dinghy gleamed in the afternoon Malibu sun, its last load coming down the stairs—the professor with his briefcase, tobacco jar, and binoculars. The offshore breeze ruffled Andromeda's tropical sundress, a festive little shift he'd bought for her in Hawai'i. Her back was straight, round shoulders firm, despite the imminent farewell.

"Well, this is the last of it," Jedediah said, setting his things in the dinghy. "I'm off to see the Wizard, the wonderful Wizard of Oz."

Andromeda chuckled, but she was too young and had too tame a life to realize just how big a leap Jedediah was making. The briefcase symbolized the trip's scholarly purpose, but Jedediah knew he was actually sailing off the edge of his world—at least he hoped to. All she knew was that he was probably sailing out of her life.

"Are you worried about the storm?" she said instead of asking her real question.

"No, it'll either pass or peter out by the time I get down there. NOAA's last report said it's stalled about eleven hundred miles south-southeast of the Big Island. Actually, I'm much more worried about you . . . about us. I wish you'd reconsider, Andy."

She shook her head, bangs quivering, and little wet diamonds fell from her eyes.

"You can always catch a flight to Hilo, and if you miss me there, to Christmas Island, or even Pago Pago."

"I'm glad we had those few days in Hawai'i," she said, changing the subject. "I'm especially glad for those two late-night chats on that black-sand beach."

"About life in academia."

"I'll remember what you said about making a commitment to true inquiry, and fostering the faith required to pursue that."

"Regardless of tenure politics and whatever priorities and money society holds out to you. Einstein's the one to model, Andy. Part of his genius was that he made whatever sacrifices were necessary—even working in a patent office—to live a life pursuing his own questions."

Her face brightened at that thought, reflecting inborn idealism inherited from her father. She stepped close to Jedediah and squeezed his arm. "So often talking with you is like seeing first light."

"Of course, you have one disadvantage Einstein didn't have. You're a woman, like the brilliant physicist that married him, contributed to his theories, and whom he ultimately discarded."

"And then there's Vera Ruben," she added stoutly, referring to the Carnegie astronomer who while suffering decades of gender discrimination by colleagues discovered dark matter.

Jedediah put his arm around her. "Thank God we live in a different era. I may be sad you're not coming with me, but I think you're sailing the right course."

A single large cloud out to sea passed over the sun.

"Well," she said, snuggling closer, "I hope it's not just dumb ambition. Like you, I may decide the university is too limiting for me, but I need to discover that on my own."

Jedediah smiled, even as his own heart ached. "I wish I could have met you decades ago, but I can't overstate how glad I am our souls finally caught up with one another. The irony is that had you not shown up that night with your binoculars . . ." He pointed at the turnoff above the cliff. ". . . I might still be poring over my papers instead of weighing anchor. Advising you on your project, telling you about mine, and answering your daunting questions—both scholarly and personal—gave me real focus. Our talks about Mauna Kea, the Big Eye, and the Hawaiians also helped."

"How's that?"

"They underscored how with each passing year the life lessons of wayfinding cultures fade. Maybe that won't happen as rapidly now, what with the Polynesian Voyaging Society and their *Hokule'a* spreading those ideas across the globe. But just in case, I want to get down there before the islanders are as caught up in novelties as Americans, before they lose their ability to apprehend dimensions of reality that our busy technological culture makes opaque to us, before the elders who still understand those deeper dimensions die. Spending time with a bright young woman like you—and trying to act younger than I am—made me finally realize how time waits for no one. I'll miss you sorely, Andy, but I sail knowing *you're* not wasting your time."

The breeze freshened, and Jedediah looked out at his sloop. "I should get going, to take advantage of the fair winds. There's just one more thing, Andy. Please consider what I said about the Big Eye and your father. He could be a big help to us."

"Haisley won't keep his money in the pot if the telescope goes to Chile. That won't change, regardless of what I say to Dad . . . or what he says to Haisley."

"No doubt you're right, but won't you try?"

"I promise. It's the least I can do after all you've done for me. You know, Jedediah, I understand you much better after those days in Hawai'i, your feelings about the Polynesians. Before the funeral, I had never met a Hawaiian. They're definitely special. Even the Hawaiian scholars at Bishop Museum seemed so down-to-earth and affectionate."

"That part of the Hawai'i myth is still true."

Andromeda sat down on the log they'd often leaned against while watching the night skies. Her bangs sagged to one side. "Seems odd to see you off during the day. Somehow I imagined this parting moment at night, under stars . . . when Uranus is up."

"Uranus *is* up. That's why I'm leaving now." Jedediah pointed his pipe stem above the western horizon. "Look over there. You'll see my blue planet after dusk, about the time *Wayfinder* disappears beyond the horizon."

Another vessel set sail that afternoon, the *Phoenix II*, a container ship sailing from Long Beach to O'ahu whose cargo included fifty Stryker combat vehicles and five RQ-7B Shadow drones, the first shipment of a lucrative Department of Defense contract Tom Williams hoped would prevent the sale of more of his family's land. Henry Hashimura, who had pulled the necessary strings to make it happen, called the senior Tom that afternoon. Marilyn, seasoned enough to display the proper mix of excitement and apprehension, pulled Tom from a meeting. He took the call at his office desk, a koa wood antique with a view across the bay toward the harbor.

"Hi, Tom," the aging powerbroker greeted cheerily. "It's Noburo." Tom could picture Hashimura's toothy grin next to his diamond-studded gold iPhone.

"Noburo! Good afternoon!" He lit a cigarette and leaned back in his grandfather's leather chair.

"Raining in Hilo, or sunshine?"

"Sunshine, which matches my mood."

"I'm sure. I understand the *Phoenix* weighed anchor in San Diego today."

"Yes, indeed, thank you again for making it happen."

"Fortunately, the deal went down pretty smoothly. Of course, the mainland shippers aren't happy. In fact, to satisfy one of them—owned by a nephew of the Armed Services chair—our congressional delegation had to agree to revisit your contract next year instead of waiting five years from now."

Tom's heart dropped. He remembered that vague phrase on the paper, but Noburo had reassured him. Tom crushed his Camel into the ashtray and put another into his mouth. "I can't plan much with only a one-year contract."

The understatement of the morning. Tom and his son had worked out a detailed capitalization plan based on five years of military shipping income. Even with the exorbitant rates Department of Defense contracts yielded—almost twice what other contractors paid—Williams & Company needed all five years to avoid selling off land. This news would no doubt induce Tommy to advocate putting some of their oldest holdings on the market.

Noburo didn't respond, a silence over the line.

"Is that arrangement firm?" Tom finally asked.

"Yes . . . until next year. But I'm sure everything will go well this year, and the Williams & Company contract will stand against any competitors. We can tighten up your guarantees at that time . . . assuming DOD is satisfied."

And therein lies the problem, Tom thought, the Haisley Big Eye suddenly the elephant in the room. Tom, as old a hand as Noburo, let the kingpin's words lie there with no response. Thirty seconds passed before Noburo filled the void.

"How's the local mood on our next telescope?" he asked, knowing full well the answer. That morning he, too, had read the *Star-Advertiser*'s statewide poll. Fifty-six percent said the mountain "has enough telescopes and no more should be allowed," and 66 percent said "the recent military action against Native Hawaiian protesters was mishandled," another sign of the changing times. Percentages among Big Island respondents were even higher.

"I wish the Army hadn't made that mess up there," Tom said, sucking hard on his cigarette.

"Hmmm."

"Now it will take even more pressure to turn around the local opposition."

"You and your son are dynamos," Noburo said confidently, but Tom heard him light his first cigarette of the conversation. "And you've got a powerful Hawaiian on your side."

The oblique reference to Pano Kamalu stirred an unsavory feeling in Tom's gut. He should have known that calling in old chits with Noburo would be riskier in the twenty-first century, that the old machine had to play even harder ball now that the Hawaiians and their environmental cohort were forces to be reckoned with.

But Tom was still of missionary stock. "I don't like turning over rocks," he said. "Too many centipedes."

"I agree, Tom . . . of course. But Pano is a stakeholder and ambitious, and that makes him a player we can use."

Tom lit his third cigarette and crumpled the empty pack. "What did you have in mind?" A rhetorical question to avert another void.

"Pano has a long history with the mountain, as did his Hui predecessor," Hashimura said, referring to Haku Kane. "Their friends in construction—the companies and the unions—have a helluva lot to gain by the Big Eye, but Pano can't be too visible in mustering the troops. You can."

What Noburo didn't say to Williams—nothing to be gained by it now—was that people with a long history often closet skeletons along the way, and Pano had a very old one of which few were aware.

"I won't deal with Pano," Tom said. "He's on the chamber of commerce . . . fine. But I'll have nothing to do with his strong-arming."

"Of course not, Tom. Just do your job with the rest of the chamber, including that silly mayor you people elected," this last delivered with that hint of menace for which Noburo was renowned—and on which he rarely had to act.

CHAPTER 45

Discoveries

Willy McRae tried to nap as his telescope operator drove the Berkeley team down to the base camp after their fourth night searching for planets on Keck I, but Willy's delirium from the data they'd collected made that impossible. Using the telescope's high-resolution spectrometer, they'd confirmed Kepler space telescope data on another potentially habitable exoplanet in the Milky Way. Even more thrilling, they'd observed properties in that exoplanet indicating that it was closer to Earth's size than any other Goldilocks candidate yet found. Once that data was verified with rigorous processing in Berkeley, his team's discovery would make Willy's planetary explorations among the most successful on Earth, including identifying from thousands of Kepler-confirmed exoplanets two that might actually support life. After a quick breakfast and four or five hours of attempted sleep Willy would drive down to Hilo to catch his flights back to Oakland in the warm glow of his accomplishment.

Jill Kualono spotted Willy's team coming down and pushed open the gate at the guard shack. This reminded Willy of another reason to be happy: his stint on Keck, scheduled six months earlier, had begun five days after the summit clash between the islanders and the Army. A feeling of deep relief passed over him as the ranger waved him through; months would pass before he next observed, and by then all that hubbub would be behind them—or so suggested his indomitable optimism.

He tossed his backpack full of data onto the lobby couch and bounced down the stairs to the dining room.

"Eh, getta load o'pointy-head," Jeffrey Drake muttered to the Filipino cook on duty, Drake now in charge with Braddah K gone. His eyes were bloodshot from the potent doobie he'd smoked that morning, his first since his sobering encounter with Moses in the parking lot several weeks earlier. "Guy mus' be giddy on thin air to trip out li'dat at dis hour."

The other cook chuckled under his breath. "Yeah, most times dey so outta it, w'en barely make da steps!"

"Breakfast?" Drake said, standing with mock attention in his Jackson Pollack smock.

"Pull out the stops!" Willy replied with a grin so broad it displayed all his crooked teeth. "Two eggs—sunny-side up—and hash browns! Double order of toast!"

Drake leaned on his spatula, meanness flickering in his eyes. "You call that pulling out the stops? I'll tell you what pulling out the stops is—having your American Army point guns at a bunch of Hawaiians praying on the summit."

Willy's happy face collapsed, and the Filipino quickly vanished into the kitchen, ostensibly to help Erik mix some pancake batter.

"The day of reckoning is coming for you people," Drake said, pointing his spatula at the astronomer. "You haoles think you can take over everything, but don't be surprised when you get kicked off this mountain!" Drake fumbled for two eggs and cracked them open over the grill. He broke one yoke, but let it ride.

Eggs over easy take a minute to fry, a long time to face a belligerent primed to deliver more abuse. "Back in a minute," Willy muttered, leaving his tray on the counter to seek refuge at the orange juice machine.

The kitchen crew was often rowdy, occasionally even rude, but Willy had never been harassed. Indeed, Drake had snapped at *every* astronomer that morning, having just learned that Jill Kualono was the reason an FBI agent had "interrogated" him the previous

afternoon about the Keck shooting. Whatever civility Drake had res-
urrected after his heart-to-heart with Moses vanished after the FBI
encounter. Agent Makau had pressed him for the name of anyone
who could back up his claim that he was fast asleep in the dormitory
when that summit bullet flew. Fortunately, Jeffrey's stint in federal
prison hadn't come up—but how long could he count on that?

"Hey," Drake said when the astronomer returned, "I was outta
line spouting off like that."

Willy cautiously stepped up to the counter, though he'd actually
begun to lose his appetite. "Don't worry about it," he muttered.

"See . . . Potty Mouth is my nickname," Drake continued, handing Willy his plate of food. "But astronomers are known around here
as robber barons of the sky. Enjoy your breakfast." The smile served
up with the comment was rancid.

Willy fled to a table as far from the serving counter as possible—
upset as much with himself as with Drake. *I don't need to justify my
work to anyone!* he thought, sitting down with his tray. He peered
over at the cook. *Know-nothing dim bulb!* The spontaneous epithet so
tickled him that he started to giggle.

"Hash browns that strange this morning?" said the stately old
Englishman approaching the table, a timeworn British cardigan
stretched tight over his round belly. The grizzled astrophysicist from
Cambridge stood on the other side of the table with his usual toast,
marmalade, and tea—and one of his legendary morning martinis.
His potent "sleeping tonics" yielded the soundest daylong sleeps of
any observer and had given him a permanent place in base camp
lore. Along with a nickname, Dr. Sapphire, after the English-style
Bombay gin he always brought up for his concoctions. "Fancy a bit of
company?" he asked.

Willy hesitated, but what could he say? Chatting up the old-
timer was better than avoiding eye contact with the kitchen crew.
Willy motioned to a chair where the plump astronomer would best
block his view of the kitchen.

"Hunting for Goldilocks, no doubt?" the older man said as he
settled in, well aware of Willy's renown.

"Yep. It's been a good run this time. And you?"

"Indeed. Two weeks I've got on JCMT—star formation, of course."

"Of course," Willy said, also well aware of his breakfast mate's reputation. No one with less-than-stellar work would get fourteen nights on the James Clerk Maxwell Telescope, the huge submillimeter antenna built by the kingdom and now in its last grand days before decommissioning.

"Good skies for the most part. Only humbug this stint was the day I lost to the protest." He sipped his martini.

"A shame," Willy said, biting into his toast.

"'Twas, wasn't it? You Yanks have a queer way of garnering public support for astronomy. Christ, it looked like Afghanistan up here." He spread some marmalade on his unbuttered toast. "But then Americans always do things in a big way, don't you?"

"'Fraid so," Willy replied, thinking it was an odd jab from a Brit whose own former empire had also participated in the Iraq and Afghanistan debacles. He pierced the yoke of his one good egg and scooped a forkful of hash browns into his mouth.

"Keck seems to be taking the brunt of the current ballyhoo," Dr. Sapphire continued chattily, "but it's really all about the Big Eye, isn't it?"

Willy sighed. "I guess we have to do a better job explaining what we do here, the importance of our discoveries," something he'd said repeatedly during the earlier TMT controversy.

"Indeed. But then what difference would PR have made for Galileo?"

"Indeed," Willy parroted, retiring his fork to his barely touched plate. He got up from the table.

"Well, cheerio and good luck with your data," said the Cambridge man, martini glass to his lips.

Willy slept poorly that morning, anxiety about the Big Eye breaking his sleep every half hour. He gave up at noon. Hungry after abandoning his breakfast that morning, he begrudgingly ventured into the dining room again. Fortunately, the Filipino cook was serving lunch.

Moses noticed Willy eating a cheeseburger and walked over to the dining room.

"Dr. McRae," he said with a professional dignity that tempted Willy to lodge a complaint about Drake, but he thought better of it, knowing he'd be back many times in the future.

"Yes?"

"A phone call came in while you were sleeping," Moses said, holding out a sealed privacy envelope containing the message. "They told me it was urgent."

Willy took it, and Moses disappeared. The message inside was from Dr. Adam Jacob:

> Tuesday, 10:50 a.m.
>
> We're holding an emergency meeting at 3:00 pm with Haisley at the astronomy offices in Honolulu. Need you there if at all possible. Please come.
>
> —Jacob

Who is "we"? Willy wondered, running his fingers through his grizzled auburn curls. *And what's the problem now!* He never finished his cheeseburger.

Willy dashed onto an earlier flight, but with Honolulu's horrendous traffic, the cabbie got him to the Manoa campus thirty minutes after Jacob's meeting had begun. Agitated voices issued through the closed conference room door. Willy's near empty stomach turned when he heard the clipped utterings of Air Force General Michael Todt.

Opening the door interrupted the argument, and they all looked over at Willy. The uniformed Todt sat cold-eyed at one end of the long table, his note-taking adjutant at his side. Rotund Alfred Haisley, red-faced, filled the chair on the other end, his fat hands resting on an artist's rendering of his Big Eye mausoleum. Dr. Adam Jacob sat kitty-corner on the table's far side, two feet down from a file folder and a glass of water waiting for Willy. "The Bishop" of Caltech astronomy was, as usual, cool as a cucumber, but a frown supplanted his characteristic smirk.

Willy was immediately embarrassed to have brought his backpack slung over his shoulder. He was also still in the jeans he'd worn on the mountain but had managed to slip on a polo shirt for the plane.

"Good morning, gentlemen," he greeted, taking his appointed chair. He glanced across the table where another water glass and folder had been set.

"We've asked Dr. Bushmill to join us at four o'clock," Jacob said, adding to Willy's dismay. The bouncy disingenuousness of the UH director of astronomy and astrophysics always put Willy on guard.

"Willy," Haisley blurted. His name had never been uttered with such desperation. "Caltech's decided to take the Big Eye to Chile!"

Willy looked over at Jacob, then at Todt, the set jaws on both men a confirmation. "You know I can't support that."

"Alfred's threatened to pull out his money," Jacob said flatly, but his pebble eyes flashed with contempt. "Seems his commitment to the future of American astronomy now depends solely on having his crypt on Mauna Kea."

Even Todt's poker face betrayed disgust with a slight uplift of his eyebrow.

"You made that deal with him, Willy," Jacob continued in an accusatory tone, "which is why we asked you to be here today."

Tired, hungry, and still blurry from four days at altitude, Willy's usual ebullience was gone. "You all knew that more than a decade ago."

"But the politics have changed," said Jacob, "and Caltech's board of directors has decided we've got to focus on Chile so we don't get skunked like we did with the Keck outriggers and the TMT."

"Of course the Air Force is still committed to Mauna Kea," Todt said grimly, "no matter what it takes to make it happen. With our prime adversaries in the Northern Hemisphere, and our Haleakala complex already established on Maui, putting the Big Eye in South America undercuts its military purpose considerably . . . and could limit our financial participation. Our view has been communicated to the secretary of defense and Hawai'i's congressional delegation, and *they* concur with *us*."

At that moment Willy realized the whole project was suddenly in jeopardy. He wished he was wearing a suit and tie like Jacob and Haisley. But he was still the brightest man at the table—even outpacing Jacob—and the same uncanny intuition that could almost sense planets' presence in detected photons usually gave Willy vitality on his feet.

"Would you gentlemen step out for a few minutes," he said to Jacob and the Air Force officers, "and give Alfred and me a chance to chat?"

They nodded.

"And keep Bushmill from interrupting us!" Willy added as they left the room.

He pulled up a chair next to Haisley, whose hands trembled. Willy took a long, deep breath and tried to summon all his charisma.

"I won't go along with their plan, Alfred," he said evenly. "That would break my promise to you." Haisley's bulbous eyes watered behind his glasses. "But it does appear that we're up against a wall."

Willy glanced out the window at the sunny campus, an idyllic scene belying conflicts that too often marred what Willy saw as scholarship's higher purpose.

"We have powerful allies against Caltech on this one—Todt and the local politicians," Willy said, though speaking it left a sour taste in his mouth. "Obviously, everyone at UH wants the Big Eye here, and half my California colleagues would prefer we built on Mauna Kea. The other half, frankly, always preferred Chile"—an understatement after the TMT fiasco. "Were it not for your money, Alfred, even Jacob might prefer it."

"I won't go to Chile!" Haisley said, grasping the mausoleum drawing so tightly his pink knuckles went white.

Willy sat calmly, and then smiled, but the hope conveyed was feigned. "How much money do you have in that big sack of yours, Alfred?"

"Enough," he harrumphed.

"Well, let's use it, shall we?"

"What are you talking about?"

"Another $75 million, as a gift to Caltech to build detectors for the Big Eye."

"Seventy-five million! Caltech's already spent $500 million of my money just to get us to this dead end. You expect me to raise my stakes?"

"I suspect that's what it would take to turn Jacob's mind."

Haisley's round face turned red as a tomato, but he gazed out the window to digest the idea.

Willy drank down the water in Bushmill's glass and waited.

"Fifty," Haisley said finally. "I'll go fifty million if they build on the summit and guarantee the mausoleum."

"Let's see if we can convince them, shall we?"

Haisley nodded.

When the group came back, they all noticed that Haisley had regained his composure, his big face pasty again. Fortunately, Dr. Bushmill had not yet arrived. Willy explained the deal and Haisley affirmed it.

"If I can convince the Caltech board to go ahead with Mauna Kea, we'll still have to fix the political mess here in Hawai'i," Jacob said, but at least his mouth showed a trace of smirk again. "Fifty million is a hefty sum for instrument development . . . I *might* be able to get them to go along . . ."

Todt leaned forward over the table. "Especially if they realize Alfred is absolutely firm in his opposition to Chile."

"Not a penny more if it goes there!"

"Um-hmm," Jacob mused. He glanced at Todt, whose cold, stony face carried its own menacing resolve. "Mr. Haisley, can you make it sixty?"

Haisley reddened again, but remained calm. "I can do that."

"Then it's a deal," Jacob said, his smirk back in full form, "but with one crucial condition."

Haisley frowned.

Jacob turned his little eyes on Willy, their brows leaping upward. "Dr. McRae, will you agree to help us with the local PR on this? You're a huge figure in the world of astronomy, and your, well, personal magnetism could help us greatly with the Hawai'i population. Are you willing to come out of your scholarly cocoon and hustle the local community—the business folk and the great unwashed—to diffuse the opposition? Help us through the inevitable controversies during the environmental review?"

The idea offended Willy. He was a dedicated scholar, not a PR hack, and the thought of "hustling" anyone turned his stomach.

"That's a great idea!" Haisley blurted. "You're the astronomer who always gets people excited about studying the cosmos! Life on other planets! Celestial mysteries to be solved! The Carl Sagan touch, that's what you have! You could go on TV, on radio, even set up a website! Lecture all over the state . . . the world! What a great idea!"

Now it was Willy's turn to redden. Reluctantly, he consented.

CHAPTER 46

More Discoveries

Willy McRae took a red-eye home to Oakland. Though he'd slept on the plane, he felt exhausted, the glow of his planetary discovery now eclipsed by the earthly finding that the Big Eye stood on shakier ground than he'd imagined. He arrived at his home the next morning and discovered Andromeda waiting for him in the living room. His daughter's presence always excited Willy and her surprise visit put solar wind back into his mood. They chatted over Peet's coffee, bagels, and jam.

"How's school?" he asked, always delighted to hear the details.

"My thesis proposal is really strong, Dad. I'm sure they'll approve it, even if it turns their heads a bit."

They talked a half hour about the thesis, and he was deeply intrigued, but she made no mention of Jedediah Clarke's advisory role. Discussing her work launched them into a broader conversation about using space-based observatories to search for a living planet. Inevitably, that led to talk of the Big Eye—as she hoped it would when she decided to drive up from Pasadena.

"The whole project came within a hair's breadth of collapsing yesterday," Willy confided with a sigh, and proceeded to shock her with details of the Honolulu meeting. Jedediah had warned Andromeda that science politics could be brutal, but the bald-faced power brokering in the meeting still dismayed her, especially her father's role in keeping the Mauna Kea site in play. She had underestimated just how much her loyalty to Jedediah would affect her, and she found herself fulfilling her promise to him more stridently than she had planned.

"What are they going to do about all the community unrest?" she asked.

Willy groaned. "For me, that's the worst part. I had to agree to lead the public relations effort, especially in the islands."

Andromeda's jaw dropped.

"My assigned task is to inspire confidence in the value of astronomy, to show the purity of it, I guess."

"Purity? After the meeting you just described . . . and the creeps in the room?"

Willy peered into Andromeda's face with the same wide-eyed intensity as when he examined planetary images, and tried to infer what forces could have shifted her view so profoundly.

"Was there any discussion of why people are so upset?" she continued, "any attempt to understand the Hawaiian view on the matter?"

"What do you mean, Andy, 'the Hawaiian view'? A handful of hotheaded activists have stirred up the community. I'm told they're the same Luddite reactionaries who fight anything new on the island. They don't understand, let alone appreciate, the importance of our science."

"Dad, to Hawaiians it's not about the science," she said, throwing back her bangs. "It's about their sacred mountain."

"Where are you getting this stuff? Why the sudden change of heart? Surely you, of all people, realize how key this telescope is to our dream of discovering life."

"Yes, but out of respect for the Hawaiians, it should go to Chile. It will perform just as well there . . . maybe even better."

"But Haisley won't—"

"Get to bury his corpse there? Good grief, Dad! Who does he think he is, a pharaoh? Besides, you've never approved of mixing astronomy with warfare. You don't even like that our detectors are declassified military technology, and that some of *our* technical breakthroughs go straight back to *them*. How many times have you told me we have too many telescopes aimed on war satellites instead of the heavens—like that stuff on Haleakala?"

Willy's frustrations rose all over again, but magnified. Hearing his beloved daughter remind him of realities he didn't like to admit brought up a deep blue streak left over from his father's disapprovals.

"I told you, without Haisley there's no money for the ground-based telescope we need. Who's putting these ideas in your head? What do *you* know about the Hawaiians?"

"Dr. Clarke introduced me to them last week." It slipped out.

"Jedediah Clarke? That madman? What do you have to do with him?"

"He's been advising me on my thesis. Jedediah is the reason my proposal is as solid as it is."

"'Jedediah?' Advising? I thought Caltech kicked Clarke out years ago."

"It's an . . . ah . . . informal arrangement, between him and me."

"And what do you mean he introduced you to the Hawaiians last week?"

Andromeda hesitated. How could she not tell her father, her original kindred spirit, about a relationship so important to her, especially when her heart had not yet accepted that it might be over? "We went to Hawai'i together."

Together? Realization of what Andromeda was saying finally broke through his resistance, and Willy's stunned expression showed it. "For research?" he asked, hopefully.

"A holiday."

"Together?"

"We're involved, Dad."

"I see." Willy got up from the sofa and wandered about the room. "He's quite a bit older than you," he said finally.

"Only in years, not in spirit, nor in values. The reasons he retired early from Caltech are motives you would appreciate. In fact, you two share more in common than you might think . . . a creative twist to your brains being just one of them."

Willy knew that was true, that Jedediah Clarke's astrophysics contained some of the most compelling ideas he had pondered. And Clarke's passionate, offbeat papers about space-based telescopes always delighted him. What Willy couldn't reconcile was imagining his daughter with a man of Clarke's *personal* reputation, the free-wheeling bachelor with the avant-garde life.

"Did he pressure you?" Willy asked with a father's protective tone.

Andromeda almost laughed, recalling how the whole thing started when she window-peeped the famous astronomer. She shook her head. "No, Dad, if anything, it was the other way around."

Willy sat back down in the sofa and absently stared at his bookshelves.

"Look, Dad, it was platonic for months, but the more we got to know each other, discuss our ideas, the deeper the connection. It was . . . well . . . inevitable."

"What are your plans?"

Andromeda sighed deeply. "I don't really know. He's off on a research project . . . out of the country . . . and it's not clear when, or even if, he'll be back."

"You mean, it may be over?"

His hopeful tone cut deep. "Not if I have anything to do with it. We're staying in touch while he's away."

Andromeda's news, on top of his Big Eye problems, sapped all the energy that seeing her had restored. Yet Willy knew he could not challenge her choices, as his father had too often challenged his. He had made that vow to himself long ago, when she was still just a child.

"Does your mother know about this?"

"No . . . but I'll tell her tonight, when she gets back from the college."

"So you and he met with some Hawaiians, and they don't want the telescope."

"The Hawaiians have nothing against astronomy, Dad. In fact, they have a long heritage of studying the heavens—for agriculture, celestial navigation . . . and for spiritual connection. But Mauna Kea is their most sacred place, their Mount Sinai, their Fuji-san, their

Mount Olympus. No matter how much they value our quest, they cannot allow further desecration."

Willy sighed. "Like the Indians at Mount Graham . . . and Kitt Peak."

"Exactly . . . Just a minute, Dad." She pulled out her iPhone and found the snapshot Jedediah had taken of her with Aunty Moana's friends after the funeral. "Do these people look like flaming reactionaries to you?"

Willy scanned the beaming, gentle faces of Moses, Hoku, Erik, Freddie, and Sam. His daughter, now a mature young woman in her own right, stood smiling in the middle.

"No."

"And yet these people—every one of them—is opposed to the Big Eye, even these three who work at the base camp."

"Oh yes," he said, studying the image. "I recognize the camp manager . . . Moses. He's definitely no reactionary."

"And the other Hawaiians I spoke with that day were some of the friendliest people I'd ever met, even after they'd learned we were astronomers. That we had come all the way from California to honor their friend seemed to truly move them."

"You say this picture was taken at a funeral? Everybody looks so happy."

"An hour earlier they were crying . . . and telling the most amazing stories about this woman."

"I suppose we all create comfortable—even if inaccurate—images of our adversaries. I've seen it many times on university committees." He rolled his eyes. "Well, Andy, what's to be done?"

"Maybe you could talk to Haisley, try to persuade him to go to Chile."

"You heard how he reacted to that idea."

Andromeda cocked her head. "What if you convinced him that the telescope is going to get killed by its controversy, that his dream and all that money could get waylaid if they pursue Mauna Kea?"

"He might buy that, eventually, but certainly not now. Frankly, it won't matter what the Hawaiians want. All the power brokers are lined up behind Mauna Kea . . . except maybe Jacob . . . I wonder . . . ?"

"If things get really out of hand again—and Jedediah thinks they will—Jacob's argument for Chile could win the day."

"But Haisley would still have to give up his burial, and just be satisfied to live forever in the annals of astronomy."

"You have personal influence with Haisley. If anyone can sway him, it's you."

"I don't know, honey."

"Think about it, Dad. Haisley's long played up his huge donation in the media, so how can he withdraw it now? He would become persona non grata to the astronomers he idolizes."

"You've got a point there." Again Willy got up and went to the window. Andromeda observed her brilliant father "processing the data" she'd presented, and she watched as her arguments started to take hold.

"Look, Andy, even if Haisley could be convinced to honor his financial pledge, there's still the problem of the Air Force. They don't want to spend their $500 million on a telescope outside the country."

Andromeda leaped up and joined him at the window. "Then find a substitute for their money."

Willy actually laughed. "With what? From who? We've already completely fished out the usual funding grounds, and all we got was $500 million in cooperative partnerships, and that includes Caltech's part of those deals."

"I know who might pay for it," she announced, finally playing the trump card Jedediah had given her when she promised she'd approach Willy. "Mitch Gardner."

"The Maui shampoo mogul? Why the hell would he contribute to a telescope? He only supports leftwing causes, doesn't he?"

"Exactly! And he loves Hawaiians. He's already given millions to their cultural programs and even some to the sovereignty activists."

"I still don't get it, Andy."

"Mitch Gardner is an old seventies radical who made his fortune putting shampoo ginger and other tropicals into his yuppie hair products. He grows the stuff on Big Island and Maui farms and has estates on both islands. Gardner's already said publicly that he doesn't favor any more development on either mountain, Haleakala or Mauna Kea. His Hawaiian friends have convinced him of that. If he knew his money would keep the Big Eye off Mauna Kea *and* skunk the Air Force, who desecrated Haleakala with their summit surveillance compound, he might just do it . . . unless he has some other objection to astronomy."

"Five hundred million is a lot of clams, especially to stop a project rather than create one."

"He's got oodles of cash, Dad. Gardner's one of the richest men on the planet, much wealthier than Haisley. And from what you've described, Dr. Jacob could care less who gives the money—he's already proven that by teaming up with the Air Force."

The sparkle returned to Willy's sky-blue eyes and he grinned with all his crooked teeth. "You are a smart cookie, Andy. Do you know that? I think you just successfully hustled your father."

Andromeda grinned back, but she didn't reveal how conflicted she'd been in deciding to approach him, or that it was the goddess Urania appearing in her dream that morning that had compelled her to drive up to Oakland. "Science and culture must never become separated," the Greek muse of astronomy had said, peering into a numinous pond of reflected stars. "True innovators discover solutions where none seem to exist."

"Thanks, Dad," she replied, "but one big question remains. How does one get an audience with the great radical tycoon?"

"Ahh, you have a point there. I may be pretty well known in astronomy circles, but Gardner wouldn't know me from Adam."

"Yes, but Gardner does know Jedediah Clarke. One of Gardner's many houses sits next to Jedediah's bungalow in Malibu. They've partied together for years," she said, not mentioning the Maui Wowie the two occasionally smoked when Gardner was in town. "Jedediah has already laid some groundwork, even hinted to Gardner that he might ask a favor."

"Oh, I see. So I really have been hustled."

"Uh-huh, but all for good causes—a fine telescope in the mountains of Chile *and* the goodwill of the Hawaiians."

Indeed, Willy had no idea just how critical getting his participation was in an already carefully strategized plan. At the funeral

Moses had revealed to Jedediah the Hawaiians' planned march to the summit in a few weeks, and the astronomer, fearing another confrontation, decided to recruit Andromeda and her father in his crazy idea. Willy, of course, was unaware of the secret protest, but its imminence was why Jedediah stood ready to contact Gardner as soon as Andromeda sent word via email to *Wayfinder*'s laptop. He thought that if Willy could secure Gardner's commitment before the protest, the march would more likely be peaceful.

Andromeda immediately emailed news of her success to Jedediah. He wrote back that evening, reporting that he'd made contact with Gardner and that the billionaire was willing to consider Willy's proposal. Willy called Gardner's scheduler the very next day, but the mogul's calendar had no openings until a Saturday two weeks hence—just one week before the protest.

CHAPTER 47

Meeting with the Mogul

Mitch Gardner's sprawling residence near Hana looked more like a Buddhist temple than a tycoon's home. The Japanese design of the house, with its swooping eaves, shoji doors, and understated wood and stone details, immediately calmed Willy, who had grown anxious during the long wait. A lovely middle-aged receptionist in beige cotton pants and blouse guided the astronomer through the elegant foyer to a lava rock path lined with bonsai trees, landscaped stones, and Japanese lamps. A life-size bronze of Lao Tzu stood near what she called "the revelations pond," where four men waited in exquisite rattan chairs.

Mitch Gardner and the three Hawaiians rose as Willy approached, and the receptionist withdrew. Gardner was taller and older than in the news photos Willy had seen. Decades of sunshine had deeply lined his tanned face, and his once youthful features—dazzling eyes and smile—now carried the resolute solemnity of an elder. His graying ponytail almost reached his black Louis Vuitton jeans, and a striking lei of spiraling black pupu shells hung above his blousy aqua shirt.

"Good morning, Dr. McRae," he greeted with a firm handshake and a bold, deep voice. "Let me introduce my friends, who have also read your email outlining the proposal"—the one Andromeda had helped him draft. All three Hawaiians wore shorts and dark T-shirts printed with various elegant designs. Like Gardner, they wore flip-flops.

"Thank you for seeing me," Willy said as they all sat down.

"I'm *delighted* to finally meet you!" Gardner said. "The guy looking for another living planet! I caught two of your Berkeley lectures on YouTube a couple of years ago. You reminded me of Sagan. I met Carl in the '90s at a global warming conference. You're the kind of scientists we need right now, guys with smarts, passion . . . and a moral compass."

Willy blushed.

"So you know Jedediah," Gardner continued. "Well, he's a bit of an oddball, but he's another scientist for our times."

An elderly Japanese woman—Gardner's personal *sado* trainer—approached from the back of the house with a lacquered bamboo *shikki* tray, on which she had beautifully arranged a ceramic teapot, five teacups, and a platter of mango *mochi*. Gardner leaned forward in his chair after she had gracefully served the group.

"Let's get started," he said. "Your proposal, of course, is preposterous, which is one of the reasons I was so intrigued by it. It's a crazy idea and a lotta dough, but you know, it just might work." He turned to the Hawaiians. "You guys read it. Now you see the man behind it. Any thoughts?"

The eldest of the trio, also sporting a ponytail, snow-white, spoke.

"We have one question that was not addressed in your proposal," he said to Willy. "What about the people on that mountain in Chile? What if they don't want your telescope?"

"Here's my understanding," Willy said, leaning forward. "There were controversies when the Europeans began to build their observatories down there—mostly about how Chileans would benefit from foreigners building on their mountain range. Astronomers were forced—rightly—to pay better wages to local laborers than they'd intended and to give Chilean astronomers observing time on the telescopes."

"I see."

"These disputes were nothing like what we've experienced in recent years on Mauna Kea. It's true that the indigenous people of northern

Chile, like Hawaiians, revere mountains and the earth mother that dwells there, but meetings between them and the astronomers—over the Giant Magellan and ELT—suggest much more local support than opposition. Some of Earth's largest observatories already stand on Cerro Tololo and Cerro Paranal, so they understand what we're talking about. Those particular peaks, while revered as part of the Atacama range, are apparently not nearly as culturally sensitive as Mauna Kea."

"If that's true, Mitch, then we have no objection to this man's plan. But if the Chilean tribes do object, we will oppose it too. Can you live with that, Mitch?"

"I can—and will act accordingly." He turned to Willy. "Can you, Dr. McRae?"

"Yes. If that happens, we'll just go back to the drawing board . . . and find a different site that doesn't offend the local population."

The Hawaiian elder looked over at his companions. They nodded their assent.

"Then it's done." Gardner said, reaching over to shake hands with Willy.

"That was fast," said the stunned astronomer.

Gardner sipped his tea and smiled. "Decisions are easy when you're padded with wealth. And if you know who you are and have good friends to advise you, it's possible to do the right thing now and again. My staff will draw up the papers, which will clearly state my conditions for the donation—that the Big Eye go to Chile rather than Mauna Kea, that the Air Force withdraw its involvement, and that objections from the Chilean tribes will mean finding another, more suitable location. I'm also adding another $50 million to the main donation to sweeten Caltech's pot and give you a little more leverage with them. Ten million of that sum will be designated for use by the Chilean tribes. I trust you can shepherd all this through whatever internal politics remain. Jedediah says you're in a position to do that."

"I am."

"Jedediah also expressed some urgency and said that immediate public expression of my donation would be helpful. My staff will help you coordinate the publicity. In the meantime, I'll email you a letter of intent that you can use in your negotiations with Caltech and Alfred Haisley. I'll also send a personal letter to Haisley if you think that might help."

"I'm breathless. Thank you."

"Thank *you*—for flying over to meet us . . . and for giving a damn."

Gardner got up and began walking back to the house, his grizzled ponytail swinging over his back.

"Oh," he said, looking over his shoulder, "I hope it's *you* who finds that planet, the one that reminds us, as you said in your lecture, that 'we're all of one species here on Earth.' If my contribution to the telescope can help meet that goal, I'll consider it money well spent."

His flip-flops slapped confidently on the rock path while Willy, dumbfounded, stood mute by the pond.

"Mahalo," said the eldest of the Hawaiians, now all standing. The others nodded and a round of traditional hugs ensued.

As Gardner stepped out of his flip-flops to enter the house, he turned back once again. "Dr. McRae," he said in a deep voice that carried across the garden. "I'm sure you know this, but it might help sort out your surprise. When one's karma is good—like yours—doing the right thing, or having it done for you, is almost effortless."

That night, as Jedediah Clarke dozed below deck on *Wayfinder*, he dreamt of Poli'ahu. Her luminescent smile and the brilliant, whirling snows around her convinced him that the meeting with Gardner had gone well. The next morning an email from Andromeda and a text from Mitch Gardner confirmed that.

CHAPTER 48
Final Plans Drawn

Willy McRae felt a new bounce in his step after meeting with Mitch Gardner and the Hawaiians. He now had powerful means to restore the project's purity, and he felt his own integrity renewed. He pursued the hasty negotiations with the same charismatic zeal with which he'd birthed the project years earlier at Haisley's party.

Adam Jacob would no doubt be relieved to have someone other than demanding generals funding his Caltech telescope, especially if that also meant avoiding another fiasco like the one they'd suffered with their Thirty Meter Telescope. Those Chilean-site advantages would probably even outweigh "The Bishop's" primary attachment to Mauna Kea—possessing the only GOD that could peer into *both* the Northern and Southern Hemisphere skies, a distinct plus in the brutal competition for astronomical discoveries.

The tougher nut would be Alfred Haisley, but Willy was determined to redirect the beer mogul's focus from his prosaic fixation on a stateside mausoleum to a "transcendent *international* mission guiding us to a living planet," as he would exhort the donor, "and on a mountain where your namesake telescope will remain untarnished by earthly military schemes or protracted indigenous protests." He would also tell Haisley that going to Chile was the only path that would assure that the Big Eye would be built.

Mitch Gardner, writing to Haisley "as one successful businessman to another," told the donor that "your reputation, already firmly
established with astronomers, will expand to a much broader audience—to the international fans of Carl Sagan and Neil de Grasse
Tyson—because you kept your dream alive by choosing a peaceful
middle way."

Willy recruited Andromeda as his "colleague in arms" at the
negotiations, forging a father-daughter collaboration like they'd
never had before. He even wondered if he might eventually finagle
her participation on one of the Big Eye science committees, a plum
appointment for a Caltech student not yet holding a PhD.

While negotiations ensued in California, and the two McRaes
honed their strategy to publicize Gardner's donation, Big Island
Hawaiians quietly organized their protest march to the summit
through one-on-one word of mouth. Over centuries, Hawaiians had
mastered how to keep knowledge of secret events under wraps, trusting discreet elders and their overlapping extended families to spread
the word out of view, like the flows of subterranean springs that feed
the lowlands from mountain heights. Aging activists—veterans of
myriad demonstrations and occupations in the 1970s—schooled the
young ones on how to network quietly to generate huge crowds with
only a day or two's notice.

As effectively as Hawaiians had enforced a strict prohibition—a
kapu—on violence during their years-long TMT protests, they now
imposed a similar discipline to prohibit even the slightest reference
to the march on social media. It was an ironic kapu limiting the very
tools through which they'd stunned astronomers and police during
the TMT clash with extraordinary last-minute sign-wavings, hearing turnouts, and summit road blockades.

Indeed, hundreds had put the Mauna Kea march on their
November calendars, and a committee of "Guardians for the
Mauna"—a newly branded descendant of the celebrated *Kia'i*, protectors, of TMT fame—busily printed placards and amassed the
Hawaiian flags they'd brandished during that earlier fight. With
approval of the Guardians' committee, two highly trusted millennials skilled with social media also created an online ruse to be

launched twelve hours before the march. An elaborate conversation on Facebook, Twitter, and Instagram would suggest that Native Hawaiians would gather that Saturday for a sunrise prayer vigil on the summit of Maui's Haleakala to "heal injuries inflicted on humanity by the military's notorious surveillance compound there." To minimize confusion, cautionary hints of the possible ruse were included in the spoken messages spread through the coconut wireless, warnings that would later be reinforced by planting into the first Facebook and Twitter posts an ancient navigation proverb about fixing one's eyes on the right island and staying together on course.

Even Ranger Jill, whose Kualono half of her family lived on O'ahu, hadn't heard about the Mauna Kea march yet. Moses, of course, was informed, and he shrewdly scheduled his base camp staff to include only workers sympathetic enough not to interfere with the procession, which was set to begin at the visitor center parking lot that Saturday at dawn. Because Josh Mattos worked at the Gemini Telescope, his relatives had so far left him and his immediate family out of the loop. Others with observatory jobs were also kept in the dark or, if they could be trusted, were urged to call in sick that day. The continuing approach of tropical storm Alana, by then upgraded to a Category 2 hurricane, kept officials at Civil Defense, Hawai'i County Police, the National Guard, and the Army preoccupied with storm-related emergency planning.

It was now Thursday, just two days before the march, and organizers worried that operatives in the local Homeland Security network might still catch wind of their plans. NSA and CIA elements of that network included a rogues' gallery of ex-military planted throughout the islands after 9/11 in innocuous federal posts, including in national parks, post offices, NOAA agencies, and various US government telescopes. The Guardians hoped the fake sunrise event on Haleakala—where Hawaiians opposing the Daniel K. Inouye Solar Telescope had been arrested in 2015—would redirect any suspicious operatives to Maui the night before.

Meanwhile, Josh Mattos began executing his own plan to keep the Big Eye off the summit, the first step being an early-morning visit to his parents at their old Waimea home.

"Been staying outta trouble, Dad?" Josh said with male bravado, plopping into the old couch in front of the picture window. His father, hair still damp from his morning shower and dressed in denim from neck to boot, sat slumped in his old La-Z-Boy. Mauna Kea stood in silence outside, its towering profile haloed by streaks of high clouds, the first signs of the hurricane building to the south.

"Much as any old cowhand stays out of trouble," Johnny replied.

Seven weeks had passed since they'd last talked in person, and the four phone calls in between were stilted by Josh's concealed agitation and his father's lingering embarrassment at having broken down in front of his son. Only now—with his decision firm, the plan finalized, and the necessary supplies obtained—did Josh feel settled enough to see his father face-to-face.

"Where's Mom today?"

"At Aunty Lei's, making lauhala mats. Can you stay for lunch? She should be back by then."

"Doubtful." He glanced up at the mountain, wishing he could have seen his mother again too. "Got lots to do today."

"Why? What's up?"

"Oh, ya know, one 'ting after anottah on da home front."

Johnny immediately recognized the lie, more by his son's feigned smile than his words. That bogus grin was something else he'd picked up in Afghanistan.

"Cup o' coffee, son?"

"Sounds good."

Josh followed his lumbering father into the kitchen and sat down at the table in front of the family poi bowl. Johnny filled two old Hilo Hattie mugs with dark brew.

"Of all da horses you w'en rode on da ranch, Dad, which was yer favorite?"

The old cowboy thought only a moment. "No question about that—Ku'uipo." Sweetheart. A blue-eyed Appaloosa with a spotted white butt galloped into Johnny's mind, sporting a handmade saddle embossed with tapa designs by his father. "Tenacious, that gal . . . ," he said, sitting down across the table from Josh. "Never flinched, even up Mauna Kea's steepest slopes."

"She w'en nevah dare wit' *you* in da saddle!"

Johnny laughed, his own grand horse teeth showing. "No, I don't suppose she did."

"We've both had good times on Mauna Kea, haven't we, Dad?" Josh's eyes watered and his dark cheeks flushed.

"We have."

"Last time I was here, you was pretty upset."

Johnny stared into the poi bowl.

"Well, Dad, I done a lot o' t'inkin' since den, and I decided I not going stay wit' Gemini much longer. I jes' been fakin' dat all dis pilikia on da mountain doesn't break my heart too."

"What about Betty and the kids? How you gonna make a living?"

Josh brushed the question away with his muscled hand. "No worry. I'll find somet'ing. See, I know my ancestors stay up dere . . . so . . . I making my own plans for save da mountain."

Johnny sighed deeply. "It may be too late son. Besides, what's there to do? Sometimes, I wish Madam Pele would just take out the whole lot."

"Dat would do it," Josh said, nodding. "In da meantime, gotta defend dose ancestors, right? I mean, what choice we got?"

Johnny nodded absently, immobilized by disappointments—a turbulent marriage, his wounded son, the changed islands, and now the astronomers' siege of the mountain. "Gosh, I'm tired today," he said, rubbing the back of his ruddy neck.

Josh stood up and glugged the rest of his coffee. "Well, I'll get outta yer hair. You jes' rest now." Johnny joined him in standing up, and the two men embraced.

"Love ya, Dad," Josh whispered into his ear. "Please don' evah forget dat."

"I know, son. Aloha."

Josh kissed his father's bristled cheek, and then let go.

It wasn't until that afternoon while mending barbwire on his backyard fence that Johnny realized his son had meant that good-bye to be his last. He dropped his pliers and grasped the fence post, his heart racing. But that shock carried with it a second jolt from his na'au. *Was it my son who shot at the Keck mirror?*

Johnny marched over to the carport where Nani was putting away leftover lauhala leaves from her weaving session with Aunty Lei.

"I think our son's about to do some damn fool thing!" he hollered, his face as pained as the dread erupting in his chest.

Nani's heart dropped, her biggest worry about her son flying into her mind. "Oh, God! He's gonna kill himself."

"No," Johnny said with sudden stoicism. "It's some goddamn thing he thinks he has to do to avenge the mountain!"

Tears filled Nani's big eyes at another truth she'd long recognized. "Josh isn't the same since the war," she said. "His sweet nature is gone."

"He's lost his bearings, Nani. I hardly recognize my own son!"

And yet . . . , she thought, *how alike he is to you, volatile and full of raging passions.* "You men are always turning your grief into conflict," she said, "picking fights, making stands, going off half-cocked in the name of some principle or other."

"Dammit, Nani, don't start!"

Her face went blank, her eyes dark and remote, peering inward. Johnny had seen it many times before and knew to shut up until whatever she was trying to discern with her na'au became clear. "Auwe!" she finally muttered, her face reanimated but looking much older. "This is bad."

"What is it?"

"Something Aunty Lei told me this morning. Now I see why she shared it . . . and why I must now share it with you."

Nani trembled as she described how Lei's dearest cousin, the kaula Uncle Pe'a Morgan, had two nights earlier dreamt that "everything on the mountaintop was swept clean."

"Uncle Pe'a assumed it was a premonition about the coming storm," she explained. "But he was puzzled by one image in the dream . . . a young warrior in a loincloth standing on the windy summit ridge, his spear pointing down toward the north plateau."

Johnny's usual reservoir of energy—capped for weeks by despondency—suddenly poured forth, and he leaped into action. Several calls to Josh's cell yielded only his now ironic message: "You w'en try reach me but failed. T'anks anyway. Leave one name and numbah." Johnny hopped into his black pickup to drive straight to Hilo. As he pulled the Ranger out of the driveway, instinct told him to throw in a few things for the mountain, just in case.

Erik and Hoku had spent that Thursday morning preparing for their own trek on Mauna Kea to spread Aunty Moana's ashes. Her remains, held in a wooden box crafted by one of the "village" carpenters from a piece of fallen mamane near Hale Pohaku, waited on the windowsill of Hoku's seaside bungalow, where she and Erik plotted their clandestine hike to a place and at a time identified by Uncle Pe'a. Erik had shared their plan only with Moses, who as one of the mountain guardians might be needed to lend a hand. It was Moses who would get them through the now locked gate to the summit. He'd also given Erik all weekend off to accommodate the trek, believing that earthly concerns like kitchen schedules and observatory rules—even a clandestine protest—must be put aside for ceremonies set in accordance with the position of the stars and other celestial bodies.

"It'll be damn cold at that hour," Erik told Hoku, urging her to throw even more warm clothes into her duffle. "Moses will give us parkas when we meet him at the gate."

"I've only been up there at night in the summer," Hoku admitted, finding another sweatshirt in a drawer. "What's it like in late fall?"

"Cold but beautiful when it's clear, heavenly, but miserable—even dangerous—in foul weather."

"Are you worried about the hurricane? This morning's paper said it's still tracking toward the island."

"Not so much," Erik said. "But if it does get nasty up there, I have a key to the summit lunchroom. It's built like a bunker, and has a heater too."

In truth, Erik hadn't paid much attention to the storm; he couldn't bear to. He was determined to honor Aunty Moana, who during his despair had harbored him in her love. He had hoped, perhaps foolishly trusted, that the storm would veer off or stall, keeping the way clear to the summit so they could perform their Saturday-morning task at a place and hour set by kahunas.

CHAPTER 49

Tempests on the Way

By Friday morning, Hurricane Alana had sucked all of the archipelago's moist November air into its growing vortex south of the island, and bright morning sunshine burst through the bedroom window of Jill Kualono's studio apartment, stirring her and Special Agent Muku Makau to get up out of bed after their latest steamy liaison. Their affair had certainly spiced up Muku's FBI investigation of the Keck sniping incident and strengthened the couple's bond as investigative comrades.

The naked FBI agent lumbered over to the kitchen area and scanned Jill's refrigerator for something to stem his hunger while she turned on the coffeemaker, furtively admiring his muscled body in the morning light.

"I wonder what's happening with the hurricane?" he said, sitting down at the table with a piece of cold pizza left over from their working session the night before.

"Try check the Civil Defense website," she said, sauntering past him on her way to get dressed and brushing her breasts across the top of his head. "They'll have the latest scoops."

He grinned as he watched her waddle theatrically to the bathroom. "Cocky tita!" No better compliment could he have made to further excite her, and an accurate description of both her ranger style and the way she'd manhandled him in bed.

Muku opened his laptop, still set up on the table. By the time she returned, showered and in uniform for her weekend shift, he'd found the 6:00 a.m. update and read it aloud:

"Hurricane Alana is now 400 miles south of the Big Island of Hawai'i, moving north at 11 miles per hour. Alana is now a Category 2 hurricane with sustained winds of 105 miles per hour. A hurricane watch remains in effect for the entire state of Hawai'i. Current models suggest that the storm will likely pass 200 miles southwest of the Big Island early Saturday morning, bringing high winds and heavy rains to the southern half of the island. While the likelihood of the hurricane coming on land is small at this time, residents and visitors should still take precautions in the event that the storm shifts direction and evacuations become necessary."

"That's a relief," Jill said, pulling her foul-weather gear out of the closet. "But it'll still be nasty on the mountain when she goes by."

"Maybe I'll go up too and do my research from that base camp office they're letting me use. By tonight you may need some warming up."

"What you mean is you'll want some!"

He laughed, delighted at the rapport they'd developed during the investigation. After all that lovemaking his professional rules began to break down and he decided to confide his hunch about the sniper's identity.

"C'mere tita," he said with feigned dominance, calling up a file on the laptop. "I wanna try out an idea on you."

She brought over their coffees and sat down next to him, her hand gripping his naked thigh.

"None of that," he said, returning to his special agent—haole—voice. "I want you to look at these pictures while I take a shower."

Jill was taken aback by the images on the screen, shocked—but not really surprised—that undercover FBI agents had taken pictures of everyone at the earlier protest vigil. It also peeved her that Muku had kept this a secret from her until now. As she scanned the digital images, the Hawaiian half of her got ever more upset, reminded of just how much the state's security network tracked Hawaiian activists.

"Sorry I kept this part of our investigation from you," Muku said when he returned, sitting down at the table in a fresh pair of slacks and an aloha shirt. "We couldn't risk any further reaction to what had happened up there."

"Amazing what a blow job will do," she snapped. "Men!"

"C'mon, it's not like that at all. I really need your help." He nudged the laptop toward her and scrolled through the pictures until he came to the ones during Aunty Moana's heart attack.

Christ! Dey even took pictures o' dat! she thought, shaking her head.

"I wanna get your opinion on something," he said, still not quite grasping her mood.

She crossed her arms. "Yeah?"

"See the guy helping the woman having the heart attack? Any idea who he is?"

Jill leaned forward over the laptop and studied the picture. "He's a Gemini technician, Josh Mattos."

"Hawaiian?"

She frowned at the implication. "Portuguese-Hawaiian—just like me."

"Look at these five shots taken of him before, during, and after she fell to the ground."

She hunched closer to the screen. "So?"

"What do you make of him?"

"Seems pretty agitated—but who wouldn't be seeing a heart attack?"

"Yeah, but look, even before she fell, when he was still just watching the crowd."

Jill nodded. "I see what you mean. Seems real jittery."

"In fact, he looks more rattled *before* the heart attack than after."

Jill scanned the photos. "Yeah, you're right. You know, Muku, I think this is the technician who did two tours in Afghanistan—came back maybe three, four years ago."

"Wo! . . . And that would explain something else. A guy with actual combat experience might have the M16 skills to just miss the Keck mirror from a quarter-mile away . . . and in the dark."

"M16?"

"That's the kind of bullet the county cops found when they searched the dome. The .270 Magnum shell you found on the cone had been there a while. Sorry not to tell you about that either, but I was under strict orders.

Her jaw clenched. *These easy deceptions come from Muku's haole blood*, she thought, well aware of the inner toll of conflicting ancestries.

"Until I studied these pictures, I figured it was your loudmouth cook, Drake, especially after I found out he'd done three years in a federal penitentiary for civil disobedience."

"I didn't know that."

"Apparently was too effective . . . smart, persistent, the point man . . . and he pissed off the government."

How could I not know that? she thought. *After all those years up there, how is that possible? Surely Moses knew.* She glanced out the window. *And knew how to keep it under wraps.*

"But now my guts tell me the Afghan vet is our sniper," Muku continued. "Why he showed up at the protest is beyond me. But sometimes it's like that. Criminals often return to the scene, especially if they're a little lolo. Or he might have been checking it out for another attack. You said he sounded like he planned to do more damage when he blubbered over the phone."

Jill sipped her coffee, struggling to regain composure after feeling betrayed. "He told me—between tears—that the shooting 'was just the beginning,' that he was 'really gonna wreck something.'"

"Problem is," Muku said, getting up and walking into the shaft of light coming through the window, "our new security measures—the public restrictions, the supervised gate—are useless against an insider with summit access through his job."

"Yeah, but I'll be watching for him. You should definitely come up too. I've got a feeling he might make his move this weekend."

"Why this weekend?"

"Just a hunch," she said. There was no way Jill would share with an FBI agent, even a Hawaiian one, what her friends and distant cousins had tried to keep clear of her antennae, that the Hawaiians were marching Saturday. That's why she'd arranged with Moses to work that weekend, just in case she needed to decide whose side she was on. Having her own personal FBI agent on hand could prove useful either way.

~

On the other end of town, Erik was dreaming. Aunty Moana, as a plump little girl with shining eyes, sat on a snow-white blanket atop Mauna Kea. "Everyone has the soul of a child," she said, beaming with that same warm smile Erik knew so well, "no matter what their experiences make them look like on the outside."

A ringing phone startled Erik awake, driving the details of his dream deep into his subconscious. He fumbled for the receiver. "Yeah?" he said, staring dumbly out the Airstream window.

"Erik, it's Hoku! Come over, right away! Your seal just showed up at my house."

It took Erik less than ten minutes to dress and drive over in Baby Blue. He dashed up the walk past the weathered tiki of Kanaloa and knocked on her bright yellow door.

"Come in!" she hollered. "I'm out by the pond!"

Erik immediately spotted the monk seal through the casement windows as he crossed the studio to the French doors leading out back. Hoku, wrapped in her pareu, sat at the edge of the freshwater pool, marveling at the six-foot creature lying on a sandy wash twenty feet down the lava rock shore. Erik knelt next to Hoku, and the silvery seal lifted its robed head, fixing its gaze on the young man.

"*Auuoooooowaa!*" the seal barked, rising up on its stout front flippers.

Hoku grasped Erik's arm. "What's the message?"

"Message?"

"From the kupua!" she said impatiently. "She wouldn't be here without a reason. Concentrate!"

"*Auuoooooowaa!*" the seal barked again.

Erik's words came unbidden. "Maka'ala."

"Maka'ala? Do you even know what that means?"

He nodded. "Aunty taught me . . . 'Eyes open.'"

"So it's a warning."

"Yeah, but about what?"

"Think, Erik."

"I'm trying." He closed his eyes.

"Is it about going up with Aunty's ashes?"

"No . . . something else . . . something that will happen on the mountain."

"The protest?"

Erik peered into the creature's black, sheeny eyes. It blinked. "I don't think so. We'll have put Aunty to rest before the march begins. No . . . something else . . . something we don't know about."

The seal ruffled the folds of its ashen collar and lumbered closer to the pair.

Erik half rose in apprehension. "What's happening?"

"I don't know," Hoku said, tightening her grip. "Stay put!"

The seal swung its quarter-ton body around and shuffled back toward the sea, its flippers scrapping across the lava. "She's leaving!" Erik gasped.

The ancient pinniped slipped into the water, its silver coat flashing under the cobalt swells. A moment later, the ghostly head popped up well offshore.

"Auuoooooowaaa!" she barked, then vanished into the blue depths.

A surge of emotion welled up inside Erik, and tears began streaming from his dark-blue eyes. "Why did she go? Did I scare her away?"

"No," Hoku said, taking his hand. "All hoʻailona—our nature signs—recede once the message is received and understood . . . the bird leaves, the cloud dissipates, the lunar rainbow fades."

"Why am I crying?"

"It's overwhelming to come face to face with the larger forces. Was there anything else, Erik?"

"Only that we have to be very careful."

"I got that too."

Hoku made them breakfast. She was in a chatty mood after the morning's excitement, but Erik was unusually quiet, drifting on thoughts and feelings. Recognizing this, Hoku left him alone. She plucked the Hilo newspaper off the front stoop and over a cup of tea began perusing the day's stories. "Erik, look at this!" She slid the paper across the table. Right under its masthead was a 20-point headline:

Big Eye Blinks: $550 Million Donation Keeps Giant Scope off Mauna Kea

Next to the story was a smiling picture of Mitch Gardner with a caption that read "Shampoo CEO convinces Haisley and Caltech to build in Chile."

"Wow! That's big news!" Erik said.

"I can't believe it. Aunty would be so happy!"

Neither of them could have known that the astronomers they'd met at Aunty Moana's funeral had played a key role in altering the political universe in which the Big Eye project now moved. The article did report that UC Berkeley's chief "planet hunter," Willy McRae, had facilitated the agreement and attended the Maui press conference with the two rich donors, officials from Caltech, and the three Hawaiian elders Willy had met at Gardner's estate. Andromeda's presence in the audience was not mentioned, but half her willowy form could be seen in the press conference photo.

"After all those years, someone from that side finally acted pono," Hoku said, still not quite believing it.

Johnny Mattos had risen early that morning after sleeping fitfully in the guest room of his son's three-bedroom home in Hilo. He and Josh's wife, Betty, had stayed up until after midnight waiting for Josh's return. Her calls to his cell Thursday night and that morning had yielded no replies. Betty was a wreck. Her brave demeanor, which had held the family together in the years after Josh's discharge, had finally shattered. Their two young children sensed something amiss, and Betty had put them in her mother's care for the weekend.

"I didn't even recognize Josh when he left after lunch," Betty confided to Johnny with a wail that sent shivers up the old cowboy's spine. "He hugged the kids as if he was never gonna see them again!" She grasped Johnny's arm with both hands. "Is he gonna harm himself?"

"No, I don't think so, Betty. I checked all his usual haunts," Johnny said quickly, "and his surfboard and fishing gear are still in the garage." Johnny didn't mention that both of his son's rifles were gone, the Winchester and an Army surplus M16 he'd purchased right after his discharge. "The folks at Gemini say he called in sick yesterday and this morning . . . but I think he's on the mountain. I'm going up and see if I can find him." Johnny also didn't share his suspicions about the Keck shooting or his deeper worry that his son now relied on a moral compass he'd used to survive in Afghanistan. Johnny knew that vengeance had taken over Josh's heart and feared that his own grief-stricken tirades had given his son a false justification for violence.

That evening, as Braddah K surfed the first huge waves generated by the hurricane, he had his own revelation. As a Kuamoʻo with a long line of ancestors bearing responsibility for Mauna Kea, he would join the Hawaiians' march to the sacred summit and live out whatever destiny lay there.

By coincidence, Willy McRae was already on the mountain, having decided after the Maui press conference to fly over with Andromeda to give her a tour of the astronomers' base camp and the Kecks.

CHAPTER 50

Reclaiming the Mountain

One hour before dawn, under cloudy skies and in blustery winds, three hundred Hawaiians, environmentalists, and other Big Eye opponents converged at the base camp's visitor center, including families with children. They crowded their vehicles into the parking lot and lined both sides of the roadway. Some carried signs declaring MAUNA KEA IS SACRED – NO BIG EYE HERE! and PROTECT THE MAUNA! A number held poster-size photos of Aunty Moana with lettering proclaiming WE RESPECT OUR KUPUNA (our elders and ancestors), and several clutched MAHALO MITCH GARDNER! signs. KAPU ALOHA placards were everywhere. Numerous Hawai'i flags, some hung upside down as symbols of distress, fluttered madly in the wind. Because of the recently publicized decision to build the Big Eye in Chile, organizers had redefined the march as a "prayer tribute to the mountain" and asked participants to leave behind the most strident signs, including one declaring MAUNA KEA IS A BURIAL FOR KUPUNA NOT MAINLAND FAT CATS!

Many marchers wore traditional kihei draped over their warmer clothes or their faded Ku Kia'i Mauna ("Guardians of the Mountain") T-shirts from the TMT protests. Countless wore leis of maile vine and ti leaves or had fresh blossoms in their hair. Several reporters, including a television crew from Big Island Video News, tipped off at the last moment by Sam Chun, mingled with the crowd, but most of the state's media had flocked to the tiny mock protest on Haleakala, along with numerous police and Homeland Security operatives mis-cued by the organizers' fake social media campaign.

Sam and Koa Makali'i huddled out of the wind in Sam's Honda CR-V, strategizing how best to organize a throng larger than they'd expected. The night before both had joined dozens of other Hawaiians at a traditional ocean cleansing in Keaukaha to "purify their hearts and minds" before the march. At a soul-searching meeting earlier that Friday, event leaders had decided to go ahead with the long-planned march despite news reports that Haisley and Caltech officials had agreed to take the Big Eye to Chile. Most of the organizers had felt that a mass demonstration was still needed to shore up a decision that remained hard for them to believe. Several at the meeting had suggested postponing the march because "Kanaloa's gonna do our work for us," referring to the sea winds of Hurricane Alana. But NOAA's Friday afternoon update reported that the hurricane had stalled one hundred miles south-southwest of the island. "We may get drenched," Sam Chun had said, "but they'll know we won't back down if their commitment to Chile gets shaky."

At the meeting all vowed to do everything in their power to keep the march peaceful "through the sanctity of aloha." For some this would ensure nothing jeopardized the agreement, but for most it was their longstanding commitment not to violate the ancient kapu against warfare on the sacred mountain—a kapu they felt responsi-ble to enforce not just on their own people but on the police and the military, a much harder task.

When two young men showed up at the Friday meeting bearing a tall, fearsome tiki of the war god Kuka'ilimoku, Uncle Pe'a had taken them aside to warn them not to bring it to the next day's march. "Even Kamehameha, who had long worshiped that Ku, ultimately turned away from him," he told the puzzled youths. "That god was not ours. It was brought to our islands centuries ago by Pa'ao and his invading Tahitian empire."

"But Uncle, in school . . ."

"I don't care what they told you in school. Listen to your elders! See with your own eyes! That god thrives on fear and anger. It does not belong in the wao akua, the heavenly realm of our gods!"

"But Uncle, the tiki gives us strength."

"Indeed it does, but what kind of strength? From dark or light? For love or conflict?"

"The strength to fight the foreigners!"

"No! That male war god has intruded on our archipelago far too long! No place is more unfitting for him than on this mauna . . . Mauna a Wakea, where creation flourishes, not destruction, a holy realm tended by sacred female deities. This is a place so pure that even aliʻi warriors of old dared not enter the summit with weapons— or even warrior intent!"

The tall, aging kaula motioned the young men to step forward. "Come close," he said in a hushed voice. "Do you remember the Ku tiki that activists brought up during the prayer vigil last month—the one they've brought to protests for many years?"

"We saw it on social media," said one of them.

"Do you know what happened to it that day?"

They shook their heads.

"It cracked in half . . . and by no human hand! The old activist who tends it set the tiki in the cinder on Kukahauʻula, facing the summit puʻu. As soldiers poured out of their vehicles, an old woman began chanting, asking our ancestors and the gods for protection. At that very moment, a loud crack was heard! The activist and those standing with him turned to look and saw the broken tiki fall. Later the elders met to discuss the incident and concluded it was a message from Ke Akua, that the days of revering that war god are finally over, once and for all, and that if we want peace on this planet, all such gods—everywhere—must be set aside." Uncle Peʻa paused and sparkles rose in his eyes. "And look what happened . . . a compromise was struck and now it appears the telescope will go to Chile after all."

The two young men had been shaken by the elder's rebuke. Before that meeting, they had only heard of Uncle Peʻa, a revered kaula whose ancestry ran all the way back to Hawaiiloa, the very first

Polynesian to make landfall in the archipelago. They agreed to leave their tiki behind the next day.

Braddah K's instinct to attend the march—that his destiny awaited him there—was affirmed when he got out of his car in the orange ambience of the visitor center's sodium lamps and spotted several of his own clan milling about the building and the road. Even old Uncle Pe'a was there. A cousin from Waimea noticed K and rushed up to greet him, placing a long garland of maile leaves around his neck. The gathering's mood was warm despite the cold, with people chatting, laughing, and sharing breath as they waited for instructions. Even so, K hesitated to join them, still worried that a violent confrontation might occur and unleash painful memories too hard for him to bear. Needing time alone with his feelings, he sought temporary refuge in the shadows beneath the eaves of the old stone cabin for which Hale Pohaku had been named.

As the crowd shivered in the windy, predawn gloom, Moses assigned Jeffrey Drake to deliver to them several large thermovats of coffee and the ten dozen doughnuts he'd brought up from Hilo the night before.

"You better have a local take 'em out," Drake said, warily shaking his head.

"No. This task is yours, Jeffrey," Moses replied. "Go down and catch their vibe."

Drake looked long and hard at the man who'd once hired him right out of prison. "Giving me another chance, eh?" he said finally.

Moses smiled. "That right. This time take it."

Drake inched the kitchen van through the crowd and parked it on the concrete lanai in front of the visitor center, a hundred eyes watching. Well aware that both sides of the van displayed the Mauna Kea Cooperative's flashy observatory logo, Drake took a deep breath before opening his door. *Wish I wasn't wearing this damn uniform*, he thought, fully expecting protesters to hassle him when he emerged in his kitchen crew smock bearing the same logo on its breast.

Jeffrey quickly began moving the big thermovats from the van to the broad stone wall above the lanai. Seeing him struggling with the weighty jugs, several men stepped over to help. "Whoa! Dis is heavy!" said one of them. "Whatcha got in here?"

"Hot coffee fo' you folks . . . from da camp manager," he announced, dropping into pidgin. "And dere's doughnuts and cups in da back of da van."

"Oh, brah! Mahalo nui!" said the man, followed by similar responses from many others.

"Somet'ing to warm you up dis morning!" Jeffrey added, taking on a bit of the crowd's cheerful mood. "Cream and sugah ovah dere . . ."

"Dis coffee's da bomb!" said a young Gen Zer with a ponytail and tattoos.

"Ono doughnuts! Safeway, yeah?" said a plump woman with a bundled-up little girl in tow.

"I like the ones with the sprinkles!" the girl said with a smile that nearly broke Jeffrey's heart. *That's who this prayer march is for . . .* , he thought, then shook his head. *As if it will matter . . .*

Within minutes the throng packed the lanai, filling each other's cups while discussing their imminent walk up the mountain.

"Hey! Lemme pour one cup fo' dis hard-working cook," said one of the women. "Thank you, braddah!" she added, giving him a hug.

One of the organizers—a kihei-clad elder in his seventies— stepped over to Jeffrey and set his gnarled hands on his shoulders. "We appreciate your thoughtfulness this morning, son. Your hot coffee has fortified us for the task ahead. People needed this. They were nervous . . . unsettled . . . worried what will happen if the police and Army come. This food and drink . . . your aloha . . . was a godsend. Mahalo." With that, he placed his forehead against Jeffrey's and for the first time in Drake's life he exchanged breath with another human being.

Jeffrey stepped away from the van, ostensibly to get out of the wind. Full of emotion, he slouched against the visitor center wall and sipped the remains of his coffee. Decades had passed since he'd felt the buoyancy of a crowd or had had this kind of aloha directed his way. *Not since those heady days at Pohakuloa,* he recalled. Tears came to his eyes. *Jesus!* he thought, quickly wiping them away with the sleeve of his smock. The marchers' positive vibe was such a contrast to the fear and cynicism he'd carried out there. He felt embarrassed. He glanced down at the observatory logo on his breast. *They didn't give a hoot about that.*

As Sam and Koa began organizing the marchers into a roadwide procession, Jeffrey marveled at the coordinating skill of their core team and the loyal discipline of the crowd. Their camaraderie and aloha was palpable. *This reminds me of how we used to be during the protests at Pohakuloa . . . how I used to be.* Again, his eyes welled up. *I wish I could resurrect those feelings . . . that spirit of optimism . . . and be that way again.*

Just after dawn, the soulful blast of conches resounded off nearby cinder cones and the march began, led by Sam, Koa, and veterans of the TMT protests who had attended the previous night's cleansing. Right behind them walked Uncle Pe'a, who early that morning had received a strong message in his na'au. He had immediately tried to reach Hoku to warn her that Kanaloa's fierce winds might bring a blizzard to the mountaintop, but she and Erik had already left. Failing to reach them, he had decided to attend the march—to be at least partway up the mountain in case his special skills with the deities were needed.

For almost an hour Jill had watched the gathering marchers through binoculars from the sundeck off the camp's dining room, but she waited until they started moving up the road to notify the police and Civil Defense. Agent Makau, confronted with Jill's formidable will, had reluctantly agreed to contact his people only after she'd made her calls. Jill figured it would take at least fifteen minutes for troops at Pohakuloa Training Area to mobilize and another twenty for them to reach the base camp. Police in Hilo and Waimea would take much longer. That would give the Hawaiians enough time to make a powerful statement before being forced to withdraw. Moses had warned her when she arrived at the base camp Friday night that if Hawaiians were stopped at the gate, or if the march was halted before they felt some sense of having done their duty, "passions could boil over, and we'll all be responsible for the trouble after that." For this reason—and out of ancestral loyalty to her Hawaiian half—Jill acceded to her boss's decision to open the gate, but insisted that Moses, as camp manager, do it.

"My excuse for violating company rules," he said, "is to keep the peace."

Willy and Andromeda were still sleeping in their base camp rooms when the march began. They had visited three summit observatories until midnight, chatting with astronomers on the Kecks and Subaru and with the notorious Dr. Sapphire of martini fame, who was back studying star formation on the giant JCMT antenna.

The last of the marchers passed through the gate as the blustery winds picked up another notch, plucking placards out of two people's hands, and the first cold raindrops bled from the sky. Everyone at the base camp was too preoccupied with the throng moving up the road to notice the radio announcement that Hurricane Alana had started moving again, this time back toward the island. The tempest was now thirty-five miles due south, moving north-northeast at seventeen miles per hour, making an imminent landfall possible. By the time the convoy of PTA troops turned off the Saddle Road to head up Mauna Kea, a dark shroud of weeping clouds had pushed up against the mountain's southern face.

At about the time protesters began gathering at the visitor center, Hoku and Erik arrived at the Lake Waiau trailhead, driving the kitchen's yellow Ford Ranger that Moses had lent them and wearing the parkas he'd given them when he opened the gate. Moses had also reminded Erik that if the weather got dodgy, the couple should take cover in the summit lunchroom. Hoku and Erik were painfully aware that only a month earlier they'd been at that trailhead with Aunty Moana. Now their mentor's ashes, carefully wrapped in white tapa cloth, lay inside the wooden box on the seat between them, only inches from where she'd sat that night.

As far as Hoku and Erik knew, they were the only ones on the mountaintop. The last astronomers and technicians had abandoned the domes when the first high clouds blew in at 3:00 a.m., three hours before the first summit patrol ranger usually arrived. The few technicians scheduled to work that Saturday still waited in Hilo and Waimea for the latest word on the erratic hurricane. In keeping with ancient tradition, no one but Uncle Pe'a, who had prepared the tapa-wrapped bundle for burial, knew its intended location.

On the tapa he had stained nautical symbols of wind, waves, sails, and stars.

Hoku removed the tapa bundle from the wooden box and cradled it under her arm. When she opened the door the frigid gales nearly blew the handle out of her grasp, and Erik dashed around the truck to help her. As they started their trek down the trail, the rising wind rattled the folding foxhole shovel strapped to Erik's backpack, and the first driving snow blew out of the clouds. "Maka'ala," he whispered to himself, remembering the monk seal's warning.

They had no idea that two miles away, trembling in his truck behind a windy cinder cone at the far end of the Smithsonian array, Josh Mattos bided his time until dawn, when he would drive up to Keck to plant his bomb. The approach of the hurricane that weekend greatly simplified the execution of his plan. He'd watched the last astronomers and their T.O.s leave hours ago, and assumed rangers would keep the road closed and the mountaintop clear of people. Josh couldn't bear the thought of any more killing. It was a telescope he wanted to maim, a symbol of the science that had sullied his father's mountain, of the Air Force who'd hijacked astronomy's amazing technology as another tool of war, and of the US military who'd hijacked his life. He didn't know—and couldn't have imagined—that cooler heads had succeeded in shifting the Big Eye to Chile, and in the process left the Air Force without its satellite-imaging telescope.

Josh's father was also on the mountaintop. Johnny had gotten around the locked gate Friday evening by maneuvering his truck up the original access trail north of the base camp, bulldozed for Gerard Kuiper in 1964. Two hours of winch work had moved the two boulders the camp's road crew had placed there decades earlier, and it took him another half hour using the truck's granny gears to crawl up the heavily eroded track.

Bundled up in his old hunting jacket, with a down vest underneath and a stocking cap pulled over his ears, he sat in his pickup atop the summit ridge, watching for his son's truck. He'd parked near Josh's observatory in case he'd go there. From that vantage point, Johnny could also spot any activity near all but one summit observatory. Only the Smithsonian antennas, sprawled across the north plateau, were hidden from his view by the giant cones on which the Kecks and the Subaru Telescope had been built. Johnny had driven to Gemini as soon as the nighttime observers left, having spent the earlier hours dozing in the very spot Erik and Hoku would later park their truck.

Thick fog and driving snow swirled about Hoku and Erik as they trudged along the cinder trail to Lake Waiau. The unreality of the all-white scene added to their sense of mission. To Hoku, the snow and foggy mist felt like embraces from the goddesses Poliʻahu and Lilinoe, divine aloha that kept her body warm and tempered her worries about the arriving storm. Indeed, she felt more confident than ever. Hoku sensed the presence of Aunty Moana with each step, now and again seeing her smiling face in the bulging, racing clouds.

Erik felt the spirit of his father whirling around him and heard his reassuring voice in the wind. "Storms make you realize the man you are," Erik heard him say. "Use the strengths you acquired on the river. You know how to paddle in fogs and gales without losing your way, so why not navigate the *main* channel? There's no need to shelter in backwater bays anymore! Be a man, son!"

CHAPTER 51

Confronting the Real Enemy

The Hawaiian procession was a mile above the base camp when an Army convoy carrying sixty soldiers in riot gear raced up to Hale Pohaku. By then the marchers had donned rain jackets, ponchos, or black garbage bags to shield themselves from rain. Many wore stocking caps, some adorned with Ku Kiaʻi Mauna patches.

The eight-vehicle convoy included Humvees, a Stryker tank, and troop trucks, including an empty one at the rear for prisoners. Behind the lead Humvee was the Stryker, equipped with an Active Denial System heat ray. Originally designed for crowd control in Afghanistan—and shipped to the island just that week—its broad microwave beam, emitted from a large square panel atop the vehicle, could repel scores of people with a charge that made them feel as if their flesh was on fire.

The same lieutenant colonel with the war-seasoned face who had dispersed the summit vigil in September drove the lead Humvee, but he was not in charge. His superior, a young colonel from Maryland with a smooth face and steely gray eyes, had been assigned to PTA after the last "fiasco"—with strict orders not to compromise security again.

"Any disorder will be met with swift force," he had declared at the quick briefing thirty minutes earlier. "If the protesters don't disband immediately, mass arrests will be made . . . of everyone. We won't make the same mistake Hawai'i authorities made during the TMT protests!"

The colonel trained his combat binoculars on the steep slope above the astronomers' compound. His jaw tightened as he scanned the long mass of marchers moving slowly up the cinder road above the first switchback. "They've got five times the troops that we have," he estimated in military vernacular that caused his second in command to take a deep breath. *We're gonna do it all over again*, the lieutenant colonel thought, *in spades*.

The young officer halted the convoy at the guard shack where Moses and Jill stood waiting in rain slickers. He rolled down his window and damp mist blew in.

"I'm the camp manager," Moses shouted above the wind and the vehicles' noisy rumble, "and this is our chief ranger, Jill Kualono."

The colonel, startled to see Native Hawaiians in authority, glanced over at his second.

"The crowd's been peaceful, so far," Moses continued, "and includes children and elders. We've had no incidents, and I don't expect there to be any."

"County police here yet?"

"Negative," Jill replied in her toughest ranger voice, "ETA fifteen minutes."

"We'll have it under control by then," the young officer said, glancing back at the Stryker equipped with the heat ray.

"It's under control *now*," Moses said calmly. "The astronomers are down here sleeping and no one else is going up in this weather."

"How many rangers on duty?" the colonel asked Jill, the pitch of his voice a notch higher.

"Two, but I'm the only one commissioned for law enforcement."

The colonel glanced skeptically at her sidearm (which she'd put on for just that effect).

"I was a Waikiki street cop for ten years before this job," she said, pressing her face into his window. "But I don't plan to prove anything here today. This is just a peaceful march up the mountain. The biggest danger to life and property this morning will come from weather"—she pierced his hard gray eyes with her brown ones—"unless people lose their heads."

The colonel's face reddened. "I hope you're right about that, ma'am. We'll soon see."

Forty-mile-an-hour winds moaned across the camp buildings as the convoy moved through the gate. The marchers, alerted by the distant roar of the convoy's ascending vehicles, tensed, and a rush of apprehension passed through the crowd.

"We've got big trouble, Sam," Koa Makali'i said to Chun. "What do we do now?"

"First and foremost, stay calm. They can't make a battle if we don't fight."

Koa peered at the line of vehicles rumbling up the road, resisting her rising ire. A picture of Queen Lili'uokalani imprisoned in her palace flashed through her mind. "That's right," she said finally. "We can't allow the bastards to turn this into their game."

She pointed at two young Hawaiians nearby. "You two, walk through the crowd, tell everyone to stay calm, and keep an orderly procession. We'll chant 'E Ho Mai' until they get here. Only the march leaders are to say anything to the soldiers. No catcalls! Stay in aloha! Understand?"

The two nodded and disappeared into the throng to pass the word.

Sam looked surprised. He didn't know that right after midnight, Koa's navigator ancestors had sailed into her dreams on a double-hulled voyaging canoe bearing a message: "We will be with you today as long as you keep faith with us and with the gods who guided us over many a stormy sea. Hold tight to your rudder of aloha and you will not lose your way. We will not abandon ship if you don't."

"*E ho mai ka 'ike mai luna mai e*," she began. Grant us the wisdom from above. The other leaders joined in and the crowd followed, a potent chorus even in the wailing wind.

"Hold tight to your rudder of aloha and you will not lose your way."

Four thousand feet above them, Hoku and Erik reached the spot where they'd left the trail to take Aunty Moana and Uncle Peʻa to the rim of Puʻu Waiau. Just then the fierce, snow-packed winds paused a moment and the distant upright stones they'd seen that night caught the attention of both of them—ancient sentinels left by Aunty Moana's clan to guide their descendants. Goose bumps rose along Hoku's spine and Erik gasped.

"I mua!" Hoku declared as their brief window filled in again with blinding snow. Onward!

They continued down the trail and five minutes later crested the cone of Puʻu Waiau. Through a torrent of blowing snow, the dim outlines of the lake came into view. Hoku pointed toward the spot Uncle Peʻa had identified as the proper resting place for Aunty Moana's remains. With renewed energy, they marched forward through what was now a powerful blizzard. Hoku had never seen anything like it, and for her it took on mystical dimensions that kept her mind off the frigid cold in her face, legs, and toes. Despite the near-horizontal barrage of pelting snow, she and Erik could see the sky to the south turning black.

Sam, Koa, and Uncle Peʻa walked back through the long, chanting procession to meet the military convoy while the other leaders guided the group forward past the second switchback. By then winds had risen beyond gale force, and driving rain blew so hard that people at the front of the procession could not see those in the rear. Finally through the throng, Sam, Koa and Uncle Peʻa stood alone in the middle of the road as the convoy rumbled up to them. The colonel directed his second to stop the Humvee a few yards in front of the trio. He lowered his helmet's face shield, unholstered his riot baton, and got out. Four soldiers from his Humvee hurried to his side, and the heat ray operator, watching via video monitor inside the Stryker, positioned his joystick at the ready.

It was only then that Sam noticed the strange weapon atop the vehicle. *What in hell is that?*

"This is a government road on state-owned property!" the young colonel shouted into the rainy wind. "Have you got a permit for a public demonstration?"

"We don't need a permit to climb our sacred mountain!" said Koa.

"If you have no permit, you cannot proceed."

Sam expected the authorities to take this tack, but as an attorney, he knew that legally they stood on shaky ground. "That claim won't hold up in court," he said calmly, despite the alarm rising in his chest. "Our state constitution ensures Native Hawaiian access."

"He's our lawyer," Koa declared, thrusting her finger toward Sam.

"That may be, but I'm under orders to disband this group."

By then the three-member TV crew had made its way to the standoff, their camera shrouded under a rain cape. The soaked reporter in the group held out her mic to catch the argument while the cameraman began shooting. Just upwind, the third crewmember struggled to keep driving rain off the lens with a black plastic tarp that flapped loudly in the gale.

"Seize that camera!" the colonel barked to his soldiers, all dripping with rain.

"That's a mistake," Sam said, "that you'll pay for tomorrow."

The camera kept rolling.

The colonel gestured to the four soldiers beside him. "Proceed."

The reporter thrust her microphone into the commander's face. "Colonel, by what authority—"

"Homeland Security! Civil Defense! You name it, I got it!"

The soldiers stormed the crew and tore the camera out of the videographer's arms, then went for the reporter's mic.

At that moment, the seasoned lieutenant colonel appeared at his superior's side.

"Sir, may I speak with you a moment. Information from command."

The young officer paused to think. It was only then that he realized he was woozy from the altitude. Uncertain, he acceded. "In the Humvee," he declared, pointing at the vehicle. "You four soldiers, stand by."

"What's the message from command?" he asked when they were back in the Humvee.

"You're to stand down," said the lieutenant colonel.

"What officer sent that directive?"

"I did . . . on behalf of my soldiers."

"You can't—"

"With all due respect, sir, we're making a big mistake here."

"I'll be the judge of that!"

"No, you won't. The generals will make that determination . . . based on our reports. If there's violence this morning, and in front of the media, you'll be put back to my level," a reference to both his rank and his reprimand after the last mountain confrontation.

"You're a fine one to talk. Under your command, the protesters overwhelmed your Stryker and cowered your gunner!"

"Not exactly. She stood down to keep the peace . . . just as all hell was about to break loose."

"And was demoted."

"Yes, that was the Army's assessment. But she did the right thing, the only thing at the moment that could have avoided bloodshed . . . and saved the Army's ass."

"You're out of line, soldier!" the colonel growled though his face shield. "I'm tasked with maintaining order, and that means disbanding these protesters!" he said as if reading out of a field manual.

"You won't do that unless you start talking with them, not barking orders. They're civilians not—"

"Radical extremists? We've been tracking these Hawaiians for years. This is all about undermining American authority here, to establish their own rogue nation and kick the military off the islands! They don't want that telescope because we'll use it to defend the United States! Anti-Americanism is the real enemy here today!"

The reactionary outburst shocked the older soldier. "No!" he shouted, clutching the young colonel's arm and peering into his face. "The real enemy is ignorance," he said in a lower but still resolute voice, "and the fear I see in your eyes that comes from it."

"Careful, soldier . . ."

"It's the same dumbshit ignorance that took us into Iraq and Afghanistan!" He pressed on recklessly. "And Vietnam before that! I recognize it only because I did three hairy stints in Iraq while you were still toting your books to officers training class! No, young man, they're not radical extremists. They're a bunch of islanders trying to defend their mountain. And the biggest tragedy of it all is that our soldiers will pay for their officers' folly . . . like they always do. I'm not gonna let you jeopardize the safety and reputation of *my* trainees because of *your* ignorance . . . and I'm more than happy to explain all this at a court-martial if I have to."

Two blasts of rain-filled wind slammed the Humvee with such force that it shook as if the earth had quaked, causing the colonel to brace himself against the windows. The older soldier suppressed a smile.

The young officer's steely eyes burned, but he said nothing. Deep in his male psyche, beyond the reach of schoolbook lessons, he recognized the personal authority of an older, seasoned man who, despite his lower rank, was his alpha.

"Now go back out there with your shield up off your face so they can see you, and use all your professional training—and your strong will—to *talk* them off the mountain!"

"I'll try it," he declared without flinching, "but if that doesn't work, I expect you to follow my commands without protest."

"Yes, sir!" he replied with a perfect salute.

The colonel radioed the sergeant assigned to the soldiers detaining the news team. "Back off from the TV crew," he said, "and await further orders." He then called the heat ray operator in the Stryker: "No engagement without a clear signal from me."

"Copy that."

"Good moves," said the lieutenant colonel. "Sound judgment."

The young man took a deep breath, pushed his shield up off his face, and grabbed the door handle. By then snow mixed with the rain, and the winds were wilder than ever.

The marchers at the back of the procession had seen the soldiers manhandle the TV crew, and a dozen of them broke ranks to rush down the road to help. By the time the colonel stepped back out of the Humvee, they had assembled behind Sam, Koa, and Uncle Pe'a. A big beefy Hawaiian stepped out of the group to stand beside the elder. It was Braddah K, his broad shoulders and dark hair plastered with snow.

"I'm descended from da first Hawaiians w'en climb dis mountain," he said in a firm, low voice almost lost in the windy deluge. "My ancestors are buried here, and my family has kuleana for dis mauna.

So . . . on behalf of my ʻohana . . . I welcome you to our mountain."

The colonel was so taken aback that he failed to anticipate Braddah K's next move. The four nervous soldiers watched the big Hawaiian advance, and anticipating the colonel's command, reached for their batons.

Braddah K placed his maile lei on the young officer's shoulders and with a firm bear hug kissed him on the cheek. "Aloha," he said.

With Aunty Moana's remains now lodged among her ancestors— Poliʻahu's blizzard already concealing the buried tapa-wrapped bundle under snow—Hoku and Erik trekked back up the drifting trail. The frozen tears Hoku had cried during her burial chant glistened on her cheeks. *From now on, Aunty Moana's love will be my strength*, Erik thought as he trudged through a foot-high drift. *If she could keep faith with losses graver than any I've endured, I can too.*

Three miles away, on a snowy track leading from the north plateau to the cinder "escape road" behind the Keck telescopes, Josh Mattos began his final journey to the top of Mauna Kea. He four-wheeled through the raging blizzard, the explosives he'd prepared cushioned with blankets in the crew cab of his truck and his two rifles racked above them. He passed the Smithsonian antennas flanking the road, their snow-heaped dishes making them look like bizarre sentries with giant sombreros. When he finally turned off the north plateau to climb the heavily drifted road to the Kecks, he was no longer in the lee of the summit ridge and the full force of Alana's winds smacked his truck.

That's when his father spotted the big Silverado from his perch next to the Gemini dome. Johnny extinguished the portable camping heater that had warmed his cab all morning and slammed his truck into gear.

CHAPTER 52
Kanaloa's Winds

Seventy-five-mile-an-hour winds rocked the yellow pickup as Erik and Hoku huddled in its cab, waiting for the engine to generate enough warmth to turn on the heater. Their beet-red faces were wet, wind-burned, and cold, and their thawing feet ached inside icy boots. Hoku, on the passenger side, shivered violently, her teeth chattering.

The towering cinder cones around them—their peaks cloaked in dark, swirling vapors—shielded them from the tempest's strongest winds. Even so, brutal gusts pummeled the truck as if by giant fists hurled from above, and horizontal snow flew by the windshield, rendering everything beyond it white. Snow crystals piled up against the glass, a warning that eventually the truck, too, would become part of the buried landscape. Now and again eddying winds opened portholes in the storm, revealing a ghostly profile of the nearest dome—the tall cylindrical building of the James Clerk Maxwell Telescope.

Erik found a kitchen towel in the cluttered space behind the seat and wiped the moisture off Hoku's trembling face. "Aunty Moana would probably find all this exciting," he said to assuage the fear he saw in Hoku's eyes.

"I've never been this cold in all my life!"

"The wind-chill during that last mile of the trail was probably minus ten or more," he said, wiping his own face. "Pretty typical for winters back home."

"No wonder you're not in agony. Your Viking ancestors knew how to handle it. Mine came from the tropics."

"Hang in there, Hoku. We'll have some heat in here soon."

He poured coffee into two Styrofoam cups from the thermos Moses had given them at the gate three hours earlier. It was now lukewarm, but still yielded steam in the frigid cab. "Let's see what's happening with the hurricane," he said, turning on the radio. "Up here we catch stations all over the state."

The kitchen crew had set the dial on KAPA, a Hawaiian station in Kona, which that day played Mauna Kea songs in solidarity with the marchers. Just concluding was a stirring tribute to the snow goddess, "Poli'ahu I Ke Kapu" by Waimea-born Hawane Rios.

"Maika'i!" Hoku said, her spirit lifting a bit. "That's comforting."

As the song finished, the announcer Sistah Lulu came on. "Here's da latest scoops off da social media," she said, tracking the day's events on her iPhone. "We got a crowd estimate now, direct from da march . . . one text from my sistah-in-law. At least three hundred people, she say! She also say da winds and rain *really* intense now, dat it's prob'ly snowing on the summit. As you folks know a'ready, Alana hit da Big Island a few minutes ago . . . so gotta be pretty wild up dere on the mauna!"

"Uh-oh," Erik said.

Hoku's mouth dropped. "You think we can get back down?" she asked.

"No problem," he replied, far less certain than his tone. Even with four-wheel drive, the road above ten thousand feet would be treacherous. Whatever snow had fallen would already have blown into drifts, and ice from freezing rain downslope no doubt slickened the road's lower portions. They'd also be driving southwest, straight into the storm. "But to be on the safe side," he added, "let's head up to the summit lunchroom . . . if that road's still passable."

"What the . . . ?" Erik gasped as a break in the windblown snow again revealed the towering dome of the James Clerk Maxwell Telescope. "A vehicle just drove up to the JCMT!" They watched as a chubby man, made more so by his bulky parka, struggled to get out of his Ford Explorer. Bent low against the wind, with his briefcase tugging in the gusts, he plodded through drifts to the observatory door and a moment later disappeared inside. The porthole closed again and they looked at each other.

"Weird," Hoku said. "What's he doing up here in this weather?"

"I don't know. He's not a telescope operator I recognize . . . must be an astronomer."

"Why would he come now?"

"It doesn't make sense," Erik said. "I've heard of emergency runs in bad weather, usually to top off dewars with liquid nitrogen so the detector's chips stay cold if the summit gets sealed off for days. But they should have sent a T.O. to do it. And *nobody's* supposed to drive up in a storm alone."

A pounding on Hoku's door startled both of them. This time it came from a human fist. Hoku opened the electric window as snow blasted inside.

"My son's crazy!" shouted the swarthy old man leaning inside the window. Water mixed with snow dripped off his nose and cheeks, and he labored for breath. "He's come unhinged! And I think he's gonna sabotage an observatory!"

Hoku, already spooked by the storm, leaned in toward Erik and pressed the window's control button. The rising glass pushed the old man's arms off the window.

"Wait! Wait! My son's gonna blow up that dome!" he cried, pointing his trembling gloved finger toward the JCMT.

"I think this guy's for real," Erik said, leaning over Hoku. "Get inside!" he yelled through the glass. Erik pulled Hoku into the middle of the seat, and Johnny Mattos squeezed his big frame into the truck, slamming the door behind him.

"He was after the Keck," he said, winded and panting, "the Californians' telescope! But the blizzard kept him off the summit! I tried 911 but I get no signal from my cell!"

"Calm down!" Erik declared, suddenly taking charge. *Storms make you realize the man you are.* "You need to tell us what this is all about!"

"Yes," Johnny said, struggling to quell his panic. "Yes, of course." He took a deep breath and swallowed. "You know about the Keck mirror . . . about the shooting last summer?"

"Yes."

"Well, I think my son was the sniper."

Erik and Hoku glanced at each other, absorbing the remark. The cab, its windows fogged from everyone's breath, suddenly felt claustrophobic. Erik switched on the defrost, its air just beginning to warm.

"When I finally figured that out," Johnny said, still panting, "I realized he might try something else . . . do more damage. He's got an M16 with him, but he also knows how to make explosives . . . from his time in the Army. I came up here to stop him." Johnny placed his sopped glove over his forehead, his eyes watering. "The war ruined him . . . set him off balance. He tried to get it together . . . he really did . . . even got himself a regular job."

Erik reached across Hoku to grasp the old man's arm. "But why attack a telescope!"

"Oh God!" Johnny moaned, unable to express his own complicity. "On top of everything else, he feels shame about working for Gemini."

"Working for Gemini! What's his name?"

"Josh . . . Josh Mattos."

"Hoku! He was the one with the defibrillator at the summit vigil, the guy who got Aunty Moana's heart beating again!"

Johnny jerked back against the window. "What?"

"We can't go into it now," Erik said, "but I know who he is. Why do you think he's trying to blow up JCMT?"

Johnny seemed to finally catch his breath. "It's the biggest one he can reach in the blizzard. He tried to get to the summit—that back road behind Keck—but it's blocked with snow." He pointed again at the British observatory. "I saw him park on the other side of that dome. I tried to catch up with him, but my truck got waylaid in drifts on that switchback just below the summit."

"You walked all the way from up there? That's more than a mile!"

Johnny nodded. "When I discovered his guns gone I thought he was gonna finish the job he started when he shot at the Keck, but I have a feeling he's planning worse. Josh learned explosives in the Army. He knows how to do it."

Again a porthole opened in the storm, and the tall profile of the parka-clad soldier appeared in the drifts at the base of the dome. He was bending over, fidgeting with something near the wall.

"Oh Christ!" Johnny cried, flinging open the truck door. Ice crystals blew inside as the old hunter strode into the storm.

Erik leaped out and intercepted him in the drift fronting the truck.

"I'll go!" Erik hollered through the snowy wind. "I haven't been walking a mile," he lied. "You stay in the truck and keep trying 911 on your cell!"

"It's *my* kuleana!" Johnny hollered back.

"Then we'll go together. You start, and I'll catch up. I need to tell Hoku what's happening. Give me your cell."

Johnny dug inside his jean jacket and found the phone.

"Don't rush!" Erik declared. "You'll be of no use if you're out of breath before we reach him. What's your name?"

"Johnny . . . Johnny Mattos."

"OK, Johnny, I'll be right back."

The old cowboy trudged forward into the white out while Erik plowed back through the drifts. The heat inside the truck gave him a moment of relief.

"We're gonna go after him together, Hoku. Try to get a signal on your cell and call 911, but don't waste the batteries if you can't get through." He handed her Johnny's phone. "Here's an extra cell. It's old, but he might have a different service provider—and additional juice. Also, try the base camp once or twice. The number's here on the dash. Will you be OK?"

Hoku nodded.

Erik slammed the door shut and headed into the howling storm. A minute later, the winds shifted again and the observatory popped into view. The distant figure set another parcel further along the wall then disappeared around the back of the building. Johnny, two hundred feet in front of Erik, was still two hundred yards from the dome.

As Erik closed the gap between them, he noticed that beneath Johnny's hunting jacket a holstered pistol hung from his belt. He couldn't be sure in the blowing snow, but it looked an awful lot like a six-shooter.

CHAPTER 53
Maelstrom Revelations

The base camp was abuzz when Willy and Andromeda walked in from the dormitory, their slumbers broken by the wailing wind and the earlier roar of the Army convoy climbing the cinder road.

"What's going on?" Andromeda asked Jeffrey Drake as she waited in the last of the breakfast line. Her father, scowling, stood behind her.

"Another terrible confrontation," Drake said soberly. "More misunderstandings."

Willy, surprised at the cook's civil tone, narrowed his eyes. *Is this the same creep that humiliated me last time I was here?* he thought.

"Why? What's happened?" Andromeda asked.

"Hundreds of Hawaiians marching to the summit . . . and an Army convoy to stop them."

"So that's what I heard an hour ago."

"Another protest?" Willy said. "But the Big Eye's going to Chile."

"They know that. We took some coffee and doughnuts down to the marchers this morning and they told me it's no longer a protest. It's a prayer vigil to honor the mountain . . . dedicated to peace and aloha." Jeffrey almost choked saying those last words, the palpable—disorienting—love he'd felt from the crowd still with him. "They're also carrying mahalo signs for Mitch Gardner," Drake added, "and told me they're grateful to whoever put that deal together."

Willy blushed and Andromeda smiled.

"Then why the military convoy?"

Pain crossed Drake's face. "Some people have a hard time recognizing love . . . or accepting it."

"Look! The Army's heading back down!" Freddie hollered from the lobby, where he'd been watching with binoculars out the glass front doors. "Looks like the Hawaiians are coming down too!"

"Any arrests?" Jeffrey asked when he got to the entrance, his voice so shaky that Freddie did a double take to be certain it was Drake.

"Can't tell yet. They're still too far up the mountain."

Willy and Andromeda abandoned their trays and joined the knot of astronomers craning to see out the front doors. A shower of marble-sized hail pelted the glass and bounced off the vehicles in the lot. The awed onlookers stepped back.

The long line of Army vehicles and the throng of islanders behind them, their Hawaiian flags wildly flapping, were barely visible in the barrage of wind, rain, and hail, but the vivid picture of confrontation stunned Willy. He stumbled away from the doors, steadying himself on the check-in counter fronting the base camp's office. Only then did he fully realize how right Andromeda and Jedediah had been about the Hawaiians' feelings—and the potential for a terrible clash.

Five minutes later, the hail stopped and the crowd at the entrance could clearly see that everyone was coming back down. "I don't see anyone cuffed in zip ties," Freddie said, peering through the binos. "The marchers look drenched, but some of them are smiling."

"Thank God it's over," Moses replied, resting a big hand on Freddie's shoulder. "I hope no one's been hurt and that everybody can get off the mountain before this storm gets any worse." *And that Erik and Hoku are safe inside the summit lunchroom*, he thought.

Thirty minutes later, the hurricane's leading edge slammed the base camp. Two windows got shattered by lumber flung off a storage pile, and the old eucalyptus tree near the visitor center snapped in half. Shingles flew off roofs and the dining room lights flickered. Moses walked briskly to the coffee urn where Jill and Muku were filling mugs after abandoning the now roofless guard shack.

"More trouble," Moses said to Jill.

She slouched against the counter. "Now what?"

"We're missing an astronomer. Old Doc Sapphire's not in the camp, and Jeffrey Drake thinks he went back up to retrieve his MacBook before the summit got blocked by snow. According to Drake, the old Brit realized he'd left it behind while sipping his morning martini."

"Who's the idiot that let him through the gate!" the ranger shouted.

"One of the T.O.s."

"Shit! Now someone's gotta go get him!" Jill said, shaking her head, "and that no doubt means me."

"I'll go with you, Jill," said Muku.

"Which dome?"

"JCMT."

"Well, we *might* make it that far, but I'm not taking any chances. There's probably enough crackers and peanut butter in their lunchroom to keep him fed for a week, if need be."

"If he has the sense to stay put," Moses said, "and if the dome doesn't get badly damaged." Again, he thought of Erik and Hoku.

"You really think the summit will get hit that hard?" Muku asked.

"I just got a call from Civil Defense. Alana's now a Category 3 hurricane and she hit the southeast side of the island twenty minutes ago. If she stays on her current course, she'll plow right over us. There's already lots of damage on the coast and power poles down all over the place. The only reason we still have power is we're on the priority grid."

"Then why aren't we evacuating the camp?" Jill said with rising exasperation.

"Civil Defense says it's probably too late."

"Yeah, no kidding," Muku quipped, shaking his head.

"I've got Freddie and Jeffrey battening down the hatches, but I'm afraid Alana's already on us."

"Don't hurricanes weaken once they hit land?" Muku asked.

"Usually, yes," Moses nodded, "but if they don't, they can actually intensify as they go upslope. No one really knows for sure what that means on an island this tall. There were no scientists here the last time a hurricane plowed over the Big Island, back in the late 1800s . . . and that storm was smaller than Alana. After talking with the NOAA guys, Civil Defense thinks the summit could get devastated."

"Nothing like giving us a little notice!" Jill carped.

"I said the same thing. They told me we're probably safe down here at the base camp . . . unless the hurricane intensified when it climbed up the saddle."

Jill shook her head. "Not good."

"The whole thing is strange," Moses said, gazing through the dining room windows at the tumult outside. "That hurricane was clearly heading northwest and away from the island until four o'clock this morning. Even two hours ago, it looked like it was gonna miss us."

Jill turned to Muku. "If we're gonna go up, we better go now. But I'm telling you, Moses, I'm taking no chances with our lives just because some dumbshit, gin-tipsy astronomer gambled his life for a laptop!"

Johnny Mattos stopped in his tracks a hundred yards from the British observatory. "What's that other vehicle?" he asked Erik, now right beside him.

"There's an astronomer inside the dome."

"God no!" He plunged forward.

"You won't save anyone if you run out of steam!" Erik said. "Slow down!"

Johnny paid no attention, and the two men were almost running.

The last seventy-five yards were the worst. JCMT sat on a rise and the steep, boulder-strewn slope below it taxed their legs and lungs. Johnny, now hypothermic, shivered uncontrollably, yet this mountain of a man kept putting one boot ahead of the other.

He's moving on pure will! Erik thought, well aware of his own acute fatigue. "We're almost there," Erik said to reassure them both. "We'll need a plan of action."

"I'll handle it," Johnny declared. "He's my son."

"What's the gun for?"

Johnny ignored the question.

Halfway up the rise, they could see the yellow detonator wire linking all the explosives.

"You cut the wire while I stop my son," Johnny said, struggling to pull his Leatherman tool out of its holster on his belt. But his frozen fingers wouldn't work, and the unsuccessful effort spent the last of the old man's energy. He fell to his knees, cussing. Erik tried to help him out of the snow, but Johnny couldn't make his legs work.

"I'm done," he gasped, fighting to catch his breath. "Here," he said, reaching under his jacket for the pistol holstered there, "take this."

"I won't use it." Love and hate can't occupy the same space.

"Mad dogs must be shot!"

"He's your son!"

"Not anymore!"

"I'll talk him out of it!"

"You're crazy!"

"Johnny, everyone has the soul of a baby . . . no matter what their experience makes them look like."

"He'll kill you first, and he knows how to do it!" Johnny said, big tears streaming off his face and into the wind.

"Then I'll die." *Be a man.*

Erik felt a surge of energy, as if his own father was with him, and he forged ahead with renewed conviction. He glanced back at Johnny Mattos. His big shoulders convulsed in grief as the snow drifted in around him.

Jill drove her bright red pickup straight into the purple clouds whirling around the mountaintop. Sheets of horizontal rains and wind-lifted cinders strafed the truck as Jill four-wheeled through deep trenches surging with ash-reddened water.

"Dis is one mean storm!" Muku yelled on adrenaline. He reached over and squeezed her thigh. "One mean tita driver too!" Jill would have returned the gesture, but she dared not take a hand off the wheel.

Another thousand feet up, sleet began plastering the windshield and turned the truck's VHF antenna into an ice-crusted sculpture.

The south wind shrieked through a tiny gap in the rear window's seal, unnerving both of them.

Erik finally crested the rise on which the giant dome stood. He dug into his parka's pocket for Johnny's Leatherman, but it wasn't there. He searched the other pocket. "Oh no!" he muttered, only then realizing that in the argument about the gun, and with his head hypoxic, he hadn't actually taken the tool.

The ex-soldier was seventy-five yards away, rolling the yellow wire back to his truck.

"Josh!" Erik hollered through the wailing, snowy wind, cupping his hands around his mouth like a megaphone. Above them pieces of debris—dome panels, roofing tiles, and lots of tourist litter—was flying off the summit ridge, bouncing down cones or twirling in the wild winds.

Josh spun around, astonished to see the outlines of another man standing in the storm.

"Your father sent me!" Erik shouted, resuming his march through the drifts.

"Get outta here if you don't wanna die!" Josh shouted back.

"The blast's gonna kill you too!"

"Don't matter. I dead a'ready!"

"There's an astronomer inside the dome!" Erik shouted, pointing at the steel behemoth. "You really want to kill an innocent man?"

Josh glanced through the driving snow at the JCMT Explorer parked in the loading dock. He had wondered what it was doing there.

"Your father's here too, stuck in a snowdrift on the other side of the dome!"

"Bull!"

"Johnny risked his life to find you." By then Erik was close enough to see surprise, then consternation pass over Josh's face. "That's four innocent men that will die in the blasts," Erik said, now almost close enough to stop shouting.

"Don't include me! I not innocent!"

"Everyone has the soul of a baby. That includes you." Erik continued to trudge forward.

Josh reached inside his parka and pulled out the M9 service pistol he'd smuggled out of Afghanistan. His eyebrows were crusted white with snow. "You talkin' crazy!"

"You love this mountain, don't you?" Erik said.

Josh didn't answer.

"You love it as much as your father does."

"It's in our blood, dammit!"

"Well, you're not the only one. There's hundreds of Hawaiians marching up the road right now to show the world they also love Mauna Kea."

"C'mon. In dis storm?"

"In this hurricane! And that old woman you saved the last time the Hawaiians came up, she loved the mountain too. She knew her heart was damaged, by all the crap she'd endured, but she came anyway, to test her hopes and make her stand for the mountain."

"Yeah, well, she died."

"Trying to keep the love alive. She's here today, you know, right now, standing next to you."

The winds suddenly hushed as if a great blanket had been pulled over the mountain, and deep blue sky shown above them. Josh dropped the spool of blasting wire and stood, dumbfounded, in the inexplicable calm.

"Aunty Moana was a healer," Erik said, no longer shouting. "Because of her, others who love Mauna Kea convinced the astronomers to take their Big Eye to Chile. It's not coming here, Josh! Do you hear me? The telescope's going to South America! The summit is safe! It's safe because people intervened and changed everything. It was love that made people do the right thing—not hate. Now it's your turn."

Sunlight broke over the edge of the hurricane's eye, bathing the mountain in golden light. The fresh snow glittered below their feet. Josh fell to his knees, one hand clutching the gun, the other the spool. His mouth warped into a grimace.

"Dat's what she w'en told me!" he cried, his lips trembling. "She w'en dying right dere in my arms, and she say, 'We need your heart too!'"

"That's what she's saying right now, Josh. Do you hear her?"

"I do." He dropped the gun into the snow and thrust his hands up to his face, sobbing uncontrollably.

Erik walked up and cradled him in his arms. "Let's go get your dad," he said softly.

Josh, still weeping, nodded.

CHAPTER 54
After the *Huli*

Jedediah Clarke was steering Wayfinder over huge swells left from the hurricane when he heard a distress call come over the VHF radio. Squally winds still moaned through the rigging in the aftermath of the storm, and the radio crackled from lightning far to the north, but Jedediah thought he heard the words "mayday" and "cargo vessel *Phoenix*." He lashed the rudder to a cleat, unhooked his safety harness, and raced down the companionway to the nav station.

"Mayday! Mayday! Mayday! This is *Phoenix II*, *Phoenix II*, *Phoenix II*. Mayday, *Phoenix II*. Position 21 35 North 156 25 West . . ."

Jedediah slid into the seat and ran his gloved finger over the chart to locate the ship's position.

". . . We're breaking up in hurricane seas, require immediate assistance. Twelve people aboard, taking lifeboats. I repeat, this is the cargo vessel *Phoenix II* abandoning ship twenty-two miles northeast of Maui, at 21 35 North, 156 25 West. Any vessel in the vicinity, please render assistance immediately. We're breaking up in hurricane seas . . ."

Jedediah grabbed the handset and waited for a closer vessel to respond. He was more than three hundred miles south of the sinking ship, well out of range to pick up survivors, but he knew that in bad weather he might be the only one catching the broadcast. He had anxiously tracked Alana for days and had abandoned his own plans to dock in Hilo on his way to the South Seas, instead dropping well south on a course to the Line Islands.

"*Phoenix II*, this is Coast Guard station Barber's Point, Hawai'i. A rescue ship and aircraft are on their way . . ."

Jedediah breathed a sign of relief. He cranked up the volume and returned to the cockpit.

Just as the hurricane had passed over Mauna Kea, the winds of its trailing half had whipped up a wildly confused sea windward of the Big Island and Maui, battering the Williams & Company's bouncing cargo ship. Like everyone else, its officers had been surprised by the hurricane's sudden turn back to the island and tried to outrun it. The first of two giant rogue waves generated by the tempest had nearly capsized the ship, pushing it high into the air, then driving it deep into the sea where the second rogue slammed its aft quarter. The old steel hull torqued beyond capacity, ripping the ship apart at the seams. Fifty Stryker vehicles bound for O'ahu's Schofield Barracks had snapped their tie downs and piled up against the hold's port side, crushing the five Shadow drones and hastening the ship's plunge to the bottom.

Over the next three hours, Jedediah listened to the radio traffic as a Coast Guard chopper plucked the ship's crew out of the lifeboats one by one and transported them to a waiting cutter. Between snippets of rescue drama, he ruminated on the vivid dream he'd had the night before in the rocking berth of *Wayfinder*. A luminescent woman in a white robe had appeared at the foot of his bed, just in front of the nav station. Her icy-blue eyes emitted soft light that illuminated the whole cabin. A smiling elder with a moon face stood beside her, and behind them, visible up the companionway, Hawaiian faces crowded the hatch and the starlit cockpit.

"All will be well now," the shining spirit of the dream had said, the old woman—Aunty Moana—nodding beside her, "for my people, and for the astronomers. Mahalo."

Poli'ahu's message about the astronomers puzzled Jedediah. If Alana blew right over the island, he thought, surely it had wreaked havoc on the observatories.

It was actually winds from the back half of the storm—not during its initial arrival—that had packed the worst punch, tearing the wind-pummeled domes apart, drenching the telescopes, and marring several of the Keck's multimillion-dollar mirrors with flying debris. Windblown pieces of twisted steel collided with the Smithsonian antennas, nearly ripping one off its concrete base. Other debris collected all across the abandoned TMT site.

Fortunately, Jill and Muku had reached the JCMT dome while the hurricane's eye was still passing over the summit, giving them just enough time to help Erik and Josh retrieve the elder Mattos who by that time lay unconscious and frostbitten in the snow. Jill had revived him with smelling salts while Muku confiscated his revolver. The trio wrapped him in a wool blanket and carried him back to the ranger's warm truck on a litter. As soon as Johnny was safe inside the truck's crew cab, Muku had handcuffed Josh and pushed him in beside his father, then trudged back to the dome to secure the explosives and Josh's M9, still laying in the snow. By then Hoku had managed to rock the kitchen pickup free of the snowdrift around its wheels and drive it up to the JCMT. Winds had just begun to pick up again as Hoku and Erik escorted the old British astronomer—who had been cowering in its tiny control room—back to their truck.

As Jill guided Erik, Hoku, and Dr. Sapphire back down the treacherous mountain road, the hurricane's trailing winds had begun losing steam after climbing up and over the high volcanic island. But it still took an hour in hellacious weather to maneuver the two pickups down the heavily eroded road and get all seven people safely back to the base camp. Two county police officers rushed over to Jill's truck to take custody of Josh Mattos, and an Army ambulance summoned from PTA took his father to the hospital in Waimea.

Over hot coffee and Portuguese bean soup—made specially by Jeffrey Drake for the four frozen souls—Erik, Hoku, Jill, and Muku debriefed their harrowing experiences. Erik's story of how he'd stopped the bomber flabbergasted Jill, and Muku couldn't decide which had thrown the tita more off balance, Erik's ballsy act or that he and Hoku had trekked into a blizzard to bury Aunty Moana's ashes. Muku then recalled what his grandfather, who'd fought in the battle of Luzon, had once told him about heroism: "Love is a human being's greatest instinct and the biggest reason we bother to survive."

"Ohhhh," said Jill, throwing her arms around him.

When the diminishing storm rolled over Maui, its winds had dropped below one hundred miles per hour, but that was still fierce enough to cause $8 million of damage to the military compound atop Haleakala. Devastation along the coasts of both islands was much worse. Storm surges flooded all the coastal cities, sweeping several homes off their foundations and littering every south-facing beach with huge coral chunks and boulders. Gales ripped away dozens of roofs and left vehicles, power poles, and tons of twisted debris strewn over roadways. Flash floods and mudslides closed highways and inundated homes. Miraculously, no one was killed by the storm, but hundreds were injured and at least a thousand were made homeless.

When the remnant hurricane passed over Oʻahu, gale force winds and storm surges lashed everything on the coast and power went out in greater Honolulu. Only a few people evacuated their houses, most preferring to ride out the storm at home, using every spare minute to secure doors, windows, and vehicles against the onslaught. One of those was Henry Hashimura, whose Black Point mansion sat on the edge of the exposed peninsula. With the same stubborn defiance that he'd guided his political revolution against the white oligarchy, the elderly Noburo joined his housekeeping staff in securing the estate. His valiant exertions may have satisfied his will but proved too much for his sullied heart, and he collapsed while dragging his thronelike lounger off his vast lanai. Ten minutes passed before anyone noticed, and he died alone, drenched by the spray of thundering waves.

"It could have been worse," said Tommy Williams at a hastily called chamber of commerce meeting the next day at the shipping company's Hilo headquarters. "About two-and-a-half billion dollars in damage to this island."

Same as the price tag for the Big Eye, thought Namaka Hee, the ex-model prudently keeping that observation to herself.

"It's bad enough," said contractor Herbert Oshiro. "Preliminary reports indicate at least thirty million to the Mauna Kea observatories alone." Oshiro didn't mention that he'd already estimated the huge windfalls for his firm once the island's rebuilding efforts got underway.

"And Noburo is dead," murmured the elder Williams, sitting across from the dusty oil painting of his great-grandfather's *Phoenix*. He ached at the thought of yet another icon of the old days gone. But his deeper grief had come with the news that the *Phoenix II* had sunk, its precious cargo—meant to save his family's lands—now on the ocean floor.

Across town, at Hoku's studio, another hurricane debrief was underway. Hoku, Erik, and Uncle Pe'a drank mamaki tea in a circle of chairs in the middle of the one-room bungalow. Huge swells left over from the storm thundered against the rocky shore, but sun filtering through wisps of high cloud filled the room with golden afternoon light. Tree limbs, splintered boards, and a host of ocean-borne plastic littered the shoreline outside.

Uncle Pe'a got up with the help of his ornate staff and walked to the window. "You did the right thing taking Moana's ashes up despite the storm. It was vital for everything that followed that her remains joined the others on the mountain."

"What do you think will happen now, Uncle?" Hoku asked.

The old kahuna gazed out at the unsettled sea. "I think the astronomers will be moved by these events."

"You really think so?" Erik asked.

Uncle Pe'a nodded. "And I know Hawaiians will be. Even the few hotheads at the march seemed to have restored their faith. I don't think that can be undone. Do you remember when it snowed in Iraq during the worst of the violence?"

"I read about that in my dad's newspaper," Erik said. "The first time anyone there had seen a snowfall."

"Without a doubt, it was a sign," the elder continued. "And despite all the fear and hatred, the Iraqis took it as such. They stood in the streets marveling at the falling flakes that they could never have imagined. Countless stories were reported of people contemplating the snow's significance, and for the first time since the war began not a single act of violence occurred that day anywhere in the country. Now Iraqis have a hopeful story to pass on to their children, a contrasting narrative to bolster their spirits against the religious violence that drags on and on."

"I saw something else amazing happen during our storm," Hoku said, smiling at Erik, "a real change in you. You were confident and brave."

"I had Aunty Moana with me . . . *her* courage and determination."

Uncle Peʻa walked back from the window and squeezed the young man's shoulder with his long fingers. "I disagree. Oh yes, Moana was there all right. Everything you've told me about what happened confirms that. But it was *your* courage and determination—no longer dormant—that stopped the bomber and saved the lives of his father and the old astronomer. That, too, can never be undone."

He leaned his ornate staff against his chair and put his other hand on Hoku's shoulder. "Just as Hoku's changed heart—to trust the good—can never be undone, not without doing violence to her basic character. Actions taken in true faith build trust in your heart, and that changes the energy of the universe . . . one person at a time. Good job you two!" He beamed.

"I want to share something else," the old kaula said, easing into his chair across from them. "When we were all marching up the road in those wild winds, before the really heavy rains came, I saw something dark whirling above the mountain. At first I thought it was a great flock of birds, but as I focused on them, I saw that they were not birds but an agitated cloud of negative energy . . . the rot fostered during a half century of disrespect for Mauna Kea . . . swept away by the marchers' faith and the winds of Kanaloa. Then I knew the huli was underway." The overturning.

"That explains the way I felt when Erik and I walked down into Puʻu Waiau. Despite the blizzard and the howling winds, inside I felt calm . . . even serene. I sensed that something big had changed."

"I'm not surprised, Hoku . . . and someone else noticed the exodus of that agitated cloud. You both know Keola Kuamoʻo."

"Braddah K."

"He saw it too and sought me out. 'Uncle what is that?' he asked. I told him 'it was the past, Keola, finally driven away by hope.'"

"I have some other happy news," Hoku said, feeling the time was right to share it. She got up from her chair and walked to her easel where a white cloth hung over the oil in progress she had shown Erik weeks earlier. "I finally finished the painting."

She lifted the cloth. The vibrant oil still held all the features Erik remembered—the shimmering peak rising out of turbulent seas; a starless sky mottled with purples, blacks, and burgundies; and the meteor flaming toward the mountain with its yin/yang human face of serene green eyes and anguished blue mouth. But the white profile of the mountain was no longer vacant, filled in with cubist shapes of its bold topography—triangular cones, V-shaped gulches, and a shining lake. Midway up the mountain was a band of wildly etched mamane trees speckled with bright yellow blossoms. Inside the great cones, as textural motifs, she'd painted dozens of tiny Hawaiian faces, ancient and new, each expressing some facet of Polynesian wisdom—truth, love, humility, hard work, or beauty. And interspersed among the faces, she'd brushed in vivid icons of frigatebirds, whales, octopus, and seals.

"When did you get a chance to do all that?" Erik asked.

"The week after Aunty's funeral."

Uncle Pe'a pointed his carved staff at one of the little faces, its toothy smile rendered almost representational. "Moana?"

Hoku nodded.

"Have you decided on a name for the painting?"

"*Light Coming through Dark.*"

After his supper, Erik sat alone under the stars on the rocky ledge in front of Sunny Boy's bungalow, thinking about the maelstrom he'd just survived. He gazed up at Mauna Kea. Only the starlit summit cones were visible above the billowy clouds, leaving the impression of a floating island in the sky.

Then, for the first time in two years, he remembered standing at the Ala Wai bus stop with the old South Seas vagabond that he'd crewed for on the passage from Samoa. "The ship Ishmael had boarded sank," the skipper had said, "downed by primal forces more powerful than Captain Ahab's will. But Ishmael himself survived, and by a coffin expelled from the sinking ship."

Erik looked out to sea and smiled with warm melancholy. "But in *this* saga," he muttered, "the Polynesians also escaped alive . . . in fact, they thrived."

The Choice

It would take five years to repair the damage wrought by Hurricane Alana, but the deeper healing—among people—began immediately. Islanders of all ages and ethnicities pulled together to clear the debris and rebuild their homes, businesses, and schools. A rush for FEMA money ensued, including for some questionable no-bid contracts to firms with old Democratic Party ties, but just as many companies and unions donated their help as did those who tussled over the disaster money. And none of the homeless, including the people in the storm-swamped Hawaiian village next to Erik's Airstream, went without help. Two young state senators, feisty Big Island Gen Zers elected after Alana's devastation, persuaded the legislature to finally build some livable housing for Hawaiʻi's destitute.

Astronomers concluded that the UH 88-inch telescope and the old Canada-France-Hawaiʻi Telescope were "damaged beyond reasonable repair" and decided the time had come to tear them down. Hawaiians were relieved when astronomers announced they would not seek replacement facilities on the two sites, instead committing to restore those parts of the ridge to something close to their original condition. Some Canadian and French astronomers objected. They'd long anticipated a CFHT upgrade, but its funding—shaky since the TMT fiasco—dried up after the hurricane tore open its dome, drenched the telescope, and flooded its control room. CFHT officials mentioned none of that, instead attributing their closure decision to "a sincere desire to rebuild common ground in our island community."

With the aging United Kingdom Infrared Telescope already targeted for decommissioning, the decisions to remove the 88-inch and CFHT meant that only a single dome—the Gemini—would remain on the upper summit ridge. Even UH astronomy director Dr. James Bushmill acknowledged on KITV News that "decommissioning some 'Mona Kea' telescopes might help heal our longstanding rift with our Hawaiian hosts." In truth, his own astronomy faculty had compelled him to forfeit the UH site, and to join other campus professors in an educational effort "to finally bring the astronomy community's cultural awareness into the twenty-first century." Astronomers also realized that the storm that meteorologists had prophetically named "the awakening" was no ordinary hurricane. Its stunning impact gave them the courage to throw off professional loyalties and advocate on behalf of the whole island community.

Even Caltech astronomers eventually embraced Adam Jacob's pact with Alfred Haisley and Mitch Gardner to take the Big Eye to South America. They realized that a century of hurricanes bypassing the Big Island was probably a fluke, and the warming planet would likely make hurricanes as frequent in Hawai'i as in the Caribbean. That the islanders didn't want the telescope was something they would never publicly acknowledge.

As might be expected, General Todt and his Air Force comrades became even more adamant about beefing up their capacity to watch for enemy space weaponry and immediately received congressional funding to repair and expand their surveillance compound on Haleakala. Washington also sent money to replace the sunken Strykers and drones, but the military's sway with island politicians would never be the same, Alana's unnerving wreckage a crippling blow after the earlier Red Hill scandal at Pearl Harbor.

The Williams & Company men, shocked by the loss of the *Phoenix*, also decided to take a different tack toward the future. Instead of selling off family land for hotels and real estate development, or rebuilding their shipping with military contracts, they jumped on the growing bandwagon for sustainable Hawai'i alternatives to oil, urgently popular after the failed occupations of Iraq and Afghanistan and the scourge of ISIS terrorism they'd spawned—and now the hurricane's vivid display of future climate change. Williams & Company would build wind generators on their Hamakua Coast acreage. Tom senior approached several younger members of the post-Hashimura Democratic establishment to corral new alternative energy appropriations to help capitalize their "Winds for the Future" plan, and Sam Chun accepted Tom's invitation to serve on the project's advisory committee.

Meanwhile, Uncle Pe'a began what he considered his last but most important endeavor before leaving the physical realm to join his ancestors—find the ancient bones removed from the summit area during early telescope construction. Two retired construction workers—emboldened by the storm—confirmed that burials had been disturbed during the construction of at least three observatories. For his mission Uncle Pe'a recruited Hoku, who knew intimately the valleys, cones, and caves of the vast terrain surrounding the summit, including on the north plateau. He also enlisted the extraordinary sixth sense of Aunty Moana's mentor, the oracle crone with the queen's pipe.

Hui chief Pano Kamalu, rattled by the storm and haunted for weeks by turbulent dreams, fell into a funk so deep that his main rival—a brutish O'ahu drug thug akin to the vicious mob figures right after statehood—ousted him from the Hui hierarchy. Eventually Pano found his way to the top of Mauna Kea, where his ancestors directed him to seek redemption under the tutelage of elders in his own family.

The huli winds of Alana also created a new challenge for Erik Peterson. With three telescopes being phased out and others inoperable during repairs, use of the base camp dormitories dropped precipitously, and Moses had to lay off his most recent hires, including Erik. This distasteful directive was the last Moses would carry out for the Mauna Kea Cooperative, deciding it was time to retire. He persuaded his bosses to hire Braddah K in his place, keeping intact the base camp's long line of ancestral links to the mountain.

Jill, too, was challenged, but by her own accord. No longer romantically distracted by Muku Mukai after the FBI agent returned to his tamer Oʻahu duties, she experienced a rare moment of introspection. Inspired by Erik's story of Aunty Moana's tough-love mentoring, Jill decided that she, too, needed a Hawaiian elder to guide her. Erik introduced her to Uncle Peʻa, who connected the hot-blooded officer with a gruff but loving former National Park Service ranger who agreed to teach her the ancient Hawaiian martial art of *lua* if she'd commit to getting her temper under control. (And Muku, overcome by Erik's unselfish bravery, never told Jill that while checking out her Keck shooting suspects he'd discovered that the young man's canoe had been spotted near the Riverboat Captain's Inn on the night Murdock Kemp's cabin cruiser sank, and that the Cottonwood police had removed Erik's name from their "persons of interest" list only after Kemp's girlfriend admitted she might not have properly secured the boat.)

Jeffrey Drake left his base camp job a week after the storm and began a spiritual pilgrimage that took him to India, Burma, Thailand, and Japan. The last anyone heard, he had taken a research post in the Bangkok field office of Amnesty International.

Moses managed to finagle an extra month of work for Erik to give him time to look for another job. While he hoped Erik would stay on the island, Moses assumed that after earning sufficient money to return to the South Seas, the young vagabond would decide to go there. Moses contacted Jedediah Clarke using an email address he obtained from Andromeda, who had since transferred from Caltech to UC Berkeley to finish her thesis. Moses asked the iconoclastic old professor if he might need crew. Jedediah sent an enthusiastic reply from Rarotonga:

"After that brutal solo passage from Malibu to the Line Islands, I decided never again to go without crew. This very day I made inquiries in Avarua—no luck!?!—and when I got back to *Wayfinder* I found your email about Erik! That he was also once a pro photographer gets me all the more excited. I could use someone with a good camera to document the people and places I'm investigating. And he cooks too! Send him down!"

It seemed as though providence was again working in Erik's favor, just as it had in leading him to Mauna Kea two years earlier—except for one thing.

"I'm not sure the South Seas is in my future," he told Hoku, Freddie, Sam, and Sunny Boy as they drank beers on the DJ's seaside lanai in Keaukaha. The sun had just dropped behind Mauna Kea, and only Jupiter—the Roman god of the heavens—shimmered above the mountain's purple profile.

"But Hawai'i w'en get in yer blood," Freddie said, accompanying Sunny Boy's 'ukulele on his guitar.

The old disc jockey paused to lift his beer. "Dat's right, haole boy," he said. "What more you want den what we git in Hilo?"

"Home . . . Minnesota."

Sam was stunned. "I t'ought you said you w'en nevah go back?"

"That was before Alana."

"You stay scared?"

"Just the opposite, Sam. Mauna Kea gave me the strength to do battle with my demons, and Aunty Moana showed me how to do it. Now I can go home and fight for the river."

"He more lolo den me," Sunny Boy said. "Whatcha t'ink Hoku? Our boy los' his marbles?"

No one understood better than Hoku the struggles Erik had endured and overcome, but listening to her spiritual brother talk of leaving broke her heart. "He's got to follow his own na'au," she said, "and if we really love him, we'll support whatever he decides." Her dark eyes teared up. "But we'll miss you, Erik."

"I still own my houseboat at the river's bend," he said. "It's pretty funky—and no doubt five Minnesota winters have taken their toll—but there's plenty of room for all of you to come visit." He was looking at Hoku's face when he said it.

Freddie reached into the cooler for another beer, determined now to really get drunk. "Whatcha gonna do for work?"

"I'll get my old photo business up and running and spend part of each week making portraits, maybe even some art videos, of the river, to remind people of the beauty they've taken for granted . . . or never really knew. And when people are used to my being back home,

I'm gonna run for the Cottonwood City Council and stand with the other locals . . . and with anyone who loves the river or Cottonwood . . . to fight for small business and a return to down-home democracy. Who says we can't make progress by consciously taking steps backward to embrace our valued traditions?"

Freddie cracked his knuckles. "You t'ink that'll take wit' people ovah dere . . . in da 'other world,' as you like say?"

"I don't know . . . but Aunty Moana showed me that if you act in the world as if the world is the way you want it to be, others who'd like to live there will join you." Freddie's skeptical face provoked a less confident thought: *I'll give it a go anyway . . . and do my best to avoid joining Jack in the river.*

Sunny Boy stopped strumming. "Eh, brah. I no git it! You got every'ting you dream fo' here." He glanced at Hoku. "Why try fix somet'ing busted ovah dere?"

"It's lolo, I know, but 'I w'en come from ovah dere,'" he said, parroting Sunny Boy's pidgin and punching him in the arm. "As long as the wisdom of Hawai'i remains here alone, that other world will never change for the better. Maybe I can shed some of that light with my camera . . . and my life . . . and carry back some of the aloha you guys taught me."

"But, Erik, can yer *soul* survive?" Freddie said, pointing the neck of his beer bottle at the Minnesotan's chest.

"The river will help me. God knows it's tried while I've been away."

"Bettah break out da 'okolehau!" Freddie said, pulling an unopened bottle of the local hooch from his backpack. Sunny Boy teetered into his kitchen and returned a moment later with five vintage shot glasses—three sporting gaudy "Hang Loose" shakas—that Freddie filled to their rims.

Hoku stood up and raised her glass toward Mauna Kea, now barely visible in the twilight. "Here's to Erik and his river."

They all toasted, not a dry eye among them.

When the party broke up, well after midnight, Erik and Hoku, both tipsy, ambled down to the rocks below Sunny Boy's bungalow. They could hear the old DJ humming as he stumbled around the kitchen cleaning up. Jupiter glowed like a beacon directly over the summit ridge.

Erik took Hoku's hand. "I hope you'll come visit me someday . . . and see my river."

He sensed her probing eyes in the dark. "It just might happen," she said, squeezing his hand.

"I have one more question, Hoku. No one has ever explained to me what that strange brilliant light was that I saw approaching the island way back when. Do you have any idea?"

"Now I can tell you what Aunty told me. She said it was your own inner light connecting with the divine energy of the mountain, that had you truly abandoned your hope, you would not have seen it. You would have found this island to be like all the others you left behind . . . and none of this could have happened."

Hoku wrapped Erik in her arms and placed her forehead atop his, the tips of their noses touching. Breathing together, they shared the mana of all their mentors—including their fathers, Aunty Moana, Mauna Kea, and the mighty Mississippi—and then said good night. Erik wandered down the shore to the old sitting stones near Aunty Moana's vacant shack. He took his former place on the stone closest to her hale, his heart full and his mind made up. An 'iwa passed over the little cove, its winged profile black against the dazzling stars.

Hoʻopau! ('The End')

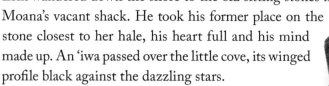

AFTERWORD

Novelists ask readers to suspend their disbelief no matter how fantastic their story or how unfamiliar the reader is with the realities the author's fiction seeks to illuminate. This presents a double challenge to the contemporary Hawai'i novelist. First, Hawai'i's intrinsic qualities—astonishing landscapes, ancient cultural traditions, peculiar characters drawn from Hawai'i's extraordinary diversity, and an island society heavily marked by a turbulent colonial history—make island realities often feel like fiction. Second, much of what non-islanders have written about Hawai'i perpetuates stereotypes of the place and its people, and American literature, movies, and even news accounts have fostered a pop image of Hawai'i more akin to fiction than fact.

With these two problems in mind, I tried to make *Mauna Kea* a compelling, imaginative tale that also faithfully illuminates today's Hawai'i, particularly the remote and volcanic Big Island, whose wonders, ethnic diversity, and cultural conflicts make it a truly unique and important place in the world.

While the characters and events of my narrative are pure fiction, its historic, cultural, and scientific backdrops parallel reality. The astronomical quest to find extraterrestrial life on Earth-like planets in our galaxy (and the rifts among astronomers on how best to do that), while simplified for readability, are reasonably accurate, including references to their Giant Optical Devices (GODs). The novel's portrayal of the long-standing clash over Mauna Kea development, while fictionalized, is true in spirit (and accurate in many details), including the widely publicized Thirty Meter Telescope controversy and the protests it provoked, as well as astronomers' dreams of future telescopes there. References to famous American scientists, among them the iconoclastic Richard Feynman, are consistent with history.

The story's weather scenarios—including fierce blizzards and hurricanes—are entirely possible. Indeed, similar events have occurred at one time or another, including the unprecedented 1968 winter storm during construction of the University of Hawai'i 88-inch telescope and the 1871 hurricane that wreaked havoc on the Big Island.

The novel's "magical realism" fits closely with Hawaiian cultural perspectives, practices, and events found in the historical and cultural literature and enunciated by contemporary cultural practitioners, particularly those who practice on Mauna Kea. The strange phenomena portrayed in the story were often inspired by actual events, in some cases from firsthand accounts shared with the author by people working on the mountain, including non-Hawaiians who to this day remain puzzled by their experiences. Fictional references to disturbed burials mirror persistent (sometimes highly specific) rumors over the years, including those described to me by early observatory construction workers.

The novel's political, economic, and military landscape, while fictionalized, draws upon genuine aspects of Hawai'i's milieu at various times since statehood, including the nearly sixty-year Mauna Kea land-use conflict (half of which I witnessed firsthand) and similar battles over military, tourist, and real estate development. Episodes in the story that take place on the US mainland reflect the American milieu during roughly that same period. Those elements, largely portrayed through Erik Peterson's flashbacks, seek to illuminate the twenty-first century America from which he escapes, a place steeped in its own mythology (e.g., "the land of opportunity" and "the world's greatest democracy"). The steady US military buildup in the archipelago, particularly after World War II, is accurately portrayed in the novel. (It's no coincidence that former CIA cybersecurity expert Edward Snowden worked in a National Security Agency compound on O'ahu when he stole classified intelligence files that he leaked to the media.)

The novel's characters are fictional renderings or fanciful composites of the sorts of people one encounters in Hawai'i—Native Hawaiians, local and haole islanders, astronomers, observatory employees, politicians, activists, business leaders, and underworld operatives—but they certainly do not represent specific individuals now or in the past. Two real (now deceased) politicians are mentioned in the story. Hawai'i's longtime US Senator Daniel Inouye was an iconic leader in the Asian American struggle against prejudice and discrimination, who, nonetheless, also played a key role in the Americanization of post-statehood Hawai'i, including leveraging his political power to promote Mauna Kea astronomy and expand US military use of the islands. Minnesota's US Senator Paul Wellstone revived that state's progressive populist traditions during the 1990s and then, at the height of his growing national influence, died with his wife, daughter, and several aides in a mysterious plane crash in northern Minnesota.

I have taken literary license with some technical details that might clutter or confuse an already complex story. For example, the observatories' institutional arrangements have been simplified, including the name and fictional portrayal of the organization that manages the base camp and its rangers. Similarly, Oshiro Construction is a fictional composite of the various construction companies that over many decades transformed Mauna Kea's once pristine summit into a sprawling complex of techno-industrial buildings and infrastructure.

Islanders may notice that I took slight liberties with some pidgin and Hawaiian dialogues to ensure that non-island readers could understand them. I was also selective in my use of Hawaiian words (and in some cases simplified their glossary definitions) so as not to overwhelm or frustrate readers not yet familiar with that wonderfully vivid language. I chose to include glottal stops ('okina) in the text but, for readers' ease, left out the macrons (kahakō). For those readers interested in learning the proper Hawaiian pronunciations, both diacritical marks are included in the pronunciation guide and glossary that follows, presented in accord with Pukui and Elbert's *Hawaiian Dictionary*.

In recent years, the mountain's name is sometimes spelled as a single word—Maunakea—especially among University of Hawai'i scholars. I chose the more commonly used two-word spelling, primarily because the mountain cultural practitioners that I know (including those who reviewed my drafts) almost all spell it that way.

I sincerely hope that you, the reader, have enjoyed *Mauna Kea: A Novel of Hawai'i*, and that through its characters and story have felt the enchantment of Mauna Kea and the Native Hawaiians who love and defend it. I also hope its portrayal of their enduring tradition of aloha gives you hope in a turbulent world where ethnocentric prejudice and violence continue to impede the resolution of conflict and too often thwart more wholesome and sustainable paths to progress.

Mahalo nui loa.
Tom Peek
Volcano, island of Hawai'i
March 2023

ACKNOWLEDGMENTS

Each novel a writer creates grows out of his or her previous tales and the life experiences that went into them, so gratitude for any subsequent book is cumulative. In my case, that starts with the readers of my first novel, *Daughters of Fire*, who generously shared their thoughts and feelings after its publication.

That feedback substantially informed the cultural foundation and story arc for *Mauna Kea*, especially the ideas, suggestions, and moral support I received from islanders who'd read the earlier work. Most precious to me were the encouraging responses of Native Books founder Maile Meyer; *kupunas* Sylvester Apiki Pauelua, Clarence "Ku" Ching, Kaliko Kanaele, Ed Galu Stevens, and Betty Stevens; Hawai'i author Tom Coffman; Hawai'i-born Pacific literature professor Susan Najita; Bess Press stalwart Dimpna Figuracion; and my Big Island friends Nelson Ho, Greg Herbst, Keola Awong, Toni Case, and Kaluna West.

As for *Mauna Kea: A Novel of Hawai'i*, there are many to thank.

First, a wholehearted mahalo goes to my wife, Catherine Robbins, who read multiple drafts, always providing honest criticism and keen insight, and whose unwavering encouragement over the project's seven years kept me plugging away. Catherine's deep love for Mauna Kea—where we first met decades ago and on whose volcanic slopes we trekked together and with our kupuna—is reflected in every page, as well as on the book's cover, which is graced by her stunning oil painting *Lilinoe*.

I'm also deeply grateful to Aunty Leina'ala Apiki McCord, whose spirit and lessons always accompany me on the mountain. Early on she encouraged me to write about her islands and culture, reviewed an early draft of my first novel, and shortly before her death in 2001 gave me crucial feedback on the historical prologue for *Mauna Kea*. But her greatest gift was sharing her Hawaiian world with her *hanai* son from the Upper Mississippi who was trying to connect his home island

and Viking ancestry in Minnesota with what he'd come to know and love about Hawai'i. After Aunty joined her ancestors, other elders and cultural practitioners continued with equal patience to guide me on my journey. My dear friend Kealoha Pisciotta, whom I met when we both worked on Mauna Kea, has long been a key source of insight and inspiration, and a guide on how to keep faith with aloha in the face of adversity. Thank you all for trusting my heart and encouraging me to explore things not entirely conceivable to my Western mind.

I also owe a debt of gratitude to other Hawaiian friends who invited me into their rich culture, including some with long ancestral ties to Mauna Kea. One of these people, Moses Kealamakia, with whom I've spent many hours on the mountain, and from whom I've learned much about its deepest meanings and islanders' abiding connection to it, read a near-final draft. His helpful comments and loving encouragement gave me confidence to proceed. Mahalo kāua!

Special thanks also goes to my Mauna Kea comrade Nelson Ho, a longtime Sierra Club protector of the mountain whose love for Mauna Kea matches that of anyone previously mentioned. During late-night sessions on my lanai and while camping high up on our beloved mountain, Nelson lent his ear to numerous chapters in progress, offering astute suggestions all along the way. He later reviewed the full manuscript, again offering important insights and advice. Nelson's understanding of Hawai'i's complex political and cultural landscapes and his intimate knowledge of the decades-long telescope controversy—to say nothing of his steadfast moral support—were invaluable.

Mahalo nui to Native Hawaiian artist and educator Kaluna West, whose stunning painting of Lake Waiau gives me chicken skin whenever I see it. His astute and enthusiastic comments on a near-final draft—and his continued soulful encouragement for the project—are hugely appreciated.

Much thanks to my dear friend Dr. Bradford Smith, whose love of science, nature, the cosmos—and Hawai'i—was the subject of numerous lively discussions on our lanais. Brad, a renowned elder of American astronomy and planetary exploration, shared countless insights about his field that deeply informed the astronomical elements of the novel's narrative and inspired the creation of my iconoclastic character Dr. Jedediah Clarke. Sadly, Brad died before the novel was finished, and his absence left a black hole in our lives that nonetheless continues to emit a powerful beam of energy our way.

Mahalo to former Mountain Superintendent Tom Krieger and the Mauna Kea Support Services staff for their aloha and encouragement when I was an early astronomy guide at Hale Pohaku. Tom, recognizing a fellow sailor caught up in the beauty of the Pacific, gave me my first job in Hawai'i and in so doing made possible all that followed—including my novels.

Other stalwart friends and family members tested various drafts of the manuscript for content and readability, including Pacific literature professor Susan Najita, cultural anthropologist Dr. Michael Osmera, writer and poet Gene Ervine, poet Dr. Jaime Jacinto, beta-reader extraordinaire Rob Kennedy, faithful comrade Scott Sandager and his avid-reader wife Mary Ann Mathieu, and the prose-savvy couple Anne Peek and Tom Ehlinger. Others provided insightful feedback on individual chapters read to them on my lanai, including Kealoha Pisciotta, Keomailani Von Gogh, novelist Arthur Rosenfeld, and fellow Grey Cloud Island river rat Jerry Taube. Thank you all for your insights and support!

Renowned artist John Dawson created the book's beautiful pen-and-ink drawings and the eye-popping illustrated map that opens the tale, artwork inspired by his own read of the novel. Collaborating with John and his wife and colleague, Kathleen Oshiro Dawson, is always a delight!

Mahalo also to Koa Books founder Arnie Kotler, who had the island knowledge and professional brawn to publish my first Hawai'i novel, *Daughters of Fire*, knowing that it might ruffle a few feathers, and to Buddy Bess and David DeLuca at Bess Press, who've kept the book in print. A further thanks goes to Arnie who, later working as a literary agent, found a kindred publishing midwife for *Mauna Kea*, David Wilk at All Night Books. Arnie has long felt that Hawai'i, with its vibrant Native Hawaiian culture and extraordinary ethnic diversity, is an "incubator" of potent perspectives and ideas sorely needed well beyond the islands.

Mahalo nui loa to David Wilk at All Night Books for taking on this project and creatively and conscientiously guiding his excellent team to produce a beautiful book any author would be proud of. On that team, master copy editor Karen Seriguchi applied her knowledge, skills, and eagle eye to the final manuscript, assuring that the high editorial standards of previous eras continued with this book. Mahalo, Karen, for being my safety net! Thanks also to Alexia Garaventa for the book's beautiful page and cover design.

Many thanks to my brilliant friends John Dvorak and Arthur Rosenfeld—distinguished authors both—whose advice and commiserations kept my writer's flame alive during the long, rough-and-tumble quest to hone my tales and then find publishers to share them with the world.

Mahalo to those who've offered other vital moral support during my writing endeavors: the Peek 'ohana, especially my parents and first writing mentors, Mary and Rolly Peek; my friends Tomomasa Hyakuna, Bob Evans, Dr. Keith Huston, James D. Houston, Barbara George, Diane McGregor, Michele Taube, and Pat and Janet Durkin; computer whiz Roger Lidia who kept my aging PCs up to date enough to finish each project; accounting genius Jerry Wells, who has long helped keep this budget-challenged artist solvent; and my writing students, whose own efforts continue to remind me that the pen is a powerful tool for the flowering of one's soul. Mahalo to any others whom I may have failed to mention whose aid or encouragement helped bring my novels to fruition.

I'm also grateful for the inspiring lives and words of many writers, particularly Natalie Goldberg, James Norman Hall, Herman Melville, Robert Louis Stevenson, Joseph Conrad, W. Somerset Maugham, Robert Dean Frisbie, and Mark Twain. And of course, I am forever indebted to Mauna Kea, Kilauea, and the island of Hawai'i for keeping me in touch with life's deepest realities after I returned from hitchhiking by boat across the South Seas.

Mahalo a nui to all!

Were it not for the aforementioned, this book would not be in your hands. Yet I alone am responsible for the story—including any mistakes or misinterpretations—and I humbly ask forgiveness if I have offended anyone with my tale. *E kala mai ia'u.*

PRONOUNCING HAWAIIAN WORDS

The Hawaiian alphabet has twelve letters. Hawaiian vowels (a, e, i, o, u) are pronounced similarly to the way they are in Latin, Spanish, Italian, and Japanese:

a is "ah" (as in "father")	*o* is "oh" (as in "note")
e is "eh" (as in "bet")	*u* is "oo" (as in "blue")
i is "ee" (as in "niece")	

Hawaiian consonants (*h, k, l, m, n, p, w*) are similar to those in English, except that *w* is sometimes pronounced as a soft *v* when it follows *a, e,* or *i*, such as in the traditional pronunciation of Hawai'i ("Hah-vah~ee-ee").

When a word has a glottal stop (*'okina*) between vowels, such as in *pu'u*, both vowels are enunciated distinctly with a slight pause between them ("poo-oo"). When a word in the glossary has a macron (*kahakō*) over a vowel, such as in Kāne, hold that vowel's sound a bit longer ("Kaah-neh").

Generally, when two vowels are side by side (with or without a glottal stop or macron), both are distinctly enunciated (*akua* is "ah-koo-ah"). Some vowel pairs (certain diphthongs) are pronounced by gently sliding into the second sound from the first:

ae is "ah~eh"	(*'ae*)	*au* is "ah~oo"	(*'aumakua*)
ai is "ah~ee"	(*lānai*)	*ei* is "eh~ee"	(*lei*)
ao is "ah~oh"	(*haole*)	*oi* is "oh~ee"	(*poi*)

GLOSSARY OF HAWAIIAN
AND OTHER WORDS

'ae	Yes.
'āhinahina	Silversword plant, a native species of Mauna Kea whose spiky leaves are the color of moonlight (also *hinahina*).
"Ah oui, je comprends"	(French) "Ah yes, I understand."
'āina	Homeland, land, "that which feeds."
akua	God or gods, sometimes used to refer to the Christian God.
alana	Awakening, arising.
'Alenuihāhā	Notorious sea channel between the islands of Hawai'i and Maui; literally, "great billows smashing."
ali'i	Royalty descended from thirteenth-century Tahitian colonizers; their strict, stratified social system later evolved into a peaceful constitutional monarchy that nineteenth-century ali'i tried to protect after a subsequent colonization by Americans, whose descendants overthrew the monarchy and persuaded Congress to annex the islands to the US.
aloha	Love, affection, compassion, kindness; to share the "divine breath of life"; often used as a greeting; also reflects the ideas of respect, humility, truth, and honor.
aloha nō	Deepest aloha.
"ancêtre à moi et la vôtre"	(French) "An ancestor to you and me."
"A'ole nao!"	"Oh no!"
"'Auē noho'i ē"	"How terrible!"
'auku'u	Black-crowned night heron, seen as a messenger for the ancestors.

auwē	Oh no, alas! Also *auē*.
'aumakua	Family or ancestral spirits often embodied in animals, rocks, clouds, or plants.
āwiki mai	Be swift, hurry!
bumbye	(pidgin) By and by, eventually.
coconut wireless	(slang) Refers to islanders' tradition of passing information by word of mouth through family and friends.
"E kala mai"	"I'm sorry."
FEMA	Acronym for the Federal Emergency Management Agency.
FLETC	Acronym for the Federal Law Enforcement Training Centers; California locations, where Hawai'i officers usually train, include Los Angeles and Chico; pronounced "fleh-tsee."
hā	Breath
hala	The pandanus tree (*Pandanus odoratissimus*), a coastal plant symbolic of traditional Polynesian culture; the leaves (*lauhala*) are used for hats, baskets, bowls, mats, sails, and other woven objects.
hale	House, hut.
Haleakalā	Maui's tallest mountain, a dormant volcano from which the demigod Māui lassoed the sun to lengthen the day and permit his mother, the goddess Hina, to dry her *tapa* cloth; literally, "house used by the sun"; site of several astronomical facilities. Despite continual objections from islanders and the National Park Service, which operates a park on Haleakalā, the Department of Defense has conducted military surveillance activities there since 1942.
Hale Pōhaku	Stone House, in reference to a lava rock hunting cabin built high up Mauna Kea by the Civilian Conservation Corps (CCC) as part of a public works program after the Great Depression; place name for the location of the astronomers' base camp.
"Hāmau!"	"Silence! Hush!"
"Hana hou"	"Do it again"; "Encore!"
haole	Foreigner, now often means Caucasian.

haupia	Coconut pudding, a traditional dessert formerly of coconut cream and arrowroot, now usually made with cornstarch.
Hawai'i	The name of both the island (the Big Island) and the archipelago; elsewhere in Polynesia the name of the underworld or ancestral home; in Hawai'i the name is said to have no meaning.
heiau	Stone temple, usually a platform.
hewa	Wrong or sinful, gravely offensive; grave offense.
hewa loa	Great sin or offense.
hibiscus	(English) The state flower of Hawai'i.
Hilo	Second-largest city in the Hawaiian Islands; perhaps named for the new moon or a Polynesian navigator.
hi'uwai	Spiritual cleansing in water, healing bath.
hō'ailona	Sign or omen, also 'ailona.
hōkū	Star.
holomoana	Seafarer, also *holokai*.
Hongwanji	(Japanese) "Temples of the primal vow" of the Jodo Shinshu ("True Pure Land") sect of Buddhism; the non-Romanized word is *Hongan-ji*.
honi	Traditional exchange of breath between two people; can also mean kiss.
ho'okupu	Ceremonial offering, especially to a deity or a chief.
ho'ololi	To change, turn over, transform (used here as the name of the Hawaiian "squatters village").
"Ho'onana!"	"Look!"
hui	Association or society.
hula	One of the traditional Hawaiian dances, many quite ancient.
hula hālau	Hula troupe or school.
huli	To turn over or reverse, also *ho'o huli*.
hūnā	Confidential, covert; something to be hidden; sometimes in reference to *kahuna*.
imu	Traditional Polynesian underground oven.
"I mua!"	"Onward!" or "Forward!"

ʻio	Hawaiian hawk whose appearance is highly auspicious.
ʻiwa	Great frigatebird whose wingspread can reach over seven feet; a body form of the ancestral spirit of sailors.
iwi	Bones.
"Ka!"	"Oh!"
kaʻao	Legend, tale; fanciful; fiction (referred to here as KAAO Radio, where Sunny Boy Rocha works).
kāhili	Standard of feathers symbolizing the monarchy.
kahu	Guardian or honored attendant; the title (in modern times misapplied to Christian ministers) implies an intimate and confidential relationship between a god and its guardian or keeper.
kahuna	General term for priest, sorcerer, or expert in any profession or craft.
kahuna kilo kilo	Priest of sky omens.
kai	Sea or area near the sea.
Kaiwi	Channel between Molokaʻi and Oʻahu, sometimes called the Molokaʻi Channel; literally, "the bone."
kālua	Cooked in "the pit" or *imu*, sometimes in reference to "kālua pig" or "kālua pork," a traditional delicacy.
kamaʻaina	Native born, literally, "land child."
kamani	Large, beautiful trees (*Calophyllum inophyllum*) whose spreading canopies often shade Hawaiʻi's shoreline.
Kāne	Foremost of the Hawaiian gods who is credited with creation, light, waters of life, abundance, and procreation; water in Lake Waiau is associated with this deity ("the waters of Kāne").
kapa	*Tapa* cloth, traditional Polynesian cloth made from *wauke* or *māmaki* bark.
kapu	Taboo, sacred, prohibited.
Kapu Aloha	The tradition and protocol of strict adherence to the principle of aloha.
Kapiko o Waiʻau	A water goddess of Lake Waiau ("umbilical of swirling water").
kāula	A type of *kahuna*—prophet, seer, oracle.

Ke Akua	God, the god, sometimes in reference to the Polynesian "Supreme One," whose name is never uttered.
Keaukaha	Coastal settlement and Hawaiian Home Lands area near Hilo; literally, "the passing current."
keiki	Child, children, offspring.
kīhei	Rectangular *tapa* garment tied over one shoulder with a knot, often worn ceremonially.
kilo hōkū	Hawaiian astronomer, one who observes the sky.
kilo honua	One who reads signs in the earth.
kilo kilo	Priest of sky omens.
kine	(pidgin) Kind, type; a related expression is the fill-in pidgin term *da kine* whose meaning is contextual (similar to "whatchamacallit").
koa	A famous Hawaiian hardwood tree of the acacia family (*Acacia koa*); brave, bold, valiant.
Kū	Hawaiian god of male-generating power who resided in Hawai'i prior to Tahitians' arrival in the thirteenth century.
Kūka'ilimoku	War god brought to Hawai'i by thirteenth-century invaders from Tahiti; a favored god of King Kamehameha during the wars leading to unification of the islands.
Kūkahau'ula	Hawaiian name for Mauna Kea's summit ridge (Pu'u o Kūkahau'ula); literally, "Kū of the red-hewed dew."
kū kia'i mauna	"Guardians of the mountain," an expression used at ceremonies and protests over telescope development on Mauna Kea, widely used during the clash over the Thirty Meter Telescope.
kukui	Candlenut tree (*Aleurites moluccana*) whose seeds were widely used to produce light and so symbolizes enlightenment.
kuleana	Responsibility, province, jurisdiction, or concern.
kupua	Demigod or cultural hero, especially a supernatural being possessing several forms.
kupuna	Elder, ancestor; starting point, source.
ku'uipo	Sweetheart.

lānai	Veranda, porch.
lauhala	Long, sharp leaves of the *hala* (pandanus) tree, used for hats, baskets, bowls, mats, sails, and other woven objects.
lau lau	Pork, fish, beef, or taro tops wrapped in *taro* (*kalo*) leaves and steamed in a ti leaf; a popular food throughout Polynesia, usually cooked in an *imu*, or underground oven.
lavalava	(Samoan) Sarong worn like a skirt knotted at the waist.
lele	Sacrificial altar or stand.
lei	Traditional garland of flowers, leaves, shells, or nuts.
Lilinoe	Mauna Kea's goddess of mist, the younger sister of Poli'ahu; she resides in a cinder cone just below the volcano's summit.
lōlō	Crazy.
Lono	Hawaiian god of peace, agriculture, and fertility; in European myth, the god for which the natives of Kealakekua Bay mistook Captain James Cook.
lua	Ancient Hawaiian martial art involving hand-to-hand fighting; many of its techniques are secret.
lūau	A Hawaiian feast, named for the taro leaves often served at one; the more traditional term is *pā'ina*; also (more traditionally) *lū'au*; chicken *lū'au*, a traditional favorite, consists of chicken pieces sprinkled with sea salt, then layered with taro leaves and baked in coconut milk.
luna	Sugar plantation foreman.
mahalo	Thank you; often accentuated by adding *nui* (big, greatest, much, many) or *nui loa* (very much, immense).
maile	A fragrant woodland vine used for special leis.
maika'i	Good, righteous, very fine.
Makali'i	The constellation Pleiades, the seven "little eyes" of Pleiades; in Japanese, *Subaru*.
mālama	Take care of, tend, protect.
"Mālama pono"	"Take good care of your soul."
malasada	(Portuguese) A sugared doughnut without a hole.

malihini	Stranger, newcomer.
māmaki	A native plant in the nettle family (*Pipturus albidus*) with which Hawaiians make a medical tea.
māmane	A native leguminous tree (*Sophora chrysophylia*) that thrives high up Mauna Kea; home to the native *palila* bird.
manini	Small common fish (surgeonfish or convict tang) considered tasty to islanders; the name is also used as an expression meaning "insignificant" or "small fry."
marae	(South Pacific) A sacred place, including ceremonial stone shrines and altars, like those built by Hawai'i's earliest inhabitants on Mauna Kea, Mauna Loa, and Pōhakuloa.
matua	(Samoan) Elder.
mauna	Mountain, mountainous region.
Mauna Kea	The tallest mountain in the Pacific Basin (13,796 feet) and home to numerous international telescopes; Mauna Kea's summit is considered a *piko* (or umbilical cord) that ties the earth to the sky; among its names are Mauna a Wākea (mountain of the Sky Father Wākea), Mauna Ākea (a variation of the same), and Mauna Kea (white mountain); sometimes spelled Maunakea.
maururu	(Mangarevan) Thank you.
mean	(pidgin) Radical, too much, over the top.
moana	Ocean, open sea.
mochi	(Japanese) A traditional sweet made from pounded rice flour.
"mon ami"	(French) "My friend."
Mo'oinanea	This matriarch of all lizard (*mo'o*) gods and goddesses is a guardian of Mauna Kea; legend holds that she often dwells in the mountain's Lake Waiau.
na'au	Gut instinct or intuitive knowledge.
Nāhiku	The Big Dipper constellation.
nīele	Nosy, prying.
nohea	Handsome.
"N'oublie pas!"	(French) "Don't forget!"

'ohana	Family or clan.
'ōhi'a	A common native tree 'ōhi'a *lehua* (*Metrosideros macropus*); its *lehua* blossoms are beautiful pom-poms of red, orange, yellow, and similar hues; symbol of the volcano goddess Pele.
'ōkolehau	Whisky distilled from ti root, using methods originally taught to the Hawaiians by American whalers; literally, "iron bottom," in reference to the whalers' blubber try pots used to distill it.
'ono	Delicious.
'opihi	A small shellfish (limpet) much prized for its delicious flavor, an essential part of any traditional *lūau*.
pahu	Traditional sharkskin drum.
paka lōlō	"Crazy weed" or numbing tobacco, marijuana.
palaka	A checkered shirt traditionally worn by plantation workers, usually blue and white of block-print cloth.
palila	Native honey creeper that lives only on the upper slopes of Mauna Kea.
paniolo	Hawaiian cowboy, the name derived from the Spanish word *Español*.
Papa	Earth Mother in Hawaiians' creation myth; wife of Wākea, the Sky Father.
pareu	(Tahitian) A cloth wrap, often colorful; in Hawai'i *kīkepa*.
Pele	Hawaiians' volcano goddess, sometimes referred to as Tutu Pele or Madam Pele (see the author's novel *Daughters of Fire* for a deeper understanding of this important deity).
pilau	Stinking, rotten, putrid.
pilikia	Trouble, distress.
pōhaku	Rock, stone.
Pōhakuloa	Land division in the saddle between Mauna Kea and Mauna Loa and the location of numerous Native Hawaiian shrines, altars, and other cultural sites; now the location of the US government's Pohakuloa Training Area (PTA) and its live-fire bombing range; literally, "long stone."
poi	Traditional Polynesian mash made from taro root.

poke	Raw fish cut into chunks and traditionally served with sea salt and seaweed (*limu*).
Poliʻahu	Luminescent snow goddess of Mauna Kea.
pono	Virtuous, moral, correct, true nature.
popoi	(Mangarevan) Fermented breadfruit mash.
pū	Conch shell horn.
pueo	Hawaiian owl, a type of *ʻaumakua* or ancestral spirit.
pūpū	Appetizer; general name for marine or land shells (sometimes anglicized as "pūpū shells").
pupule	Crazy.
puʻu	Hill or cinder cone.
sadō	(Japanese) Traditional tea ceremony, "the way of tea."
SETI	Search for Extraterrestrial Intelligence, a program to search for intelligent life beyond Earth; the SETI Institute is supported by NASA, NSF, other federal agencies, and foundations.
shaka	(pidgin) Hand gesture with thumb and pinky extended.
shibai	(pidgin, from the Japanese) A sham, not true, hypocritical.
shikki	(Japanese) Traditional lacquerware.
tabi	(Japanese) Split-toe footware, often seen as reef shoes.
tapa	Polynesian cloth made from bark; in Hawaiʻi *kapa*.
taro	A root prepared in various ways as the traditional Polynesian starch; in Hawaiʻi *kalo*.
ti	Plant whose leaves are used to wrap offerings, wrap food for cooking, and make skirts, leis, and other items; viewed as auspicious or protective, it is planted near dwellings and other structures *(ki)*.
tiki	Wooden god image; in Hawaiʻi usually called *kiʻi*.
tita	(pidgin) Tough, local woman.
tsunami	(Japanese) Seismic sea wave.
tūtū	Grandfather or grandmother.

ʻuaʻu	Hawaiian petrol, seabirds that hunt the deep ocean during the day returning to their nests in the high country of Mauna Kea, Mauna Loa, Pohakuloa, and Haleakala.
uē	Weeping, lamenting, mourning (also *uwē*).
uhiwai	Heavy fog or mist.
ʻukulele	A small four-string guitar brought to Hawaiʻi by nineteenth-century Portuguese immigrants from the Azore Islands; literally, "leaping flea," nickname of the man who popularized the instrument.
wahi kapu	Sacred place.
wahine	Woman, women.
Waiau	Legendary lake 13,007 feet above sea level; named for the water goddess Kapiko o Waiau ("umbilical of the swirling water"); literally, "swirling water" or "water current."
wai puna	Spring water; figuratively, "sweetheart."
Wākea	Sky Father in Hawaiians' creation myth, in some traditions source of the name Mauna Kea; mythical ancestor of all Hawaiians; husband of Papa, the Earth Mother.
wao akua	A distant mountainous region inhabited by spirits, a realm of the gods; often the highest part of a volcano.
wēkiu	"Uppermost," name for the endangered native *wēkiu* bug, which lives only on Mauna Kea.
wānana	To foretell.

GLOSSARY OF PRIMARY CHARACTERS' NAMES

Erik Peterson	(Norse) Alone
Hōkū Holokai	Star; seafarer
Aunty **Moana Kuahiwi**	The open sea; mountain
Moses **Kawaʻaloa**	The long canoe
Jedediah Clarke	(Hebrew) Friend of God
Andromeda McCrea	(Greek) Ruler over men and the galaxy named after the Greek goddess Andromeda
Willy **McCrea**	(Irish) Son of grace
Tom (**Thomas**) Williams	(biblical) The skeptical apostle "doubting Thomas"
Freddie (**Alfred**) Hartwig	(Anglo-Saxon) Elf counsel, wise helper
Sam **Chun**	(Chinese) End of winter, beginning of spring
Sunny Boy **Rocha**	(Portuguese) One who is of (or from) the rock
Jill Delima **Kualono**	Mountaintop region
Jeffrey Drake	(German) God's peace; (German and Norse) dragon
Uncle **Peʻa Morgan**	Canoe sail; (Celtic) one who lives by the sea
Johnny **Mattos**	(Portuguese) Bush, forest, or scrubland
Josh (**Joshua**) Mattos	(Hebrew) Lord's salvation—in biblical reference to the leader of the Israelite tribes after the death of Moses and who earlier commanded a militia for the prophet
Kuamoʻo family	Keel of a canoe or backbone

About the Author

Tom Peek lived his early life on Grey Cloud Island in the backwaters of Minnesota's Upper Mississippi River. After hitchhiking by boat through the South Seas, he settled on the island of Hawai'i three decades ago. There he's been, among other things, an astronomy and mountain guide on Mauna Kea, an eruption ranger and exhibit writer on Kilauea, and an insider participant in the efforts to protect both sacred volcanoes. An award-winning novelist and acclaimed writing teacher, he lives near Kilauea's erupting summit crater.

About the Illustrator

John D. Dawson was raised in San Diego and has lived on Hawai'i Island for three decades. A graduate of the Art Center School, Los Angeles, now the ArtCenter College of Design, Dawson has illustrated books for national publishers as well as stamps for the US Postal Service, including its entire Nature of America series. He's also done commissions for the United Nations, National Park Service, National Geographic Society, National Wildlife Federation, and Audubon Society. His fine art watercolors and acrylics are represented by the Volcano Art Center gallery in Hawai'i Volcanoes National Park.

About the Cover Artist

Catherine Robbins, raised in the coastal mountains outside San Francisco, has lived on Hawai'i Island for four decades. She is a self-taught artist whose bold and evocative oil paintings of the island's volcanoes and plants have moved other artists to dub her "the Georgia O'Keeffe of Hawai'i." Her oils are represented by several Hawai'i Island galleries and found in private collections in Europe, North America, Japan, and Hawai'i.